Fanta...
of Time...

SIGNET DOUBLE SCIENCE FICTION:

THE
SEEDLING
STARS

and

GALACTIC
CLUSTER

★★★★★★★★★★★★★★★★★★★★★★★★★★★★★★★★★★★

The Seedling Stars

and

Galactic Cluster

★★★★★★★★★★★★★★★★★★★★★★★★★★★★★★★★★★★

by

JAMES BLISH

Ⓞ

A SIGNET BOOK

NEW AMERICAN LIBRARY

TIMES MIRROR

ACKNOWLEDGMENTS

The Seedling Stars:

Book I of this volume was first published in *Fantasy and Science Fiction* magazine as "A Time to Survive," and is copyright 1955 by Fantasy House, Inc.
Book II was first published in *IF Worlds of Science Fiction* magazine and is copyright 1954 by Quinn Publishing Co., Inc.
Book III, in considerably different form, appeared in *Super Science Stories* as "Sunken Universe," copyright 1942 by Fictioneers, Inc., and in part in *Galaxy Science Fiction* as "Surface Tension," copyright 1952 by the Galaxy Publishing Corporation.
Book IV was first published in *IF Worlds of Science Fiction* as "Watershed" and is copyright 1955 by Quinn Publishing Co., Inc.

Galactic Cluster:

"Tomb Tapper" copyright 1956 by Street & Smith Publications, Inc., reprinted from *Astounding Science Fiction;* "King of the Hill" originally copyright © 1955 by Royal Publications Inc., for *Infinity Science Fiction;* "Common Time," copyright 1953 by Columbia Publications, Inc., from the August 1953 issue of *Science Fiction Quarterly;* "A Work of Art," copyright © 1956 as "Art Work" by Columbia Publications, Inc., from the July 1956 issue of *Science Fiction Stories;* "To Pay the Piper," originally published in *If—Worlds of Science Fiction,* copyright 1956 by Quinn Publishing Company, Inc.; "Nor Iron Bars" originally copyright © 1956 and 1957 as "Detour to the Stars" and "Nor Iron Bars" by Royal Publications, Inc., for *Infinity Science Fiction;* "Beep" copyright 1954 by Galaxy Publishing Corporation; "This Earth of Hours" © 1959 by Mercury Press, Inc., from the June 1959 issue of *The Magazine of Fantasy and Science Fiction.*

The quotation from *Personae* by Ezra Pound, copyright 1926 by Ezra Pound, is reprinted by permission of New Directions.

The
Seedling
Stars

TO H. L. GOLD

BOOK ONE

SEEDING PROGRAM

1

The spaceship resumed humming around Sweeney without his noticing the change. When Capt. Meiklejon's voice finally came again from the wall speaker, Sweeney was still lying buckled to his bunk in a curious state of tranquillity he had never known before, and couldn't possibly have described, even to himself. Though he had a pulse, he might otherwise have concluded that he was dead. It took him several minutes to respond.

"Sweeney, do you hear me? Are—you all right?"

The brief hesitation in the pilot's breathing made Sweeney grin. From Meiklejon's point of view, and that of most of the rest of humanity, Sweeney was all wrong. He was, in fact, dead.

The heavily insulated cabin, with its own airlock to the outside, and no access for Sweeney at all to the rest of the ship, was a testimonial to his wrongness. So was Meiklejon's tone: the voice of a man addressing, not another human being, but something that had to be kept in a vault.

A vault designed to protect the universe outside it—not to protect its contents from the universe.

"Sure, I'm all right," Sweeney said, snapping the buckle and sitting up. He checked the thermometer, which still registered its undeviating minus 194° F.—the mean surface temperature of Ganymede, moon number III of Jupiter. "I was dozing, sort of. What's up?"

"I'm putting the ship into her orbit; we're about a thousand miles up from the satellite now. I thought you might want to take a look."

"Sure enough. Thanks, Mickey."

The wall speaker said, "Yeah. Talk to you later." Sweeney grappled for the guide rail and pulled himself over to the cabin's single bull'seye port, maneuvering with considerable precision. For a man to whom 1/6 Earth gravity is normal, free fall—a situation of no gravity at all—is only an extreme case.

Which was what Sweeney was, too. A human being—but an extreme case.

He looked out. He knew exactly what he would see; he had studied it exhaustively from photos, from teletapes, from maps, and through telescopes both at home on the Moon and on Mars. When you approach Ganymede at inferior conjunction, as Meiklejon was doing, the first thing that hits you in the eye is the huge oval blot called Neptune's Trident—so named by the earliest Jovian explorers because it was marked with the Greek letter *psi* on the old Howe composite map. The name had turned out to have been well chosen: that blot is a deep, many-pronged sea, largest at the eastern end, which runs from about 120° to 165° in longitude, and from about 10° to 33° North latitude. A sea of what? Oh, water, of course—water frozen rock-solid forever, and covered with a layer of rock-dust about three inches thick.

East of the Trident, and running all the way north to the pole, is a great triangular marking called the Gouge, a torn-up, root-entwined, avalanche-shaken valley which continues right around the pole and back up into the other hemisphere, fanning out as it goes. (*Up* because north to space pilots, as to astronomers, is down.) There is nothing quite like the Gouge on any other planet, although at inferior conjunction, when your ship is coming down on Ganymede at the 180° meridian, it is likely to remind you of Syrtis Major on Mars.

There is, however, no real resemblance. Syrtis Major is perhaps the pleasantest land on all of Mars. The Gouge, on the other hand, is—a gouge.

On the eastern rim of this enormous scar, at long. 218°, N. lat. 32°, is an isolated mountain about 9,000 feet high, which had no name as far as Sweeney knew; it was marked with the letter *pi* on the Howe map. Because of its isolation, it can be seen easily from Earth's Moon in a good telescope when the sunrise terminator lies in that longitude, its peak shining detached in the darkness like a little star. A semicircular shelf juts westward out over the Gouge from the base of Howe's *pi,* it sides bafflingly sheer for a world which shows no other signs of folded strata.

It was on that shelf that the other Adapted Men lived.

Sweeney stared down at the nearly invisible mountain with its star-fire peak for a long time, wondering why he was not reacting. Any appropriate emotion would do: anticipation, alarm, eagerness, anything at all, even fear. For that matter, having been locked up in a safe for over two months should by now have driven him foaming to get out, even if only to join the Adapted Men. Instead, the tranquillity persisted. He was unable to summon more than a momentary curiosity over Howe's *pi* before his eye was drawn away to Jupiter himself, looming monstrous and insanely-colored only 600,000 miles away, give or take a few thousand. And even that planet had attracted him only because it was brighter; otherwise, it had no meaning.

"Mickey?" he said, forcing himself to look back down into the Gouge.

"Right here, Sweeney. How does it look?"

"Oh, like a relief map. That's how they all look. Where are you going to put me down? Don't the orders leave it up to us?"

"Yeah. But I don't think there's any choice," Meiklejon's voice said, less hesitantly. "It'll have to be the big plateau—Howe's H."

Sweeney scanned the oval mare with a mild distaste. Standing on that, he would be as conspicuous as if he'd been planted in the middle of the Moon's Mare Crisium. He said so.

"You've no choice," Meiklejon repeated calmly. He burped the rockets several times. Sweeney's weight returned briefly, tried to decide which way it wanted to throw itself, and then went away again. The ship was now in its orbit; but whether Meiklejon had set it up to remain put over its present co-ordinates, or instead it was to cruise criss-cross over the whole face of the satellite, Sweeney couldn't tell, and didn't ask. The less he knew about that, the better.

"Well, it's a long drop," Sweeney said. "And that atmosphere isn't exactly the thickest in the system. I'll have to fall in the lee of the mountain. I don't want to have to trudge a couple of hundred miles over Howe's H."

"On the other hand," Meiklejon said, "if you come down too close, our friends down there will spot your parachute. Maybe it'd be better if we dropped you into the Gouge, after all. There's so much tumbled junk down there that the radar echoes must be tremendous—not a chance of their spotting a little thing like a man on a parachute."

"*No*, thank you. There's still optical spotting, and a foil parachute looks nothing like a rock spur, even to an Adapted Man. It'll have to be behind the mountain, where I'm in both optical *and* radar shadow at once. Besides, how could I climb out of the Gouge onto the shelf? They didn't plant themselves on the edge of a cliff for nothing."

"That's right," Meiklejon said. "Well, I've got the catapult pointed. I'll suit up and join you on the hull."

"All right. Tell me again just what you're going to do while I'm gone, so I won't find myself blowing the whistle when you're nowhere around." The sound of a suit locker being opened came tinnily over the intercom. Sweeney's chute harness was already strapped on, and getting the respirator and throat-mikes into place would only take a moment. Sweeney needed no other protection.

"I'm to stay up here with all power off except maintenance for 300 days," Meiklejon's voice, sounding more distant now, was repeating. "Supposedly by that time you'll have worked yourself in good with our friends down there and will know the setup. I stand ready to get a message from you on a fixed frequency. You're to send me only a set of code letters; I feed them into the computer, the comp tells me what to do and I act accordingly. If I don't hear from you after 300 days, I utter a brief but heartfelt prayer and go home. Beyond that, God help me, I don't know a thing."

"That's plenty," Sweeney told him. "Let's go."

Sweeney went out his personal airlock. Like all true interplanetary craft, Meiklejon's ship had no overall hull. She consisted of her essential components, including the personnel globe, held together by a visible framework of girders and I-beams. It was one of the longest of the latter, one which was already pointed toward Howe's H, which would serve as the "catapult."

Sweeney looked up at the globe of the satellite. The old familiar feeling of falling came over him for a moment; he looked down, reorienting himself to the ship, until it went away. He'd be going in that direction soon enough.

Meiklejon came around the bulge of the personnel globe, sliding his shoes along the metal. In his bulky, misshapen spacesuit, it was he who looked like the unhuman member of the duo.

"Ready?" he said.

Sweeney nodded and lay face down on the I-beam, snapping the guide-clips on his harness into place around it. He could feel Meiklejon's mitts at his back, fastening the JATO unit; he could see nothing now, however, but the wooden sled that would protect his body from the beam.

"Okay," the pilot said. "Good luck, Sweeney."

"Thanks. Count me off, Mickey."

"Coming up on five seconds. Five. Four. Three. Two. One. *Hack*."

The JATO unit shuddered and dealt Sweeney a nearly paralyzing blow between his shoulder-blades. For an instant the acceleration drove him down into his harness, and the sled spraddled against the metal of the I-beam.

Then, suddenly, the vibration stopped. He was flying free. A little belatedly, he jerked the release ring.

The sled went curving away from under him, dwindling rapidly among the stars. The pressure at his back cut out as the JATO unit, still under power, flamed ahead of him. The instantly-dissipated flick of heat from its exhaust made him ill for a moment; then it had vanished. It would hit too hard to leave anything where it landed but a hole.

Nothing was left but Sweeney, falling toward Ganymede, head first.

From almost the beginning, from that day unrememberably early in his childhood when he had first realized that the underground dome on the Moon was all there was to the universe for nobody but himself, Sweeney had wanted to be human; wanted it with a vague, impersonal ache which set quickly into a chill bitterness of manner and outlook at his unique everyday life, and in dreams with flares of searing loneliness which became more infrequent but also more intense as he matured, until such a night would leave him as shaken and mute, sometimes for several days at a stretch, as an escape from a major accident.

The cadre of psychologists, psychiatrists and analysts assigned to him did what they could, but that was not very much. Sweeney's history contained almost nothing that was manipulable by any system of psychotherapy developed to help human beings. Nor were the members of the cadre ever able to agree among themselves what the prime goal of such therapy should be: whether to help Sweeney to live with the facts of his essential inhumanity, or to fan instead that single spark of hope which the non-medical people on the Moon were constantly holding out toward Sweeney as the sole reason for his existence.

The facts were simple and implacable. Sweeney was an Adapted Man—adapted, in this instance, to the bitter cold, the light gravity, and the thin stink of atmosphere which prevailed on Ganymede. The blood that ran in his veins, and the sol substrate of his every cell, was nine-tenths liquid ammonia; his bones were Ice IV; his respiration was a complex hydrogen-to-methane cycle based not upon catalysis by an iron-bearing pigment, but upon the locking and unlocking of a double sulfur bond; and he could survive for weeks, if he had to, upon a diet of rock dust.

He had always been this way. What had made him so had happened to him literally before he had been conceived: the application, to the germ cells which had later united to form him, of an elaborate constellation of techniques—selective mitotic poisoning, pinpoint X-irradiation, tectogenetic microsurgery, competitive metabolic inhibition, and perhaps fifty more whose names he had never even heard—which collectively had been christened "pantropy." The word, freely retranslated, meant "changing everything"—and it fitted.

As the pantropists had changed in advance the human pattern in Sweeney's shape and chemistry, so they had changed his education, his world, his thoughts, even his ancestors. You didn't make an Adapted Man with just a wave of the wand, Dr. Alfven had once explained proudly to Sweeney over the intercom. Even the ultimate germ cells were the emergents of a hundred previous generations, bred one from another before they had passed the zygote stage like one-celled animals, each one biassed a little farther toward the cyanide and ice and everything nice that little boys like Sweeney were made of. The psych cadre picked off Dr. Alfven at the end of that same week, at the regular review of the tapes of what had been said to Sweeney and what he had found to say back, but they need hardly have taken the trouble. Sweeney had never heard a nursery rhyme, any more than he had ever experienced the birth trauma or been exposed to the Oedipus complex. He was a law unto himself, with most of the whereases blank.

He noticed, of course, that Alfven failed to show up when his next round was due, but this was commonplace. Scientists came and went around the great sealed cavern, always accompanied by the polite and beautifully uniformed private police of the Greater Earth Port Authority, but they rarely lasted very long. Even among the psych cadre there was always a peculiar tension, a furious constraint which erupted periodically into pitched shouting battles. Sweeney never found out what the shouting was about because the sound to the outside was always cut as soon as the quarrels began, but he noticed that some of the participants never showed up again.

"Where's Dr. Emory? Isn't this his day?"

"He finished his tour of duty."

"But I want to talk to him. He promised to bring me a book. Won't he be back for a visit?"

"I don't think so, Sweeney. He's retired. Don't worry about him, he'll get along just fine. I'll bring you your book."

It was after the third of these incidents that Sweeney was let out on the surface of the Moon for the first time—guarded, it was true, by five men in spacesuits, but Sweeney didn't care. The new freedom seemed enormous to him, and his own suit, only a token compared to what the Port cops had to wear, hardly seemed to exist. It was his first foretaste of the liberty he was to have, if the many hints could be trusted, after his job was done. He could even see the Earth, where people lived.

About the job he knew everything there was to know, and knew it as second nature. It had been drummed into him from his cold and lonely infancy, always with the same command at the end:

"We must have those men back."

Those six words were the reason for Sweeney; they were also Sweeney's sole hope. The Adapted Men had to be recaptured and brought back to Earth—or more exactly, back to the dome on the Moon, the only place besides Ganymede where they could be kept alive. And if they could not all be recaptured—he was to entertain this only as a possibility—he must at least come back with Dr. Jacob Rullman. Only Rullman would be sure to know the ultimate secret: how to turn an Adapted Man back into a human being.

Sweeney understood that Rullman and his associates were criminals, but how grievous their crime had been was a question he had never tried to answer for himself. His standards were too sketchy. It was clear from the beginning, however, that the colony on Ganymede had been set up without Earth's sanction, by methods of which Earth did not approve (except for special cases like Sweeney), and that Earth wanted it broken up. Not by force, for Earth wanted to know first what Rullman knew, but by the elaborate artifice which was Sweeney himself.

We must have those men back. After that, the hints said—never promising anything directly—Sweeney could be made human, and know a better freedom than walking the airless surface of the Moon with five guards.

It was usually after one of these hints that one of those suddenly soundless quarrels would break out among the staff. Any man of normal intelligence would have come to suspect

13

that the hints were less than well founded upon any real expectation, and Sweeney's training helped to make him suspicious early; but in the long run he did not care. The hints offered his only hope and he accepted them with hope but without expectation. Besides, the few opening words of such quarrels which he had overheard before the intercom clicked off had suggested that there was more to the disagreement than simple doubt of the convertibility of an Adapted Man. It had been Emory, for instance, who had burst out unexpectedly and explosively:

"But suppose Rullman was right—?"

Click.

Right about what? Is a lawbreaker ever "right?" Sweeney could not know. Then there had been the technie who had said "It's the cost that's the trouble with terra-forming"— what did that mean?—and had been hustled out of the monitoring chamber on some trumped-up errand hardly a minute later. There were many such instances, but inevitably Sweeney failed to put the fragments together into any pattern. He decided only that they did not bear directly upon his chances of becoming human, and promptly abandoned them in the vast desert of his general ignorance.

In the long run, only the command was real—the command and the nightmares. *We must have those men back.* Those six words were the reason why Sweeney, like a man whose last effort to awaken has failed, was falling head first toward Ganymede.

The Adapted Men found Sweeney halfway up the great col which provided the only access to their cliff-edge colony from the plateau of Howe's H. He did not recognize them; they conformed to none of the photographs he had memorized; but they accepted his story readily enough. And he had not needed to pretend exhaustion—Ganymede's gravity was normal to him, but it had been a long trek and a longer climb.

He was surprised to find, nevertheless, that he had enjoyed it. For the first time in his life he had walked unguarded, either by men or by mechanisms, on a world where he felt physically at home; a world without walls, a world where he was essentially alone. The air was rich and pleasant, the winds came from wherever they chose to blow, the temperature in the col was considerably below what had been allowable in the dome on the Moon, and there was sky all around him, tinged with indigo and speckled with stars that twinkled now and then.

He would have to be careful. It would be all too easy to

accept Ganymede as home. He had been warned against that, but somehow he had failed to realize that the danger would be not merely real, but—seductive.

The young men took him swiftly the rest of the way to the colony. They had been as incurious as they had been anonymous. Rullman was different. The look of stunned disbelief on the scientist's face, as Sweeney was led into his high-ceilinged, rock-walled office, was so total as to be frightening. He said: "What's this!"

"We found him climbing the col. We thought he'd gotten lost, but he says he belongs to the parent flight."

"Impossible," Rullman said. "Quite impossible." And then he fell silent, studying the newcomer from crown to toe. The expression of shock dimmed only slightly.

The long scrutiny gave Sweeney time to look back. Rullman was older than his pictures, but that was natural; if anything, he looked a little less marked by age than Sweeney had anticipated. He was spare, partly bald, and slope-shouldered, but the comfortable pod under his belt-line which had shown in the photos was almost gone now. Evidently living on Ganymede had hardened him some. The pictures had failed to prepare Sweeney for the man's eyes: they were as hooded and unsettling as an owl's.

"You'd better tell me who you are," Rullman said at last. "And how you got here. You aren't one of us, that's certain."

"I'm Donald Leverault Sweeney," Sweeney said. "Maybe I'm not one of you, but my mother said I was. I got here in her ship. She said you'd take me in."

Rullman shook his head. "That's impossible, too. Excuse me, Mr. Sweeney, but you've probably no idea what a bombshell you are. You must be Shirley Leverault's child, then—but how did you get here? How did you survive all this time? Who kept you alive, and tended you, after we left the Moon? And above all, how did you get away from the Port cops? We knew that Port Earth found our Moon lab even before we abandoned it. I can hardly believe that you even exist."

Nevertheless, the scientist's expression of flat incredulity was softening moment by moment. He was, Sweeney judged, already beginning to buy it. And necessarily: there Sweeney stood before him, breathing Ganymede's air, standing easily in Ganymede's gravity, with Ganymede's dust on his cold skin, a fact among inarguable facts.

"The Port cops found the big dome, all right," Sweeney said. "But they never found the little one, the pilot plant. Dad blew up the tunnel between the two before they landed—he

15

was killed in the rock-slide. Of course I was still just a cell in a jug when that happened."

"I see," Rullman said thoughtfully. "We picked up an explosion on our ship's instruments before we took off. But we thought it was the Port raiders beginning to bomb, unexpected though that was. Then they didn't destroy the big lab either, after all?"

"No," Sweeney said. Rullman surely must know that; radio talk between Earth and Moon must be detectable at least occasionally out here. "There were still some intercom lines left through to there; my mother used to spend a lot of time listening in on what was going on. So did I, after I was old enough to understand it. That was how we found out that the Ganymedian colony hadn't been bombed out, either."

"But where did you get your power?"

"Most of it from our own strontium⁹⁰ cell. Everything was shielded so the cops couldn't detect any stray fields. When the cell finally began to give out, we had to tap Port's main accumulator line—just for a little bit at first, but the drain kept going up." He shrugged. "Sooner or later they were bound to spot it—and did."

Rullman was momentarily silent, and Sweeney knew that he was doing the pertinent arithmetic in his head, comparing the 20-year half-life of strontium⁹⁰ with Sweeney's and the Adapted Men's chronology. The figures would jibe, of course. The Port cops' briefing had been thorough about little details like that.

"It's still quite astounding, having to rethink this whole episode after so many years," Rullman said. "With all due respect, Mr. Sweeney, it's hard to imagine Shirley Leverault going through such an ordeal—and all alone, too, except for a child she could never even touch, a child as difficult and technical to tend as an atomic pile. I remember her as a frail, low-spirited girl, trailing along after us listlessly because Robert was in the project." He frowned reminiscently. "She used to say, 'It's his job.' She never thought of it as anything more than that."

"*I* was her job," Sweeney said evenly. The Port cops had tried to train him to speak bitterly when he mentioned his mother, but he had never been able to capture the emotion that they wanted him to imitate. He had found, however, that if he rapped out the syllables almost without inflection, they were satisfied with the effect. "You misjudged her, Dr. Rullman—or else she changed after Dad was killed. She had guts enough for ten. And she got paid for it in the end. In the only coin the Port cops know how to pay."

"I'm sorry," Rullman said gently. "But at least you got away. I'm sure that's as she would have wanted it. Where did the ship you spoke of come from?"

"Why, we always had it. It belonged to Dad, I suppose. It was stored in a natural chimney near our dome. When the cops broke into the monitoring room, I went out the other side of the dome, while they were—busy with mother, and beat it. There wasn't anything I could have done—"

"Of course, of course," Rullman said, his voice low and quiet. "You wouldn't have lasted a second in their air. You did the right thing. Go on."

"Well, I got to the ship and got it off. I didn't have time to save anything but myself. They followed me all the way, but they didn't shoot. I think there's still one of them upstairs now."

"We'll sweep for him, but there's nothing we can do about him in any case except keep him located. You bailed out, I gather."

"Yes. Otherwise I wouldn't have had a chance—they seemed to want me back in the worst way. They must have the ship by now, and the coordinates for the colony too."

"Oh, they've had those coordinates since we first landed," Rullman said. "You were lucky, Mr. Sweeney, and bold, too. You bring back a sense of immediacy that I haven't felt for years, since our first escape. But there's one more problem."

"What is it? If I can help—"

"There's a test we'll have to make," Rullman said. "Your story seems to hold water; and I really don't see how you could have become what you are, unless you were really one of us. But we have to be certain."

"Sure," Sweeney said. "Let's go."

Rullman beckoned and led him out of the office through a low stone door. The corridor through which they passed was so like all those Sweeney had seen on the Moon that he scarcely bothered to notice it. Even the natural gravity and circulating, unprocessed air were soothing rather than distracting. It was the test that worried Sweeney, precisely because he knew that he would be helpless to affect the outcome. Either the Port Authority's experts had put him together cunningly enough to pass any test, or—

—or he would never have the chance to become human.

Rullman nodded Sweeney through another door into a long, low-ceilinged room furnished with half a dozen laboratory benches and a good deal of glassware. The air was more active here; as on the Moon, there were ventilators roiling it. Someone came around a towering, twisted fractionating apparatus in which many small bubbles orbited, and moved toward them. It was, Sweeney saw, a small glossy-haired girl, with white hands and dark eyes and delicately precise feet. She was wearing the typical technie's white jacket, and a plum-colored skirt.

"Hello, Dr. Rullman. Can I help?"

"Sure, if you can neglect that percolator a while, Mike. I want to run an ID typing; we've got a new man here. All right?"

"Oh, I think so. It'll take a minute to get the sera out." She moved away from them to another desk and began to take out ampoules and shake them before a hooded light. Sweeney watched her. He had seen female technies before, but none so modelled, so unconstrained, or so—close as this. He felt light-headed, and hoped that he would not be asked to speak for a little while. There was sweat on his palms and a mumbling of blood in his inner ear, and he thought perhaps he might cry.

He had been plunged into the midst of his untested, long-delayed adolescence, and he liked it no better than anyone ever had.

But his diamond-etched caution did not blur completely. He remembered to remember that the girl had been as little surprised to see him as the two young men who had found him climbing the col had been. Why? Surely Dr. Rullman was not the only Adapted Man to know everyone in the colony by sight, and hence the only one able to feel consternation at the sight of a strange face. By this time, the settlers on Ganymede should know each other's slightest wrinkles, should have committed to memory every gesture, mannerism, dimple, shading, flaw or virtue that would help them to tell each other from the hostile remainder of overwhelming mankind.

The girl took Sweeney's hand, and for a moment the train of thought fell apart completely. Then there was a sharp stab in the tip of his right middle finger, and Mike was expressing droplets of blood into little puddles of bluish solution, spotted in sets of three on a great many slips of thin glass. Microscope slides; Sweeney had seen them before. As for the blood, she could have more if she wanted it.

But he returned doggedly to the question. Why had the young men and Mike failed to be surprised by Sweeney? Was it their age-group that counted? The original colonists of Ganymede would know both each other and their children by sight, while the youngsters to whom everything was essentially new would see nothing strange in a new face.

Children: then the colonists were fertile. There had never

been a hint of that, back on the Moon. Of course it meant nothing to Sweeney personally. Not a thing.

"Why, you're trembling," the girl said in a troubled voice. "It was only a little nick. You'd better sit down."

"Of course," Rullman said immediately. "You've been under quite a strain, Mr. Sweeney; forgive me for being so thoughtless. This will be over in just a moment."

Sweeney sat down gratefully and tried to think about nothing. Both the girl and Rullman were now also seated, at the bench, examining with microscopes the little puddles of diluted blood Mike had taken from Sweeney.

"Type O, Rh negative," the girl said. Rullman was taking notes. "MsMs, P negative, cdE/cde, Lutheran a-negative, Kell-Cellano negative, Lewis a-minus b-plus."

"Hmm," Rullman said, unilluminatingly, all as one sound. "Also Duffy a-negative, Jk-a, U positive, Jay positive, Bradbury-immune, platelets IV, and non-sickling. A pretty clean sweep. Mean anything to you, Mike?"

"It should," she said, looking at Sweeney speculatively. "You want me to match him, then."

Rullman nodded. The girl came to Sweeney's side and the spring-driven lancet went *snick* against another of his fingertips. After she went back to the bench, Sweeney heard the sound again, and saw her brush her own left middle fingertip against a slide. Silence.

"Compatible, Dr. Rullman."

Rullman turned to Sweeney and smiled for the first time. "You pass," he said. He seemed genuinely glad. "Welcome, Mr. Sweeney. Now if you'll come back to my office, we'll see what we can do about placing you in living quarters, and of course in a job—we've plenty of those. Thanks, Mike."

"You're welcome. Goodbye, Mr. Sweeney. It looks like I'll be seeing a lot more of you."

Sweeney nodded and gulped. It was not until he was back in Rullman's office that he could control his voice.

"What was that all about, Dr. Rullman? I mean, I know you were typing my blood, but what did it tell you?"

"It told me your *bona fides*," Rullman said. "Blood groups are inheritable; they follow the Mendelian laws very strictly. Your blood pattern gave me your identity, not as an individual, but as a member of a family. In other words, they showed that you really are what you claim to be, a descendant of Bob Sweeney and Shirley Leverault."

"I see. But you matched me against the girl, too. What did that test?"

"The so-called private factors, the ones that appear only

19

within a family and not in the general population," Rullman said. "You see, Mr. Sweeney, as we reckon such matters here, Michaela Leverault is your niece."

2

For at least the tenth time in two months, Mike was looking at Sweeney with astonishment, troubled and amused at once. "Now where," she said, "did you get *that* idea?"

The question, as usual, was dangerous, but Sweeney took his time. Mike knew that he was always slow to answer questions, and sometimes seemed not to hear them at all. The need for such a protective habit was luridly obvious to Sweeney, and he was only postponing the moment when it should become just as obvious to the Ganymedians; only the plainly pathological introversion of his character as a whole had excused him even thus far from a suspicion that he was ducking the hard ones.

Sooner or later, Sweeney was sure, that suspicion would arise. Sweeney had had no experience of women, but he was nevertheless convinced that Mike was an exceptional sample. Her quickness of penetration sometimes seemed close to telepathy. He mulled the question, leaning on the railing around the hedge below the mountain, looking reflectively into the Gouge, constructing his answer. Each day he had to shorten that mulling-time, though the questions grew no less difficult for his pains.

"From the Port cops," he said. "I've got only two answers to that question, Mike. Anything I didn't get from my mother, I got from spying on the cops."

Mike, too, looked down into the mists of the Gouge. It was a warm summer day, and a long one—three and a half Earth days long, while the satellite was on the sunward side of Jupiter, and coming, with Jupiter, closer and closer to the sun. The wind which blew over the flute-mouthpiece of rock on this side of the mountain was as gentle and variable as a flautist's breath, and did not stir the enormous tangled stolons and runners which filled the bottom of the great valley, or the wrap-around leaves which were plastered to them like so many thousands of blue-green Möbius strips.

It was not quiet down there, but it seemed quiet. There were many more thrums and rummums of rolling rocks and

20

distant avalanches than one heard during the cold weather. The granite-skinned roots were growing rapidly while their short time was come, burrowing insistently into the walls of the valley, starting new trees and new rocks. In the cliffs, the warm weather changed water-of-crystallization from Ice IV to Ice III, the bound water snapping suddenly from one volume to another, breaking the rock strata apart. Sweeney knew how that worked; that was exfoliation; it was common on the Moon, though on the Moon it was caused by the re-freezing of Ice I in the gypsum strata. But the end-result was the same: rock-slides.

All these incessant erratic rumbles and muted thunders were the sounds of high summer in the Gouge. They were as peaceful to Sweeney's ears as bee-buzz is to an Earthman, though Sweeney had never encountered bee-buzz except in books. And like growing things everywhere, the terrific gnarled creepers down below sent up into the Adapted Men's air a fresh complacent odor, the specific smell of vegetable battle-unto-death which lulls animal nostrils and animal glands into forgetting past struggles of their own.

Ganymede was, as a matter of fact, a delightful world, even for a dead man. Or solely for a dead man.

"I can't understand why the Port cops would waste time batting lies back and forth," Mike said at last. "*They* know we weren't doing any commerce-raiding. We've never been so much as off Ganymede since we landed here. And we couldn't get off if we wanted to, now. Why should they pretend that we did? Why would they talk about it as if it was a fact, especially since they didn't know you were listening? It's senseless."

"I don't know," Sweeney said. "It never entered my head that you *weren't* commerce-raiding. If I'd had any notion that they weren't telling the truth, I'd have listened for clues to tell me why they weren't. But it never entered my head. And now it's too late; all I can do is guess."

"You must have heard something. Something you don't remember consciously. I can guess, too, but it's your guess that's important. You were listening to them; I wasn't. Try, Don."

"Well," Sweeney said, "maybe they didn't know that what they were saying was untrue. There's no law that says a Port cop has to be told the truth by his bosses. They're back on Earth; I was on the Moon, and so were they. And they sounded pretty convinced; the subject kept coming up, all the time, just casually, as if everybody knew about it. They all believed that Ganymede was raiding passenger liners as far

21

in as the orbit of Mars. It was a settled fact. That's how I heard it."

"That fits," Mike said. Nevertheless, she was not looking at Sweeney; instead, she bent her head farther down over the rim of the Gouge, her hands locked together before her in dim space, until her small breasts were resting lightly on the railing. Sweeney took a long breath. The effluvium of the vines suddenly seemed anything but lulling.

"Tell me, Don," she said. "When did you hear the cops begin to talk this subject up? For the first time, I mean?"

His veering attention snapped back into the frigid center of his being so suddenly that it left behind a bright weal, as if a lash had been laid across his exposed brain. Mike was dangerous; dangerous. He had to remember that.

"When?" he said. "I don't know, Mike. The days were all alike. It was toward the end, I think. When I was a kid I used to hear them talk about us as if we were criminals, but I couldn't figure out why. I guessed that it was because we were different, that's all. It was only at the end that they began to talk about specific crimes, and even then it didn't make much sense to me. My mother and I hadn't ever pirated any ships, that was for sure."

"Only at the last. That's what I thought. They began to talk like that for the first time when your power began to fail. Isn't that right?"

Sweeney gave that one a long think, at least twice as long as would ordinarily have been safe before Mike. He already knew where Mike's questions were leading him. In this instance, a quick answer would be fatal. He had to appear to be attempting, with some pain, to dredge up information which was meaningless to him. After a while, he said:

"Yes, it was about then. I was beginning to cut down on tapping their calls; it didn't take much power, but we needed all we had. Maybe I missed hearing the important parts; that's possible."

"No," Mike said grimly. "I think you heard all of it. Or all you were meant to hear. And I think you interpreted what you heard in exactly the way they wanted you to, Don."

"It could be," Sweeney said slowly. "I was only a kid. I would have taken what I heard at face value. But that would mean that they knew we were there. I wonder. I don't remember exactly, but I don't think we had begun to sneak power from them yet. We were still thinking about putting a sun-cell on the surface, in those days."

"No, no. They must have known you were there years before you began to tap their power. Rullman's been talking about that lately. There are simple ways of detecting even a phone-line tap, and your strontium battery couldn't have been undetected very long, either. They waited only until they could be sure they'd get you when they finally raided you. It's the way they think. In the meantime, they fed you hokum when you eavesdropped."

So much for the story the cops had told Sweeney to tell. Only the extreme of stupidity which it assumed in the Adapted Men had protected it this long; nobody defends himself, at least at first, upon the assumption that his opponent thinks he is a microcephalic idiot. The deception had lasted two months, but it would never last 300 days.

"Why would they do that?" Sweeney said. "They were going to kill us as soon as they could—as soon as they could work out a way to do it without damaging our equipment. What did they care what we thought?"

"Torture," Mike said, straightening and locking her hands around the railing with the automatic tetany of a bird's claws touching a perch. She looked across the Gouge at the distant, heaped range on the other side. "They wanted you to think that everything your people had planned and done had come to nothing—that we had wound up as nothing but vicious criminals. Since they couldn't get to you and your mother immediately, they amused themselves with strafing you while they worked. Maybe they thought it'd help soften you up—goad you into making some mistake that would make the job of getting in to you easier. Or maybe they did it just because they enjoyed it. Because it made them feel good."

After a short silence, Sweeney said, "Maybe that was it. Maybe not. I don't know, Mike."

She turned to him suddenly and took him by the shoulders. Her eyes were crystal blue. "How could you know?" she said, her fingers digging into his deltoid muscles. "How could you know *anything* when there was nobody to tell you? The Earth must be full of lies about us now—lies, and nothing but lies! You've got to forget them—forget them all—just as though you'd just been born. You *have* just been born, Don, believe me. Only just. What they fed you on the Moon was lies; you've got to start learning the truth here, learning it from the beginning, like a child!"

She held him a moment longer. She was actually shaking him. Sweeney did not know what to say; he did not even know what emotion to mimic. The emotion he felt was still almost unknown; he did not dare let it show, let alone let it loose. While the girl looked furiously into his eyes, he could not even blink.

After all, he really had been born some time ago. Born dead.

The painful, tenfold pressure on his shoulders changed suddenly to a residual tingling over a deep ache, and Mike's hands dropped to her sides. She looked away, across the Gouge again. "It's no use," she said indistinctly. "I'm sorry. That's a hell of a way for a girl to talk to her uncle."

"That's all right, Mike. I was interested."

"I'm sure of it. . . . Let's go for a walk, Don. I'm sick of looking into the Gouge." She was already striding back toward the looming mountain under which the colony lived.

Sweeney watched her go, his icy blood sighing in his ears. It was terrible to be unable to think; he had never known the dizziness of it until he had met Mike Leverault, but now it seemed determined never to leave him—it abated sometimes, but it never quite went away. He had been ruefully glad, at the very beginning, that the close "blood" tie between himself and Mike, a genetic tie which was quite real since he was in fact Shirley Leverault's Adapted son, would prevent his becoming interested in the girl in accordance with Earth custom. But in fact it had had no such effect. Earth tabus had no force for him, and here on Ganymede, that particular tabu had been jettisoned summarily. Rullman had told him why.

"Don't give it a second thought," he had said on that very first day, grinning into Sweeney's stunned face. "We haven't any genetic reasons for forbidding inbreeding; quite the contrary. In a small group like ours, the strongest and most immediate evolutionary influence is genetic drift. Unless we took steps to prevent it, there'd be a loss of unfixed genes with every new generation. Obviously we can't allow that, or we'd wind up with a group in which there'd be no real individuals: everybody would be alike in some crucial and absolutely unpredictable respect. No tabu is worth that kind of outcome."

Rullman had gone on from there. He had said that simply permitting inbreeding could not in itself halt genetic drift; that in some respects it encouraged it; and that the colony was taking positive measures to circumvent drift, measures which would begin to bear fruit within eight generations. He had begun by this time to talk in terms of alleles and isomorphs and lethal recessives, and to scribble such cryptograms as $rrR:rRR/('rA)rr/R'Rr$ on the sheet of mica before him; and then, suddenly, he had looked up and realized that he had lost his audience. That, too, had amused him.

Sweeney had not minded. He knew he was ignorant. Besides, the colony's plans meant nothing to him; he was on

Ganymede to bring the colony to an end. As far as Mike was concerned, he knew that nothing would govern him but his monumental loneliness, as it governed everything else that he did and felt.

But he had been astonished to discover that, covertly at least, that same loneliness governed everyone else in the colony, with the sole possible exception of Rullman.

Mike looked back, and then, her face hardening, quickened her pace. Sweeney followed, as he knew he had to; but he was still struggling to think.

Much of what he had learned about the colony, if it was true—and at least everything he had been able to check had passed that test—had involved his unlearning what he had been taught by the Port cops. The cops, for instance, had said that the alleged commerce-raiding had had two purposes: secondarily to replenish food and equipment, but primarily to augment the colonists' numbers by capturing normal people for Adaptation.

There was no commerce-raiding going on now, that much was certain, and Sweeney was inclined to believe Mike's denial that there had ever been any in the past. Once one understood the ballistics of space-travel, one understood also that piracy is an impossible undertaking, simply because it is more work than it is worth. But beyond this persuasive practical objection, there was the impossibility of the motive the Port cops had imputed to the Ganymedians. The primary purpose was nonsense. The colonists were fertile, and hence did not need recruits; and besides, it was impossible to convert a normal adult human being into an Adapted Man—pantropy had to begin before conception, as it had been begun with Sweeney.

Calamitously, the reverse also appeared to be true. Sweeney had been unable to find anybody in the colony who believed it possible to convert an Adapted Man back into a human being. The promise the Port cops had held out to him—though they had never made it directly—thus far appeared to be founded upon nothing better than dust. If it were nevertheless possible to bring a man like Sweeney back to life, only Rullman knew about it, and Sweeney had to be hypercautious in questioning Rullman. The scientist had already made some uncomfortable deductions from the sparse facts and ample lies with which Sweeney had, by order of the Port cops, provided him. Like everyone else on Ganymede, Sweeney had learned to respect the determination and courage which were bodied forth in everything Rullman did and said; but unlike anybody else on Ganymede, he feared Rullman's understanding.

And in the meantime—while Sweeney waited, with a fatalism disturbed only by Mike Leverault, for Rullman to see through him to the other side of the gouge which was Sweeney's frigid tangled substitute for a human soul—there remained the question of the crime.

We must have those men back. Why? *Because we need to know what they know.* Why not ask them? *They won't tell us.* Why not? *Because they're afraid.* What of? *They committed a crime and must be punished.* What did they do?

SILENCE

So the question of the crime still remained. It had not been commerce-raiding; even had the Ganymedians achieved the impossible and had pirated spacecraft, that would not have been the *first* crime, the one which had made the Adapted Men flee to Ganymede in the first place, the crime from which the whole technique of pantropy had sprung. What high crime had the parents of the Adapted Men committed, to force them to maroon their children on Ganymede for what they must have believed was to be forever?

The responsibility was not the children's, that much was also obvious. The children had never been on the Earth at all. They had been born and raised on the Moon, in strict secrecy. The cops' pretense that the colonists themselves were wanted back for some old evil was another fraud, like the story about commerce-raiding. If a crime had been committed on Earth, it had been committed by the normal Earthmen whose frigid children roamed Ganymede now; it could have been committed by no-one else.

Except, of course, by Rullman. Both on the Moon and on Ganymede it was the common assumption that Rullman had been an Earth-normal human being once. That was impossible, but it was agreed to be so. Rullman himself turned the question away rather than deny it. Perhaps the crime had been his alone, since there was nobody else who could have committed it.

But *what* crime? Nobody on Ganymede could, or would, tell Sweeney. None of the colonists believed in it. Most of them thought that nothing was held against them but their difference from normal human beings; the exceptional few thought that the development of pantropy itself was the essential crime. Of that, clearly, Rullman was guilty, if "guilty" was the applicable word.

Why pantropy, or the responsibility for developing it, should be considered criminal was a mystery to Sweeney, but there was a great deal else that he didn't know about Earth laws and standards, so he wasted no more time in puzzling over it. If Earth said that inventing or using pantropy was a crime, that was what it was; and the Port cops had already told him that he must not fail to bring back Rullman, no matter how grievously he failed to fulfill all his other instructions. It was an answer, and that was enough.

But why hadn't the cops said so in the first place? And why, if pantropy was a crime, had the cops themselves compounded that identical crime—by creating Sweeney?

Belatedly, he quickened his pace. Mike had already disappeared under the lowering brow of the great cavern. He could not remember noticing, now, which of the dozen smaller entrances she had used, and he himself did not know where more than two of them led. He chose one at random.

Four turns later, he was hopelessly lost.

This was unusual, but it was not entirely unexpected. The network of tunnels under Howe's *pi* was a labyrinth, not only in fact but by intention. In drilling out their home, the Adapted Men had taken into consideration the possibility that gun-carrying men in spacesuits might some day come looking for them. Such a man would never find his way out from under the mountain, unless an Adapted Man who had memorized the maze led him out; and he would never find an Adapted Man, either. Memorization was the only key, for no maps of the maze existed, and the colonists had a strictly enforced law against drawing one.

Sweeney had perhaps half of the maze committed to memory. If he did not meet someone he knew—for after all, nobody was hiding from *him*—he could count upon entering a familiar section sooner or later. In the meantime, he was curious to see anything that there was to be seen.

The first thing of interest that he saw was Dr. Rullman. The scientist emerged from a tunnel set at a 20° angle to the one Sweeney was in at the moment, going away from Sweeney and unaware of him. After an instant's hesitation, Sweeney followed him, as silently as possible. The noisy ventilation system helped to cover his footfalls.

Rullman had a habit of vanishing for periods ranging from half a day to a week. Anybody who knew where he went and what he did there did not talk about it. Now was a chance, perhaps, for Sweeney to find out for himself. It was possible, of course, that Rullman's disappearances were related to the forthcoming meteorological crisis on Ganymede, about which Sweeney had been hearing an increasing number of hints. On the other hand . . . what was on the other hand? There could be no harm in investigating.

Rullman walked rapidly, his chin ducked into his chest, as though he were travelling a route so familiar that habit could be entrusted with carrying him along it. Once Sweeney almost lost him, and thereafter cautiously closed up the interval between them a little; the labyrinth was sufficiently complex to offer plenty of quick refuges should Rullman show signs of turning back. As the scientist moved, there came from him an unpredictable but patterned series of wordless sounds, intoned rather than spoken. They communicated nothing, actuated no mechanisms, gave Rullman no safe-conduct—as was evidenced by the fact that Sweeney was travelling the same course without making any such noise. Indeed, Rullman himself seemed to be unaware that he was making it.

Sweeney was puzzled. He had never heard anybody hum before.

The rock beneath Sweeney's feet began to slope downward, gently but definitely. At the same time, he noticed that the air was markedly warmer, and was becoming more so with almost every step. A dim sound of laboring machinery was pulsing in it.

It got hotter, and still hotter, but Rullman did not hesitate. The noise—which Sweeney could now identify definitely as that of pumps, many of them—also increased. The two men were now walking down a long, straight corridor, bordered by closed doors rather than maze exits; it was badly lit, but Sweeney nevertheless allowed Rullman to get farther ahead of him. Toward the other end of this corridor, the heat began to diminish, to Sweeney's relief, for he had begun to feel quite dizzy. Rullman gave no indication that he even noticed it.

At this end Rullman ducked abruptly into a side entrance which turned out to be the top of a flight of stone steps. Quite a perceptible draft of warm air was blowing down it. Warm air, Sweeney knew, was supposed to rise in a gravitational field; why it should be going in the opposite direction he could not imagine, especially since there appeared to be no blowers in operation on this level. Since it was blowing toward Rullman, it would also carry any noise Sweeney made ahead of him. He tiptoed cautiously down.

Rullman was not in sight when Sweeney left the stairwell. There was before Sweeney, instead, a long, high-ceilinged passageway which curved gently to the right until vision was cut off. Along the inside of the curve, regularly spaced, were crouching machines, each one with a bank of laterally-coiled metal tubing rearing before it. These were the sources of the sounds, Sweeney had heard.

Here, it was cold again; abnormally cold, despite the heavy current of warm air blowing down the stairwell. Something, Sweeney thought, was radically wrong with the behaviour of the thermodynamic laws down here.

He slouched cautiously ahead. After only a few steps, past the first of the laboring mechanisms—yes, it was coldest by the shining coils, as if cold were actually radiating from them —he found an undeniable airlock. Furthermore, it was in use: the outer door was sealed, but a little light beside it said that the lock was cycling. Opposite the lock, on the other wall, one of a row of spacesuit lockers hung open and tenantless.

But it was the legend painted on the airlock valve which finally made everything fall into place. It said:

PANTROPE LABORATORY ONE
Danger — Keep Out!

Sweeney dodged away from the airlock with a flash of pure panic, as a man wanted for murder might jump upon seeing a sign saying "50,000 volts." It was all clear now. There was nothing wrong with the thermodynamics of this corridor that was not similarly "wrong" inside any refrigerator. The huge engines were pumps, all right—heat pumps. Their coils were frost-free only because there was no water vapor in Ganymede's air; nevertheless, they were taking heat from that air and transferring it to the other side of that rock wall, into the pantrobe lab.

No wonder the laboratory was sealed off from the rest of the maze by an airlock—and that Rullman had had to put on a spacesuit to go through it.

It was hot on the other side. Too hot for an Adapted Man.

But *what* Adapted Man?

What good was pantropy to Rullman here? That phase of history was supposed to be over and done with. Yet what was going on in this laboratory obviously was as alien to the environment of Ganymede as Ganymede's environment was to Earth's.

A is to B as B is to—what? To C? Or *to* A?

Was Rullman, in the face of the impossibility of such a project, *trying to re-adapt his people to Earth?*

There should be dials or meters on this side of the wall which would give more information as to what it was like on the other side. And there they were, in a little hooded embrasure which Sweeney had overlooked in the first shock. They said:

059		0614
	—	0030

Degrees F.   Millibars

047		0140

Dew Point O_2 Tens mm Hg

Some of these meant nothing to Sweeney: he had never before encountered pressure expressed in millibars, let alone the shorthand way it was registered on the meter before him; nor did he know how to compute relative humidity from the dew point. With the Fahrenheit scale he was vaguely familiar, vaguely enough to have forgotten how to convert it into Centigrade readings. But—

Oxygen tension!

There was one planet, and one only, where such a measurement could have any meaning.

Sweeney ran.

He was no longer running by the time he had reached Rullman's office, although he was still thoroughly out of breath. Knowing that he would be unable to cross back over the top of the pantrobe lab again, feeling that heat beating up at him and knowing at least in part what it meant, he had gone in the opposite direction, past the gigantic heat-exchangers, and blundered his way up from the other side. The route he had followed had covered over three erratic miles, and several additional discoveries which had shaken him almost as hard as had the first one.

He was entirely unsure that he was even rational any more. But he had to know. Nothing was important to him now but the answer to the main question, the permanent founding or dashing of the hope under which he had lived so long.

Rullman was already back in the office, almost surrounded by his staff. Sweeney pushed his way forward among the Ganymedians, his jaw set, his diaphragm laboring.

"This time we're going to close all the safety doors," Rullman said into the phone. "The pressure fronts are going to be too steep to allow us to rely on the outside locks alone. See to it that everybody knows where he's to be as soon as the alert sounds, and this time make it stick; we don't want anybody trapped between doors for the duration. This time it may swoop down on us at damn short notice."

The phone murmured and cut out.

"Hallam, how's the harvesting? You've got less than a week, you know."

"Yes, Dr. Rullman—we'll be through in time."

"And another thing—oh, hello, Donald. What's the matter? You're looking a little pasty. I'm pretty busy, so make it fast, please."

"I'll make it fast," Sweeney said. "I can put it all into one question if I can talk to you privately. For just a few seconds."

Rullman's reddish eyebrows went up, but after examining Sweeney's face more closely, the scientist nodded and rose. "Come next door, then. . . . Now then, youngster, spit it out. With the storm coming up, we don't have time for shilly-shallying."

"All right," Sweeney said, taking a long breath. "This is it: Is it possible to change an Adapted Man back into a human being? An Earth-normal human being?"

Rullman's eyes narrowed very slowly; and for what seemed a long time, he said nothing. Sweeney looked back. He was afraid, but he was no longer afraid of Rullman.

"You've been down below, I see," the scientist said at last, drumming at the base of his chin with two fingers. "And from the terms you use, it strikes me that Shirley Leverault's educational methods left—well, the cliché springs to mind—something to be desired. But we'll let those things pass for now.

"The answer to your question, in any case, is: *No*. You will never be able to live a normal life in any other place than Ganymede, Donald. And I'll tell you something else that your mother should have told you: You ought to be damned glad of it."

"Why should I?" Sweeney said, almost emotionlessly.

"Because, like every other person in this colony, you have a Jay-positive blood type. This wasn't concealed from you when we found it, on the first day you joined us, but evidently it didn't register—or had no special significance for you. Jay-positive blood doesn't mean anything on Ganymede, true enough. *But Jay-positive Earth-normal people are cancer-*

31

prones. They are as susceptible to cancer as hemophiliacs are to bleeding to death—and upon equally short notice.

"If by some miracle you *should* be changed to an Earth-normal man, Donald, you would be under immediate sentence of death. So I say you should be glad that it can't happen—damn glad!"

3

The crisis on Ganymede—though of course it would not even be an incident, were there nobody there to live through it—comes to fruition roughly every eleven years and nine months. It is at the end of this period that Jupiter—and hence his fifteen-fold family of moons and moonlets—makes his closest approach to the Sun.

The eccentricity of Jupiter's orbit is only 0.0484, which amounts to very little for an ellipse which averages 483,300,000 miles from its focal points. Nevertheless, at perihelion Jupiter is nearly ten million miles closer to the Sun than he is at aphelion; and the weather on Jupiter, never anything less than hellish, becomes indescribable during that approach. So, on a smaller but sufficient scale, does the weather on Ganymede.

The perihelion temperature on Ganymede never rises high enough to melt the ice of Neptune's Trident, but it does lift through the few niggardly degrees necessary to make the vapor pressure of Ice III known in Ganymede's air. Nobody on Earth could dream of calling the resulting condition "humidity," but Ganymede's weather turns upon such microscopic changes; an atmosphere containing *no* water will react rapidly to even a fractional vapor content. For one thing, it will pick up more heat. The resulting cycle does not go through more than a few turns before it flattens out, but the end-product is no less vicious.

The colony, Sweeney gathered, had come through one such period without any but minor difficulties, simply by withdrawing entirely under the mountain; but for many reasons that course was no longer possible. There were now semi-permanent installations—weather stations, observatories, radio beacons, bench-marks and other surveying monuments—which could be dismantled only with the loss of much time before the crisis, and re-established with still more loss afterwards.

32

Furthermore, some of them would be needed to report and record the progress of the crisis itself, and hence had to stay where they were.

"And don't get the idea," Rullman told a mass meeting of the colonists, gathered in the biggest cavern of the maze, "that even the mountain can protect us all the way through this one. I've told you before, but I'll remind you again, that the climax this year coincides with the peak of the sunspot cycle. Everybody's seen what that does to the weather on Jupiter proper. We can expect similar effects, to scale, on Ganymede. There's going to be trouble no matter how well we prepare. All we can hope for is that the inevitable damage will be minor. Anybody who thinks we're going to get off scot-free has only to listen for a minute."

In the calculated, dramatic pause which followed, everybody listened. The wind was audible even down here, howling over the outlets and intakes of the ventilation system, carried, amplified and encrusted with innumerable echoes, by the metal miles of the air ducts. The noise was a reminder that, at the height of the coming storm, the exterior ports would all be closed, so that everyone under the mountain would have to breathe recirculated air. After a moment, a mass sigh—an involuntary intake of breath against the easily imagined future—passed through Rullman's audience. He grinned.

"I don't mean to frighten you," he said. "We'll get along. But I don't want any complacency either, and above all, I won't stand for any sloppiness in the preparations. It's particularly important that we keep the outside installations intact this time, because we're going to need them before the end of the next Jovian year—a long time before that, if everything continues to go well."

The grin was suddenly quenched. "I don't need to tell some of you how important it is that we get that project completed on schedule," Rullman said, quietly. "We may not have much time left before the Port cops decide to move in on us—it amazes me that they haven't already done so, particularly since we're harboring a fugitive the cops troubled to chase almost into our atmosphere—and we can't plan on their giving us any leeway.

"For those of you who know about the project only in outline, let me emphasize that there is a good deal more hanging from it than immediately meets the eye. Man's whole future in space may be determined by how well we carry it off; we can't afford to be licked—neither by the Earth nor by the weather. If we are, our whole long struggle for survival will

33

have been meaningless. I'm counting on everyone here to see to it that that doesn't happen."

It was difficult to be sure of what Rullman was talking about when he got onto the subject of the "project." It had something to do with the pantrope labs, that much was clear; and it had to do also with the colony's original spaceship, which Sweeney had run across that same day, stored in a launching chimney almost identical with the one on the Moon out of which Sweeney had been rocketed to begin his own free life, and fitted—if judgment based upon a single brief look could be trusted—either for a long voyage by a few people, or for a short trip by a large group.

Beyond that, Sweeney knew nothing about the "project," except for one additional fact of which he could make nothing: it had something to do with the colony's long-term arrangements for circumventing the loss of unfixed genes. Possibly—nobody would be less able to assess the possibility than Sweeney—the only connection this fact had with the "project" was that it *was* long-term.

Sweeney, in any event, knew better than to ask questions. The storm that was going on inside him took precedence, anyhow; as far as he was concerned, it was even more important than the storms that were sweeping Ganymede, or any that might sweep that world in the foreseeable future. He was not used to thinking in terms of a society, even a small one; Rullman's appeals to that Ideal were simply incomprehensible to him. He was the solar system's most thorough-going individualist—not by nature, but by design.

Perhaps Rullman sensed it. Whether he did or not, the assignment he gave Sweeney might have been perfectly calculated to throw a lonely man into the ultimate isolation he feared; to put the burden of an agonizing decision entirely upon the shoulders of the man who had to carry it; or—to isolate a Port spy where he could do the least harm while the colony's attention was fully occupied elsewhere. Or possibly, even probably, he had none of these motives in mind; what counted, in any event, was what he did.

He assigned Sweeney to the South polar weather station, for the duration of the emergency.

There was almost nothing to do there but watch the crystals of methane "snow" bank against the windows, and keep the station tight. The instruments reported back to base by themselves, and needed no further attention. At the height of the crisis, perhaps, Sweeney might find himself busy for a while; or, he might not. That remained to be seen.

In the meantime, he had plenty of time to ask questions—

and nobody to ask them of but himself, and the hooting, constantly rising wind.

There was an interlude. Sweeney hiked, on foot, back to Howe's H to recover the radio transceiver he had buried there, and then hiked back to the weather station. It took him eleven days, and efforts and privations of which Jack London might have made a whole novel. To Sweeney it meant nothing; he did not know whether or not he would want to use the radio after he got back with it; and as for the saga of his solo journey, he did not know that it was a saga, or even that it had been unusually difficult and painful. He had nothing against which to compare it, not even fiction; he had never read any. He measured things by the changes they made in his situation, and possession of the radio had not changed the questions he was asking himself; it had only made it possible to act upon the answers, once he had any answers.

Coming back to the station, he saw a pinnah-bird. It burrowed into the nearest drift as soon as it saw him, but for the preceding instant he had had company. He never saw it again, but now and then he thought about it.

The question, put simply, was: What was he going to do now?

That he was thoroughly in love with Mike Leverault could no longer be argued. It was doubly difficult to come to grips with the emotion, however, because he did not know the name of it, and so had to reason each time with the raw experience itself, rather than with the more convenient symbol. Each time he thought about it, it shook him all over again. But there it was.

As for the colonists, he was certain that they were not criminals in any way, except by Earth's arbitary fiat. They were a hard-working, courageous, decent lot, and had offered to Sweeney the first disinterested friendliness he had ever known.

And, like all the colonists, Sweeney could not help but admire Rullman.

There, in those three propositions, rested the case against using the radio.

The time for reporting to Meiklejon was almost up. The inert transceiver on the table before Sweeney had only to send a single one of five notes, and the colony on Ganymede would be ended. The notes were coded:

WAVVY: *Have custody need pickup*
NAVVY: *Have custody need help*
VVANY: *Need custody have help*
AAVYV: *Need custody need pickup*
YYAWY: *Have custody have pickup*

35

What response the computer on board the ship would make, what course of action it would dictate in response to any one of those signals was unknown, but that was now almost beside the point. Any response would be inappropriate, since not one of the five signals fitted the actual situation—despite all the intellectual travail which had gone into tailoring them.

If no note were sent, Meiklejon would go away at the end of 300 days. That might mean that Rullman's "project," whatever that was, would go through—but that wouldn't save the colony. It would take Earth a minimum of two generations to breed and mature another Sweeney from the artificially maintained ovaries of mercifully long-dead Shirley Leverault, and it was hardly likely that Earth would even try. Earth probably knew more than Sweeney did about the "project"—it would be difficult to know less—and if Sweeney himself failed to stop it, the next attempt would most likely arrive as a bomb. Earth would stop wanting "those men" back, once it became evident that she couldn't get them even through so subtle a double agent as Sweeney.

Item: chain reaction. There was, Sweeney knew, a considerable amount of deuterium on Ganymede, some of it locked in the icy wastes of Neptune's Trident, a lesser amount scattered through the rocks in the form of lithium deuteride. A fission bomb going off here would stand an excellent chance of starting a fusion explosion which would detonate the whole satellite. If any still-active fragment of that explosion should hit Jupiter, only a bare 665,000 miles away now, that planet would be quite large enough to sustain a Bethé or carbon cycle; it was diffuse, but it alone among the planets had the mass. The wave front of *that* unimaginable catastrophe would boil Earth's seas in their beds; it might also—the probability was about $3/8$—trigger a nova outburst from the Sun, though nobody would stay alive to be grateful very long if it didn't.

Since Sweeney knew this, he had to assume that it was common knowledge, and that Earth would use chemical explosives only on Ganymede. But would it? Common knowledge and Sweeney had had precious little contact so far.

Still, it hardly mattered. If Earth bombed the colony, it would be all up with him, regardless. Even the limited companionship, the wordless love, the sense that he might yet be born, all would be gone. He would be gone. So might the little world.

But if he signalled Meiklejon and the computer, he would be taken alive away from Mike, away from Rullman, away from the colony, away and away. He would stay his own dead self. He might even have a new chance to learn that same endless lesson about the shapes loneliness can take; or, Earth might work a miracle and turn him into a live, Jay-positive human being.

The wind rose and rose. The congruent furies of the storms inside and outside Sweeney mounted together. Their congruence made a classic example, had he been able to recognize it, of the literary device called "the pathetic fallacy"— but Sweeney had never read any fiction, and recognizing nature in the process of imitating art would have been of no use to him anyhow.

He did not even know that, when the crisis of the exterior storm began to wear away the windward edge of the weather station's foundations with a million teeth of invisible wrath, his lonely battle to save the station might have made an epic. Whole chapters, whole cantos, whole acts of what might have been conscious heroism in another man, in a human being, were thrown away while Sweeney went about his business, his mind on his lonely debate.

There was no signal he could send that would tell Meiklejon or the computer the truth. He did not have custody of the men Earth wanted, and he didn't want to have it, so it would be idiotic to ask for help to get it. He no longer believed that Earth "must have those men back," either for Earth's purposes—mysterious though they remained—or for his own, essentially hopeless though his own appeared to be.

But any signal would take him off Ganymede—if he wanted to be taken.

The crisis, he saw, was over. He made the station fast.

He checked the radio once more. It worked. He snapped the turning pointer to one of its copper contacts and closed the key, sending Meiklejon VVANY. After half an hour, the set's oscillator began to peep rhythmically, indicating that Meiklejon was still in Ganymede's sky, and had heard.

Sweeney left the set on the table in the station, went back to the mountain, and told Rullman what he was and what he had done.

Rullman's fury was completely quiet, and a thousand times more frightening than the most uncontrolled rage could have been. He simply sat behind his desk and looked at Sweeney, all the kindness gone out of his face, and the warmth out of his eyes. After a few moments, Sweeney realized that the blankness of Rullman's eyes meant that he was not seeing him at all; his mind was turned inward. So was his rage.

"I'm astonished," he said, in a voice so even that it seemed to contain no surprise at all. "Most of all, I'm astonished at myself. I should have anticipated something like this. But I didn't dream that they had the knowledge, or the guile, to stake everything on a long-term program like this. I have been, in short, an idiot."

His voice took on, for a moment, a shade of color, but it was so scathing that it made Sweeney recoil. And yet no single word of condemnation of Sweeney had yet been forthcoming from Rullman; the man was, instead, strafing himself. Sweeney said tentatively:

"How could you have known? There were a lot of points where I might have given myself away, but I was doing my damndest not to. I might have kept the secret still longer, if I'd wanted it that way."

"You?" Rullman said. The single syllable was worse than a blow. "You're as blameless as a machine, Donald. I know too much about pantropy to think otherwise. It's very easy to isolate an Adapted infant, prevent him from becoming a human being at all, if you've sufficient ill-will to want to. Your behavior was predictable, after all."

"Was it?" Sweeney said, a little grimly. "I came and told you, didn't I?"

"And what if you did? Can that change matters now? I'm sure that Earth included that very high probability in its plans. Insofar as you have loyalties at all, they were bound to become divided; but it was probably calculated that they would stay divided—that is, would not change completely. And so here you are, trying to play both ends against the middle—you yourself being the middle—by betraying your masquerade to me at the same time you betray the colony to Earth. Nothing can be accomplished by that."

"Are you sure?"

"Quite sure," Rullman said stonily. "I suppose they offered you an inducement. Judging by the questions you've asked me before, they must have promised to make an Earth-normal human being out of you—as soon as they found out from us how to do that. But the fact of the matter is that it can't be done at all, and you know it. And now there's no future for you with us, either. I'm sorry for you, Donald, believe me; it's not your fault that they made you into a creature instead of a person. But you are nothing now but a bomb that's already gone off."

Sweeney had never known his father, and the hegemony of the Port cops had been too diffuse to instill in him any focussed, automatic respect for persons standing *in loco par-*

entis. He discovered, suddenly, that he was furious with Rull-man.

"That's a silly damn speech," he said, staring down and across the desk at the seated, slightly bowed man. "Nothing's gone off yet. There's plenty of information I can give you that you might use, if you want to work to get it. Of course if you've given up in advance—"

Rullman looked up. "What do you know?" he said, with some puzzlement. "You said yourself that it would be the computer on board this Capt. Meiklejon's ship that would decide the course of action. And you can't communicate effectively with Meiklejon. This is a strange time to be bluffing, Donald."

"Why would I bluff? I know more about what Earth is *likely* to do with my message than anybody else in the colony. My experience with Earth is more recent. I wouldn't have come to you at all if I'd thought the situation to be hopeless—and if I hadn't carefully picked the one message to send to Meiklejon that I thought left the colony some hope. I'm not straddling. I'm on your side. To send no message at all would have been the worst possible thing to do. This way, we may have a grace period."

"And just how," Rullman said slowly, "can you expect me to trust you?"

"That's your problem," Sweeney said brusquely. "If I really am still straddling, it's because the colony's failed to convince me that my future lies here. And if that's the case, I'm not alone—and it's the colony's own fault for being so secretive with its own people."

"Secretive?" Rullman said, with open astonishment now. "About what?"

"About the 'project.' About the original crime Earth wants you for. About why Earth wants you back—you in particular, Dr. Rullman."

"But—that's common knowledge, Donald. All of it."

"Maybe so. But it isn't common to *me*—and most of the original settlers take it all so much for granted that they can't talk about it, except in little cryptic references, like a private joke everybody's supposed to know. But everybody doesn't; did you know that? I've found that about half your second generation here has only the foggiest notion of the past. The amount of information available here to a newcomer— whether he's newly arrived like me, or just plain newborn— you could stick in a pinnah-bird's eye. And that's dangerous. It's why I could have betrayed the colony *completely* if I hadn't decided against it, and you couldn't have stopped me."

Rullman leaned back and was quiet for quite a long time.

"Children often don't ask questions when they think they're already expected to know the answers," he murmured. He looked considerably more thunderstruck than he had when Sweeney made his original announcement. "They like to appear knowing even when they aren't. It gives them status in their own eyes."

"Children and spies," Sweeney said. "There are certain questions neither of them can ask, and for almost the same reasons. And the phonier the children's knowledge actually is, the easier for the spy to get around among the adults."

"I begin to see," Rullman said. "We thought we were immune to spying, because an Earth spy couldn't live here without elaborate, detectable protections. But that was a problem in physics, and that kind of problem is soluble. We should have assumed so from the beginning. Instead, we made ourselves socially as vulnerable as possible."

"That's how I see it. I'll bet that my father wouldn't have let you get away with it if he'd been able to get away with you. He was supposed to have been an expert in that kind of thing. I don't know; I never knew him. And I suppose it's beside the point, anyhow."

"No," Rullman said. "It's very much to the point, and I think you've just proven it, Donald. Your father couldn't prevent it, but perhaps he's given us an instrument for repairing it."

"Meaning me?"

"Yes. Ringer or no ringer, the blood you carry—and the genes—have been with us from the beginning, and I know how they show their effects. I see them now. Sit down, Donald. I begin to hope. What shall we do?"

"First of all," Sweeney said, "please, please tell me what this colony is all about!"

It was a difficult assignment.

Item: the Authorities. Long before space travel, big cities in the United States had fallen so far behind any possibility of controlling their own traffic problems as to make purely political solutions chimerical. No city administration could spend the amount of money needed for a radical cure, without being ousted in the next elections by the enraged drivers and pedestrians who most needed the help.

Increasingly, the traffic problems were turned over, with gratitude and many privileges, to semi-public Port, Bridge and Highway Authorities: huge capital-investment ventures modelled upon the Port of New York Authority, which had shown its ability to build and/or run such huge operations as the Holland and Lincoln Tunnels, the George Washington Bridge, Teterboro, LaGuardia, Idlewild and Newark airports, and many lesser facilities. By 1960 it was possible to travel from the tip of Florida to the border of Maine entirely over Authority-owned territory, if one could pay the appropriate tolls (and didn't mind being shot at in the Poconos by embattled land-owners who were still resisting the gigantic Incadel project).

Item: the tolls. The Authorities were creations of the states, usually acting in pairs, and as such enjoyed legal protections not available to other private firms engaged in interstate commerce. Among these protections, in the typical enabling act, was a provision that "the two said states will not . . . diminish or impair the power of the Authority to establish, levy and collect tolls and other charges . . ." The federal government helped; although the Federal Bridge Act of 1946 required that the collection of tolls must cease with the payment of amortization, Congress almost never invoked the Act against any Authority. Consequently, the tolls never dropped; by 1953 the Port of New York Authority was reporting a profit of over twenty million dollars a year, and annual collections were increasing at the rate of ten per cent a year.

Some of the take went into the development of new facilities—most of them so placed as to increase the take, rather than solve the traffic problem. Again the Port of New York Authority led the way; it built, against all sense, a third tube for the Lincoln Tunnel, thus pouring eight and a half million more cars per year into Manhattan's mid-town area, where the city was already strangling for want of any adequate ducts to take away the then-current traffic.

Item: the Port cops. The Authorities had been authorized from the beginning to police their own premises. As the Authorities got bigger, so did the private police forces.

By the time space travel arrived, the Authorities owned it. They had taken pains to see that it fell to them; they had learned from their airport operations—which, almost alone among their projects, always showed a loss—that nothing less than total control is good enough. And characteristically, they never took any interest in any form of space-travel which did not involve enormous expenditures; otherwise they could take no profits from sub-contracting, no profits from fast amortization of loans, no profits from the laws allowing them fast tax write-offs for new construction, no profits from the indefinitely protracted collection of tolls and fees after the initial cost and the upkeep had been recovered.

At the world's first commercial spaceport, Port Earth, it cost ship owners $5000 each and every time their ships touched the ground. Landing fees had been outlawed in private atmosphere flying for years, but the Greater Earth Port Authority operated under its own set of precedents; it made landing fees for spacecraft routine. And it maintained the first Port police force which was bigger than the armed forces of the nation which had given it its franchise; after a while, the distinction was wiped out, and the Port cops *were* the armed forces of the United States. It was not difficult to do, since the Greater Earth Port Authority was actually a holding company embracing every other Authority in the country, including Port Earth.

And when people, soon after spaceflight, began to ask each other, "How shall we colonize the planets?," the Greater Earth Port Authority had its answer ready.

Item: terraforming.

Terraforming—remaking the planets into near-images of the Earth, so that Earth-normal people could live on them. Port Earth was prepared to start small. Port Earth wanted to move Mars out of its orbit to a point somewhat closer to the sun, and make the minor adjustments needed in the orbits of the other planets; to transport to Mars about enough water to empty the Indian Ocean—only a pittance to Earth, after all, and not 10 per cent of what would be needed later to terraform Venus; to carry to the little planet top-soil about equal in area to the state of Iowa, in order to get started at growing plants which would slowly change the atmosphere of Mars; and so on. The whole thing, Port Earth pointed out reasonably, was perfectly feasible from the point of view of the available supplies and energy resources, and it would cost less than thirty-three billion dollars. The Greater Earth Port Authority was prepared to recover that sum at no cost in taxes in less than a century, through such items as $50 rocket-mail stamps, $10,000 Mars landing fees, $1,000 one-way strap-down tickets, 100-per-desert-acre land titles, and so on. Of course the fees would continue after the cost was recovered—for maintenance.

And what, after all, the Authority asked reasonably, was the alternative? Nothing but domes. The Greater Earth Port Authority hated domes. They cost too little to begin with, and the volume of traffic to and from them would always be miniscule. Experience on the Moon had made that painfully clear. And the public hated domes, too; it had already shown a mass reluctance to live under them.

As for the governments, other than that of the United

States, that the Authority still tolerated, none of them had any love for domes, or for the kind of limited colonization that the domes stood for. They needed to get rid of their pullulating masses by the bucket-full, not by the eye-dropper-full. If the Authority knew that emigration increases the home population rather than cuts it, the Authority carefully refrained from saying so to the governments involved; they could rediscover Franklin's Law for themselves. Domes were out; terraforming was in.

Then came pantropy.

If this third alternative to the problem of colonizing the planets had come as a surprise to the Authority, and to Port Earth, they had nobody to blame for it but themselves. There had been plenty of harbingers. The notion of modifying the human stock genetically to live on the planets as they were found, rather than changing the planets to accommodate the people, had been old with Olaf Stapledon; it had been touched upon by many later writers; it went back, in essence, as far as Proteus, and as deep into the human mind as the werewolf, the vampire, the fairy changeling, the transmigrated soul.

But suddenly it was possible; and, not very long afterwards, it was a fact.

The Authority hated it. Pantropy involved a high initial investment to produce the first colonists, but it was a method which with refinement would become cheaper and cheaper. Once the colonists were planted, it required no investment at all; the colonists were comfortable on their adopted world, and could produce new colonists without outside help. Pantropy, furthermore, was at its *most* expensive less than half as costly as the setting-up of the smallest and least difficult dome. Compared to the cost of terraforming even so favorable a planet as Mars, it cost nothing at all, from the Authority's point of view.

And there was no way to collect tolls against even the initial expense. It was too cheap to bother with.

WILL YOUR CHILD BE A MONSTER?

If a number of influential scientists have their way, some child or grandchild of yours may eke out his life in the frozen wastes of Pluto, where even the sun is only a spark in the sky—and will be unable to return to Earth until after he dies, *if then!*

Yes, even now there are plans afoot to change innocent unborn children into alien creatures who would die terribly the moment that they set foot upon the green planet of their ancestors. Impatient with the slow but steady pace of man's conquest of Mars, prominent ivory-tower thinkers are working out ways to produce all kinds of travesties upon the human form—travesties which will be able to survive, somehow, in the bitterest and most untamed of planetary infernos.

The process which may produce these pitiful freaks— at enormous expense—is called "pantropy." It is already in imperfect and dangerous existence. Chief among its prophets is white-haired, dreamy-eyed Dr. Jacob Rullman, who . . .

"Stop," Sweeney said.

He put his fingertips to his temples, and then, trembling, took them away again and looked at Rullman. The scientist put down the old magazine clipping, which even in its telfon sheath was as yellow as *paella* after its half-life in Ganymede's air. Rullman's own hands were quite steady; and what there was left of his hair was as reddish-brown as ever.

"Those lies!—I'm sorry. But they work, I know they work. That's what they filled me up with. It's different when you realize how vicious they are."

"I know," Rullman said, gently. "It's easy to do. Bringing up an Adapted child is a special process, the child is always isolated and anxious to imitate, you may tell it anything you wish; it has no choice but to believe, it's desperate for closer contact, for acceptance, for the embraces it can never have. It's the ultimate in bottle-babies: the breast that might have fed it may be just on the other side of the glass, but it also lies generations in the past. Even the voice of the mother comes along a wire—if it comes along at all. I know, Donald, believe me. It happened to me, too. And it's very hard."

"Jacob Rullman was—"

"My remote, immediate father. My mother died early. They often do, of the deprivation, I believe; like yours. But my father taught me the truth, there in the Moon caves, before he was killed."

Sweeney took a deep breath. "I'm learning all that now. Go on."

"Are you sure, Donald?"

"Go on. I need to know, and it's not too late. Please."

"Well," Rullman said reflectively, "the Authority got laws passed against pantropy, but for a while the laws didn't have many teeth; Congress was leary of forbidding vivisection at the same time, and didn't know exactly what it *was* being asked to forbid; Port didn't want to be too explicit. My father was determined to see pantropy tried while the laws still provided some loopholes—he knew well enough that they'd be stiffened as soon as Port thought it safe to stiffen them. And he was convinced that we'd never colonize the stars by dome-building or terraforming. Those might work on some of our local planets—Mars, Venus—but not outside."

"Outside? How would anybody get there?"

"With the interstellar drive, Donald. It's been in existence for decades, in fact for nearly half a century. Several exploratory voyages were made with it right after it was discovered, all of them highly successful—though you'll find no mention of them in the press of the time. Port couldn't see any profit emerging out of interstellar flight and suppressed the news, sequestered the patents, destroyed the records of the trips— insofar as it could. But all the Port ships have the overdrive, just in case. Even our ship has it. So does your ferry-pilot friend up there."

Sweeney shut up.

"The thing is this: most planets, even right here inside the solar system, won't sustain domes to begin with, and can't be terraformed in any even imaginable way. Jupiter, for instance. And too many others will yield to either procedure too slowly, and too unprofitably, to tempt Port. Over interstellar distances, Port won't even try, since there'd be no trade or traffic it could collect against.

"Pantropy was the obvious answer—not for Port, certainly, but for man's future in general. Somehow, my father sold that idea to some politicians, and to some people with money, too. He was even able to find several survivors of those early interstellar expeditions, people who knew some of the extra-solar planets *and* the operation of the overdrive. All these people wanted to make at least one demonstration experiment in pantropy, an open-ended one which would lead to others if it succeeded.

"We are that experiment: this colony on Ganymede.

"Port had it outlawed before it was fairly started, but by the time they found the Moon labs it was too late; we got away. It was then that they put teeth into the laws, and made them retroactive; they had to kill pantropy, and they knew it.

"And that is why our very existence is a crime, Donald. And it is an absolute requirement of Port's policy that the colony be a failure, and that they *be able to prove it*. That's why they want us back. They want to be able to exhibit us, to show what helpless freaks we are on Earth, and to tell their people that we couldn't get along on Ganymede either, and had to be bailed out of our own mess.

45

"After that—well, there are those phony commerce-raiding charges you told me about. We'll be tried. We'll be executed, most likely, by exposing us in public to Earth-normal conditions. It would be a fine object-lesson; indeed, the finishing touch."

Sweeney crouched down in his chair, utterly revolted by the first complete emotion he had ever experienced: loathing for himself. He understood, now, the overtones in Rullman's voice. Everyone had been betrayed—everyone!

The voice went on without mercy, piling up the ashes. "Now, as for the project, our project that is, that's equally as simple. We know that in the long run human beings can't colonize the stars without pantropy. We know that Port won't allow pantropy to be used. And we know, therefore, that we ourselves have to carry pantropy to the stars, before Port can head us off. One, two, three, infinity.

"So that's what we're going to do, or *were* going to do. We've got our old ship fitted out for the trip, and we've got a new generation of children—just a small number—trained to operate it, and adapted for—well, for someplace. The kids can't live on Earth, and they can't live on Ganymede; but they can live on one of six different extra-solar planets we've picked out—each one of which is at a different compass-point, and at a different distance from Sol. I know the names of only two of them, the kids are the only ones who know the rest. Which one they'll actually go to will be decided only after they're aloft and on their way. Nobody who stays behind will be able to betray them. Earth will never find them.

"There will be the beginning of the most immense 'seeding program' in man's history: seeding the stars with people.

"If we can still manage to get it off the ground."

In the silence that followed, the door of Rullman's office opened quietly, and Mike Leverault came in, looking preoccupied and carrying a clipboard. She stopped when she saw them, and Sweeney's heart constricted on the thawing slush inside its stiffly pumping chambers.

"Excuse me," she said. "I thought . . . Is there something wrong? You both look so grim—"

"There's something wrong," Rullman said. He looked at Sweeney.

A corner of Sweeney's mouth twitched, without his willing it. He wondered if he were trying to smile, and if so, about what.

"There's no help for it," he said. "Dr. Rullman, your colonists will have to revolt against you."

The starshell burst high, perhaps three miles up. Though it was over the western edge of the plateau, enough light spilled down to the floor of the Gouge to checker the rocking, growling halftrack.

The sound, however, was too faint to break through the noise of the turbines, and Sweeney wasn't worried about the brief light. The truck, pushing its way north at a good twenty miles an hour beneath the wild growth, would be as difficult to detect from the air as a mouse running among roots.

Besides, nobody would be likely to be looking into the Gouge now. The evidences of battle sweeping the highlands were too compelling; Sweeney himself was following them tensely.

Mike was doing the driving, leaving Sweeney free to crouch in the tool- and instrument-littered tonneau by the big aluminum keg, watching the radar screen. The paraboloid basketwork of the radar antenna atop the truck was not sweeping; it was pointing straight back along the way he and Mike had come, picking up a microwave relay from the last automatic station that they had passed. The sweeping was being done for Sweeney, by the big radio-telescope atop Howe's *pi*.

Sweeney paid little attention to the near, low, fast streaks on the screen. They were painted there by rocket ordnance of low calibre—a part of the fighting which had no bearing on the overall pattern. That pattern was already clear: it showed, as it had for days, that the insurgent forces still held the mountain and its heavy weapons, but that the attacking salient from the loyalists' camp up north was maintaining the initiative, and was gathering strength.

It had developed into a running stalemate. Though the insurgents had obviously managed to drive the loyalists out of Howe's *pi*, perhaps by some trick with the ventilators, perhaps by some form of guerrilla warfare, they were equally evidently no match for the loyalists in the field. There they were losing ground twice as fast as they had originally taken it. The supporting fire from the mountain didn't seem to be helping them much; it was heavy, but it was terribly inaccurate. The frequent starshells told their own story of bad visibility and worse intelligence. And the loyalists, ousted though they were, had all the planes; they had the effrontery to fly them over the lines with riding lights.

What the loyalists would do when confronted with the problem of retaking the mountain was another question. Nothing short of very heavy stuff would make much of a dent on Howe's *pi*. And, even overlooking the fact that the heavy stuff was all inside the mountain, it would be suicide for *either* force to use it on Ganymede. The fighting hadn't become that bitter, yet. But it yet might.

And the Earth ships that showed on the screen inside the halftrack knew it. That much showed clearly by their disposition. They were there, almost surely, because they had deduced that Sweeney was leading the insurgents—but they showed no desire to draw in and give Sweeney a hand. Instead, they stood off, a little inside the orbit of Callisto, about 900,000 miles from Ganymede—far enough to give themselves a good running start if they saw an atomic spark on Ganymede, close enough to bail Sweeney out once it seemed that he had gained the victory anyhow.

Mike's voice, shouting something unintelligible, came back to him mixed in with the roaring of the halftrack's turbines.

"What's the matter?" he shouted, cocking his head.

". . . that rock-tumble ahead. If it's as . . . before . . . probably break the beam."

"Stop her," Sweeney shouted. "Want another reading."

The halftrack halted obediently, and Sweeney checked his screen against Rullman's readings, which showed on tumblers snicking over on a counter near his elbow. It checked; 900,-000 was close enough. Maybe a little closer, but not much. The wave-front of a full satellary explosion would cross that distance in about five seconds, carrying instant obliteration with it; but five seconds would be long enough to allow the automatics on the Earth ships to slam them away on transfinite drive.

He slapped her on the shoulder, twice. "Okay so far. Go ahead."

Her reply was lost, but he saw her crash-helmet nod, and the truck began to cant itself slowly and crazily up a long, helter-skelter causeway of boulders and rubble: a sort of talus-slope, one of many rolled each year into the Gouge by exfoliation in the cliffs. Mike turned and smiled back at him gleefully, and he smiled back; the treads were clanking too loudly to permit any other answer.

The whole scheme had depended from the beginning upon so long a chain of *ifs* that it could still fall apart at any moment and at any flawed link. It had been dependable only at the beginning. The signal Sweeney had sent Meiklejon— VVANY—had told Meiklejon nothing, since he didn't know the code; but it had told the computer that Sweeney still lacked custody of the Adapted Men that Earth wanted, but that he had the help he thought he would need in getting that custody eventually. That much was a known. What orders the computer would rap out for Meiklejon in response comprised the first of the *ifs*.

The computer might, of course, react with some incredibly bold piece of gamemanship too remote from normal human thinking to be even guessable; Shannon's chess-playing machines sometimes won games from masters that way, though more usually they could barely hold their own against dubs. Since there was no way to anticipate what such a gambit would be like, neither Sweeney nor Rullman had wasted any time trying to pretend that there was.

But the other alternative was much more likely. The machine would assume that Sweeney was safe, as was evidenced by the arrival of the coded signal; and that if he had help he could only have gathered about him a secret core of disaffected colonists, a "Loyal Ganymedian Underground" or equivalent. Earth would assume, and would build the assumption into the computer, that many of the colonists were dissatisfied with their lives; it was a hope that Earth could turn into a fact without being aware of the delusion, since nobody on Earth could suspect how beautiful Ganymede was. And the computer would assume, too, that it might be only a matter of time before Sweeney also had custody, and would be sending Meiklejon WAVVY—or maybe even YYAWY.

"How will we know if it does?" Rullman had demanded.

"If it does, then the deadline will pass without Meiklejon's making a move. He'll just stick to his orbit until the computer changes his mind. What else could it tell him to do, anyhow? He's just one man in a small ship without heavy armament. And he's an Earthman at that—he couldn't come down here and join my supposed underground group even if the idea occurred to him. He'll sit tight."

The halftrack heaved itself over an almost cubical boulder, slid sidewise along its tilted face, and dropped heavily to the bed of smaller rounded stones. Sweeney looked up from the radar controls to see how the big aluminum keg was taking the ride. It was awash in a sea of hand tools—picks, adzes, sledges, spikes, coils of line rapidly unwinding—but it was securely strapped down. The miracle of fireworks chemistry (and specifically, Ganymedian chemistry) still slumbered in-

49

side it. He clambered forward into the cab beside Mike and strapped himself down to enjoy the ride.

There was no way to predict or to calculate how long an extension of the deadline the machine on Meiklejon's ship would allow Sweeney for the launching of his insurrection. The colony worked as though there would be no grace period at all. When the deadline passed without any sign that Meiklejon even existed—though the radio-telescope showed that he was still there—Sweeney and Rullman did not congratulate each other. They could not be sure that the silence and the delay meant what they had every good reason to hope that it meant. They could only go on working.

The movements of machines, men, and energy displays which should look to Meiklejon like a revolt of the colonists burst away from Howe's *pi* eleven days later. All the signs showed that it had been the loyalists who had set up their base near the north pole of Ganymede. Sweeney and Mike had driven through the Gouge before, for that purpose, planting in a radar-crazy jungle a whole series of small devices, all automatic, all designed to register on Meiklejon's detectors as a vast bustle of heavy machinery. The visible strategic movements of the opposing armies had suggested the same loyalist concentration at the pole.

And now Sweeney and Mike were on their way back.

The computer appeared to be waiting it out; Meiklejon had evidently fed the data to it as a real rebellion. Sweeney's side obviously was carrying the field at first. The computer had no reason to run a new extrapolation up to the first day the loyalist forces had managed to hold their lines; and then it had to run squarely up against the question of how the loyalists could take the mountain even if, in the succeeding weeks, they should sweep the field clear of Sweeney.

"Kid stuff," Sweeney had said. "It hasn't any reason to think differently. Too simple to make it extrapolate beyond the first derivative."

"You're very confident, Donald."

Sweeney stirred uneasily in the bucket seat as he recalled Rullman's smile. No Adapted Man, least of all Sweeney, had had any real childhood; no "kid stuff." Fortunately the Port cops had thought it essential to Sweeney's task that he know theory of games.

The halftrack settled down to relatively smooth progress once more, and Sweeney got up to check the screen. The talus-slope, as Mike had anticipated, cut off reception from the radar relay station behind them; Sweeney started the antenna sweeping. Much of the field was cropped by the near edge of the Gouge, but that effect would begin to disappear gradually from the screen now. The floor of the Gouge rose steadily as one approached the north pole, although it never quite reached the level of the plains. He could already capture enough sky to be satisfied that the Earth ships were just where they had been before.

That had been the last risk: that Meiklejon, alarmed at the computer's continued counsels of inaction, would radio Earth for advice from higher authorities. Obviously a colonists' revolt on Ganymede, one that could be painted as a "We want to go home" movement, would be ideal for Earth's purposes. Earth would not only insist on Meiklejon's sitting tight as his computer had told him to do—but would also hasten to bring up reinforcements for Sweeney, just in case.

Both Sweeney and Rullman had known how likely that was to happen, and had decided to take the chance, and make preparations against it. The chance had not paid off—the Earth ships were here—but it still looked as though the preparations might.

As content as was possible under the circumstances, Sweeney went forward. Before reaching for his safety belt, he stopped to kiss Mike, to the considerable detriment of her control of the lurching truck.

The explosion threw him, hard, halfway across the empty bucket seat.

He struggled up, his head ringing. The truck's engines seemed to have stopped; beneath the ringing, he could hear nothing but the sound of the blowers.

"Don! Are you all right? What was that?"

"Ugh," he said, sitting down. "Nothing broken. Hit my head a crack. It was high explosive, from the sound. A big one."

Her face was pinched and anxious in the soft glow from the dashboard. "One of ours? Or—"

"I don't know, Mike. Sounded like it hit back down the ravine a distance. What's the matter with the engine?"

She touched the starter. It whined, and the engine caught at once. "I must have stalled it," she said apologetically. She put it in gear. "But it doesn't feel right. The traction's bad on your side."

Sweeney swung the cab door open and dropped to the stony ground. Then he whistled.

"What is it?"

"That was closer than I thought," he called back. "The righthand track is cut almost in half. A flying rock splinter, I suppose. Toss me the torch."

She leaned far out across his seat, reaching the arc-cutter to him, and then the goggles. He made his way to the rear of the truck and snapped the switch. The electric arc burned sulfur-blue; a moment later, the damaged track was unwinding from around the four big snowmobile tires like an expiring snake. Dragging the cord behind him, Sweeney cut the left track off, too, and then returned to the cab, rewinding the cord as he went.

"Okay, but take it slow. Those tires are going to be cut to ribbons by the time we hit that base."

Her face was still white, but she asked no more questions. The halftrack began to crawl forward, a halftrack no longer. At a little over two miles farther on, the first of the eight tires blew, making them both jump. A hasty check showed that it was the right outside rear one. Another two and a half miles, and the right inside drive tire blew out, too. It was bad to have two gone on the same side of the truck, but at least they were on different axles and in alternate position. The next one to go, five miles farther on—the ground became less littered as it rose—was the left inside rear.

"Don."

"Yes, Mike."

"Do you think that was an Earth bomb?"

"I don't know, Mike. I doubt it; they're too far away to be throwing stuff at Ganymede except at random, and why would they do that? More likely it was one of our torpedoes, out of control." He snapped his fingers. "Wait a minute. If we're throwing H.E. at each other, now, the cops will have noticed, and *that* we can check."

Bang!

The halftrack settled down to the right and began to slobber at the ground. No check was needed to tell Sweeney that that one had been the right outside driver. Those two wheels would be hitting on bare rims within the next thousand feet or so of travel; the main weight of the vehicle was back there —the steering tires took very little punishment, comparatively.

Gritting his teeth, he unbuckled the safety and scrambled back to the radar set, checking the aluminum drum automatically as he went.

There was much more sky showing on the screen now. It was impossible to triangulate the positions of the Earth ships now that the transmission from Howe's *pi* was cut off, but the pips on the screen were markedly dimmer. Sweeney guessed that they had retreated at least another hundred thousand miles. He grinned and leaned into Mike's ear.

"It was one of ours," he said. "Rullman's stepping up on the heavy artillery, that's all. One of his torpedo pilots must have lost one in the Gouge. The Port cops have detected the step-up, all right—they've backed off. It's beginning to look more and more as though the rebels might try to smear the loyalist base with a fission bomb, and they don't want to be cheek to cheek with the planet when that happens. How far do we have to go, still?"

Mike said, "We're—"

Bang! Mike grabbed for the switch, and the engine died.

"—here," she finished, and then, amazingly, began to giggle.

Sweeney swallowed, and then discovered that he was grinning, too. "With three track-tires intact," he said. "Hooray for us. Let's get on the job."

Another starshell broke open in the sky, not as near as before. Sweeney went around to the back of the truck, Mike picking her way after him, both of them looking ruefully at the wreathes of shredded silicone rubber which once had been two excellent tires. Two of the rims were quite bare; the fifth deflated tire, which had not been driven on, was only a puncture and might be salvaged.

"Unstrap the barrel and roll 'er out the tailgate," Sweeney said. "Easy. Now let's lower 'er to the ground, and over there."

All around them, concealed among the rocks and the massive, gnarled trunks, were the little instruments whose busy electronic chattering made this spot sound like a major military encampment to the ships lying off Ganymede. Photographs, of course, would not be expected to show it: the visible light was insufficient, the infra-red still weaker, and ultra-violet plates would be stopped by the atmosphere. Nobody would expect to *see* anything from space by any method, not in the Gouge; but the detectors would report power being expended, and power sources moving about—and rebel torpedoes homing purposefully on the area. That should be enough.

With Mike's help, Sweeney stood the aluminum barrel on end roughly in the center of this assemblage. "I'm going to take that punctured tire off," he said. "We've got fifteen minutes until take-off time, and we may need it later. Know how to wire up this thing?"

"I'm not an idiot. Go change your tire."

While Sweeney worked, Mike located the main input lead for the little invisible chatterers and spliced a line into it. To this she rigged a spring-driven switch which would snap to "Off" as soon as current was delivered to a solenoid which actuated its trigger. One strand of reel-wound cable went to the solenoid, another to a red-splashed terminal on the side of the aluminum keg. She checked the thumb-plunger at the other end of the cable. Everything was ready. When that plunger was pushed, the little chatterers would go Off, at the same moment that the barrel went On.

"All set, Mike?"

"Ready and waiting. Five minutes until take-off time."

"Good," Sweeney said, taking the reel from her. "You'd better get in the truck and take it on across the pole—over the horizon from here."

"Why? There's no real danger. And if there is, what good would I be over there alone?"

"Look, Mike," Sweeney said. He was already walking backwards, still to the north, paying out cable. "I just want to get that truck out of here; maybe we can use it, and once that barrel starts, it just might set the truck on fire. Besides, supposing the cops decide to take a close look down here? The truck's visible, or at least it's suspiciously regular. But they couldn't see *me*. It'd be far better to have the truck over the horizon. Fair enough?"

"Oh, all right. Just don't get yourself killed, that's all."

"I won't. I'll be along after the show's over. Go on, beat it."

Scowling, though not very convincingly, she climbed back into the truck, which pulled slowly away up the grade. Sweeney could hear its bare rims screeching against upthrusts of rock long after it had disappeared, but finally it was out of earshot as well.

He continued to walk backward, unwinding the cable from the reel until it was all gone, and the phony encampment was a full mile south of him. He took the thumb switch in his right hand, checked his watch, and crouched down behind a long low spur to wait.

A whole series of starshells made a train of blue suns across the sky. Somewhere a missile screamed, and then the ground shook heavily. Sweeney fervently hoped that the "insurgent" torpedomen weren't shaving it too fine.

But it wouldn't be long now. In just a few seconds, the survival ship—the ship aimed at one of six unknown stars, and carrying the new generation of Adapted children—would take off from Howe's *pi*.

Twenty seconds.

Fifteen.

Ten.

Nine.

Eight.

Seven.

Six.

Sweeney pushed the plunger.

The aluminum keg ignited with a hollow cough, and an intense ball of light, far too bright to be shut out either by the welding goggles or by closed eyelids or by both, rose into Ganymede's sky. The heat struck against Sweeney's skin as strongly as the backwash of the JATO unit had done, so long ago. The concussion, which followed about nine seconds later, flattened him and made his nose bleed.

Uncaring, he rolled over and looked upward. The light had already almost died. There was now a roiling column of white smoke, shot through with lurid, incandescent colors, hurling itself skyward at close to a mile a minute.

It was altogether a hell of a convincing-looking fission bomb—for a fake.

The column didn't begin to mushroom until it was almost five miles high, but by that time Sweeney was sure that there wasn't an Earth ship anywhere within ten astronomical units of Ganymede. Nobody would stop to make inquiries, especially when all the instruments in the "encampment" had stopped transmitting simultaneouly with the "blast."

It might perhaps occur to Port later that the "blast" might have been a huge, single-shot Roman candle fired from an aluminum keg, propelled by a mixture of smoke-flare compounds and low-grade chemical explosives. But by that time, the survival ship would be gone beyond all possibility of tracing its path.

As a matter of fact, it was gone already. It had left on the count, uncounted by Sweeney, of Zero.

Sweeney got up, humming cheerfully—and quite as tunelessly as Rullman—and continued to plod north. On the other side of the pole, the Gouge was supposed to continue to become shallower as it proceeded into the Jupiter-ward hemisphere of Ganymede. There was a twilight zone there, illuminated by the sun irregularly because of libration while Ganymede was on the sunward side of Jupiter, and quite regularly as the satellite went toward and away from occultation with the big primary. Of course the occultation periods would be rather cold, but they lasted less than eight hours apiece.

Elsewhere on Ganymede, the other colonists were heading for similar spots, their spurious war equipment destroyed, their purpose fulfilled. They were equipped variously, but all as well as Sweeney; and he had a sound ten-wheeled snowmobile, on which the six remaining tires could be redistributed to make the vehicle suitable for heavy tractoring, and with a

55

tonneau loaded with tools, seeds, slips and cuttings, medical supplies, reserve food and fuel. He also had a wife.

Earth would visit Ganymede, of course. But it would find nothing. The inside of Howe's *pi* had been razed when the survival ship had taken off. As for the people, they would be harmless, ignorant, and *widely* scattered.

Peasants, Sweeney thought. Whistling, he crossed the north pole. Nothing but peasants.

At last he saw the squat shape of the truck, crouched at the mouth of a valley. At first Mike was not visible, but finally he spotted her, standing with her back to him on a rise. He clambered up beside her.

The valley was narrow for about a hundred feet ahead, and then it opened out in a broad fan of level land. A faint haze hovered over it. To an Earthman, nothing could have looked more desolate—but no Earthman was looking at it.

"I'll bet that's the best farm land on Ganymede," Sweeney whispered. "I wish——"

Mike turned and looked at him. He cut the wish off unspoken, but there was no doubt that Mike had fathomed it. But Rullman was no longer on Ganymede to share its beauties—this one, or any other. Though he would never see the end of the journey, and could not have survived at its goal, he had gone with the children on the ship—and taken his exportable knowledge with him.

He had been, Sweeney knew, a great man. Greater, perhaps, than his father.

"Go on ahead with the truck, Mike," Sweeney said softly. "I'll walk on behind you."

"Why? It'll ride easy on that soil—the extra weight won't matter."

"I'm not worrying about the weight. It's just that I want to walk it. It's—well, hell, Mike, don't you know that I'm just about to be born? Whoever heard of a kid arriving with a fourteen-ton truck?"

BOOK TWO

THE THING
IN THE ATTIC

. . . And it is written that after the Giants came to Tellura from the far stars, they abode a while, and looked upon the surface of the land, and found it wanting, and of evil omen. Therefore did they make man to live always in the air and in the sunlight, and in the light of the stars, that he would be reminded of them. And the Giants abode yet a while, and taught men to speak, and to write, and to weave, and to do many things which are needful to do, of which the writings speak. And thereafter they departed to the far stars, saying, Take this world as your own, and though we shall return, fear not, for it is yours.

—THE BOOK OF LAWS

1

Honath the Purse-Maker was haled from the nets an hour before the rest of the prisoners, as befitted his role as the arch-doubter of them all. It was not yet dawn, but his captors led him in great bounds through the endless, musky-perfumed orchid gardens, small dark shapes with crooked legs, hunched shoulders, slim hairless tails, carried, like his, in concentric spirals wound clockwise. Behind them sprang Honath on the end of a long tether, timing his leaps by theirs, since any slip would hang him summarily.

He would of course be on his way to the surface, some 250 feet below the orchid gardens, shortly after dawn in any event. But not even the arch-doubter of them all wanted to begin the trip—not even at the merciful snap-spine end of a tether —a moment before the law said, Go.

The looping, interwoven network of vines beneath them, each cable as thick through as a man's body, bellied out and down sharply as the leapers reached the edge of the fern-tree forest which surrounded the copse of horsetails. The whole party stopped before beginning the descent and looked eastward, across the dim bowl. The stars were paling more and more rapidly; only the bright constellation of the Parrot could still be picked out without doubt.

"A fine day," one of the guards said, conversationally. "Better to go below on a sunny day than in the rain, Purse-Maker."

Honath shuddered and said nothing. Of course, it was always raining down below in Hell, that much could be seen by a child. Even on sunny days, the endless pinpoint rain of transpiration, from the hundred million leaves of the eternal trees, hazed the forest air and soaked the black bog forever.

He looked around in the brightening, misty morning. The eastern horizon was black against the limb of the great red sun, which had already risen about a third of its diameter; it was almost time for the small, blue-white, furiously hot consort to follow. All the way to that brink, as to every other horizon, the woven ocean of the tree tops flowed gently in long, unbreaking waves, featureless as some smooth oil. Only nearby could the eye break that ocean into its details, into the world as it was: a great, many-tiered network, thickly overgrown with small ferns, with air-drinking orchids, with a thousand varieties of fungi sprouting wherever vine crossed vine and collected a little humus for them, with the vivid parasites sucking sap from the vines, the trees, and even each other. In the ponds of rainwater collected by the closely fitting leaves of the bromelaids, tree-toads and peepers stopped down their hoarse songs dubiously as the light grew, and fell silent one by one. In the trees below the world, the tentative morning screeches of the lizard-birds—the souls of the damned, or the devils who hunted them, no one was quite sure which—took up the concert.

A small gust of wind whipped out of the hollow above the glade of horsetails, making the network under the party shift slightly, as if in a loom. Honath gave with it easily, automatically, but one of the smaller vines toward which he had moved one furless hand hissed at him and went pouring away

58

into the darkness beneath—a chlorophyll-green snake, come up out of the dripping aerial pathways in which it hunted in ancestral gloom, to greet the suns and dry its scales in the quiet morning. Farther below, an astonished monkey, routed out of its bed by the disgusted serpent, sprang into another tree, reeling off ten mortal insults, one after the other, while still in mid-leap. The snake, of course, paid no attention, since it did not speak the language of men; but the party on the edge of the glade of horsetails snickered appreciatively.

"Bad language they favor, below," another of the guards said. "A fit place for you and your blasphemers, Purse-Maker. Come now."

The tether at Honath's neck twitched, and then his captors were soaring in zig-zag bounds down into the hollow toward the Judgment Seat. He followed, since he had no choice, the tether threatening constantly to foul his arms, legs, or tail, and—worse, far worse—making his every movement mortally ungraceful. Above, the Parrot's starry plumes flickered and faded into the general blue.

Toward the center of the saucer above the grove, the stitched leaf-and-leather houses clustered thickly, bound to the vines themselves, or hanging from an occasional branch too high or too slender to bear the vines. Many of these purses Honath knew well, not only as visitor but as artisan. The finest of them, the inverted flowers which opened automatically as the morning dew bathed them, yet which could be closed tightly and safely around their occupants at dusk by a single draw-string, were his own design as well as his own handiwork. They had been widely admired and imitated.

The reputation that they had given him, too, had helped to bring him to the end of the snap-spine tether. They had given weight to his words among others—weight enough to make him, at last, the arch-doubter, the man who leads the young into blasphemy, the man who questions the Book of Laws.

And they had probably helped to win him his passage on the Elevator to Hell.

The purses were already opening as the party swung among them. Here and there, sleepy faces blinked out from amid the exfoliating sections, criss-crossed by relaxing lengths of dew-soaked rawhide. Some of the awakening householders recognized Honath, of that he was sure, but none came out to follow the party—though the villagers should be beginning to drop from the hearts of their stitched flowers like ripe seed-pods by this hour of any normal day.

A Judgment was at hand, and they knew it—and even those who had slept the night in one of Honath's finest houses would not speak for him now. Everyone knew, after all, that Honath did not believe in the Giants.

Honath could see the Judgment Seat itself now, a slung chair of woven cane crowned along the back with a row of gigantic mottled orchids. These had supposedly been transplanted there when the chair was made, but no one could remember how old they were; since there were no seasons, there was no particular reason why they should not have been there forever. The Seat itself was at the back of the arena and high above it, but in the gathering light Honath could make out the white-furred face of the Tribal Spokesman, like a lone silver-and-black pansy among the huge vivid blooms.

At the center of the arena proper was the Elevator itself. Honath had seen it often enough, and had himself witnessed Judgments where it was called into use, but he could still hardly believe that he was almost surely to be its next passenger. It consisted of nothing more than a large basket, deep enough so that one would have to leap out of it, and rimmed with thorns to prevent one from leaping back in. Three hempen ropes were tied to its rim, and were then cunningly interwound on a single-drum windlass of wood, which could be turned by two men even when the basket was loaded.

The procedure was equally simple. The condemned man was forced into the basket, and the basket lowered out of sight, until the slackening of the ropes indicated that it had touched the surface. The victim climbed out—and if he did not, the basket remained below until he starved or until Hell otherwise took care of its own—and the windlass was rewound.

The sentences were for varying periods of time according to the severity of the crime, but in practical terms this formality was empty. Although the basket was dutifully lowered when the sentence had expired, no one had ever been known to get back into it. Of course, in a world without seasons or moons, and hence without any but an arbitrary year, long periods of time are not easy to count accurately. The basket may often have arrived thirty or forty days to one side or the other of the proper date. This was only a technicality, however, for if keeping time was difficult in the attic world, it was probably impossible in Hell.

Honath's guards tied the free end of his tether to a branch and settled down around him. One abstractedly passed a pine cone to him, and he tried to occupy his mind with the business of picking the juicy seeds from it, but somehow they had no flavor.

More captives were being brought in now, while the Spokesman watched with glittering black eyes from his high perch. There was Mathild the Forager, shivering as if with ague, the fur down her left side glistening and spiky, as though she had inadvertently overturned a tank plant on herself. After her was brought Alaskon the Navigator, a middle-aged man only a few years younger than Honath himself; he was tied up next to Honath, where he settled down at once, chewing at a joint of cane with apparent indifference.

Thus far, the gathering had proceeded without more than a few words being spoken, but that ended when the guards tried to bring Seth the Needlesmith from the nets. He could be heard at once, over the entire distance to the glade, alternately chattering and shrieking in a mixture of tones that might mean fear or fury. Everyone in the glade but Alaskon turned to look, and heads emerged from purses like new butterflies from cocoons.

A moment later, Seth's guards came over the lip of the glade in a tangled group, now shouting themselves. Somewhere in the middle of the knot Seth's voice became still louder; obviously he was clinging with all five members to any vine or frond he could grasp, and was no sooner pried loose from one than he would leap by main force, backwards if possible, to another. Nevertheless, he was being brought inexorably down into the arena, two feet forward, one foot back, three feet forward . . .

Honath's guards resumed picking their pine cones. During the disturbance, Honath realized, Charl the Reader had been brought in quietly from the same side of the glade. He now sat opposite Alaskon, looking apathetically down at the vine-web, his shoulders hunched forward. He exuded despair; even to look at him made Honath feel a renewed shudder.

From the high Seat, the Spokesman said: "Honath the Purse-maker, Alaskon the Navigator, Charl the Reader, Seth the Needlesmith, Mathild the Forager, you are called to answer to justice."

"Justice!" Seth shouted, springing free of his captors with a tremendous bound, and bringing up with a jerk on the end of his tether. "This is no justice! I have nothing to do with—"

The guards caught up with him and clamped brown hands firmly over his mouth. The Spokesman watched with amused malice.

"The accusations are three," the Spokesman said. "The first, the telling of lies to children. Second, the casting into doubt of the divine order among men. Third, the denial of the Book

61

of Laws. Each of you may speak in order of age. Honath the Purse-Maker, your plea may be heard."

Honath stood up, trembling a little, but feeling a surprisingly renewed surge of his old independence.

"Your charges," he said, "all rest upon the denial of the Book of Laws. I have taught nothing else that is contrary to what we all believe, and called nothing else into doubt. And I deny the charge."

The Spokesman looked down at him with disbelief. "Many men and women have said that you do not believe in the Giants, Purse-Maker," he said. "You will not win mercy by piling up more lies."

"I deny the charge," Honath insisted. "I believe in the Book of Laws as a whole, and I believe in the Giants. I have taught only that the Giants were not real in the sense that we are real. I have taught that they were intended as symbols of some higher reality, and were not meant to be taken as literal Persons."

"What higher reality is this?" the Spokesman demanded. "Describe it."

"You ask me to do something the writers of the Book of Laws themselves couldn't do," Honath said hotly. "If they had to embody the reality in symbols rather than writing it down directly, how could a mere pursemaker do better?"

"This doctrine is wind," the Spokesman said. "And it is plainly intended to undercut authority and the order established by the Book. Tell me, Purse-Maker, if man need not fear the Giants, why should they fear the law?"

"Because they are men, and it is to their interest to fear the law. They aren't children, who need some physical Giant sitting over them with a whip to make them behave. Furthermore, Spokesman, this archaic belief *itself* undermines us. As long as we believe that there are real Giants, and that some day they'll return and resume teaching us, so long will we fail to seek answers to our questions for ourselves. Half of what we know was given to us in the Book, and the other half is supposed to drop to us from the skies if we wait long enough. In the meantime, we vegetate."

"If a part of the Book be untrue, there can be nothing to prevent that it is all untrue," the Spokesman said heavily. "And we will lose even what you call the half of our knowledge—which is actually the whole of it, to those who see with clear eyes."

Suddenly, Honath lost his temper. "Lose it, then!" he shouted. "Let us unlearn everything we know only by rote, go back to the beginning, learn all over again, and continue to learn, from our own experience. Spokesman, you are an old man, but there are still some of us who haven't forgotten what curiosity means!"

"Quiet!" the Spokesman said. "We have heard enough. We call on Alaskon the Navigator."

"Much of the Book is clearly untrue," Alaskon said flatly, rising. "As a handbook of small trades it has served us well. As a guide to how the universe is made, it is nonsense, in my opinion; Honath is too kind to it. I've made no secret of what I think, and I still think it."

"And will pay for it," the Spokesman said, blinking slowly down at Alaskon. "Charl the Reader."

"Nothing," Charl said, without standing, or even looking up.

"You do not deny the charges?"

"I've nothing to say," Charl said, but then, abruptly, his head jerked up, and he glared with desperate eyes at the Spokesman. "I can read, Spokesman. I have seen words of the Book of Laws that contradict each other. I've pointed them out. They're facts, they exist on the pages. I've taught nothing, told no lies, preached no unbelief. I've pointed to the facts. That's all."

"Seth the Needlesmith, you may speak now."

The guards took their hands gratefully off Seth's mouth; they had been bitten several times in the process of keeping him quiet up to now. Seth resumed shouting at once.

"I'm no part of this group! I'm the victim of gossip, envious neighbors, smiths jealous of my skill and my custom! No man can say worse of me than that I sold needles to this pursemaker—sold them in good faith! The charges against me are lies, all of them!"

Honath jumped to his feet in fury, and then sat down again, choking back the answering shout almost without tasting its bitterness. What did it matter? Why should he bear witness against the young man? It would not help the others, and if Seth wanted to lie his way out of Hell, he might as well be given the chance.

The Spokesman was looking down at Seth with the identical expression of outraged disbelief which he had first bent upon Honath. "Who was it cut the blasphemies into the hardwood trees, by the house of Hosi the Lawgiver?" he demanded. "Sharp needles were at work there, and there are witnesses to say that your hands held them."

"More lies!"

"Needles found in your house fit the furrows, Seth."

"They were not mine—or they were stolen! I demand to be freed!"

"You will be freed," the Spokesman said coldly. There was no possible doubt as to what he meant. Seth began to weep and to shout at the same time. Hands closed over his mouth again. "Mathild the Forager, your plea may be heard."

The young woman stood up hesitantly. Her fur was nearly dry now, but she was still shivering.

"Spokesman," she said, "I saw the things which Charl the Reader showed me. I doubted, but what Honath said restored my belief. I see no harm in his teachings. They remove doubt, instead of fostering it, as you say they do. I see no evil in them, and I don't understand why this is a crime."

Honath looked over to her with new admiration. The Spokesman sighed heavily.

"I am sorry for you," he said, "but as Spokesman we cannot allow ignorance of the Law as a plea. We will be merciful to you all, however. Renounce your heresy, affirm your belief in the Book as it is written from bark to bark, and you shall be no more than cast out of the tribe."

"I renounce it!" Seth said. "I never shared it! It's all blasphemy and every word is a lie! I believe in the Book, all of it!"

"You, Needlesmith," the Spokesman said, "have lied before this Judgment, and are probably lying now. You are not included in the dispensation."

"Snake-spotted caterpillar! May your—*ummulph*."

"Purse-Maker, what is your answer?"

"It is, No," Honath said stonily. "I've spoken the truth. The truth can't be unsaid."

The Spokesman looked down at the rest of them. "As for you three, consider your answers carefully. To share the heresy means sharing the sentence. The penalty will not be lightened only because you did not invent the heresy."

There was a long silence.

Honath swallowed hard. The courage and the faith in that silence made him feel smaller and more helpless than ever. He realized suddenly that the other three would have kept that silence, even without Seth's defection to stiffen their spines. He wondered if he could have done so.

"Then we pronounce the sentence," the Spokesman said. "You are one and all condemned to one thousand days in Hell."

There was a concerted gasp from around the edges of the arena, where, without Honath's having noticed it before, a silent crowd had gathered. He did not wonder at the sound. The sentence was the longest in the history of the tribe.

Not that it really meant anything. No one had ever come

back from as little as one hundred days in Hell. No one had ever come back from Hell at all.

"Unlash the Elevator. All shall go together—and their heresy with them."

2

The basket swayed. The last of the attic world that Honath saw was a circle of faces, not too close to the gap in the vine web, peering down after them. Then the basket fell another few yards to the next turn of the windlass and the faces vanished.

Seth was weeping in the bottom of the Elevator, curled up into a tight ball, the end of his tail wrapped around his nose and eyes. No one else could make a sound, least of all Honath.

The gloom closed around them. It seemed extraordinarily still. The occasional harsh scream of a lizard-bird somehow emphasized the silence without breaking it. The light that filtered down into the long aisles between the trees seemed to be absorbed in a blue-green haze, through which the lianas wove their long curved lines. The columns of tree-trunks, the pillars of the world, stood all around them, too distant in the dim light to allow them to gauge their speed of descent; only the irregular plunges of the basket proved that it was even in motion any longer, though it swayed laterally in a complex, overlapping series of figure-eights traced on the air in response to the rotation of the planet—a Foucault pendulum ballasted with five lives.

Then the basket lurched downward once more, brought up short, and tipped sidewise, tumbling them all against the hard cane. Mathild cried out in a thin voice, and Seth uncurled almost instantly, clawing for a handhold. Another lurch, and the Elevator lay down on its side and was still.

They were in Hell.

Cautiously, Honath began to climb out, picking his way over the long thorns on the basket's rim. After a moment, Charl the Reader followed, and then Alaskon took Mathild firmly by the hand and led her out onto the surface. The footing was wet and spongy, yet not at all resilient, and it felt cold; Honath's toes curled involuntarily.

"Come on, Seth," Charl said in a hushed voice. "They

won't haul it back up until we're all out. You know that."

Alaskon looked around into the chilly mists. "Yes," he said. "And we'll need a needlesmith down here. With good tools, there's just a chance—"

Seth's eyes had been darting back and forth from one to the other. With a sudden chattering scream, he bounded out of the bottom of the basket, soaring over their heads in a long, flat leap, and struck the high knee at the base of the nearest tree, an immense fan palm. As he hit, his legs doubled under him, and almost in the same motion he seemed to rocket straight up into the murky air.

Gaping, Honath looked up after him. The young needlesmith had timed his course to the split second. He was already darting up the rope from which the Elevator was suspended. He did not even bother to look back.

After a moment, the basket tipped upright. The impact of Seth's weight hitting the rope evidently had been taken by the windlass team to mean that the condemned people were all out on the surface; a twitch on the rope was the usual signal. The basket began to rise, bobbing and dancing. Its speed of ascent, added to Seth's, took his racing dwindling figure out of sight quickly. After a while, the basket was gone, too.

"He'll never get to the top," Mathild whispered. "It's too far, and he's going too fast. He'll lose strength and fall."

"I don't think so," Alaskon said heavily. "He's agile and strong. If anyone could make it, he could."

"They'll kill him if he does."

"Of course they will," Alaskon said, shrugging.

"I won't miss him," Honath said.

"No more will I. But we could use some sharp needles down here, Honath. Now, we'll have to plan to make our own—if we can identify the different woods, down here where there aren't any leaves to help us tell them apart."

Honath looked at the Navigator curiously. Seth's bolt for the sky had distracted him from the realization that the basket, too, was gone, but now that desolate fact hit home. "You actually plan to stay alive in Hell, don't you, Alaskon?"

"Certainly," Alaskon said calmly. "This is no more Hell than —up there—is Heaven. It's the surface of the planet, no more, no less. We can stay alive if we don't panic. Were you just going to sit here until the furies came for you, Honath?"

"I hadn't thought much about it," Honath confessed. "But if there is any chance that Seth will lose his grip on that rope —before he reaches the top and they knife him—shouldn't we wait and see if we can catch him? He can't weigh more than 35 pounds. Maybe we could contrive some sort of a net—"

"He'd just break our bones along with his," Charl said. "I'm for getting out of here as fast as possible."

"What for? Do you know a better place?"

"No, but whether this is Hell or not, there are demons down here. We've all seen them from up above, the snake-headed giants. They must know that the Elevator always lands here and empties out free food. This must be a feeding-ground for them—"

He had not quite finished speaking when the branches began to sigh and toss, far above. A gust of stinging droplets poured along the blue air, and thunder rumbled. Mathild whimpered.

"It's only a squall coming up," Honath said. But the words came out in a series of short croaks. As the wind had moved through the trees, Honath had automatically flexed his knees and put his arms out for handholds, awaiting the long wave of response to pass through the ground beneath him. But nothing happened. The surface under his feet remained stolidly where it was, flexing not a fraction of an inch in any direction. And there was nothing nearby for his hands to grasp.

He staggered, trying to compensate for the failure of the ground to move, but at the same moment another gust of wind blew through the aisles, a little stronger than the first, and calling insistently for a new adjustment of his body to the waves which passed along the treetops. Again the squashy surface beneath him refused to respond; the familiar give-and-take of the vine-web to the winds, a part of his world as accustomed as the winds themselves, was gone.

Honath was forced to sit down, feeling distinctly ill. The damp, cool earth under his furless buttocks was unpleasant, but he could not have remained standing any longer without losing his meager prisoner's breakfast. One grappling hand caught hold of the ridged, gritty stems of a clump of horsetail, but the contact failed to allay the uneasiness.

The others seemed to be bearing it no better than Honath. Mathild in particular was rocking dizzily, her lips compressed, her hands clapped to her delicate ears.

Dizziness. It was unheard of up above, except among those who had suffered grave head injuries or were otherwise very ill. But on the motionless ground of Hell, it was evidently going to be with them constantly.

Charl squatted, swallowing convulsively. "I—I can't stand," he moaned. "It's magic, Alaskon—the snake-headed demons—"

"Nonsense," Alaskon said, though he had remained standing only by clinging to the huge, mud-colored bulb of a cycadella. "It's just a disturbance of our sense of balance. It's a—motionlessness-sickness. We'll get used to it."

"We'd better," Honath said, relinquishing his grip on the horsetails by a sheer act of will. "I think Charl's right about this being a feeding-ground, Alaskon. I hear something moving around in the ferns. And if this rain lasts long, the water will rise here, too. I've seen silver flashes from down here many a time after heavy rains."

"That's right," Mathild said, her voice subdued. "The base of the ferntree grove always floods; that's why the treetops are so much lower there."

The wind seemed to have let up a little, though the rain was still falling. Alaskon stood up tentatively.

"Then let's move on," he said. "If we try to keep under cover until we get to higher ground—"

A faint crackling sound, high above his head, interrupted him. It got louder. Feeling a sudden spasm of pure fear, Honath looked up.

Nothing could be seen for an instant but the far-away curtain of branches and fern-fronds. Then, with shocking suddenness, something small and black irrupted through the blue-green roof and came tumbling toward them. It was a man, twisting and tumbling through the air with grotesque slowness, like a child turning in its sleep. They scattered.

The body hit the ground with a sodden thump, but there were sharp overtones to the sound, like the bursting of a gourd. For a moment nobody moved. Then Honath crept forward.

It had been Seth, as Honath had realized the moment the black figurine had burst through the branches far above. But it had not been the fall that had killed him. He had been run through by at least a dozen needles—some of them, beyond doubt, tools from his own shop, their points edged hair-fine by his own precious strops of leatherwood-bark, soaked until they were soft, pliant, and nearly transparent in the mud at the bottom of sun-warmed bromelaid tanks.

There would be no reprieve from above. The sentence was one thousand days. This burst and broken huddle of fur was the only alternative.

And the first day had barely begun.

They toiled all the rest of the day to reach higher ground, clinging to the earth for the most part because the trees, except for a few scattered gingkoes, flowering dogwoods and live oaks, did not begin to branch until their tunks had soared more than eighteen feet above the ground. As they stole cautiously closer to the foothills of the Great Range and the ground became firmer, they were able to take to the air for short stretches, but they were no sooner aloft among the willows than the lizard-birds came squalling down on them by the dozens, fighting among each other for the privilege of nipping these plump and incredibly slow-moving monkeys.

No man, no matter how confirmed a free-thinker, could have stood up under such an onslaught by the creatures he had been taught as a child to think of as his ancestors. The first time it happened, every member of the party dropped like a pine-cone to the sandy ground and lay paralyzed under the nearest cover, until the brindle-feathered, fan-tailed screamers tired of flying in such tight circles and headed for clearer air. Even after the lizard-birds had given up, they crouched quietly for a long time, waiting to see what greater demons might have been attracted by the commotion.

Thus far, none of the snake-headed Powers had shown themselves—though several times Honath had heard suggestively heavy movements in the jungle around them.

Luckily, on the higher ground there was much more cover available, from low-growing shrubs and trees—palmetto, sassafras, several kinds of laurel, magnolia, and a great many sedges. Up here, too, the endless jungle began to break to pour around the bases of the great pink cliffs, leaving welcome vistas of open sky, only sketchily crossed by woven bridges leading from the vine-world to the cliffs themselves. In the intervening columns of blue air a whole hierarchy of flying creatures ranked themselves, layer by layer: First the low-flying beetles, bees and two-winged insects; then the dragon-flies which hunted them, some with wingspreads as wide as two feet; then the lizard-birds, hunting the dragon-flies and anything else that could be nipped without fighting back; and at last, far above, the great gliding reptiles coasting along the brows of the cliffs, riding the rising currents of air, their long-jawed hunger stalking anything that flew—as they sometimes stalked the birds of the attic world, and the flying fish along the breast of the distant sea.

The party halted in an especially thick clump of sedges. Though the rain continued to fall, harder than ever, they were all desperately thirsty. They had yet to find a single brome-laid; evidently the tank-plants did not grow in Hell. Cupping their hands to the weeping sky accumulated surprisingly little water; and no puddles large enough to drink from accumulated on the sand. But at least, here under the open sky,

69

there was too much fierce struggle in the air to allow the lizard-birds to congregate and squall above their hiding place.

The white sun had already set, and the red sun's vast arc still bulged above the horizon only because the light from its limb had been wrenched higher into Tellura's sky by its passage through the white sun's intense gravitational field. In the lurid glow the rain looked like blood, and the seamed faces of the pink cliffs had all but vanished. Honath peered dubiously out from under the sedges at the still-distant escarpments.

"I don't see how we can hope to climb those," he said, in a low voice. "That kind of limestone crumbles as soon as you touch it, otherwise we'd have had better luck with our war against the cliff tribe."

"We could go around the cliffs," Charl said. "The foothills of the Great Range aren't very steep. If we could last until we get to them, we could go on up into the Range itself."

"To the volcanoes?" Mathild protested. "But nothing can live up there, nothing but the white fire-things. And there are the lava-flows, too, and the choking smoke—"

"Well, we can't climb these cliffs, Honath's quite right," Alaskon said. "And we can't climb the Basalt Steppes, either —there's nothing to eat along them, let alone any water or cover. I don't see what else we can do but try to get up into the foothills."

"Can't we stay here?" Mathild said plaintively.

"No," Honath said, even more gently than he had intended. Mathild's four words were, he knew, the most dangerous words in Hell—he knew it quite surely, because of the imprisoned creature inside him that cried out to say "Yes" instead. "We have to get out of the country of the demons. And maybe—just maybe—if we can cross the great Range, we can join a tribe that hasn't heard about our being condemned to Hell. There are supposed to be tribes on the other side of the Range, but the cliff people would never let our folk get through to them. That's on our side now."

"That's true," Alaskon said, brightening a little. "And from the top of the Range, we could come *down* into another tribe —instead of trying to climb up into their village out of Hell. Honath, I think it might work."

"Then we'd better try to sleep right here and now," Charl said. "It seems safe enough. If we're going to skirt the cliffs and climb those foothills, we'll need all the strength we've got left."

Honath was about to protest, but he was suddenly too tired to care. Why not sleep it over? And if in the night they were found and taken—well, that would at least put an end to the struggle.

It was a cheerless and bone-damp bed to sleep in, but there was no better alternative. They curled up as best they could. Just before he was about to drop off at last, Honath heard Mathild whimpering to herself, and, on impulse, crawled over to her and began to smooth down her fur with his tongue. To his astonishment, each separate, silky hair was loaded with dew. Long before the girl had curled herself more tightly and her complaints had dwindled into sleepy murmurs, Honath's thirst was assuaged. He reminded himself to mention the method in the morning.

But when the white sun finally came up, there was no time to think of thirst. Charl the Reader was gone. Something had plucked him from their huddled midst as neatly as a fallen breadfruit—and had dropped his cleaned ivory skull just as negligently, some two hundred feet farther on up the slope which led toward the pink cliffs.

3

Late that afternoon, the three found the blue, turbulent stream flowing out of the foothills of the Great Range. Not even Alaskon knew quite what to make of it. It looked like water, but it flowed like the rivers of lava that crept downward from the volcanoes. Whatever else it could be, obviously it wasn't water; water stood, it never flowed. It was possible to imagine a still body of water as big as this, but only as a moment of fancy, an exaggeration derived from the known bodies of water in the tank-plants. But this much water in motion? It suggested pythons; it was probably poisonous. It did not occur to any of them to drink from it. They were afraid even to touch it, let alone cross it, for it was almost surely as hot as the other kinds of lava-rivers. They followed its course cautiously into the foothills, their throats as dry and gritty as the hollow stems of horsetails.

Except for the thirst—which was in an inverted sense their friend, insofar as it overrode the hunger—the climbing was not difficult. It was only circuitous, because of the need to stay under cover, to reconnoiter every few yards, to choose the most sheltered course rather than the most direct. By an unspoken consent, none of the three mentioned Charl, but their eyes were constantly darting from side to side, searching for a glimpse of the thing that had taken him.

That was perhaps the worst, the most terrifying part of the tragedy: that not once since they had been in Hell had they actually seen a demon, or even any animal as large as a man. The enormous, three-taloned footprint they had found in the sand beside their previous night's bed—the spot where the thing had stood, looking down at the four sleeping men from above, coldly deciding which of them to seize—was the only evidence they had that they were now really in the same world with the demons—the same demons they had sometimes looked down upon from the remote vine-webs.

The footprint—and the skull.

By nightfall, they had ascended perhaps a hundred and fifty feet. It was difficult to judge distances in the twilight, and the token vine bridges from the attic world to the pink cliffs were now cut off from sight by the intervening masses of the cliffs themselves. But there was no possibility that they could climb higher today. Although Mathild had borne the climb surprisingly well, and Honath himself still felt almost fresh, Alaskon was completely winded. He had taken a bad cut on one hip from a serrated spike of volcanic glass against which he had stumbled, and the wound, bound with leaves to prevent its leaving a spoor which might be followed, evidently was becoming steadily more painful.

Honath finally called a halt as soon as they reached the little ridge with the cave in back of it. Helping Alaskon over the last boulders, he was astonished to discover how hot the Navigator's hands were. He took him back into the cave and then came out onto the ledge again.

"He's really sick," he told Mathild in a low voice. "He needs water, and another dressing for that cut. And we've got to get both for him somehow. If we ever get to the jungle on the other side of the Range, we'll need a navigator even worse than we need a needlesmith."

"But how? I could dress the cut if I had the materials, Honath. But there's no water up here. It's a desert; we'll never get across it."

"We've got to try. I can get him water, I think. There was a big cycladella on the slope we came up, just before we passed that obsidian spur that hurt Alaskon. Gourds that size usually have a fair amount of water inside them—and I can use a piece of the spur to rip it open—"

A small hand came out of the darkness and took him tightly by the elbow. "Honath, you can't go back down there. Suppose the demon that—that took Charl is still following

72

us? They hunt at night—and this country is all so strange . . ."

"I can find my way. I'll follow the sound of the stream of glass or whatever it is. You pull some fresh leaves for Alaskon and try to make him comfortable. Better loosen those vines around the dressing a little. I'll be back."

He touched her hand and pried it loose gently. Then, without stopping to think about it any further, he slipped off the ledge and edged toward the sound of the stream, travelling crabwise on all fours.

But he was swiftly lost. The night was thick and completely impenetrable, and he found that the noise of the stream seemed to come from all sides, providing him no guide at all. Furthermore, his memory of the ridge which led up to the cave appeared to be faulty, for he could feel it turning sharply to the right beneath him, though he remembered distinctly that it had been straight past the first side-branch, and then had gone to the left. Or had he passed the first side-branch in the dark without seeing it? He probed the darkness cautiously with one hand.

At the same instant, a brisk, staccato gust of wind came whirling up out of the night across the ridge. Instinctively, Honath shifted his weight to take up the flexing of the ground beneath him—

He realized his error instantly and tried to arrest the complex set of motions, but a habit-pattern so deeply ingrained could not be frustrated completely. Overwhelmed with vertigo, Honath grappled at the empty air with hands, feet, and tail and went toppling.

An instant later, with a familiar noise and an equally familiar cold shock that seemed to reach throughout his body, he was sitting in the midst of—

Water. Icy water, and water that rushed by him improbably with a menacing, monkeylike chattering, but water all the same.

It was all he could do to repress a hoot of hysteria. He hunkered into the stream and soaked himself. Things nibbled delicately at his calves as he bathed, but he had no reason to fear fish, small species of which often showed up in the tanks of the bromelaids. After lowering his muzzle to the rushing, invisible surface and drinking his fill, he ducked himself completely and then clambered out onto the banks, carefully neglecting to shake himself.

Getting back to the ledge was much less difficult. "Mathild," he called in a hoarse whisper. "Mathild, we've got water."

"Come in here quick then. Alaskon's worse. I'm afraid, Honath."

Dripping, Honath felt his way into the cave. "I don't have any container. I just got myself wet—you'll have to sit him up and let him lick my fur."

"I'm not sure he can."

But Alaskon could, feebly, but sufficiently. Even the coldness of the water—a totally new experience for a man who had never drunk anything but the soup-warm contents of the bromelaids—seemed to help him. He lay back at last, and said in a weak but otherwise normal voice: "So the stream was water after all."

"Yes," Honath said. "And there are fish in it, too."

"Don't talk," Mathild said. "Rest, Alaskon."

"I'm resting. Honath, if we stick to the course of the stream . . . . Where was I? Oh. We can follow the stream through the Range, now that we know it's water. How did you find that out?"

"I lost my balance and fell into it."

Alaskon chuckled. "Hell's not so bad, is it?" he said. Then he sighed, and rushes creaked under him.

"Mathild! What's the matter? Is he—did he die?"

"No . . . no. He's breathing. He's still sicker than he realizes, that's all . . . Honath—if they'd known, up above, how much courage you have—"

"I was scared white," Honath said grimly. "I'm still scared."

But her hand touched his again in the solid blackness, and after he had taken it, he felt irrationally cheerful. With Alaskon breathing so raggedly behind them, there was little chance that either of them would be able to sleep that night; but they sat silently together on the hard stone in a kind of temporary peace, and when the mouth of the cave began to outline itself, as dimly at first as the floating patches of color seen behind the closed eye, with the first glow of the red sun, they looked at each other in a conspiracy of light all their own.

Hell, Honath reflected, wasn't so bad, after all.

With the first light of the white sun, a half-grown oxyaena cub rose slowly from its crouch at the mouth of the cave, and stretched luxuriously, showing a full set of saber-like teeth. It looked at them steadily for a moment, its ears alert, then turned and loped away down the slope.

How long it had been crouched there listening to them, it was impossible to know. They had been lucky that they had stumbled into the lair of a youngster. A full-grown animal would have killed them all, within a few seconds after its cat's eyes had collected enough dawn to identify them positively. The cub, since it had no family of its own as yet, evidently

74

had only been puzzled to find its den occupied, and uninclined to quarrel about it.

The departure of the big cat left Honath frozen, not so much frightened as simply stunned by so unexpected an end to the vigil. At the first moan from Alaskon, however, Mathild was up and walking softly to the Navigator, speaking in a low voice, sentences which made no particular sense and perhaps were not intended to. Honath stirred and followed her.

Halfway back into the cave, his foot struck something and he looked down. It was the thigh bone of some medium-large animal, imperfectly cleaned, but not very recent—possibly the keepsake the oxyaena had hoped to rescue from the usurpers of its lair. Along a curved inner surface there was a patch of thick gray mold. Honath squatted and peeled it off carefully.

"Mathild, we can put this over the wound," he said. "Some molds help prevent wounds from festering . . . How is he?"

"Better, I think," Mathild murmured. "But he's still feverish. I don't think we'll be able to move on today."

Honath was unsure whether to be pleased or disturbed. Certainly, he was far from anxious to leave the cave, where they seemed at least to be reasonably comfortable. Possibly they would also be reasonably safe, for the low-roofed hole almost surely still smelt of oxyaena, and possible intruders would recognize the smell—as the men from the attic world could not—and keep their distance. They would have no way of knowing that the cat had only been a cub to begin with, and that it had vacated the premises, though of course the odor would fade before long.

Yet it was important to move on, to cross the Great Range if possible, and in the end to win their way back to the world where they belonged; even to win vindication, no matter how long it took. Even should it prove relatively easy to survive in Hell—and there were few signs of that, thus far—the only proper course was to fight until the attic world was totally reconquered. After all, it would have been the easy and the comfortable thing, back there at the very beginning, to have kept one's incipient heresies to oneself and remained on comfortable terms with one's neighbors. But Honath had spoken up and so had the rest of them, in their fashions.

It was the ancient internal battle between what Honath wanted to do, and what he knew he ought to do. He had never heard of Kant and the Categorical Imperative, but he knew well enough which side of his nature would win in the long run. But it had been a cruel joke of heredity which had fastened a sense of duty onto a lazy nature. It made even small decisions aggressively painful.

But for the moment at least, the decision was out of his hands. Alaskon was too sick to be moved. In addition, the strong beams of sunlight which had been glaring in across the floor of the cave were dimming by the instant, and there was a distant, premonitory growl of thunder.

"Then we'll stay here," he said. "It's going to rain again, and hard this time. Once it's falling in earnest, I can go out and pick up some fruit—it'll screen me even if anything is prowling around in it. And I won't have to go as far as the stream for water, as long as the rain keeps up."

The rain, as it turned out, kept up all day, in a growing downpour which completely curtained the mouth of the cave by early afternoon. The chattering of the nearby stream grew quickly to a roar.

By evening, Alaskon's fever seemed to have dropped almost to normal, and his strength nearly returned as well. The wound, thanks more to the encrusted matte of mold than to any complications within the flesh itself, was still ugly-looking, but it was now painful only when the Navigator moved carelessly, and Mathild was convinced that it was mending. Alaskon himself, having been deprived of activity all day, was unusually talkative.

"Has it occurred to either of you," he said in the gathering gloom, "that since that stream is water, it can't possibly be coming from the Great Range? All the peaks over there are just cones of ashes and lava. We've seen young volcanoes in the process of building themselves, so we're sure of that. What's more, they're usually hot. I don't see how there could possibly be any source of water in the Range—not even run-off from the rains."

"It can't just come up out of the ground," Honath said. "It must be fed by rain. By the way it sounds now, it could even be the first part of a flood."

"As you say, it's probably rain water," Alaskon said cheerfully. "But not off the Great Range, that's out of the question. Most likely it collects on the cliffs."

"I hope you're wrong," Honath said. "The cliffs may be a little easier to climb from this side, but there's still the cliff tribe to think about."

"Maybe, maybe. But the cliffs are big. The tribes on this side may never have heard of the war with our treetop folk. No, Honath, I think that's our only course from here."

"If it is," Honath said grimly, "we're going to wish more than ever that we had some stout, sharp needles among us."

Alaskon's judgment was quickly borne out. The three left the cave at dawn the next morning, Alaskon moving somewhat stiffly but not otherwise noticeably incommoded, and resumed following the stream bed upwards—a stream now swollen by the rains to a roaring rapids. After winding its way upwards for about a mile in the general direction of the Great Range, the stream turned on itself and climbed rapidly back toward the basalt cliffs, falling toward the three over successively steeper shelves of jutting rock.

Then it turned again, at right angles, and the three found themselves at the exit of a dark gorge, little more than thirty feet high, but both narrow and long. Here the stream was almost perfectly smooth, and the thin strip of land on each side of it was covered with low shrubs. They paused and looked dubiously into the canyon. It was singularly gloomy.

"There's plenty of cover, at least," Honath said in a low voice. "But almost anything could live in a place like that."

"Nothing very big could hide in it," Alaskon pointed out. "It should be safe. Anyhow it's the only way to go."

"All right. Let's go ahead, then. But keep your head down, and be ready to jump!"

Honath lost the other two by sight as soon as they crept into the dark shrubbery, but he could hear their cautious movements nearby. Nothing else in the gorge seemed to move at all, not even the water, which flowed without a ripple over an invisible bed. There was not even any wind, for which Honath was grateful, although he had begun to develop an immunity to the motionlessness sickness.

After a few moments, Honath heard a low whistle. Creeping sidewise toward the source of the sound, he nearly bumped into Alaskon, who was crouched beneath a thickly spreading magnolia. An instant later, Mathild's face peered out of the dim greenery.

"Look," Alaskon whispered. "What do you make of this?"

"This" was a hollow in the sandy soil, about four feet across and rimmed with a low parapet of earth—evidently the same earth that had been scooped out of its center. Occupying most of it were three gray, ellipsoidal objects, smooth and featureless.

"Eggs," Mathild said wonderingly.

"Obviously. But look at the size of them! Whatever laid them must be gigantic. I think we're trespassing in something's private valley."

Mathild drew in her breath. Honath thought fast, as much to prevent panic in himself as in the girl. A sharp-edged stone lying nearby provided the answer. He seized it and struck.

The outer surface of the egg was leathery rather than brittle; it tore raggedly. Deliberately, Honath bent and put his mouth to the oozing surface.

It was excellent. The flavor was decidedly stronger than that of birds' eggs, but he was far too hungry to be squeamish. After a moment's amazement, Alaskon and Mathild attacked the other two ovoids with a will. It was the first really satisfying meal they had had in Hell. When they finally moved away from the devastated nest, Honath felt better than he had since the day he was arrested.

As they moved on down the gorge, they began again to hear the roar of water, though the stream looked as placid as ever. Here, too, they saw the first sign of active life in the valley: a flight of giant dragonflies skimming over the water. The insects took flight as soon as Honath showed himself, but quickly came back, their nearly non-existent brains already convinced that there had always been men in the valley.

The roar got louder very rapidly. When the three rounded the long, gentle turn which had cut off their view from the exit, the source of the roar came into view. It was a sheet of falling water as tall as the depth of the gorge itself, which came arcing out from between two pillars of basalt and fell to a roiling, frothing pool.

"This is as far as we go!" Alaskon said, shouting to make himself heard at all over the tumult. "We'll never be able to get up those walls!"

Stunned, Honath looked from side to side. What Alaskon had said was all too obviously true. The gorge evidently had begun life as a layer of soft, partly soluble stone in the cliffs, tilted upright by some volcanic upheaval, and then worn completely away by the rushing stream. Both cliff faces were of the harder rock, and were sheer and as smooth as if they had been polished by hand. Here and there a network of tough vines had begun to climb them, but nowhere did such a network even come close to reaching the top.

Honath turned and looked once more at the great arc of water and spray. If there were only some way to prevent their being forced to retrace their steps—

Abruptly, over the riot of the falls, there was a piercing, hissing shriek. Echoes picked it up and sounded it again and again, all the way up the battlements of the cliffs. Honath sprang straight up in the air and came down trembling, facing away from the pool.

At first he could see nothing. Then, down at the open end of the turn, there was a huge flurry of motion.

A second later, a two-legged, blue-green reptile half as tall as the gorge itself came around the turn in a single huge bound and lunged violently into the far wall of the valley. It stopped as if momentarily stunned, and the great head turned toward them a face of sinister and furious idiocy.

The shriek set the air to boiling again. Balancing itself with its heavy tail, the beast lowered its head and looked redly toward the falls.

The owner of the robbed nest had come home—and they had met a demon of Hell at last.

Honath's mind at that instant went as white and blank as the underbark of a poplar. He acted without thinking, without even knowing what he did. When thought began to creep back into his head again, the three of them were standing shivering in semi-darkness, watching the blurred shadow of the demon lurching back and forth upon the screen of shining water.

It had been nothing but luck, not foreplanning, to find that there was a considerable space between the back of the falls proper and the blind wall of the canyon. It had been luck, too, which had forced Honath to skirt the pool in order to reach the falls at all, and thus had taken them all behind the silver curtain at the point where the weight of the falling water was too low to hammer them down for good. And it had been the blindest stroke of all that the demon had charged after them directly into the pool, where the deep, boiling water had slowed the threshing hind legs enough to halt it before it went under the falls, as it had earlier blundered into the hard wall of the gorge.

Not an iota of all this had been in Honath's mind before he had discovered it to be true. At the moment that the huge reptile had screamed for the second time, he had simply grasped Mathild's hand and broken for the falls, leaping from low tree to shrub to fern faster than he had ever leapt before. He did not stop to see how well Mathild was keeping up with him, or whether or not Alaskon was following. He only ran. He might have screamed, too; he could not remember.

They stood now, all three of them, wet through, behind the curtain until the shadow of the demon faded and vanished. Finally Honath felt a hand thumping his shoulder, and turned slowly.

Speech was impossible here, but Alaskon's pointing finger was eloquent enough. Along the back wall of the falls, centuries of erosion had failed to wear away completely the original soft limestone; there was still a sort of serrated chimney there, open toward the gorge, which looked as though it could be climbed. At the top of the falls, the water shot out from between the basalt pillars in a smooth, almost solid-looking tube, arching at least six feet before beginning to break into the fan of spray and rainbows which poured down into the gorge. Once the chimney had been climbed, it should be possible to climb out from under the falls without passing through the water again.

And after that?

Abruptly, Honath grinned. He felt weak all through with reaction, and the face of the demon would probably be leering in his dreams for a long time to come—but at the same time he could not repress a surge of irrational confidence. He gestured upward jauntily, shook himself, and loped forward into the throat of the chimney.

Hardly more than an hour later they were all standing on a ledge overlooking the gorge, with the waterfall creaming over the brink next to them, only a few yards away. From here, it was evident that the gorge itself was only the bottom of a far larger cleft, a split in the pink-and-gray cliffs as sharp as though it had been driven in the rock by a bolt of sheet lightning. Beyond the basalt pillars from which the fall issued, however, the stream foamed over a long ladder of rock shelves which seemed to lead straight up into the sky. On this side of the pillars the ledge broadened into a sort of truncated mesa, as if the waters had been running at this level for centuries before striking some softer rock-stratum which had permitted them to cut down further to create the gorge. The stone platform was littered with huge rocks, rounded by long water erosion, obviously the remains of a washed-out stratum of conglomerite or a similar sedimentary layer.

Honath looked at the huge pebbles—many of them bigger than he was—and then back down into the gorge again. The figure of the demon, foreshortened into a pigmy by distance and perspective, was still roving back and forth in front of the waterfall. Having gotten the notion that prey was hiding behind the sheet of water, the creature might well stay stationed there until it starved, for all Honath knew—it certainly did not seem to be very bright—but Honath thought he had a better idea.

"Alaskon, can we hit the demon with one of these rocks?"

The navigator peered cautiously into the gorge. "It wouldn't surprise me," he said at last. "It's just pacing back and forth in that same small arc. And all things fall at the same speed;

80

if we can make the rock arrive just as it walks under it—hmm. Yes, I think so. Let's pick a big one to make certain."

But Alaskon's ambitions overreached his strength; the rock he selected would not move, largely because he himself was still too weak to help much with it. "Never mind," he said. "Even a small one will be falling fast by the time it gets down there. Pick one you and Mathild can roll easily yourselves; I'll just have to figure it a little closer, that's all."

After a few tests, Honath selected a rock about three times the size of his own head. It was heavy, but between them he and Mathild got it to the edge of the ledge.

"Hold on," Alaskon said in a pre-occupied voice. "Tip it over the edge, so it's ready to drop as soon as you let go of it. Good. Now wait. He's on his backtrack now. As soon as he crosses—All right. Four, three, two, one, *drop it!*"

The rock fell away. All three of them crouched in a row at the edge of the gorge. The rock dwindled, became as small as a fruit, as small as a fingernail, as small as a grain of sand. The dwarfed figure of the demon reached the end of its mad stalking arc, swung furiously to go back again—

And stopped. For an instant it just stood there. Then, with infinite slowness, it toppled sidewise into the pool. It thrashed convulsively two or three times, and then was gone; the spreading waves created by the waterfall masked any ripples it might have made in sinking.

"Like spearing fish in a bromelaid," Alaskon said proudly. But his voice was shaky. Honath knew exactly why.

After all, they had just killed a demon.

"We could do that again," Honath whispered.

"Often," Alaskon agreed, still peering greedily down at the pool. "They don't appear to have much intelligence, these demons. Given enough height, we could lure them into blind alleys like this, and bounce rocks off them almost at will. I wish *I'd* thought of it."

"Where do we go now?" Mathild said, looking toward the ladder beyond the basalt pillars. "That way?"

"Yes, and as fast as possible," Alaskon said, getting to his feet and looking upward, one hand shading his eyes. "It must be late. I don't think the light will last much longer."

"We'll have to go single file," Honath said. "And we'd better keep hold of each other's hands. One slip on those wet steps and—it's a long way down again."

Mathild shuddered and took Honath's hand convulsively. To his astonishment, the next instant she was tugging him toward the basalt pillars.

The irregular patch of deepening violet sky grew slowly as

they climbed. They paused often, clinging to the jagged escarpments until their breath came back, and snatching icy water in cupped palms from the stream that fell down the ladder beside them. There was no way to tell how far up into the dusk the way had taken them, but Honath suspected that they were already somewhat above the level of their own vine-webbed world. The air smelled colder and sharper than it ever had above the jungle.

The final cut in the cliffs through which the stream fell was another chimney, steeper and more smooth-walled than the one which had taken them out of the gorge under the waterfall, but also narrow enough to be climbed by bracing one's back against one side, and one's hands and feet against the other. The column of air inside the chimney was filled with spray, but in Hell that was too minor a discomfort to bother about.

At long last Honath heaved himself over the edge of the chimney onto flat rock, drenched and exhausted, but filled with an elation he could not suppress and did not want to. They were above the attic jungle; they had beaten Hell itself. He looked around to make sure that Mathild was safe, and then reached a hand down to Alaskon; the navigator's bad leg had been giving him trouble. Honath heaved mightily, and Alaskon came heavily over the edge and lit sprawling on the high moss.

The stars were out. For a while they simply sat and gasped for breath. Then they turned, one by one, to see where they were.

There was not a great deal to see. There was the mesa, domed with stars on all sides; a shining, finned spindle, like a gigantic minnow, pointing skyward in the center of the rocky plateau; and around the spindle, indistinct in the starlight . . .

. . . Around the shining minnow, tending it, were the Giants.

4

This, then, was the end of the battle to do what was right, whatever the odds. All the show of courage against superstition, all the black battles against Hell itself, came down to this: *The Giants were real!*

They were inarguably real. Though they were twice as tall

as men, stood straighter, had broader shoulders, were heavier across the seat and had no visible tails, their fellowship with men was clear. Even their voices, as they shouted to each other around their towering metal minnow, were the voices of men made into gods, voices as remote from those of men as the voices of men were remote from those of monkeys, yet just as clearly of the same family.

These were the Giants of the Book of Laws. They were not only real, but they had come back to Tellura as they had promised to do.

And they would know what to do with unbelievers, and with fugitives from Hell. It had all been for nothing—not only the physical struggle, but the fight to be allowed to think for oneself as well. The gods existed, literally, actually. This belief was the real hell from which Honath had been trying to fight free all his life—but now it was no longer just a belief. It was a fact, a fact that he was seeing with his own eyes.

The Giants had returned to judge their handiwork. And the first of the people they would meet would be three outcasts, three condemned and degraded criminals, three jailbreakers—the worst possible detritus of the attic world.

All this went searing through Honath's mind in less than a second, but nevertheless Alaskon's mind evidently had worked still faster. Always the most outspoken unbeliever of the entire little group of rebels, the one among them whose whole world was founded upon the existence of rational explanations for everything, his was the point of view most completely challenged by the sight before them now. With a deep, sharply indrawn breath, he turned abruptly and walked away from them.

Mathild uttered a cry of protest, which she choked off in the middle; but it was already too late. A round eye on the great silver minnow came alight, bathing them all in an oval patch of brilliance.

Honath darted after the navigator. Without looking back, Alaskon suddenly was running. For an instant longer Honath saw his figure, poised delicately against the black sky. Then he dropped silently out of sight, as suddenly and completely as if he had never been.

Alaskon had borne every hardship and every terror of the ascent from Hell with courage and even with cheerfulness—but he had been unable to face being told that it had all been meaningless.

Sick at heart, Honath turned back, shielding his eyes from

the miraculous light. There was a clear call in some unknown language from near the spindle.

Then there were footsteps, several pairs of them, coming closer.

It was time for the Second Judgment.

After a long moment, a big voice from the darkness said: "Don't be afraid. We mean you no harm. We're men, just as you are."

The language had the archaic flavor of the Book of Laws, but it was otherwise perfectly understandable. A second voice said: "What are you called?"

Honath's tongue seemed to be stuck to the roof of his mouth. While he was struggling with it, Mathild's voice came clearly from beside him:

"He is Honath the Purse-Maker, and I am Mathild the Forager."

"You are a long distance from the place we left your people," the first Giant said. "Don't you still live in the vine-webs above the jungles?"

"Lord—"

"My name is Jarl Eleven. This is Gerhardt Adler."

This seemed to stop Mathild completely. Honath could understand why: the very notion of addressing Giants by name was nearly paralyzing. But since they were already as good as cast down into Hell again, nothing could be lost by it.

"Jarl Eleven," he said, "the people still live among the vines. The floor of the jungle is forbidden. Only criminals are sent there. We are criminals."

"Oh?" Jarl Eleven said. "And you've come all the way from the surface to this mesa? Gerhardt, this is prodigious. You have no idea what the surface of this planet is like—it's a place where evolution has never managed to leave the tooth-and-nail stage. Dinosaurs from every period of the Mesozoic, primitive mammals all the way up the scale to the ancient cats—the works. That's why the original seeding team put these people in the treetops instead."

"Honath, what was your crime?" Gerhardt Adler said.

Honath was almost relieved to have the questioning come so quickly to this point; Jarl Eleven's aside, with its many terms he could not understand, had been frightening in its very meaninglessness.

"There were five of us," Honath said in a low voice. "We said we—that we did not believe in the Giants."

There was a brief silence. Then, shockingly, both Jarl Eleven and Gerhardt Adler burst into enormous laughter.

Mathild cowered, her hands over her ears. Even Honath flinched and took a step backward. Instantly, the laughter stopped, and the Giant called Jarl Eleven stepped into the oval of light and sat down beside them. In the light, it could be seen that his face and hands were hairless, although there was hair on his crown; the rest of his body was covered by a kind of cloth. Seated, he was no taller than Honath, and did not seem quite so fearsome.

"I beg your pardon," he said. "It was unkind of us to laugh, but what you said was highly unexpected. Gerhardt, come over here and squat down, so that you don't look so much like a statue of some general. Tell me, Honath, in what way did you not believe in the Giants?"

Honath could hardly believe his ears. A Giant had begged his pardon! Was this some still crueler joke? But whatever the reason, Jarl Eleven had asked him a question.

"Each of the five of us differed," he said. "I held that you were not—not real except as symbols of some abstract truth. One of us, the wisest, believed that you did not exist in any sense at all. But we all agreed that you were not gods."

"And, of course, we aren't," Jarl Eleven said. "We're men. We come from the same stock as you. We're not your rulers, but your brothers. Do you understand what I say?"

"No," Honath admitted.

"Then let me tell you about it. There are men on many worlds, Honath. They differ from one another, because the worlds differ, and different kinds of men are needed to people each one. Gerhardt and I are the kind of men who live on a world called Earth, and many other worlds like it. We are two very minor members of a huge project called a 'seeding program,' which has been going on for thousands of years now. It's the job of the seeding program to survey newly discovered worlds, and then to make men suitable to live on each new world."

"To make men? But only gods—"

"No, no. Be patient and listen," said Jarl Eleven. "We don't make men. We make them suitable. There's a great deal of difference between the two. We take the living germ plasm, the sperm and the egg, and we modify it; then the modified man emerges, and we help him to settle down in his new world. That's what we did on Tellura—it happened long ago, before Gerhardt and I were even born. Now, we've come back to see how you people are getting along, and to lend a hand if necessary."

He looked from Honath to Mathild, and back again. "Do you follow me?" he said.

"I'm trying," Honath said. "But you should go down to the jungle-top, then. We're not like the others; they are the people you want to see."

"We shall, in the morning. We just landed here. But, just because you're not like the others, we're more interested in you now. Tell me: has any condemned man ever escaped from the jungle floor before?"

"No, never. That's not surprising. There are monsters down there."

Jarl Eleven looked sidewise at the other Giant; he seemed to be smiling. "When you see the films," he remarked, "you'll call that the understatement of the century. Honath, how did you three manage to escape, then?"

Haltingly, at first, and then with more confidence as the memories came crowding vividly back, Honath told him. When he mentioned the feast at the demon's nest, Jarl Eleven again looked significantly at Adler, but he did not interrupt.

"And, finally, we got to the top of the chimney and came out on this flat space," Honath said, "Alaskon was still with us then, but when he saw you and the shining thing he threw himself back down the cleft. He was a criminal like us, but he should not have died. He was a brave man, and a wise one."

"Not wise enough to wait until all the evidence was in," Adler said enigmatically. "All in all, Jarl, I'd say 'prodigious' is the word for it. This is really the most successful seeding job any team has ever done, at least in this limb of the galaxy. And what a stroke of luck, to be on the spot just as it came to term, and with a couple at that!"

"What does it mean?" Honath said.

"Just this, Honath. When the seeding team set your people up in business on Tellura, they didn't mean for you to live forever in the treetops. They knew that, sooner or later, you'd have to come down to the ground and learn to fight this planet on its own terms. Otherwise, you'd go stale and die out."

"Live on the ground all the time?" Mathild said in a faint voice.

"Yes, Mathild. The life in the treetops was to have been only an interim period, while you gathered knowledge you needed about Tellura, and put it to use. But to be the real masters of the world, you will have to conquer the surface, too.

"The device your people worked out, of sending only criminals to the surface, was the best way of conquering the planet that they could have picked. It takes a strong will and exceptional courage to go against custom; and both those qualities
86

are needed to lick Tellura. Your people exiled just such fighting spirits to the surface, year after year after year.

"Sooner or later, some of those exiles were going to discover how to live successfully on the ground, and make it possible for the rest of your people to leave the trees. You and Honath have done just that."

"Observe please, Jarl," Adler said. "The crime in this first successful case was ideological. That was the crucial turn in the criminal policy of these people. A spirit of revolt is not quite enough; but couple it with brains, and—ecce homo!"

Honath's head was swimming. "But what does all this mean?" he said. "Are we—not condemned to Hell any more?"

"No, you're still condemned, if you still want to call it that," Jarl Eleven said soberly. "You've learned how to live down there, and you've found out something even more valuable: How to stay alive while cutting down your enemies. Do you know that you killed three demons with your bare hands, you and Mathild and Alaskon?"

"Killed—"

"Certainly," Jarl Eleven said. "You ate three eggs. That is the classical way, and indeed the only way, to wipe out monsters like the dinosaurs. You can't kill the adults with anything short of an anti-tank gun, but they're helpless in embryo—and the adults haven't the sense to guard their nests."

Honath heard, but only distantly. Even his awareness of Mathild's warmth next to him did not seem to help much.

"Then we have to go back down there," he said dully. "And this time forever."

"Yes," Jarl Eleven said, his voice gentle. "But you won't be alone, Honath. Beginning tomorrow, you'll have all your people with you."

"*All* our people? But—you're going to drive them out?"

"All of them. Oh, we won't prohibit the use of the vine-webs, too, but from now on your race will have to fight it out on the surface as well. You and Mathild have proven that it can be done. It's high time the rest of you learned, too."

"Jarl, you think too little of these young people themselves," Adler said. "Tell them what is in store for them. They are frightened."

"Of course, of course. It's obvious. Honath, you and Mathild are the only living individuals of your race who know how to survive down there on the surface. And we're not going to tell your people how to do that. We aren't even going to drop them so much as a hint. That part of it is up to you."

Honath's jaw dropped.

"It's up to you," Jarl Eleven repeated firmly. "We'll return you to your tribe tomorrow, and we'll tell your people that you two know the rules for successful life on the ground—and that everyone else has to go down and live there, too. We'll tell them nothing else but that. What do you think they'll do then?"

"I don't know," Honath said dazedly. "Anything could happen. They might even make us Spokesman and Spokeswoman—except that we're just common criminals."

"Uncommon pioneers, Honath. The man and woman to lead the humanity of Tellura out of the attic, into the wide world." Jarl Eleven got to his feet, the great light playing over him. Looking up after him, Honath saw that there were at least a dozen other Giants standing just outside the oval of light, listening intently to every word.

"But there's a little time to be passed before we begin," Jarl Eleven said. "Perhaps you two would like to look over our ship."

Numbly, but with a soundless emotion much like music inside him, Honath took Mathild's hand. Together they walked away from the chimney to Hell, following the footsteps of the Giants.

BOOK THREE

SURFACE TENSION

A sky of ice, a microscopic enemy, and two hundred naked men struggling to survive in a puddle of water. **Prologue**

[DAMON KNIGHT]

Dr. Chatvieux took a long time over the microscope, leaving la Ventura with nothing to do but look at the dead landscape of Hydrot. Waterscape, he thought, would be a better word. From space, the new world had shown only one small, triangular continent, set amid endless ocean; and even the continent was mostly swamp.

The wreck of the seed-ship lay broken squarely across the one real spur of rock which Hydrot seemed to possess, which reared a magnificent twenty-one feet above sea-level. From this eminence, la Ventura could see forty miles to the horizon across a flat bed of mud. The red light of the star Tau Ceti, glinting upon thousands of small lakes, pools, ponds and puddles, made the watery plain look like a mosaic of onyx and ruby.

"If I were a religious man," the pilot said suddenly, "I'd call this a plain case of divine vengeance."

Chatvieux said: "Hmn?"

"It's as if we'd been struck down for—is it *hubris*? Pride, arrogance?"

"*Hybris*," Chatvieux said, looking up at last. "Well, is it? I don't feel swollen with pride at the moment. Do you?"

"I'm not exactly proud of my piloting," la Ventura admitted. "But that isn't quite what I mean. I was thinking about

89

why we came here in the first place. It takes a lot of arrogance to think that you can scatter men, or at least things very much like men, all over the face of the galaxy. It takes even more pride to do the job—to pack up all the equipment and move from planet to planet and actually make men, make them suitable for every place you touch."

"I suppose it does," Chatvieux said. "But we're only one of several hundred seed-ships in this limb of the galaxy, so I doubt that the gods picked us out as special sinners." He smiled. "If they had, maybe they'd have left us our ultraphone, so the Colonization Council could hear about our cropper. Besides, Paul, we don't make men. We adapt them—adapt them to Earthlike planets, nothing more than that. We've sense enough—or humility enough, if you like that better—to know that we can't adapt men to a planet like Jupiter, or to the surface of a sun, like Tau Ceti."

"Anyhow, we're here," la Ventura said grimly. "And we aren't going to get off. Phil tells me that we don't even have our germ-cell bank any more, so we can't seed this place in the usual way. We've been thrown onto a dead world and dared to adapt to it. What are the pantropes going to do with our recalcitrant carcasses—provide built-in waterwings?"

"No," Chatvieux said calmly. "You and I and all the rest of us are going to die, Paul. Pantropic techniques don't work on the body; that was fixed for you for life when you were conceived. To attempt to rebuild it for you would only maim you. The pantropes affect only the genes, the inheritance-carrying factors. We can't give you built-in waterwings, any more than we can give you a new set of brains. I think we'll be able to populate this world with men, but we won't live to see it."

The pilot thought about it, a lump of cold blubber collecting gradually in his stomach. "How long do you give us?" he said at last.

"Who knows? A month, perhaps."

The bulkhead leading to the wrecked section of the ship was pushed back, admitting salt, muggy air, heavy with carbon dioxide. Philip Strasvogel, the communications officer, came in, tracking mud. Like la Ventura, he was now a man without a function, and it appeared to bother him. He was not well equipped for introspection, and with his ultraphone totally smashed, unresponsive to his perpetually darting hands, he had been thrown back into his own mind, whose resources were few. Only the tasks Chatvieux had set him to had prevented him from setting like a gelling colloid into a permanent state of the sulks.

90

He unbuckled from around his waist a canvas belt, into the loops of which plastic vials were stuffed like cartridges. "More samples, Doc," he said. "All alike—water, very wet. I have some quicksand in one boot, too. Find anything?"

"A good deal, Phil. Thanks. Are the others around?"

Strasvogel poked his head out and hallooed. Other voices rang out over the mudflats. Minutes later, the rest of the survivors of the crash were crowding into the pantrope deck: Saltonstall, Chatvieux' senior assistant, a perpetually sanguine, perpetually youthful technician willing to try anything once, including dying; Eunice Wagner, behind whose placid face rested the brains of the expedition's only remaining ecologist; Eleftherios Venezuelos, the always-silent delegate from the Colonization Council; and Joan Heath, a midshipman whose duties, like la Ventura's and Phil's, were now without meaning, but whose bright head and tall, deceptively indolent body shone to the pilot's eyes brighter than Tau Ceti— brighter, since the crash, even than the home sun.

Five men and two women—to colonize a planet on which "standing room" meant treading water.

They came in quietly and found seats or resting places on the deck, on the edges of tables, in corners. Joan Heath went to stand beside la Ventura. They did not look at each other, but the warmth of her shoulder beside his was all that he needed. Nothing was as bad as it seemed.

Venezuelos said: "What's the verdict, Dr. Chatvieux?"

"This place isn't dead," Chatvieux said. "There's life in the sea and in the fresh water, both. On the animal side of the ledger, evolution seems to have stopped with the crustacea; the most advanced form I've found is a tiny crayfish, from one of the local rivulets, and it doesn't seem to be well distributed. The ponds and puddles are well-stocked with small metazoans of lower orders, right up to the rotifers—including a castle-building genus like Earth's *Floscularidae*. In addition, there's a wonderfully variegated protozoan population, with a dominant ciliate type much like *Paramoecium*, plus various Sarcodines, the usual spread of phyto-flagellates, and even a phosphorescent species I wouldn't have expected to see anywhere but in salt water. As for the plants, they run from simple blue-green algae to quite advanced thallus-producing types—though none of them, of course, can live out of the water."

"The sea is about the same," Eunice said. "I've found some of the larger simple metazoans—jellyfish and so on—and some crayfish almost as big as lobsters. But it's normal to find

91

salt-water species running larger than fresh-water. And there's the usual plankton and nannoplankton population."

"In short," Chatvieux said, "we'll survive here—if we fight."

"Wait a minute," la Ventura said. "You've just finished telling me that we wouldn't survive. And you were talking about us, the seven of us here, not about the genus man, because we don't have our germ-cells banks any more. What's—"

"We don't have the banks. But we ourselves can contribute germ-cells, Paul. I'll get to that in a moment." Chatvieux turned to Saltonstall. "Martin, what would you think of our taking to the sea? We came out of it once, long ago; maybe we could come out of it again on Hydrot."

"No good," Saltonstall said immediately. "I like the idea, but I don't think this planet ever heard of Swinburne, or Homer, either. Looking at it as a colonization problem alone, as if we weren't involved in it ourselves, I wouldn't give you an Oc dollar for *epi oinopa ponton*. The evolutionary pressure there is too high, the competition from other species is prohibitive; seeding the sea should be the last thing we attempt, not the first. The colonists wouldn't have a chance to learn a thing before they'd be gobbled up."

"Why?" la Ventura said. Once more, the death in his stomach was becoming hard to placate.

"Eunice, do your sea-going Coelenterates include anything like the Portuguese man-of-war?"

The ecologist nodded.

"There's your answer, Paul," Saltonstall said. "The sea is out. It's got to be fresh water, where the competing creatures are less formidable and there are more places to hide."

"We can't compete with a jellyfish?" la Ventura asked, swallowing.

"No, Paul," Chatvieux said. "Not with one that dangerous. The pantropes make adaptations, not gods. They take human germ-cells—in this case, our own, since our bank was wiped out in the crash—and modify them genetically toward those of creatures who can live in any reasonable environment. The result will be manlike, and intelligent. It usually shows the donors' personality patterns, too, since the modifications are usually made mostly in the morphology, not so much in the mind, of the resulting individual.

But we can't transmit memory. The adapted man is worse than a child in the new environment. He has no history, no techniques, no precedents, not even a language. In the usual colonization project, like the Tellura affair, the seeding teams more or less take him through elementary school before they leave the planet to him, but we won't survive long enough to give such instruction. We'll have to design our colonists with plenty of built-in protections and locate them in the most favorable environment possible, so that at least some of them will survive learning by experience alone.".

The pilot thought about it, but nothing occurred to him which did not make the disaster seem realer and more intimate with each passing second. Joan Heath moved slightly closer to him. "One of the new creatures can have my personality pattern, but it won't be able to remember being me. Is that right?"

"That's right. In the present situation we'll probably make our colonists haploid, so that some of them, perhaps many, will have a heredity traceable to you alone. There may be just the faintest of residuums of identity—pantropy's given us some data to support the old Jungian notion of ancestral memory. But we're all going to die on Hydrot, Paul, as self-conscious persons. There's no avoiding that. Somewhere we'll leave behind people who behave as we would, think and feel as we would, but who won't remember la Ventura, or Dr. Chatvieux, or Joan Heath—or the Earth."

The pilot said nothing more. There was a gray taste in his mouth.

"Saltonstall, what would you recommend as a form?"

The pantropist pulled reflectively at his nose. "Webbed extremities, of course, with thumbs and big toes heavy and thorn-like for defense until the creature has had a chance to learn. Smaller external ears, and the eardrum larger and closer to the outer end of the ear-canal. We're going to have to reorganize the water-conservation system, I think; the glomerular kidney is perfectly suitable for living in fresh water, but the business of living immersed, inside and out, for a creature with a salty inside means that the osmotic pressure inside is going to be higher than outside, so that the kidneys are going to have to be pumping virtually all the time. Under the circumstances we'd best step up production of urine, and that means the antidiuretic function of the pituitary gland is going to have to be abrogated, for all practical purposes."

"What about respiration?"

"Hm," Saltonstall said. "I suppose book-lungs, like some of the arachnids have. They can be supplied by intercostal spiracles. They're gradually adaptable to atmosphere-breathing, if our colonist ever decides to come out of the water. Just to provide for that possibility, I'd suggest that the nose be retained, maintaining the nasal cavity as a part of the otological system, but cutting off the cavity from the larynx with a

93

membrane of cells that are supplied with oxygen by direct irrigation, rather than by the circulatory system. Such a membrane wouldn't survive for many generations, once the creature took to living out of the water even for part of its lifetime; it'd go through two or three generations as an amphibian, and then one day it'd suddenly find itself breathing through its larynx again."

"Ingenious," Chatvieux said.

"Also, Dr. Chatvieux, I'd suggest that we have it adopt sporulation. As an aquatic animal, our colonist is going to have an indefinite life-span, but we'll have to give it a breeding cycle of about six weeks to keep up its numbers during the learning period; so there'll have to be a definite break of some duration in its active year. Otherwise it'll hit the population problem before it's learned enough to cope with it."

"And it'd be better if our colonists could winter over inside a good, hard shell," Eunice Wagner added in agreement. "So sporulation's the obvious answer. Many other microscopic creatures have it."

"Microscopic?" Phil said incredulously.

"Certainly," Chatvieux said, amused. "We can't very well crowd a six-foot man into a two-foot puddle. But that raises a question. We'll have tough competition from the rotifers, and some of them aren't strictly microscopic; for that matter even some of the protozoa can be seen with the naked eye, just barely, with dark-field illumination. I don't think your average colonist should run much under 250 microns, Saltonstall. Give them a chance to slug it out."

"I was thinking of making them twice that big."

"Then they'd be the biggest animals in their environment," Eunice Wagner pointed out, "and won't ever develop any skills. Besides, if you make them about rotifer size, it will give them an incentive for pushing out the castle-building rotifers, and occupying the castles themselves, as dwellings."

Chatvieux nodded. "All right, let's get started. While the pantropes are being calibrated, the rest of us can put our heads together on leaving a record for these people. We'll micro-engrave the record on a set of corrosion-proof metal leaves, of a size our colonists can handle conveniently. We can tell them, very simply, what happened, and plant a few suggestions that there's more to the universe than what they find in their puddles. Some day they may puzzle it out."

"Question," Eunice Wagner said. "Are we going to tell them they're microscopic? I'm opposed to it. It may saddle their entire early history with a gods-and-demons mythology that they'd be better off without."

"Yes, we are," Chatvieux said; and la Ventura could tell by the change in the tone of his voice that he was speaking now as their senior on the expedition. "These people will be of the race of men, Eunice. We want them to win their way back into the community of men. They are not toys, to be protected from the truth forever in a fresh-water womb."

"Besides," Saltonstall observed, "they won't get the record translated at any time in their early history. They'll have to develop a written language of their own, and it will be impossible for us to leave them any sort of Rosetta Stone or other key. By the time they can decipher the truth, they should be ready for it."

"I'll make that official," Venezuelos said unexpectedly. And that was that.

And then, essentially, it was all over. They contributed the cells that the pantropes would need. Privately, la Ventura and Joan Heath went to Chatvieux and asked to contribute jointly; but the scientist said that the microscopic men were to be haploid, in order to give them a minute cellular structure, with nuclei as small as Earthly rickettsiae, and therefore each person had to give germ-cells individually—there would be no use for zygotes. So even that consolation was denied them; in death they would have no children, but be instead as alone as ever.

They helped, as far as they could, with the text of the message which was to go on the metal leaves. They had their personality patterns recorded. They went through the motions. Already they were beginning to be hungry; the sea-crayfish, the only things on Hydrot big enough to eat, lived in water too deep and cold for subsistence fishing.

After la Ventura had set his control board to rights—a useless gesture, but a habit he had been taught to respect, and which in an obscure way made things a little easier to bear—he was out of it. He sat by himself at the far end of the rock ledge, watching Tau Ceti go redly down, chucking pebbles into the nearest pond.

After a while Joan Heath came silently up behind him, and sat down too. He took her hand. The glare of the red sun was almost extinguished now, and together they watched it go, with la Ventura, at least, wondering somberly which nameless puddle was to be his Lethe.

He never found out, of course. None of them did.

Cycle One

In a forgotten corner of the galaxy, the watery world of Hydrot hurtles endlessly around the red star, Tau Ceti. For many months its single small continent has been snowbound, and the many pools and lakes which dot the continent have been locked in the grip of the ice. Now, however, the red sun swings closer and closer to the zenith in Hydrot's sky; the snow rushes in torrents toward the eternal ocean, and the ice recedes toward the shores of the lakes and ponds . . .

1

The first thing to reach the consciousness of the sleeping Lavon was a small, intermittent scratching sound. This was followed by a disquieting sensation in his body, as if the world—and Lavon with it—were being rocked back and forth. He stirred uneasily, without opening his eyes. His vastly slowed metabolism made him feel inert and queasy, and the rocking did not help. At his slight motion, however, both the sound and the motion became more insistent.

It seemed to take days for the fog over his brain to clear, but whatever was causing the disturbance would not let him rest. With a groan he forced his eyelids open and made an abrupt gesture with one webbed hand. By the waves of phosphorescence which echoed away from his fingers at the motion, he could see that the smooth amber walls of his spherical shell were unbroken. He tried to peer through them, but he could see nothing but darkness outside. Well, that was natural; the amnionic fluid inside the spore would generate light, but ordinary water did not, no matter how vigorously it was stirred.

Whatever was outside the sphere was rocking it again, with the same whispering friction against its shell. Probably some nosey diatom, Lavon thought sleepily, trying to butt its way through an object it was too stupid to go around. Or some early hunter, yearning for a taste of the morsel inside the spore. Well, let it worry itself; Lavon had no intention of breaking the shell just yet. The fluid in which he had slept for so many months had held his body processes static, and had slowed his mind. Once out into the water, he would have to start breathing and looking for food again, and he could tell by the unrelieved darkness outside that it was too early in the spring to begin thinking about that.

He flexed his fingers reflectively, in the disharmonic motion from little finger to thumb that no animal but man can copy, and watched the widening wavefronts of greenish light rebound in larger arcs from the curved spore walls. Here he was, curled up quite comfortably in a little amber ball, where he could stay until even the depths were warm and light. At this moment there was probably still some ice on the sky, and certainly there would not be much to eat as yet. Not that there was ever much, what with the voracious rotifers coming awake too with the first gust of warm water—

The rotifers! That was it. There was a plan afoot to drive them out. Memory returned in an unwelcome rush. As if to help it, the spore rocked again. That was probably one of the Protos, trying to awaken him; nothing man-eating ever came to the Bottom this early. He had left an early call with the Paras, and now the time had come, as cold and early and dark as he had thought he wanted it.

Reluctantly, Lavon uncurled, planting his webbed toes and arching his backbone as hard as he could, pressing with his whole body against his amber prison. With small, sharp, crepitating sounds, a network of cracks raced through the translucent shell.

Then the spore wall dissolved into a thousand brittle shards, and he was shivering violently with the onslaught of the icy water. The warmer fluid of his winter cell dissipated silently, a faint glowing fog. In the brief light he saw, not far from him, a familiar shape: a transparent, bubble-filled cylinder, a colorless slipper of jelly, spirally grooved, almost as long as he was tall. Its surface was furred with gently vibrating fine hairs, thickened at the base.

The light went out. The Proto said nothing; it waited while Lavon choked and coughed, expelling the last remnants of the spore fluid from his book-lungs and sucking in the pure, ice-cold water.

"Para?" Lavon said at last. "Already?"

"Already," the invisible cilia vibrated in even, emotionless tones. Each separate hair-like process buzzed at an independent, changing rate; the resulting sound waves spread through the water, intermodulating, reinforcing or cancelling each other. The aggregate wave-front, by the time it reached human ears, was rather eerie, but nevertheless recognizable human speech. "This is the time, Lavon."

"Time and more than time," another voice said from the returned darkness. "If we are to drive Flosc from his castles."

97

"Who's that?" Lavon said, turning futilely toward the new voice.

"I am Para also, Lavon. We are sixteen since the awakening. If you could reproduce as rapidly as we—"

"Brains are better than numbers," Lavon said. "As the Eaters will find out soon enough."

"What shall we do, Lavon?"

The man drew up his knees and sank to the cold mud of the Bottom to think. Something wriggled under his buttocks and a tiny spirillum corkscrewed away, identifiable only by feel. He let it go; he was not hungry yet, and he had the Eaters—the rotifers—to think about. Before long they would be swarming in the upper reaches of the sky, devouring everything, even men when they could catch them, even their natural enemies the Protos now and then. And whether or not the Protos could be organized to battle them was a question still to be tested.

Brains are better than numbers; even that, as a proposition, was still to be tested. The Protos, after all, were intelligent after their fashion; and they knew their world, as the men did not. Lavon could still remember how hard it had been for him to get straight in his head the various clans of beings in this world, and to make sense of their confused names; his tutor Shar had drilled him unmercifully until it had begun to penetrate.

When you said "Man," you meant creatures that, generally speaking, looked alike. The bacteria were of three kinds, the rods and the globes and the spirals, but they were all tiny and edible, so he had learned to differentiate them quickly. When it came to the Protos, identification became a real problem. Para here was a Proto, but he certainly looked very different from Stent and his family, and the family of Didin was unlike both. Anything, as it turned out, that was not green and had a visible nucleus was a Proto, no matter how strange its shape might be. The Eaters were all different, too, and some of them were as beautiful as the fruiting crowns of waterplants; but all of them were deadly, and all had the whirling crown of cilia which could suck you into the incessantly grinding mastax in a moment. Everything which was green and had an engraved shell of glass, Shar had called a diatom, dredging the strange word as he dredged them all from some Bottom in his skull which none of the rest of them could reach, and even Shar could not explain.

Lavon arose quickly. "We need Shar," he said. "Where is his spore?"

"On a plant frond, far up near the sky."

Idiot! The old man would never think of safety. To sleep near the sky, where he might be snatched up and borne off by any Eater to chance by when he emerged, sluggish with winter's long sleep! How could a wise man be so foolish?

"We'll have to hurry. Show me the way."

"Soon; wait," one of the Paras said. "You cannot see. Noc is foraging nearby." There was a small stir in the texture of the darkness as the swift cylinder shot away.

"Why do we need Shar?" the other Para said.

"For his brains, Para. He is a thinker."

"But his thoughts are water. Since he taught the Protos man's language, he has forgotten to think of the Eaters. He thinks forever of the mystery of how man came here. It is a mystery—even the Eaters are not like man. But understanding it will not help us to live."

Lavon turned blindly toward the creature. "Para, tell me something. Why do the Protos side with us? With man, I mean? Why do you need us? The Eaters fear you."

There was a short silence. When the Para spoke again, the vibrations of its voice were more blurred than before, more even, more devoid of any understandable feeling.

"We live in this world," the Para said. "We are of it. We rule it. We came to that state long before the coming of men, in long warfare with the Eaters. But we think as the Eaters do, we do not plan, we share our knowledge and we exist. Men plan; men lead; men are different from each other; men want to remake the world. And they hate the Eaters, as we do. We will help."

"And give up your rule?"

"And give it up, if the rule of men is better. That is reason. Now we can go; Noc is coming back with light."

Lavon looked up. Sure enough, there was a brief flash of cold light far overhead, and then another. In a moment the spherical Proto had dropped into view, its body flaring regularly with blue-green pulses. Beside it darted the second Para.

"Noc brings news," the second Para said. "Para is twenty-four. The Syn are awake by thousands along the sky. Noc spoke to a Syn colony, but they will not help us; they all expect to be dead before the Eaters awake."

"Of course," said the first Para. "That always happens. And the Syn are plants; why should they help the Protos?"

"Ask Noc if he'll guide us to Shar," Lavon said impatiently.

The Noc gestured with its single short, thick tentacle. One of the Paras said, "That is what he is here for."

"Then let's go. We've waited long enough."

The mixed quartet soared away from the Bottom through the liquid darkness.

"No," Lavon snapped. "Not a second longer. The Syn are awake, and Notholca of the Eaters is due right after that. You know that as well as I do, Shar. Wake up!"

"Yes, yes," the old man said fretfully. He stretched and yawned. "You're always in such a hurry, Lavon. Where's Phil? He made his spore near mine." He pointed to a still-unbroken amber sphere sealed to a leaf of the water-plant one tier below. "Better push him off; he'll be safer on the Bottom."

"He would never reach the Bottom," Para said. "The thermocline has formed."

Shar looked surprised. "It has? Is it as late as all that? Wait while I get my records together." He began to search along the leaf in the debris and the piled shards of his spore. Lavon looked impatiently about, found a splinter of stonewort, and threw it heavy end first at the bubble of Phil's cell just below. The spore shattered promptly, and the husky young man tumbled out, blue with shock as the cold water hit him.

"Wough!" he said. "Take it easy, Lavon." He looked up. "The old man's awake? Good. He insisted on staying up here for the winter, so of course I had to stay too."

"Aha," Shar said, and lifted a thick metal plate about the length of his forearm and half as wide. "Here is one of them. Now if only I haven't misplaced the other—"

Phil kicked away a mass of bacteria. "Here it is. Better give them both to a Para, so they won't burden you. Where do we go from here, Lavon? It's dangerous up this high. I'm just glad a Dicran hasn't already shown up."

"I here," something droned just above them.

Instantly, without looking up, Lavon flung himself out and down into the open water, turning his head to look back over his shoulder only when he was already diving as fast as he could go. Shar and Phil had evidently sprung at the same instant. On the next frond above where Shar had spent his winter was the armored, trumpet-shaped body of the rotifer Dicran, contracted to leap after them.

The two Protos came curving back out of nowhere. At the same moment, the bent, shortened body of Dicran flexed in its armor plate, straightened, came plunging toward them. There was a soft *plop* and Lavon found himself struggling in a fine net, as tangled and impassible as the matte of a lichen. A second such sound was followed by a muttered imprecation from Phil. Lavon struck out fiercely, but he was barely able to wriggle in the web of wiry, transparent stuff.

"Be still," a voice which he recognized as Para's throbbed

behind him. He managed to screw his head around, and then kicked himself mentally for not having realized at once what had happened. The Paras had exploded the trichocysts which lay like tiny cartridges beneath their pellicles; each one cast forth a liquid which solidified upon contact with the water in a long slender thread. It was their standard method of defense.

Farther down, Shar and Phil drifted with the second Para in the heart of a white haze, like creatures far gone in mold. Dicran swerved to avoid it, but she was evidently unable to give up; she twisted and darted around them, her corona buzzing harshly, her few scraps of the human language forgotten. Seen from this distance, the rotation of the corona was revealed as an illusion, created by the rhythm of pulsation of the individual cilia, but as far as Lavon was concerned the point was solely technical and the distance was far too short. Through the transparent armor Lavon could also see the great jaws of Dicran's mastax, grinding away mechanically at the fragments which poured into her unheeding mouth.

High above them all, Noc circled indecisively, illuminating the whole group with quick, nervous flashes of his blue light. He was a flagellate, and had no natural weapons against the rotifer; why he was hanging around drawing attention to himself Lavon could not imagine.

Then, suddenly, he saw the reason: a barrel-like creature about Noc's size, ringed with two rows of cilia and bearing a ram-like prow. "Didin!" he shouted, unnecessarily. "This way!"

The Proto swung gracefully toward them and seemed to survey them, though it was hard to tell how he could see them without eyes. The Dicran saw him at the same time and began to back slowly away, her buzzing rising to a raw snarl. She regained the plant and crouched down.

For an instant Lavon thought she was going to give up, but experience should have told him that she lacked the sense. Suddenly the lithe, crouched body was in full spring again, this time straight at Didin. Lavon yelled an incoherent warning.

The Proto didn't need it. The slowly cruising barrel darted to one side and then forward, with astonishing speed. If he could sink that poisoned seizing-organ into a weak point in the rotifer's armor—

Noc mounted higher to keep out of the way of the two fighters, and in the resulting weakened light Lavon could not

101

see what was happening, though the furious churning of the water and the buzzing of the Dicran continued.

After a while the sounds seemed to be retreating; Lavon crouched in the gloom inside the Para's net, listening intently. Finally there was silence.

"What's happened?" he whispered tensely.

"Didin does not say."

More eternities went by. Then the darkness began to wane as Noc dropped cautiously toward them.

"Noc, where did they go?"

Noc signaled with his tentacle and turned on his axis toward Para. "He says he lost sight of them. Wait—I hear Didin."

Lavon could hear nothing; what the Para "heard" was some one of the semi-telepathic impulses which made up the Proto's own language.

"He says Dicran is dead."

"Good! Ask him to bring the body back here."

There was a short silence. "He says he will bring it. What good is a dead rotifer, Lavon?"

"You'll see," Lavon said. He watched anxiously until Didin glided backwards into the lighted area, his poisonous ram sunk deep into the flaccid body of the rotifer, which, after the delicately-organized fashion of its kind, was already beginning to disintegrate.

"Let me out of this net, Para."

The Proto jerked sharply for a fraction of a turn on its long axis, snapping the threads off at the base; the movement had to be made with great precision, or its pellicle would tear as well. The tangled mass rose gently with the current and drifted off over the abyss.

Lavon swam forward and, seizing one buckled edge of Dicran's armor, tore away a huge strip of it. His hands plunged into the now almost shapeless body and came out again holding two dark spheroids: eggs.

"Destroy these, Didin," he ordered. The Proto obligingly slashed them open.

"Hereafter," Lavon said, "that's to be standard procedure with every Eater you kill."

"Not the males," one of the Para pointed out.

"Para, you have no sense of humor. All right, not the males —but nobody kills the males anyhow, they're harmless." He looked down grimly at the inert mass. "Remember—destroy the eggs. Killing the beasts isn't enough. We want to wipe out the whole race."

"We never forget," Para said emotionlessly.

The band of over two hundred humans, with Lavon and Shar and a Para at its head, fled swiftly through the warm, light waters of the upper level. Each man gripped a wood splinter, or a fragment of lime chipped from stonewort, as a club; and two hundred pairs of eyes darted watchfully from side to side. Cruising over them was a squadron of twenty Didins, and the rotifers they encountered only glared at them from single red eyespots, making no move to attack. Overhead, near the sky, the sunlight was filtered through a thick layer of living creatures, fighting and feeding and spawning, so that all the depths below were colored a rich green. Most of this heavily populated layer was made up of algae and diatoms, and there the Eaters fed unhindered. Sometimes a dying diatom dropped slowly past the army.

The spring was well advanced; the two hundred, Lavon thought, probably represented all of the humans who had survived the winter. At least no more could be found. The others—nobody would ever know how many—had awakened too late in the season, or had made their spores in exposed places, and the rotifers had snatched them up. Of the group, more than a third were women. That meant that in another forty days, if they were unmolested, they could double the size of their army.

If they were unmolested. Lavon grinned and pushed an agitated colony of Eudorina out of his way. The phrase reminded him of a speculation Shar had brought forth last year: If Para were left unmolested, the oldster had said, he could reproduce fast enough to fill this whole universe with a solid mass of Paras before the season was out. Nobody, of course, ever went unmolested in this world; nevertheless, Lavon meant to cut the odds for people considerably below anything that had heretofore been thought of as natural.

His hand flashed up, and down again. The darting squadrons plunged after him. The light on the sky faded rapidly, and after a while Lavon began to feel slightly chilly. He signaled again. Like dancers, the two hundred swung their bodies in mid-flight, plunging now feet first toward the Bottom. To strike the thermocline in this position would make their passage through it faster, getting them out of the upper level where every minute, despite the convoy of Protos, concentrated danger.

Lavon's feet struck a yielding surface, and with a splash he was over his head in icy water. He bobbed up again, feeling the icy division drawn across his shoulders. Other splashes began to sound all along the thermocline as the army struck it, although, since there was water above and below, Lavon could not see the actual impacts.

Now they would have to wait until their body temperatures fell. At this dividing line of the universe, the warm water ended and the temperature dropped rapidly, so that the water below was much denser and buoyed them up. The lower level of cold reached clear down to the Bottom—an area which the rotifers, who were not very clever, seldom managed to enter.

A moribund diatom drifted down beside Lavon, the greenish-yellow of its body fading to a sick orange, its beautifully-marked, oblong, pillbox-like shell swarming with greedy bacteria. It came to rest on the thermocline, and the transparent caterpillar tread of jelly which ran around it moved feebly, trying vainly to get traction on the sliding water interface. Lavon reached out a webbed hand and brushed away a clot of vibrating rods which had nearly forced its way into the shell through a costal opening.

"Thank . . ." the diatom said, in an indistinct, whispering voice. And again, "Thank . . . Die . . ." The gurgling whisper faded. The caterpillar tread shifted again, then was motionless.

"It is right," a Para said. "Why do you bother with those creatures? They are stupid. Nothing can be done for them."

Lavon did not try to explain. He felt himself sinking slowly, and the water about his trunk and legs no longer seemed cold, only gratefully cool after the stifling heat of that he was breathing. In a moment the cool still depths had closed over his head. He hovered until he was reasonably sure that all the rest of his army was safely through, and the long ordeal of search for survivors in the upper level really ended. Then he twisted and streaked for the Bottom, Phil and Para beside him, Shar puffing along with the vanguard.

A stone loomed; Lavon surveyed it in the half-light. Almost immediately he saw what he had hoped to see: the sand-built house of a caddis-worm, clinging to the mountainous slopes of the rock. He waved in his special cadre and pointed.

Cautiously the men spread out in a U around the stone, the mouth of the U facing the same way as the opening of the worm's masonry tube. A Noc came after them, drifting like a star-shell above the peak; one of the Paras approached the door of the worm's house, buzzing defiantly. Under cover of this challenge the men at the back of the U settled on the rock and began to creep forward. The house was three times as tall as they were; the slimy black sand grains of which it was composed were as big as their heads.

There was a stir inside, and after a moment the ugly head of the worm peered out, weaving uncertainly at the buzzing Para which had disturbed it. The Para drew back, and the worm, in a kind of blind hunger, followed it. A sudden lunge brought it nearly halfway out of its tube.

Lavon shouted. Instantly the worm was surrounded by a howling horde of two-legged demons, who beat and prodded it mercilessly with fists and clubs. Somehow it made a sound, a kind of bleat as unlikely as the bird-like whistle of a fish, and began to slide backwards into its home—but the rear guard had already broken in back there. It jerked forward again, lashing from side to side under the flogging.

There was only one way now for the great larva to go, and the demons around it kept it going that way. It fell toward the Bottom down the side of the rock, naked and ungainly, shaking its blind head and bleating.

Lavon sent five Didin after it. They could not kill it, for it was far too huge to die under their poison, but they could sting it hard enough to keep it travelling. Otherwise, it would be almost sure to return to the rock to start a new house.

Lavon settled on an abutment and surveyed his prize with satisfaction. It was more than big enough to hold his entire clan—a great tubular hall, easily defended once the breach in the rear wall was rebuilt, and well out of the usual haunts of the Eaters. The muck the caddis-worm had left behind would have to be cleaned up, guards posted, vents knocked out to keep the oxygen-poor water of the depths in motion inside. It was too bad that the amoebae could not be detailed to scavenge the place, but Lavon knew better than to issue such an order. The Fathers of the Protos could not be asked to do useful work; that had been made very clear.

He looked around at his army. They were standing around him in awed silence, looking at the spoils of their attack upon the largest creature in the world. He did not think they would ever again feel as timid toward the Eaters. He stood up quickly.

"What are you gaping at?" he shouted. "It's yours, all of it. Get to work!"

Old Shar sat comfortably upon a pebble which had been hollowed out and cushioned with spirogyra straw. Lavon stood nearby at the door, looking out at the maneuvers of his legions. They numbered more than three hundred now, thanks to the month of comparative quiet which they had enjoyed in the great hall, and they handled their numbers well in the aquatic drill which Lavon had invented for them. They swooped and turned above the rock, breaking and re-assembling their formations, fighting a sham battle with invisible opponents whose shape they could remember only too well.

"Noc says there's all kinds of quarreling going on among the Eaters," Shar said. "They didn't believe we'd joined with the Protos at first, and then they didn't believe we'd all worked together to capture the hall. And the mass raid we had last week scared them. They'd never tried anything of the kind before, and they *knew* it wouldn't fail. Now they're fighting with each other over why it did. Cooperation is something new to this world, Lavon; it's making history."

"History?" Lavon said, following his drilling squadrons with a technical eye. "What's that?"

"These." The old man leaned over one arm of the pebble and touched the metal plates which were always with him. Lavon turned to follow the gesture, incuriously. He knew the plates well enough—the pure uncorroded shining, graven deeply on both sides with characters no-one, not even Shar, could read. The Protos called the plates *Not-stuff*—neither wood nor flesh nor stone.

"What good is that? I can't read it. Neither can you."

"I've got a start, Lavon. I know the plates are written in our language. Look at the first word: *ha ii ss tuh oh or ee* —exactly the right number of characters for 'history'. That can't be a coincidence. And the next two words have to be 'of the'. And going on from there, using just the characters I already know—" Shar bent and traced in the sand with a stick a new train of characters: *i/terste//ar e//e/ition.*   INTERSTELLAR EXPEDITION

"What's that?"

"It's a start, Lavon. Just a start. Some day we'll have more."

Lavon shrugged. "Perhaps, when we're safer. We can't afford to worry about that kind of thing now. We've never had that kind of time, not since the First Awakening."

The old man frowned down at the characters in the sand. "The First Awakening. Why does everything seem to stop there? I can remember in the smallest detail nearly everything that happened to me since then. But what happened to our childhoods, Lavon? None of us who survived the First Awakening seems to have had one. Who were our parents?

106

Why were we so ignorant of the world, and yet grown men and women, all of us?"

"And the answer is in the plates?"

"I hope so," Shar said. "I believe it is. But I don't know. The plates were beside me in the spore at the First Awakening. That's all I know about them, except that there's nothing else like them in the world. The rest is deduction, and I haven't gotten very far with it. Some day . . . some day."

"I hope so too," Lavon said soberly. "I don't mean to mock, Shar, or to be impatient. I've got questions, too; we all have. But we're going to have to put them off for a while. Suppose we never find the whole answer?"

"Then our children will."

"But there's the heart of the problem, Shar: we have to live to have children. And make the kind of a world in which they'll have time to study. Otherwise—"

Lavon broke off as a figure darted between the guards at the door of the hall and twisted to a halt.

"What news, Phil?"

"The same," Phil said, shrugging with his whole body. His feet touched the floor. "The Flosc's castles are going up all along the bar; they'll be finished with them soon, and then we won't dare to get near them. Do you still think you can drive them out?"

Lavon nodded.

"But why?"

"First, for effect. We've been on the defensive so far, even though we've made a good job of it. We'll have to follow that up with an attack of our own if we're going to keep the Eaters confused. Second, the castles Flosc builds are all tunnels and exits and entrances—much better than worm-houses for us. I hate to think of what would have happened if the Eaters had thought of blockading us inside this hall. And we need an outpost in enemy country, Phil, where there are Eaters to kill."

"This is enemy country," Phil said. "Stephanost is a Bottom-dweller."

"But she's only a trapper, not a hunter. Any time we want to kill her, we can find her right where we left her last. It's the leapers like Dicran and Notholca, the swimmers like Rotar, the colony-builders like Flosc that we have to wipe out first."

"Then we'd better start now, Lavon. Once the castles are finished—"

"Yes. Get your squads together, Phil. Shar, come on; we're leaving the hall."

"To raid the castles?"

"Of course."

Shar picked up his plates.

"You'd better leave those here; they'll be in your way in the fighting."

"No," Shar said determinedly. "I don't want them out of my sight. They go along."

3

Vague forebodings, all the more disturbing because he had felt nothing quite like them ever before, passed like clouds of fine silt through Lavon's mind as the army swept away from the hall on the Bottom and climbed toward the thermocline. As far as he could see, everything seemed to be going as he had planned it. As the army moved, its numbers were swelled by Protos who darted into its ranks from all sides. Discipline was good; and every man was armed with a long, seasoned splinter, and from each belt swung a stonewort-flake hand-axe, held by a thong run through a hole Shar had taught them all how to drill. There would probably be much death before the light of today faded, but death was common enough on any day, and this time it should heavily disfavor the Eaters.

But there was a chill upon the depths that Lavon did not like, and a suggestion of a current in the water which was unnatural below the thermocline. A great many days had been consumed in collecting the army, recruiting from stragglers, and in securing the hall. The intensive breeding which had followed, and the training of the new-born and the newly recruited, had taken still more time, all of it essential, but all irrevocable. If the chill and the current marked the beginning of the fall turnover . . .

If it did, nothing could be done about it. The turnover could no more be postponed than the coming of day or night. He signaled to the nearest Para.

The glistening torpedo veered toward him. Lavon pointed up.

"Here comes the thermocline, Para. Are we pointed right?"

"Yes, Lavon. That way is the place where the Bottom rises toward the sky. Flosc's castles are on the other side, where she will not see us."

"The sand bar that runs out from the north. Right. It's getting warmer. Here we go."

108

Lavon felt his flight suddenly quicken, as if he had been shot like a seed from some invisible thumb and forefinger. He looked over his shoulder to watch the passage of the rest through the temperature barrier, and what he saw thrilled him as sharply as any awakening. Up to now he had had no clear picture of the size of his forces, or the three-dimensional beauty of their dynamic, mobile organization. Even the Protos had fitted themselves into the squads; pattern after pattern of power came soaring after Lavon from the Bottom: first a single Noc bowling along like a beacon to guide all the rest, then an advance cone of Didin to watch for individual Eaters who might flee to give the alarm, and then the men, and the Protos, who made up the main force, in tight formations as beautiful as the elementary geometry from which Shar had helped derive them.

The sand-bar loomed ahead, as vast as any mountain range. Lavon soared sharply upward, and the tumbled, raw-boned boulders of the sand grains swept by rapidly beneath him in a broad, stony flood. Far beyond the ridge, towering up to the sky through glowing green obscurity, were the be-fronded stems of the plant jungle which was their objective. It was too dim with distance to allow him to see the clinging castles of the Flosc yet, but he knew that the longest part of the march was over. He narrowed his eyes and cleft the sunlit waters with driving, rapid strokes of his webbed hands and feet. The invaders poured after him over the crest of the bar in an orderly torrent.

Lavon swung his arm in a circle. Silently, the following squadrons glided into a great paraboloid, its axis pointed at the jungle. The castles were visible now; until the formation of the army, they had been the only products of close cooperation that this world had ever seen. They were built of single brown tubes, narrow at the base, attached to each other in a random pattern in an ensemble as delicate as a branching coral. In the mouth of each tube was a rotifer, a Flosc, distinguished from other Eaters by the four-leaf-clover of its corona, and by the single, prehensile finger springing from the small of its back, with which it ceaselessly molded its brown spittle into hard pellets and cemented them carefully to the rim of its tube.

As usual, the castles chilled Lavon's muscles with doubt. They were perfect, and they had always been one of the major, stony flowers of summer, long before there had been any First Awakening, or any men. And there was surely something wrong with the water in the upper level; it was warm and sleepy. The heads of the Flosc hummed contentedly at the mouths of their tubes; everything was as it should be, as it had always been; the army was a fantasm, the attack a failure before it had begun—

Then they were spied.

The Flosc vanished instantly, contracting violently into their tubes. The placid humming of their continuous feeding upon everything that passed was snuffed out; spared motes drifted about the castle in the light.

Lavon found himself smiling. Not long ago, the Flosc would only have waited until the humans were close enough, and then would have sucked them down, without more than a few struggles here and there, a few pauses in the humming while the out-size morsels were enfolded and fed into the grinders. Now, instead, they hid; they were afraid.

"Go!" he shouted at the top of his voice. "Kill them! Kill them while they're down!"

The army behind him swept after him with a stunning composite shout.

Tactics vanished. A petalled corona unfolded in Lavon's face, and a buzzing whirlpool spun him toward its black heart. He slashed wildly with his edged wooden splinter.

The sharp edge sliced deeply into the ciliated lobes. The rotifer screamed like a siren and contracted into her tube, closing her wounded face. Grimly, Lavon followed.

It was pitch dark inside the castle, and the raging currents of pain which flowed past him threw him from one pebbly wall to another. He gritted his teeth and probed with the splinter. It bit into a yielding surface at once, and another scream made his ears ring, mixed with mangled bits of words in Lavon's own language, senseless and horrible with agony. He slashed at them until they stopped, and continued to slash until he could control his terror.

As soon as he was able, he groped in the torn corpse for the eggs. The point found their life and pricked it. Trembling, he pulled himself back to the mouth of the tube, and without stopping to think pushed himself off at the first Eater to pass it.

The thing was a Dicran; she doubled viciously upon him at once. Even the Eaters had learned something about co-operation. And the Dicrans fought well in open water. They were the best possible reinforcements the Flosc could have called.

The Dicran's armor turned the point of Lavon's splinter easily. He jabbed frantically, hoping to hit a joint, but the agile creature gave him no time to aim. She charged him

110

irresistibly, and her humming corona folded down around his head, pinned his forearms to his sides—

The Eater heaved convulsively and went limp. Lavon half slashed, half tore his way free. A Didin was drawing back, pulling out its seizing-organ. The body floated downward.

"Thanks," Lavon gasped. The Proto darted off without replying; it lacked sufficient cilia to imitate human speech. Possibly it lacked the desire as well; the Didins were not sociable.

A tearing whirlpool sprang into being again around him, and he flexed his sword-arm. In the next five dreamlike minutes he developed a technique for dealing with the sessile, sucking Flosc. Instead of fighting the current and swinging the splinter back and forth against it, he gave in to the vortex, rode with it, and braced the splinter between his feet, point down. The results were even better than he had hoped. The point, driven by the full force of the Flosc's own trap, pierced the soft, wormlike body half through while it gaped for the human quarry. After each encounter, Lavon doggedly went through the messy ritual of destroying the eggs.

At last he emerged from a tube to find that the battle had drifted away from him. He paused on the edge to get his breath back, clinging to the rounded, translucent bricks and watching the fighting. It was difficult to make any military sense out of the melee, but as far as he could tell the rotifers were getting the worst of it. They did not know how to meet so carefully organized an attack, and they were not in any real sense intelligent.

The Didin were ranging from one side of the fray to the other, in two tight, vicious efficient groups, englobing and destroying free-swimming rotifers in whole flocks at a time. Lavon saw no fewer than half a dozen Eaters trapped by teams of Paras, each pair dragging a struggling victim in a trichocyst net remorselessly toward the Bottom, where she would inevitably suffocate. He was astonished to see one of the few Nocs that had accompanied his army scouring a cringing Rotar with its virtually harmless tentacle; the Eater seemed too astonished to fight back, and Lavon for once knew just how she felt.

A figure swam slowly and tiredly up to him from below. It was old Shar, puffing hard. Lavon reached a hand down to him and hauled him onto the lip of the tube. The man's face wore a frightening expression, half shock, half pure grief.

"Gone, Lavon," he said. "Gone. Lost."

"What? What's gone? What's the matter?"

"The plate. You were right. I should have known." He sobbed convulsively.

"What plate? Calm down. What happened? Did you lose one of the history plates—or both of them?"

Slowly his tutor seemed to be recovering control of his breathing. "One of them," he said wretchedly. "I dropped it in the fight. I hid the other one in an empty Flosc tube. But I dropped the first one—the one I'd just begun to decipher. It went all the way down to the Bottom, and I couldn't get free to go after it—all I could do was watch it go, spinning down into the darkness. We could sift the mud forever and never find it."

He dropped his face into his hands. Perched on the edge of the brown tube in the green glow of the waters, he looked both pathetic and absurd. Lavon did not know what to say; even he realized that the loss was major and perhaps final, that the awesome blank in their memories prior to the First Awakening might now never be filled. How Shar felt about it he could comprehend only dimly.

Another human figure darted and twisted toward him. "Lavon!" Phil's voice cried. "It's working, it's working! The swimmers are running away, what's left of them. There are still some Flosc in the castles, hiding in the darkness. If we could only lure them out in the open—"

Jarred back to the present, Lavon's mind raced over the possibilities. The whole attack could still fail if the Flosc entrenched themselves successfully. After all, a big kill had not been the only object; they had started out to capture the castles.

"Shar—do these tubes connect with each other?"

"Yes," the old man said without interest. "It's a continuous system."

Lavon sprang out upon the open water. "Come on, Phil. We'll attack them from the rear." Turning, he plunged into the mouth of the tube, Phil on his heels.

It was very dark, and the water was fetid with the odor of the tube's late owner, but after a moment's groping Lavon found the opening which lead into the next tube. It was easy to tell which way was out because of the pitch of the walls; everything the Flosc built had a conical bore, differing from the next tube only in size. Determinedly Lavon worked his way toward the main stem, going always down and in.

Once they passed beneath an opening beyond which the water was in furious motion, and out of which poured muffled sounds of shouting and a defiant buzz. Lavon stopped to probe through the hole with his sword. The rotifer gave a shrill, startled shriek and jerked her wounded tail upward, involuntarily releasing her toe-hold upon the walls of the tube. Lavon moved on, grinning. The men above would do the rest.

Reaching the central stem at last, Lavon and Phil went methodically from one branch to another, spearing the surprised Eaters from behind or cutting them loose so that the men outside could get at them as they drifted upward, propelled by the drag of their own coronas. The trumpet shape of the tubes prevented the Eaters from turning to fight, and from following them through the castle to surprise them from behind; each Flosc had only the one room, which she never left.

The gutting of the castles took hardly fifteen minutes. The day was just beginning to end when Lavon emerged with Phil at the mouth of a turret to look down upon the first City of Man.

He lay in darkness, his forehead pressed against his knees, as motionless as a dead man. The water was stuffy, cold, the blackness complete. Around him were the walls of a tube of Flosc's castle; above him a Para laid another sand grain upon a new domed roof. The rest of the army rested in other tubes, covered with other new stony caps, but there was no sound of movement or of voices. It was as quiet as a necropolis.

Lavon's thoughts were slow and bitter as drugged syrup. He had been right about the passage of the seasons. He had had barely enough time to bring all his people from the hall to the castles before the annual debacle of the fall overturn. Then the waters of the universe had revolved once, bringing the skies to the Bottom, and the Bottom to the skies, and then mixing both. The thermocline was destroyed until next year's spring overturn would reform it.

And inevitably, the abrupt change in temperature and oxygen concentration had started the spore-building glands again. The spherical amber shell was going up around Lavon now, and there was nothing he could do about it. It was an involuntary process, as dissociated from his control as the beating of his heart. Soon the light-generating oil which filled the spore would come pouring out, expelling and replacing the cold, foul water, and then sleep would come . . .

And all this had happened just as they had made a real gain, had established themselves within enemy country, had come within reach of the chance to destroy the Eaters wholesale and forever. Now the eggs of the Eaters had been laid, and next year it would have to be done all over again. And there was the loss of the plate; he had hardly begun to reflect upon what that would mean for the future.

There was a soft *chunk* as the last sand grain fell into place on the roof. The sound did not quite bring the final wave of despair against which he had been fighting in advance. Instead, it seemed to carry with it a wave of obscure contentment, with which his consciousness began to sink more and more rapidly toward sleep. They were safe, after all. They could not be ousted from the castle. And there would be fewer Eaters next year, because of all the eggs that had been destroyed, and the layers of those eggs . . . There was one plate still left . . .

Quiet and cold; darkness and silence.

In a forgotten corner of the galaxy, the watery world of Hydrot hurtles endlessly around the red star, Tau Ceti. For many months life has swarmed in its lakes and pools, but now the sun retreats from the zenith, and the snow falls, and the ice advances from the eternal ocean. Life sinks once more toward slumber, simulating death, and the battles and lusts and ambitions and defeats of a thousand million microscopic creatures retreat in to the limbo where such things matter not at all.

No, such things matter not at all when winter reigns on Hydrot; but winter is an inconstant king.

Cycle Two

1

Old Shar set down the thick, ragged-edged metal plate at last, and gazed instead out the window of the castle, apparently resting his eyes on the glowing green-gold obscurity of the summer waters. In the soft fluorescence which played down upon him, from the Noc dozing impassively in the groined vault of the chamber, Lavon could see that he was in fact a young man. His face was so delicately formed as to suggest that it had not been many seasons since he had first emerged from his spore.

But of course there had been no real reason to have expected an old man. All the Shars had been referred to traditionally as "old" Shar. The reason, like the reasons for everything else, had been forgotten, but the custom had persisted. The adjective at least gave weight and dignity to the office—

that of the center of wisdom of all the people, as each Lavon had been the center of authority.

The present Shar belonged to the generation XVI, and hence would have to be at least two seasons younger than Lavon himself. If he was old, it was only in knowledge.

"Lavon, I'm going to have to be honest with you," Shar said at last, still looking out of the tall, irregular window. "You've come to me at your maturity for the secrets on the metal plate, just as your predecessors did to mine. I can give some of them to you—but for the most part, I don't know what they mean."

"After so many generations?" Lavon asked, surprised. "Wasn't it Shar III who made the first complete translation? That was a long time ago."

The young man turned and looked at Lavon with eyes made dark and wide by the depths into which they had been staring. "I can read what's on the plate, but most of it seems to make no sense. Worst of all, the record's incomplete. You didn't know that? It is. One of the plates was lost in a battle during the first war with the Eaters, while these castles were still in their hands."

"What am I here for, then?" Lavon said. "Isn't there anything of value on the remaining plate? Did they really contain 'the wisdom of the Creators,' or is that another myth?"

"No. No, it's true," Shar said slowly, "as far as it goes."

He paused, and both men turned and gazed at the ghostly creature which had appeared suddenly outside the window. Then Shar said gravely, "Come in, Para."

The slipper-shaped organism, nearly transparent except for the thousands of black-and-silver granules and frothy bubbles which packed its interior, glided into the chamber and hovered, with a muted whirring of cilia. For a moment it remained silent, speaking telepathically to the Noc floating in the vault, after the ceremonious fashion of all the Protos. No human had ever intercepted one of these colloquies, but there was no doubt about their reality; humans had used them for long-range communication for generations.

Then the Para's cilia vibrated once more. "We are arrived, Shar and Lavon, according to the custom."

"And welcome," said Shar. "Lavon, let's leave this matter of the plates for a while, until you hear what Para has to say; that's a part of the knowledge Lavons must have as they come into their office, and it comes before the plates. I can give you some hints of what we are. First Para has to tell you something about what we aren't."

Lavon nodded, willingly enough, and watched the Proto as

115

it settled gently to the surface of the hewn table at which Shar had been sitting. There was in the entity such a perfection and economy of organization, such a grace and surety of movement, that he could hardly believe in his own new-won maturity. Para, like all the Protos, made him feel, not perhaps poorly thought-out, but at least unfinished.

"We know that in this universe there is logically no place for man," the gleaming, now immobile cylinder upon the table droned abruptly. "Our memory is the common property of all our races. It reaches back to a time when there were no such creatures as man here, nor any even remotely like men. It remembers also that once upon a day there were men here, suddenly, and in some numbers. Their spores littered the Bottom; we found the spores only a short time after our season's Awakening, and inside them we saw the forms of men, slumbering.

"Then men shattered their spores and emerged. At first they seemed helpless, and the Eaters devoured them by scores, as in those days they devoured everything that moved. But that soon ended. Men were intelligent, active. And they were gifted with a trait, a character, possessed by no other creature in this world. Not even the savage Eaters had it. Men organized us to exterminate the Eaters, and therein lay the difference. Men had initiative. We have the word now, which you gave us, and we apply it, but we still do not know what the thing is that it labels."

"You fought beside us," Lavon said.

"Gladly. We would never have thought of that war by ourselves, but it was good and brought good. Yet we wondered. We saw that men were poor swimmers, poor walkers, poor crawlers, poor climbers. We saw that men were formed to make and use tools, a concept we still do not understand, for so wonderful a gift is largely wasted in this universe, and there is no other. What good are tool-useful members such as the hands of men? We do not know. It seems plain that so radical a thing should lead to a much greater rulership over the world than has, in fact, proven to be possible for men."

Lavon's head was spinning. "Para, I had no notion that you people were philosophers."

"The Protos are old," Shar said. He had again turned to look out the window, his hands locked behind his back. "They aren't philosphers, Lavon, but they are remorseless logicians. Listen to Para."

"To this reasoning there could be but one outcome," the Para said. "Our strange ally, Man, was like nothing else in this universe. He was and is unfitted for it. He does not belong

116

here; he has been—adapted. This drives us to think that there are other universes besides this one, but where these universes might lie, and what their properties might be, it is impossible to imagine. We have no imagination, as men know."

Was the creature being ironic? Lavon could not tell. He said slowly. "Other universes? How could that be true?"

"We do not know," the Para's uninflected voice hummed. Lavon waited, but obviously the Proto had nothing more to say.

Shar had resumed sitting on the window sill, clasping his knees, watching the come and go of dim shapes in the lighted gulf. "It is quite true," he said. "What is written on the plate makes it plain. Let me tell you now what it says.

"We were made, Lavon. We were made by men who were not as we are, but men who were our ancestors all the same. They were caught in some disaster, and they made us, and put us here in our universe—so that, even though they had to die, the race of men would live."

Lavon surged up from the woven spirogyra mat upon which he had been sitting. "You must think I'm a fool," he said sharply.

"No. You're our Lavon; you have a right to know the facts. Make what you like of them." Shar swung his webbed toes back into the chamber. "What I've told you may be hard to believe, but it seems to be so; what Para says backs it up. Our unfitness to live here is self-evident. I'll give you some examples:

"The past four Shars discovered that we won't get any farther in our studies until we learn how to control heat. We've produced enough heat chemically to show that even the water around us changes when the temperature gets high enough—or low enough, that we knew from the beginning. But there we're stopped."

"Why?"

"Because heat produced in open water is carried off as rapidly as it's produced. Once we tried to enclose that heat, and we blew up a whole tube of the castle and killed everything in range; the shock was terrible. We measured the pressures that were involved in that explosion, and we discovered that no substance we know could have resisted them. Theory suggests some stronger substances—but *we need heat to form them!*

"Take our chemistry. We live in water. Everything seems to dissolve in water, to some extent. How do we confine a chemical test to the crucible we put it in? How do we maintain a solution at one dilution? I don't know. Every avenue

117

leads me to the same stone door. We're thinking creatures, Lavon, but there's something drastically wrong in the way we think about this universe we live in. It just doesn't seem to lead to results."

Lavon pushed back his floating hair futilely. "Maybe you're thinking about the wrong results. We've had no trouble with warfare, or crops, or practical things like that. If we can't create much heat, well, most of us won't miss it; we don't need more than we have. What's the other universe supposed to be like, the one our ancestors lived in? Is it any better than this one?"

"I don't know," Shar admitted. "It was so different that it's hard to compare the two. The metal plate tells a story about men who were travelling from one place to another in a container that moved by itself. The only analogue I can think of is the shallops of diatom shells that our youngsters used to sled along the thermocline; but evidently what's meant is something much bigger.

"I picture a huge shallop, closed on all sides, big enough to hold many people—maybe twenty or thirty. It had to travel for generations through some kind of medium where there wasn't any water to breathe, so the people had to carry their own water and renew it constantly. There were no seasons; no ice formed on the sky, because there couldn't be any sky in a closed shallop; and so there was no spore formation.

"Then the shallop was wrecked somehow. The people in it knew they were going to die. They made us, and put us here, as if we were their children. Because they had to die, they wrote their story on the plates, to tell us what had happened. I suppose we'd understand it better if we had the plate Shar I lost during the war—but we don't."

"The whole thing sounds like a parable," Lavon said, shrugging. "Or a song. I can see why you don't understand it. What I can't see is why you bother to try."

"Because of the plate," Shar said. "You've handled it yourself now, so you know that we've nothing like it. We have crude, impure metals we've hammered out, metals that last for a while and then decay. But the plate shines on, generation after generation. It doesn't change; our hammers and our graving tools break against it; the little heat we can generate leaves it unharmed. That plate wasn't formed in our universe—and that one fact makes every word on it important to me. Someone went to a great deal of trouble to make those plates indestructible, and to give them to us. Someone to whom the word 'stars' was important enough to be worth

118

fourteen repetitions, despite the fact that the word doesn't seem to mean anything. I'm ready to think that if our makers repeated a word even twice on a record that seems likely to last forever, then it's important for us to know what it means."

Layon stood up once more.

"All these extra universes and huge shallops and meaningless words—I can't say that they don't exist, but I don't see what difference it makes," he said. "The Shars of a few generations ago spent their whole lives breeding better algae crops for us, and showing us how to cultivate them, instead of living haphazardly on bacteria. Farther back, the Shars devised war engines, and war plans. All that was work worth doing. The Lavons of those days evidently got along without the metal plate and its puzzles, and saw to it that the Shars did, too. Well, as far as I'm concerned, you're welcome to the plate, if you like it better than crop improvement—but I think it ought to be thrown away."

"All right," Shar said, shrugging. "If you don't want it, that ends the traditional interview. We'll go our—"

There was a rising drone from the table-top. The Para was lifting itself, waves of motion passing over its cilia, like the waves which went silently across the fruiting stalks of the fields of delicate fungi with which the Bottom was planted. It had been so silent that Lavon had forgotten it; he could tell from Shar's startlement that Shar had, too.

"This is a great decision," the waves of sound washing from the creature throbbed. "Every Proto has heard it, and agrees with it. We have been afraid of this metal plate for a long time, afraid that men would learn to understand it and follow what it says to some secret place, leaving the Protos behind. Now we are not afraid."

"There wasn't anything to be afraid of," Lavon said indulgently.

"No Lavon before you, Lavon, had ever said so," the Para said. "We are glad. We will throw the plate away, as Lavon orders."

With that, the shining creature swooped toward the embrasure. With it, it bore away the remaining plate, which had been resting under it on the tabletop, suspended delicately in the curved tips of its supple ventral cilia. Inside its pellucid body, vacuoles swelled to increase its buoyancy and enable it to carry the heavy weight.

With a cry, Shar plunged through the water toward the window.

"Stop, Para!"

But Para was already gone, so swiftly that it had not even heard the call. Shar twisted his body and brought up one shoulder against the tower wall. He said nothing. His face was enough. Lavon could not look into it for more than an instant.

The shadows of the two men began to move slowly along the uneven cobbled floor. The Noc descended toward them from the vault, its tentacle stirring the water, its internal light flaring and fading irregularly. It, too, drifted through the window after its cousin, and sank slowly away toward the Bottom. Gently its living glow dimmed, flickered in the depths, and winked out.

2

For many days, Lavon was able to avoid thinking much about the loss. There was always a great deal of work to be done. Maintenance of the castles was a never-ending task. The thousand dichotomously-branching wings tended to crumble with time, especially at their bases where they sprouted from one another, and no Shar had yet come forward with a mortar as good as the rotifer-spittle which had once held them together. In addition, the breaking through of windows and the construction of chambers in the early days had been haphazard and often unsound. The instinctive architecture of the Eaters, after all, had not been meant to meet the needs of human occupants.

And then there were the crops. Men no longer fed precariously upon passing bacteria snatched to the mouth; now there were the drifting mats of specific water-fungi and algae, and the mycelia on the Bottom, rich and nourishing, which had been bred by five generations of Shars. These had to be tended constantly to keep the strains pure, and to keep the older and less intelligent species of the Protos from grazing on them. In this latter task, to be sure, the more intricate and far-seeing Proto types cooperated, but men were needed to supervise.

There had been a time, after the war with the Eaters, when it had been customary to prey upon the slow-moving and stupid diatoms, whose exquisite and fragile glass shells were so easily burst, and who were unable to learn that a friendly voice did not necessarily mean a friend. There were still people who would crack open a diatom when no one else was looking, but they were regarded as barbarians, to the puzzlement of the Protos. The blurred and simple-minded speech of the gorgeously engraved plants had brought them into the category of community pets—a concept which the Protos were utterly unable to grasp, especially since men admitted that diatoms on the half-frustrule were delicious.

Lavon had had to agree, very early, that the distinction was tiny. After all, humans did eat the desmids, which differed from the diatoms only in three particulars: Their shells were flexible, they could not move (and for that matter neither could all but a few groups of diatoms), and they did not speak. Yet to Lavon, as to most men, there did seem to be some kind of distinction, whether the Protos could see it or not, and that was that. Under the circumstances he felt that it was a part of his duty, as the hereditary leader of men, to protect the diatoms from the occasional poachers who browsed upon them, in defiance of custom, in the high levels of the sunlit sky.

Yet Lavon found it impossible to keep himself busy enough to forget that moment when the last clues to Man's origin and destination had been seized, on authority of his own careless exaggeration, and borne away into dim space.

It might be possible to ask Para for the return of the plate, explain that a mistake had been made. The Protos were creatures of implacable logic, but they respected men, were used to illogic in men, and might reverse their decision if pressed—

We are sorry. The plate was carried over the bar and released in the gulf. We will have the Bottom there searched, but . . .

With a sick feeling he could not repress, Lavon knew that that would be the answer, or something very like it. When the Protos decided something was worthless, they did not hide it in some chamber like old women. They threw it away —efficiently.

Yet despite the tormenting of his consicence, Lavon was nearly convinced that the plate was well lost. What had it ever done for Man, except to provide Shars with useless things to think about in the late seasons of their lives? What the Shars themselves had done to benefit Man, here, in the water, in the world, in the universe, had been done by direct experimentation. No bit of useful knowledge had ever come from the plates. There had never been anything in the second plate, at least, but things best left unthought. The Protos were right.

Lavon shifted his position on the plant frond, where he had been sitting in order to overlook the harvesting of an experimental crop of blue-green, oil-rich algae drifting in a clotted mass close to the top of the sky, and scratched his back gently against the coarse bole. The Protos were seldom wrong, after all. Their lack of creativity, their inability to think an original thought, was a gift as well as a limitation. It allowed them to see and feel things at all times as they were—not as they hoped they might be, for they had no ability to hope, either.

"La-von! Laa-vah-on!"

The long halloo came floating up from the sleepy depths. Propping one hand against the top of the frond, Lavon bent and looked down. One of the harvesters was looking up at him, holding loosely the adze with which he had been splitting free from the raft the glutinous tetrads of the algae.

"I'm up here. What's the matter?"

"We have the ripened quadrant cut free. Shall we tow it away?"

"Tow it away," Lavon said, with a lazy gesture. He leaned back again. At the same instant, a brilliant reddish glory burst into being above him, and cast itself down toward the depths like mesh after mesh of the finest-drawn gold. The great light which lived above the sky during the day, brightening or dimming according to some pattern no Shar ever had fathomed, was blooming again.

Few men, caught in the warm glow of that light, could resist looking up at it—especially when the top of the sky itself wrinkled and smiled just a moment's climb or swim away. Yet, as always, Lavon's bemused upward look gave him back nothing but his own distorted, bobbling reflection, and a reflection of the plant on which he rested.

Here was the upper limit, the third of the three surfaces of the universe. The first surface was the Bottom, where the water ended.

The second surface was the thermocline, definite enough in summer to provide good sledding, but easily penetrable if you knew how.

The third surface was the sky. One could no more pass through that surface than one could penetrate the Bottom, nor was there any better reason to try. There the universe ended. The light which played over it daily, waxing and waning as it chose, seemed to be one of its properties.

Toward the end of the season, the water gradually became colder and more difficult to breathe, while at the same time the light grew duller and stayed for shorter periods between darknesses. Slow currents started to move. The high waters turned chill and started to fall. The Bottom mud stirred and smoked away, carrying with it the spores of the fields of fungi. The thermocline tossed, became choppy, and melted away. The sky began to fog with particles of soft silt carried up from the Bottom, the walls, the corners of the universe. Before very long, the whole world was cold, inhospitable, flocculent with yellowing, dying creatures. The world died until the first tentative current of warm water broke the winter silence.

That was how it was when the second surface vanished. If the sky were to melt away . . .

"Lavon!"

Just after the long call, a shining bubble rose past Lavon. He reached out and poked it, but it bounded away from his sharp thumb. The gas bubbles which rose from the Bottom in late summer were almost invulnerable—and when some especially hard blow or edge did penetrate them, they broke into smaller bubbles which nothing could touch, leaving behind a remarkably bad smell.

Gas. There was no water inside a bubble. A man who got inside a bubble would have nothing to breathe.

But, of course, it was impossible to enter a bubble. The surface tension was too strong. As strong as Shar's metal plate. As strong as the top of the sky.

As strong as the top of the sky. And above that—once the bubble was broken—a world of gas instead of water? Were all worlds bubbles of water drifting in gas?

If it were so, travel between them would be out of the question, since it would be impossible to pierce the sky to begin with. Nor did the infant cosmography include any provisions for Bottoms for the worlds.

And yet some of the local creatures did burrow *into* the Bottom, quite deeply, seeking something in those depths which was beyond the reach of Man. Even the surface of the ooze, in high summer, crawled with tiny creatures for which mud was a natural medium. And though many of the entities with which man lived could not pass freely between the two countries of water which were divided by the thermocline, men could and did.

And if the new universe of which Shar had spoken existed at all, it had to exist beyond the sky, where the light was. Why could not the sky be passed, after all? The fact that bubbles could sometimes be broken showed that the surface skin had formed between water and gas wasn't completely invulnerable. Had it ever been tried?

Lavon did not suppose that one man could butt his way through the top of the sky, any more than he could burrow

123

into the Bottom, but there might be ways around the difficulty. Here at his back, for instance, was a plant which gave every appearance of continuing beyond the sky; its upper fronds broke off and were bent back only by a trick of reflection.

It had always been assumed that the plants died where they touched the sky. For the most part, they did, for frequently the dead extension could be seen, leached and yellow, the boxes of its component cells empty, floating imbedded in the perfect mirror. But some were simply chopped off, like the one which sheltered him now. Perhaps that was only an illusion, and instead it soared indefinitely into some other place—some place where men might once have been born, and might still live . . .

Both plates were gone. There was only one other way to find out.

Determinedly, Lavon began to climb toward the wavering mirror of the sky. His thorn-thumbed feet trampled obliviously upon the clustered sheaths of fragile stippled diatoms. The tulip-heads of Vortae, placid and murmurous cousins of Para, retracted startledly out of his way upon coiling stalks, to make silly gossip behind him.

Lavon did not hear them. He continued to climb doggedly toward the light, his fingers and toes gripping the plant-bole.

"Lavon! Where are you going? Lavon!"

He leaned out and looked down. The man with the adze, a doll-like figure, was beckoning to him from a patch of blue-green retreating over a violet abyss. Dizzily he looked away, clinging to the bole; he had never been so high before. He had, of course, nothing to fear from falling, but the fear was in his heritage. Then he began to climb again.

After a while, he touched the sky with one hand. He stopped to breathe. Curious bacteria gathered about the base of his thumb where blood from a small cut was fogging away, scattered at his gesture, and wriggled mindlessly back toward the dull red lure.

He waited until he no longer felt winded, and resumed climbing. The sky pressed down against the top of his head, against the back of his neck, against his shoulders. It seemed to give slightly, with a tough, frictionless elasticity. The water here was intensely bright, and quite colorless. He climbed another step, driving his shoulders against that enormous weight.

It was fruitless. He might as well have tried to penetrate a cliff.

Again he had to rest. While he panted, he made a curious

discovery. All around the bole of the water plant, the steel surface of the sky curved upward, making a kind of sheath. He found that he could insert his hand into it—there was almost enough space to admit his head as well. Clinging closely to the bole, he looked up into the inside of the sheath, probing it with his injured hand. The glare was blinding.

There was a kind of soundless explosion. His whole wrist was suddenly encircled in an intense, impersonal grip, as if it were being cut in two. In blind astonishment, he lunged upward.

The ring of pain travelled smoothly down his upflung arm as he rose, was suddenly around his shoulders and chest. Another lunge and his knees were being squeezed in the circular vise. Another—

Something was horribly wrong. He clung to the bole and tried to gasp, but there was—nothing to breathe.

The water came streaming out of his body, from his mouth, his nostrils, the spiracles in his sides, spurting in tangible jets. An intense and fiery itching crawled over the surface of his body. At each spasm, long knives ran into him, and from a great distance he heard more water being expelled from his book-lungs in an obscene, frothy sputtering. Inside his head, a patch of fire began to eat away at the floor of his nasal cavity.

Lavon was drowning.

With a final convulsion, he kicked himself away from the splintery bole, and fell. A hard impact shook him; and then the water, who had clung to him so tightly when he had first attempted to leave her, took him back with cold violence.

Sprawling and tumbling grotesquely, he drifted, down and down and down, toward the Bottom.

3

For many days, Lavon lay curled insensibly in his spore, as if in the winter sleep. The shock of cold which he had felt on re-entering his native universe had been taken by his body as a sign of coming winter, as it had taken the ozygen-starvation of his brief sojourn above the sky. The spore-forming glands had at once begun to function.

Had it not been for this, Lavon would surely have died. The danger of drowning disappeared even as he fell, as the air bubbled out of his lungs and readmitted the life-giving water. But for acute desiccation and third degree sunburn, the sunken universe knew no remedy. The healing amnionic fluid generated by the spore-forming glands, after the transparent amber sphere had enclosed him, offered Lavon his only chance.

The brown sphere, quiescent in the eternal winter of the Bottom, was spotted after some days by a prowling ameba. Down there the temperature was always an even 4°, no matter what the season, but it was unheard of that a spore should be found there while the high epilimnion was still warm and rich in oxygen.

Within an hour, the spore was surrounded by scores of astonished protos, jostling each other to bump their blunt eyeless prows against the shell. Another hour later, a squad of worried men came plunging from the castles far above to press their own noses against the transparent wall. Then swift orders were given.

Four Para grouped themselves about the amber sphere, and there was a subdued explosion as their trichocysts burst. The four Paras thrummed and lifted, tugging.

Lavon's spore swayed gently in the mud and then rose slowly, entangled in the fine web. Nearby, a Noc cast a cold pulsating glow over the operation, for the benefit of the baffled knot of men. The sleeping figure of Lavon, head bowed, knees drawn up into its chest, revolved with an absurd solemnity inside the shell as it was moved.

"Take him to Shar, Para."

The young Shar justified, by minding his own business, the traditional wisdom with which his hereditary office had invested him. He observed at once that there was nothing he could do for the encysted Lavon which would not be classifiable as simple meddling.

He had the sphere deposited in a high tower room of his castle, where there was plenty of light and the water was warm, which should suggest to the estivating form that spring was again on the way. Beyond that, he simply sat and watched, and kept his speculations to himself.

Inside the spore, Lavon's body seemed to be rapidly shedding its skin, in long strips and patches. Gradually, his curious shrunkenness disappeared. His withered arms and legs and sunken abdomen filled out again.

The days went by while Shar watched. Finally he could discern no more changes, and, on a hunch, had the spore taken up to the topmost battlements of the tower, into the direct daylight.

An hour later, Lavon moved in his amber prison.

He uncurled and stretched, turned blank eyes up toward the light. His expression was that of a man who had not yet awakened from a ferocious nightmare. His whole body shone with a strange pink newness.

Shar knocked gently on the walls of the spore. Lavon turned his blind face toward the sound, life coming into his eyes. He smiled tentatively and braced his hands and feet against the inner wall of the shell.

The whole sphere fell abruptly to pieces with a sharp crackling. The amnionic fluid dissipated around him and Shar, carrying away with it the suggestive odor of a bitter struggle against death.

Lavon stood among the shards and looked at Shar silently. At last he said:

"Shar—I've been above the sky."

"I know," Shar said gently.

Again Lavon was silent. Shar said, "Don't be humble, Lavon. You've done an epoch-making thing. It nearly cost you your life. You must tell me the rest—all of it."

"The rest?"

"You taught me a lot while you slept. Or are you still opposed to 'useless' knowledge?"

Lavon could say nothing. He no longer could tell what he knew from what he wanted to know. He had only one question left, but he could not utter it. He could only look dumbly into Shar's delicate face.

"You have answered me," Shar said, even more gently than before. "Come, my friend; join me at my table. We will plan our journey to the stars."

There were five of them around Shar's big table: Shar himself, Lavon, and the three assistants assigned by custom to the Shars from the families Than, Tanol and Stravol. The duties of these three men—or, sometimes, women—under many previous Shars had been simple and onerous: to put into effect in the field the genetic changes in the food crops which the Shar himself had worked out in little, in laboratory tanks and flats. Under other Shars more interested in metalworking or in chemistry, they had been smudged men—diggers, rock-splitters, fashioners and cleaners of apparatus.

Under Shar XVI, however, the three assistants had been more envied than usual among the rest of Lavon's people, for they seemed to do very little work of any kind. They spent long hours of every day talking with Shar in his chambers, poring over records, making miniscule scratch-marks on slate, or just looking intently at simple things about which there was no obvious mystery. Sometimes they actually worked with Shar in his laboratory, but mostly they just sat.

Shar XVI had, as a matter of fact, discovered certain rudimentary rules of inquiry which, as he explained it to Lavon, he had recognized as tools of enormous power. He had become more interested in passing these on to future workers than in the seductions of any specific experiment, the journey to the stars perhaps excepted. The Than, Tanol and Stravol of his generation were having scientific method pounded into their heads, a procedure they maintained was sometimes more painful than heaving a thousand rocks.

That they were the first of Lavon's people to be taxed with the problem of constructing a spaceship was, therefore, inevitable. The results lay on the table: three models, made of diatom-glass, strands of algae, flexible bits of cellulose, flakes of stonewort, slivers of wood, and organic glues collected from the secretions of a score of different plants and animals.

Lavon picked up the nearest one, a fragile spherical construction inside which little beads of dark-brown lava—actually bricks of rotifer-spittle painfully chipped free from the wall of an unused castle—moved freely back and forth in a kind of ball-bearing race. "Now whose is this one?" he said, turning the sphere curiously to and fro.

"That's mine," Tanol said. "Frankly, I don't think it comes anywhere near meeting all the requirements. It's just the only design I could arrive at that I think we could build with the materials and knowledge we have to hand now."

"But how does it work?"

"Hand it here a moment, Lavon. This bladder you see inside at the center, with the hollow spirogyra straws leading out from it to the skin of the ship, is a buoyancy tank. The idea is that we trap ourselves a big gas-bubble as it rises from the Bottom and install it in the tank. Probably we'll have to do that piecemeal. Then the ship rises to the sky on the buoyancy of the bubble. The little paddles, here along these two bands on the outside, rotate when the crew—that's these bricks you hear shaking around inside—walks a treadmill that runs around the inside of the hull; they paddle us over to the edge of the sky. I stole that trick from the way Didin gets about. Then we pull the paddles in—they fold over into slots, like this—and, still by weight-transfer from the inside, we roll ourselves up the slope until we're out in space. When we hit another world and enter the water again, we let the gas out of the tank gradually through the exhaust tubes represented by these straws, and sink down to a landing at a controlled rate."

"Very ingenious," Shar said thoughtfully. "But I can foresee some difficulties. For one thing, the design lacks stability."

"Yes, it does," Tanol agreed. "And keeping it in motion is going to require a lot of footwork. But if we were to sling a freely-moving weight from the center of gravity of the machine, we could stabilize it at least partly. And the biggest expenditure of energy involved in the whole trip is going to be getting the machine up to the sky in the first place, and with this design that's taken care of—as a matter of fact, once the bubble's installed, we'll have to keep the ship tied down until we're ready to take off."

"How about letting the gas out?" Lavon said. "Will it go out through those little tubes when we want it to? Won't it just cling to the walls of the tubes instead? The skin between water and gas is pretty difficult to deform—to that I can testify."

Tanol frowned. "That I don't know. Don't forget that the tubes will be large in the real ship, not just straws as they are in the model."

"Bigger than a man's body?" Than said.

"No, hardly. Maybe as big through as a man's head, at the most."

"Won't work," Than said tersely. "I tried it. You can't lead a bubble through a pipe that small. As Lavon says, it clings to the inside of the tube and won't be budged unless you put pressure behind it—lots of pressure. If we build this ship, we'll just have to abandon it once we hit our new world; we won't be able to set it down anywhere."

"That's out of the question," Lavon said at once. "Putting aside for the moment the waste involved, we may have to use the ship again in a hurry. Who knows what the new world will be like? We're going to have to be able to leave it again if it turns out to be impossible to live in."

"Which is your model, Than?" Shar said.

"This one. With this design, we do the trip the hard way —crawl along the Bottom until it meets the sky, crawl until we hit the next world, and crawl wherever we're going when we get there. No aquabatics. She's treadmill-powered, like Tanol's, but not necessarily man-powered; I've been thinking a bit about using motile diatoms. She steers by varying the power on one side or the other. For fine steering we can also hitch a pair of thongs to opposite ends of the rear axle and swivel her that way."

Shar looked closely at the tube-shaped model and pushed it experimentally along the table a little way. "I like that," he said presently. "It sits still when you want it to. With Than's spherical ship, we'd be at the mercy of any stray current at

129

home or in the new world—and for all I know there may be currents of some sort in space, too, gas currents perhaps. Lavon, what do you think?"

"How would we build it?" Lavon said. "It's round in cross-section. That's all very well for a model, but how do you make a really big tube of that shape that won't fall in on itself?"

"Look inside, through the front window," Than said. "You'll see beams that cross at the center, at right angles to the long axis. They hold the walls braced."

"That consumes a lot of space," Stravol objected. By far the quietest and most introspective of the three assistants, he had not spoken until now since the beginning of the conference. "You've got to have free passage back and forth inside the ship. How are we going to keep everything operating if we have to be crawling around beams all the time?"

"All right, come up with something better," Than said, shrugging.

"That's easy. We bend hoops."

"Hoops!" Tanol said. "On *that* scale? You'd have to soak your wood in mud for a year before it would be flexible enough, and then it wouldn't have the strength you'd need."

"No, you wouldn't," Stravol said. "I didn't build a ship model, I just made drawings, and my ship isn't as good as Than's by a long distance. But my design for the ship is also tubular, so I did build a model of a hoop-bending machine—that's it on the table. You lock one end of your beam down in a heavy vise, like so, leaving the butt striking out on the other side. Then you tie up the other end with a heavy line, around this notch. Then you run your line around a windlass, and five or six men wind up the windlass, like so. That pulls the free end of the beam down until the notch engages with this key-slot, which you've pre-cut at the other end. Then you unlock the vise, and there's your hoop; for safety you might drive a peg through the joint to keep the thing from springing open unexpectedly."

"Wouldn't the beam you were using break after it had bent a certain distance?" Lavon asked.

"Stock timber certainly would," Stravol said. "But for this trick you use *green* wood, not seasoned. Otherwise you'd have to soften your beam to uselessness, as Tanol says. But live wood will flex enough to make a good, strong, single-unit hoop—or if it doesn't, Shar, the little rituals with numbers that you've been teaching us don't mean anything after all!"

Shar smiled. "You can easily make a mistake in using numbers," he said.

"I checked everything."

"I'm sure of it. And I think it's well worth a trial. Anything else to offer?"

"Well," Stravol said, "I've got a kind of live ventilating system I think should be useful. Otherwise, as I said, Than's ship strikes me as the type we should build; my own's hopelessly cumbersome."

"I have to agree," Tanol said regretfully. "But I'd like to try putting together a lighter-than-water ship sometime, maybe just for local travel. If the new world is bigger than ours, it might not be possible to swim everywhere you might want to go."

"That never occurred to me," Lavon exclaimed. "Suppose the new world *is* twice, three times, eight times as big as ours? Shar, is there any reason why that couldn't be?"

"None that I know of. The history plate certainly seems to take all kinds of enormous distances practically for granted. All right, let's make up a composite design from what we have here. Tanol, you're the best draftsman among us, suppose you draw it up. Lavon, what about labor?"

"I've a plan ready," Lavon said. "As I see it, the people who work on the ship are going to have to be on the job full time. Building the vessel isn't going to be an overnight task, or even one that we can finish in a single season, so we can't count on using a rotating force. Besides, this is technical work; once a man learns how to do a particular task, it would be wasteful to send him back to tending fungi just because somebody else has some time on his hands.

"So I've set up a basic force involving the two or three most intelligent hand-workers from each of the various trades. Those people I can withdraw from their regular work without upsetting the way we run our usual concerns, or noticeably increasing the burden on the others in a given trade. They will do the skilled labor, and stick with the ship until it's done. Some of them will make up the crew, too. For heavy, unskilled jobs, we can call on the various seasonal pools of unskilled people without disrupting our ordinary life."

"Good," Shar said. He leaned forward and rested linked hands on the edge of the table—although, because of the webbing between his fingers, he could link no more than the fingertips. "We've really made remarkable progress. I didn't expect that we'd have matters advanced a tenth as far as this by the end of this meeting. But maybe I've overlooked something important. Has anybody any more suggestions, or any questions?"

"I've got a question," Stravol said quietly.

"All right, let's hear it."

"Where are we going?"

There was quite a long silence. Finally Shar said: "Stravol, I can't answer that yet. I could say that we're going to the stars, but since we still have no idea what a star is, that answer wouldn't do you much good. We're going to make this trip because we've found that some of the fantastic things that the history plate says are really so. We know now that the sky can be passed, and that beyond the sky there's a region where there's no water to breathe, the region our ancients called 'space.' Both of these ideas always seemed to be against common sense, but nevertheless we've found that they're true.

"The history plate also says that there are other worlds than ours, and actually that's an easier idea to accept, once you've found out that the other two are so. As for the stars—well, we just don't know yet, we haven't any information at all that would allow us to read the history plate on that subject with new eyes, and there's no point in making wild guesses unless we can test the guesses. The stars are in space, and presumably, once we're out in space, we'll see them and the meaning of the word will become clear. At least we can confidently expect to see some clues—look at all the information we got from Lavon's trip of a few seconds above the sky!

"But in the meantime, there's no point in our speculating in a bubble. We think there are other worlds somewhere, and we're devising means to make the trip. The other questions, the pendant ones, just have to be put aside for now. We'll answer them eventually—there's no doubt in my mind about that. But it may take a long time."

Stravol grinned ruefully. "I expected no more. In a way, I think the whole project in crazy. But I'm in it right out to the end, all the same."

Shar and Lavon grinned back. All of them had the fever, and Lavon suspected that their whole enclosed universe would share it with them before long. He said:

"Then let's not waste a minute. There's still a huge mass of detail to be worked out, and after that, all the hard work will just have begun. Let's get moving!"

The five men arose and looked at each other. Their expressions varied, but in all their eyes there was in addition the same mixture of awe and ambition: the composite face of the shipwright and of the astronaut.

Then they went out, severally, to begin their voyages.

It was two winter sleeps after Lavon's disastrous climb beyond the sky that all work on the spaceship stopped. By then,

Lavon knew that he had hardened and weathered into that temporarily ageless state a man enters after he has just reached his prime; and he knew also that there were wrinkles engraved on his brow, to stay and to deepen.

"Old" Shar, too, had changed, his features losing some of their delicacy as he came into his maturity. Though the wedge-shaped bony structure of his face would give him a withdrawn and poetic look for as long as he lived, participation in the plan had given his expression a kind of executive overlay, which at best made it assume a mask-like rigidity, and at worst coarsened it somehow.

Yet despite the bleeding away of the years, the spaceship was still only a hulk. It lay upon a platform built above the tumbled boulders of the sandbar which stretched out from one wall of the world. It was an immense hull of pegged wood, broken by regularly spaced gaps through which the raw beams of its skeleton could be seen.

Work upon it had progressed fairly rapidly at first, for it was not hard to visualize what kind of vehicle would be needed to crawl through empty space without losing its water; Than and his colleagues had done that job well. It had been recognized, too, that the sheer size of the machine would enforce a long period of construction, perhaps as long as two full seasons; but neither Shar and his assistants nor Lavon had anticipated any serious snag.

For that matter, part of the vehicle's apparent incompleteness was an illusion. About a third of its fittings were to consist of living creatures, which could not be expected to install themselves in the vessel much before the actual takeoff.

Yet time and time again, work on the ship had to be halted for long periods. Several times whole sections needed to be ripped out, as it became more and more evident that hardly a single normal, understandable concept could be applied to the problem of space travel. .

The lack of the history plate, which the Para steadfastly refused to deliver up, was a double handicap. Immediately upon its loss, Shar had set himself to reproduce it from memory; but unlike the more religious of his ancestors, he had never regarded it as holy writ, and hence had never set himself to memorizing it word by word. Even before the theft, he had accumulated a set of variant translations of passages presenting specific experimental problems, which were stored in his library, carved in wood. Most of these translations, however, tended to contradict each other, and none of them related to spaceship construction, upon which the original had been vague in any case.

No duplicates of the cryptic characters of the original had ever been made, for the simple reason that there was nothing in the sunken universe capable of destroying the originals, nor of duplicating their apparently changeless permanence. Shar remarked too late that through simple caution they should have made a number of verbatim temporary records —but after generations of green-gold peace, simple caution no longer covers preparation against catastrophe. (Nor, for that matter, does a culture which has to dig each letter of its simple alphabet into pulpy water-logged wood with a flake of stonewort encourage the keeping of records in triplicate.)

As a result, Shar's imperfect memory of the contents of the history plate, plus the constant and millenial doubt as to the accuracy of the various translations, proved finally to be the worst obstacle to progress on the spaceship itself.

"Men must paddle before they can swim," Lavon observed belatedly, and Shar was forced to agree with him.

Obviously, whatever the ancients had known about space-ship construction, very little of that knowledge was usable to a people still trying to build its first spaceship from scratch. In retrospect, it was not surprising that the great hulk rested incomplete upon its platform above the sand boulders, exuding a musty odor of wood steadily losing its strength, two generations after its flat bottom had been laid down.

The fat-faced young man who headed the strike delegation to Shar's chambers was Phil XX, a man two generations younger than Shar, four younger than Lavon. There were crow's-feet at the corners of his eyes, which made him look both like a querulous old man and like an infant spoiled in the spore.

"We're calling a halt to this crazy project," he said bluntly. "We've slaved away our youth on it, but now that we're our own masters, it's over, that's all. It's over."

"Nobody's compelled you," Lavon said angrily.

"Society does;—our parents do," a gaunt member of the delegation said. "But now we're going to start living in the real world. Everybody these days knows that there's no other world but this one. You oldsters can hang on to your superstitions if you like. We don't intend to."

Baffled, Lavon looked over at Shar. The scientist smiled and said, "Let them go, Lavon. We have no use for the faint-hearted."

The fat-faced young man flushed. "You can't insult us into going back to work. We're through. Build your own ship to no place!"

"All right," Lavon said evenly. "Go on, beat it. Don't stand around here orating about it. You've made your decisions and we're not interested in your self-justifications. Goodbye."

The fat-faced young man evidently still had quite a bit of heroism to dramatize which Lavon's dismissal had short-circuited. An examination of Lavon's stony face, however, seemed to convince him that he had to take his victory as he found it. He and the delegation trailed ingloriously out the archway.

"Now what?" Lavon asked when they had gone. "I must admit, Shar, that I would have tried to persuade them. We do need the workers, after all."

"Not as much as they need us," Shar said tranquilly. "I know all those young men. I think they'll be astonished at the runty crops their fields will produce next season, after they have to breed them without my advice. Now, how many volunteers have you got for the crew of the ship?"

"Hundreds. Every youngster of the generation after Phil's wants to go along. Phil's wrong about the segment of the populace, at least. The project catches the imagination of the very young."

"Did you give them any encouragement?"

"Sure," Lavon said. "I told them we'd call on them if they were chosen. But you can't take that seriously! We'd do badly to displace our picked group of specialists with youths who have enthusiasm and nothing else."

"That's not what I had in mind, Lavon. Didn't I see a Noc in these chambers somewhere? Oh, there he is, asleep in the dome. Noc!"

The creature stirred its tentacle lazily.

"Noc, I've a message," Shar called. "The Protos are to tell all men that those who wish to go to the next world with the spaceship must come to the staging area right away. Say that we can't promise to take everyone, but that only those who help us to build the ship will be considered at all."

The Noc curled its tentacle again, and appeared to go back to sleep.

4

Lavon turned from the arrangement of speaking-tube megaphones which was his control board and looked at Para. "One last try," he said. "Will you give us back the history plate?"

"No, Lavon. We have never denied you anything before. But this we must."

"You're going with us, though, Para. Unless you give us back the knowledge we need, you'll lose your life if we lose ours."

"What is one Para?" the creature said. "We are all alike. This cell will die; but the Protos need to know how you fare on this journey. We believe you should make it without the plate, for in no other way can we assess the real importance of the plate."

"Then you admit you still have it. What if you can't communicate with your fellows once we're out in space? How do you know that water isn't essential to your telepathy?"

The Proto was silent. Lavon stared at it a moment, then turned deliberately back to the speaking tubes. "Everyone hang on," he said. He felt shaky. "We're about to start. Stravol, is the ship sealed?"

"As far as I can tell, Lavon."

Lavon shifted to another megaphone. He took a deep breath. Already the water seemed stifling, although the ship hadn't moved.

"Ready with one-quarter power. . . . One, two, three, go."

The whole ship jerked and settled back into place again. The raphe diatoms along the under hull settled into their niches, their jelly treads turning against broad endless belts of crude caddis-worm leather. Wooden gears creaked, stepping up the slow power of the creatures, transmitting it to the sixteen axles of the ship's wheels.

The ship rocked and began to roll slowly along the sand bar. Lavon looked tensely through the mica port. The world flowed painfully past him. The ship canted and began to climb the slope. Behind him, he could feel the electric silence of Shar, Para, and the two alternate pilots, Than and Stravol, as if their gaze were stabbing directly through his body and on out the port. The world looked different, now that he was leaving it. How had he missed all this beauty before?

The slapping of the endless belts and the squeaking and groaning of the gears and axles grew louder as the slope steepened. The ship continued to climb, lurching. Around it, squadrons of men and Protos dipped and wheeled, escorting it toward the sky.

Gradually the sky lowered and pressed down toward the top of the ship.

"A little more work from your diatoms, Tanol," Lavon said. "Boulder ahead." The ship swung ponderously. "All right, slow them up again. Give us a shove from your side, Tol—no, that's too much—there, that's it. Back to normal; you're still turning us! Tanol, give us one burst to line us up

136

again. Good. All right, steady drive on all sides. It shouldn't be long now."

"How can you think in webs like that?" the Para wondered behind him.

"I just do, that's all. It's the way men think. Overseers, a little more thrust now; the grade's getting steeper."

The gears groaned. The ship nosed up. The sky brightened in Lavon's face. Despite himself, he began to be frightened. His lungs seemed to burn, and in his mind he felt his long fall through nothingness toward the chill slap of the water as if he were experiencing it for the first time. His skin itched and burned. Could he go up there again? Up there into the burning void, the great gasping agony where no life should go?

The sand bar began to level out and the going became a little easier. Up here, the sky was so close that the lumbering motion of the huge ship disturbed it. Shadows of wavelets ran across the sand. Silently, the thick-barreled bands of blue-green algae drank in the light and converted it to oxygen, writhing in their slow mindless dance just under the long mica skylight which ran along the spine of the ship. In the hold, beneath the latticed corridor and cabin floors, whirring Vortae kept the ship's water in motion, fueling themselves upon drifting organic particles.

One by one, the figures wheeling outside about the ship waved arms or cilia and fell back, coasting down the slope of the sand bar toward the familiar world, dwindling and disappearing. There was at last only one single Euglena, half-plant cousin of the Protos, forging along beside the spaceship into the marshes of the shallows. It loved the light, but finally it, too, was driven away into deeper, cooler waters, its single whiplike tentacle undulating placidly as it went. It was not very bright, but Lavon felt deserted when it left.

Where they were going, though, none could follow.

Now the sky was nothing but a thin, resistant skin of water coating the top of the ship. The vessel slowed, and when Lavon called for more power, it began to dig itself in among the sandgrains and boulders.

"That's not going to work," Shar said tensely. "I think we'd better step down the gear-ratio, Lavon, so you can apply stress more slowly."

"All right," Lavon agreed. "Full stop, everybody. Shar, will you supervise gear-changing, please?"

Insane brilliance of empty space looked Lavon full in the face just beyond his big mica bull's eye. It was maddening to be forced to stop here upon the threshold of infinity; and it

137

was dangerous, too. Lavon could feel building in him the old fear of the outside. A few moments more of inaction, he knew with a gathering coldness in his belly, and he would be unable to go through with it.

Surely, he thought, there must be a better way to change gear-ratios than the traditional one, which involved dismantling almost the entire gear-box. Why couldn't a number of gears of different sizes be carried on the same shaft, not necessarily all in action at once, but awaiting use simply by shoving the axle back and forth longitudinally in its sockets? It would still be clumsy, but it could be worked on orders from the bridge and would not involve shutting down the entire machine—and throwing the new pilot into a blue-green funk.

Shar came lunging up through the trap and swam himself to a stop.

"All set," he said. "The big reduction gears aren't taking the strain too well, though."

"Splintering?"

"Yes. I'd go it slow at first."

Lavon nodded mutely. Without allowing himself to stop, even for a moment, to consider the consequences of his words, he called: "Half power."

The ship hunched itself down again and began to move, very slowly indeed, but more smoothly than before. Overhead, the sky thinned to complete transparency. The great light came blasting in. Behind Lavon there was an uneasy stir. The whiteness grew at the front ports.

Again the ship slowed, straining against the blinding barrier. Lavon swallowed and called for more power. The ship groaned like something about to die. It was now almost at a standstill.

"More power," Lavon ground out.

Once more, with infinite slowness, the ship began to move. Gently, it tilted upward.

Then it lunged forward and every board and beam in it began to squall.

"Lavon! Lavon!"

Lavon started sharply at the shout. The voice was coming at him from one of the megaphones, the one marked for the port at the rear of the ship.

"Lavon!"

"What is it? Stop your damn yelling."

"I can see the top of the sky! From the *other* side, from the top side! It's like a big flat sheet of metal. We're going away from it. We're above the sky, Lavon, we're above the sky!"

Another violent start swung Lavon around toward the forward port. On the outside of the mica, the water was evaporating with shocking swiftness, taking with it strange distortions and patterns made of rainbows.

Lavon saw space.

It was at first like a deserted and cruelly dry version of the Bottom. There were enormous boulders, great cliffs, tumbled, split, riven, jagged rocks going up and away in all directions, as if scattered at random by some giant.

But it had a sky of its own—a deep blue dome so far away that he could not believe in, let alone estimate, what its distance might be. And in this dome was a ball of reddish-white fire that seared his eyeballs.

The wilderness of rock was still a long way away from the ship, which now seemed to be resting upon a level, glistening plain. Beneath the surface-shine, the plain seemed to be made of sand, nothing but familiar sand, the same substance which had heaped up to form a bar in Lavon's universe, the bar along which the ship had climbed. But the glassy, colorful skin over it—

Suddenly Lavon became conscious of another shout from the megaphone banks. He shook his head savagely and said, "What is it now?"

"Lavon, this is Tol. What have you gotten us into? The belts are locked. The diatoms can't move them. They aren't faking, either; we've rapped them hard enough to make them think we were trying to break their shells, but they still can't give us more power."

"Leave them alone," Lavon snapped. "They can't fake; they haven't enough intelligence. If they say they can't give you more power, they can't."

"Well, then, you get us out of it."

Shar came forward to Lavon's elbow. "We're on a space-water interface, where the surface tension is very high," he said softly. "If you order the wheels pulled up now, I think we'll make better progress for a while on the belly tread."

"Good enough," Lavon said with relief. "Hello below—haul up the wheels."

"For a long while," Shar said, "I couldn't understand the reference of the history plate to 'retractable landing gear,' but it finally occurred to me that the tension along a space-mud interface would hold any large object pretty tightly. That's why I insisted on our building the ship so that we could lift the wheels."

"Evidently the ancients knew their business after all, Shar."

Quite a few minutes later—for shifting power to the belly

139

treads involved another setting of the gear box—the ship was crawling along the shore toward the tumbled rock. Anxiously, Lavon scanned the jagged, threatening wall for a break. There was a sort of rivulet off toward the left which might offer a route, though a dubious one, to the next world. After some thought, Lavon ordered his ship turned toward it.

"Do you suppose that thing in the sky is a 'star'?" he asked. "But there were supposed to be lots of them. Only one is up there—and one's plenty for my taste."

"I don't know," Shar admitted. "But I'm beginning to get a picture of the way the universe is made, I think. Evidently our world is a sort of cup in the Bottom of this huge one. This one has a sky of its own; perhaps it, too, is only a cup in the Bottom of a still huger world, and so on and on without end. It's a hard concept to grasp, I'll admit. Maybe it would be more sensible to assume that all the worlds are cups in this one common surface, and that the great light shines on them all impartially."

"Then what makes it go out every night, and dim even in the day during winter?" Lavon demanded.

"Perhaps it travels in circles, over first one world, then another. How could I know yet?"

"Well, if you're right, it means that all we have to do is crawl along here for a while, until we hit the top of the sky of another world," Lavon said. "Then we dive in. Somehow it seems too simple, after all our preparations."

Shar chuckled, but the sound did not suggest that he had discovered anything funny. "Simple? Have you noticed the temperature yet?"

Lavon had noticed it, just beneath the surface of awareness, but at Shar's remark he realized that he was gradually being stifled. The oxygen content of the water, luckily, had not dropped, but the temperature suggested the shallows in the last and worst part of autumn. It was like trying to breathe soup.

"Than, give us more action from the Vortae," Lavon said. "This is going to be unbearable unless we get more circulation."

There was a reply from Than, but it came to Lavon's ears only as a mumble. It was all he could do now to keep his attention on the business of steering the ship.

The cut or defile in the scattered razor-edged rocks was a little closer, but there still seemed to be many miles of rough desert to cross. After a while, the ship settled into a steady, painfully slow crawling, with less pitching and jerking than before, but also with less progress. Under it, there was now a

140

sliding, grinding sound, rasping against the hull of the ship itself, as if it were treadmilling over some coarse lubricant the particles of which were each as big as a man's head.

Finally Shar said, "Lavon, we'll have to stop again. The sand this far up is dry, and we're wasting energy using the tread."

"Are you sure we can take it?" Lavon asked, gasping for breath. "At least we are moving. If we stop to lower the wheels and change gears again, we'll boil."

"We'll boil if we don't," Shar said calmly. "Some of our algae are dead already and the rest are withering. That's a pretty good sign that we can't take much more. I don't think we'll make it into the shadows, unless we do change over and put on some speed."

There was a gulping sound from one of the mechanics. "We ought to turn back," he said raggedly. "We were never meant to be out here in the first place. We were made for the water, not for this hell."

"We'll stop," Lavon said, "but we're not turning back. That's final."

The words made a brave sound, but the man had upset Lavon more than he dared to admit, even to himself. "Shar," he said, "make it fast, will you?"

The scientist nodded and dived below.

The minutes stretched out. The great red-gold globe in the sky blazed and blazed. It had moved down the sky, far down, so that the light was pouring into the ship directly in Lavon's face, illuminating every floating particle, its rays like long milky streamers. The currents of water passing Lavon's cheek were almost hot.

How could they dare go directly forward into that inferno? The land directly under the "star" must be even hotter than it was here.

"Lavon! Look at Para!"

Lavon forced himself to turn and look at his Proto ally. The great slipper had settled to the deck, where it was lying with only a feeble pulsation of its cilia. Inside, its vacuoles were beginning to swell, to become bloated, pear-shaped bubbles, crowding the granulated cytoplasm, pressing upon the dark nuclei.

"Is . . . is he dying?"

"This cell is dying," Para said, as coldly as always. "But go on—go on. There is much to learn, and you may live, even though we do not. Go on."

"You're—for us now?" Lavon whispered.

"We have alway been for you. Push your folly to the utter-most. We will benefit in the end, and so will Man."

The whisper died away. Lavon called the creature again, but it did not respond.

There was a wooden clashing from below, and then Shar's voice came tinnily from one of the megaphones. "Lavon, go ahead! The diatoms are dying, too, and then we'll be without power. Make it as quickly and directly as you can."

Grimly, Lavon leaned forward. "The 'star' is directly over the land we're approaching."

"It is? It may go lower still and the shadows will get longer. That may be our only hope."

Lavon had not thought of that. He rasped into the banked megaphones. Once more, the ship began to move, a little faster now, but seemingly still at a crawl. The thirty-two wheels rumbled.

It got hotter.

Steadily, with a perceptible motion, the "star" sank in Lavon's face. Suddenly a new terror struck him. Suppose it should continue to go down until it was gone entirely? Blasting though it was now, it was the only source of heat. Would not space become bitter cold on the instant—and the ship an expanding, bursting block of ice?

The shadows lengthened menacingly, stretching across the desert toward the forward-rolling vessel. There was no talking in the cabin, just the sound of ragged breathing and the creaking of the machinery.

Then the jagged horizon seemed to rush upon them. Stony teeth cut into the lower rim of the ball of fire, devoured it swiftly. It was gone.

They were in the lee of the cliffs. Lavon ordered the ship turned to parallel the rock-line; it responded heavily, slug-gishly. Far above, the sky deepened steadily, from blue to indigo.

Shar came silently up through the trap and stood beside Lavon, studying that deepening color and the lengthening of the shadows down the beach toward their own world. He said nothing, but Lavon was sure that the same chilling thought was in his mind.

"Lavon."

Lavon jumped. Shar's voice had iron in it. "Yes?"

"We'll have to keep moving. We must make the next world, wherever it is, very shortly."

"How can we dare move when we can't see where we're going? Why not sleep it over—if the cold will let us?"

"It will let us," Shar said. "It can't get dangerously cold up

142

here. If it did, the sky—or what we used to think of as the sky—would have frozen over every night, even in summer. But what I'm thinking about is the water. The plants will go to sleep now. In our world that wouldn't matter; the supply of oxygen there is enough to last through the night. But in this confined space, with so many creatures in it and no supply of fresh water, we will probably smother."

Shar seemed hardly to be involved at all, but spoke rather with the voice of implacable physical laws.

"Furthermore," he said, staring unseeingly out at the raw landscape, "the diatoms are plants, too. In other words, we must stay on the move for as long as we have oxygen and power—and pray that we make it."

"Shar, we had quite a few Protos on board this ship once. And Para there isn't quite dead yet. If he were, the cabin would be intolerable. The ship is nearly sterile of bacteria, because all the protos have been eating them as a matter of course and there's no outside supply of them, either. But still and all there would have been some decay."

Shar bent and tested the pellicle of the motionless Para with a probing finger. "You're right, he's still alive. What does that prove?"

"The Vortae are also alive; I can feel the water circulating. Which proves that it wasn't the heat that hurt Para. *It was the light.* Remember how badly my skin was affected after I climbed beyond the sky? Undiluted starlight is deadly. We should add that to the information from the plate."

"I still don't get the point."

"It's this: We've got three or four Noc down below. They were shielded from the light, and so must be still alive. If we concentrate them in the diatom galleys, the dumb diatoms will think it's still daylight and will go on working. Or we can concentrate them up along the spine of the ship, and keep the algae putting out oxygen. So the question is: Which do we need more, oxygen or power? Or can we split the difference?"

Shar actually grinned. "A brilliant piece of thinking. We may make a Shar out of you some day, Lavon. No, I'd say that we can't split the difference. Noc's light isn't intense enough to keep the plants making oxygen; I tried it once, and the oxygen production was too tiny to matter. Evidently the plants use the light for energy. So we'll have to settle for the diatoms for motive power."

"All right. Set it up that way, Shar."

Lavon brought the vessel away from the rocky lee of the cliff, out onto the smoother sand. All trace of direct light was

143

now gone, although there was still a soft, general glow on the sky.

"Now then," Shar said thoughtfully, "I would guess that there's water over there in the canyon, if we can reach it. I'll go below again and arrange—"

Lavon gasped.

"What's the matter?"

Silently, Lavon pointed, his heart pounding.

The entire dome of indigo above them was spangled with tiny, incredibly brilliant lights. There were hundreds of them, and more and more were becoming visible as the darkness deepened. And far away, over the ultimate edge of the rocks, was a dim red globe, crescented with ghostly silver. Near the zenith was another such body, much smaller, and silvered all over . . .

Under the two moons of Hydrot, and under the eternal stars, the two-inch wooden spaceship and its microscopic cargo toiled down the slope toward the drying little rivulet.

5

The ship rested on the Bottom of the canyon for the rest of the night. The great square doors were unsealed and thrown open to admit the raw, irradiated, life-giving water from outside—and the wriggling bacteria which were fresh food.

No other creatures approached them, either out of curiosity or for hunting, while they slept, although Lavon had posted guards at the doors just in case. Evidently, even up here on the very floor of space, highly organized creatures were quiescent at night.

But when the first flush of light filtered through the water, trouble threatened.

First of all, there was the bug-eyed monster. The thing was green and had two snapping claws, either one of which could have broken the ship in two like a spirogyra strand. Its eyes were black and globular, on the ends of short columns, and its long feelers were thicker through than a plant bole. It passed in a kicking fury of motion, however, never noticing the ship at all.

"Is that—a sample of the kind of life they have here?" Lavon whispered. "Does it all run as big as that?" Nobody answered, for the very good reason that nobody knew.

After a while, Lavon risked moving the ship forward against the current, which was slow but heavy. Enormous writing

144

worms whipped past them. One struck the hull a heavy blow, then thrashed on obliviously.

"They don't notice us," Shar said. "We're too small. Lavon, the ancients warned us of the immensity of space, but even when you see it, it's impossible to grasp. And all those stars —can they mean what I think they mean? It's beyond thought, beyond belief!"

"The Bottom's sloping," Lavon said, looking ahead intently. "The walls of the canyon are retreating, and the water's becoming rather silty. Let the stars wait, Shar; we're coming toward the entrance of our new world."

Shar subsided moodily. His vision of space apparently had disturbed him, perhaps seriously. He took little notice of the great thing that was happening, but instead huddled worriedly over his own expanding speculations. Lavon felt the old gap between their minds widening once more.

Now the Bottom was tilting upward again. Lavon had no experience with delta-formation, for no rivulets left his own world, and the phenomenon worried him. But his worries were swept away in wonder as the ship topped the rise and nosed over.

Ahead, the Bottom sloped away again, indefinitely, into glimmering depths. A proper sky was over them once more, and Lavon could see small rafts of plankton floating placidly beneath it. Almost at once, too, he saw several of the smaller kinds of Protos, a few of which were already approaching the ship—

Then the girl came darting out of the depths, her features blurred and distorted with distance and terror. At first she did not seem to see the ship at all. She came twisting and turning lithely through the water, obviously hoping only to throw herself over the mound of the delta and into the savage streamlet beyond.

Lavon was stunned. Not that there were men here—he had hoped for that, had even known somehow that men were everywhere in the universe—but at the girl's single-minded flight toward suicide.

"What—"

Then a dim buzzing began to grow in his ears, and he understood.

"Shar! Than! Stravol!" he bawled. "Break out crossbows and spears! Knock out all the windows!" He lifted a foot and kicked through the port in front of him. Someone thrust a crossbow into his hand.

"What?" Shar blurted. "What's the matter? What's happening?"

"Eaters!"

The cry went through the ship like a galvanic shock. The rotifers back in Lavon's own world were virtually extinct, but everyone knew thoroughly the grim history of the long battle man and Proto had waged against them.

The girl spotted the ship suddenly and paused, obviously stricken with despair at the sight of this new monster. She drifted with her own momentum, her eyes alternately fixed upon the ship and jerking back over her shoulder, toward where the buzzing snarled louder and louder in the dimness.

"Don't stop!" Lavon shouted. "This way, this way! We're friends! We'll help!"

Three great semi-transparent trumpets of smooth flesh bored over the rise, the many thick cilia of their coronas whirring greedily. Dicrans, arrogant in their flexible armor, quarreling thickly among themselves as they moved, with the few blurred, pre-symbolic noises which made up their own language.

Carefully, Lavon wound the crossbow, brought it to his shoulder, and fired. The bolt sang away through the water. It lost momentum rapidly, and was caught by a stray current which brought it closer to the girl than to the Eater at which Lavon had aimed.

He bit his lip, lowered the weapon, wound it up again. It did not pay to underestimate the range; he would have to wait. Another bolt, cutting through the water from a side port, made him issue orders to cease firing "until," he added, "you can see their eyespots."

The irruption of the rotifers decided the girl. The motionless wooden monster was of course strange to her, but it had not yet menaced her—and she must have known what it would be like to have three Dicrans over her, each trying to grab from the others the largest share. She threw herself towards the bull'seye port. The three Eaters screamed with fury and greed and bored in after her.

She probably would not have made it, had not the dull vision of the lead Dicran made out the wooden shape of the ship at the last instant. The Dicran backed off, buzzing, and the other two sheered away to avoid colliding with her. After that they had another argument, though they could hardly have formulated what it was that they were fighting about; they were incapable of exchanging any thought much more complicated than the equivalent of "Yaah," "Drop dead," and "You're another."

While they were still snarling at each other, Lavon pierced the nearest one all the way through with an arablast bolt.

146

The surviving two were at once involved in a lethal battle over the remains.

"Than, take a party out and spear me those two Eaters while they're still fighting," Lavon ordered. "Don't forget to destroy their eggs, too. I can see that this world needs a little taming."

The girl shot through the port and brought up against the far wall of the cabin, flailing in terror. Lavon tried to approach her, but from somewhere she produced a flake of stonewort chipped to a nasty point. Since she was naked, it was hard to tell where she had been hiding it, but she obviously knew how to use it, and meant to. Lavon retreated and sat down on the stool before his control board, waiting while she took in the cabin, Lavon, Shar, the other pilots, the senescent Para.

At last she said: "Are—you—the gods—from beyond the sky?"

"We're from beyond the sky, all right," Lavon said. "But we're not gods. We're human beings, just like you. Are there many humans here?"

The girl seemed to assess the situation very rapidly, savage though she was. Lavon had the odd and impossible impression that he should recognize her: a tall, deceptively relaxed, tawny woman, not after all quite like this one . . . a woman from another world, to be sure, but still . . .

She tucked the knife back into her bright, matted hair—aha, Lavon thought confusedly, there's a trick I may need to remember—and shook her head.

"We are few. The Eaters are everywhere. Soon they will have the last of us."

Her fatalism was so complete that she actually did not seem to care.

"And you've never cooperated against them? Or asked the Protos to help?"

"The Protos?" She shrugged. "They are as helpless as we are against the Eaters, most of them. We have no weapons that kill at a distance, like yours. And it's too late now for such weapons to do any good. We are too few, the Eaters too many."

Lavon shook his head emphatically. "You've had one weapon that counts, all along. Against it, numbers mean nothing. We'll show you how we've used it. You may be able to use it even better than we did, once you've given it a try."

The girl shrugged again. "We dreamed of such a weapon, but never found it. Are you telling the truth? What is the weapon?"

"Brains, of course," Lavon said. "Not just one brain, but a lot of them. Working together. Cooperation."

"Lavon speaks the truth," a weak voice said from the deck.

The Para stirred feebly. The girl watched it with wide eyes. The sound of the Para using human speech seemed to impress her more than the ship itself, or anything else that it contained.

"The Eaters can be conquered," the thin, burring voice said. "The Protos will help, as they helped in the world from which we came. The Protos fought this flight through space, and deprived Man of his records; but Man made the trip without the records. The Protos will never oppose Man again. We have already spoken to the Protos of this world, and have told them that what Man can dream, Man can do. Whether the Protos will it or not.

"Shar—your metal record is with you. It was hidden in the ship. My brothers will lead you to it.

"This organism dies now. It dies in confidence of knowledge, as an intelligent creature dies. Man has taught us this. There is nothing. That knowledge. Cannot do. With it . . . men . . . have crossed . . . have crossed space . . ."

The voice whispered away. The shining slipper did not change, but something about it was gone. Lavon looked at the girl; their eyes met. He felt an unaccountable warmth.

"We have crossed space," Lavon repeated softly.

Shar's voice came to him across a great distance. The young-old man was whispering: "But—have we?"

Lavon was looking at the girl. He had no answer for Shar's question. It did not seem to be important.

BOOK FOUR

WATERSHED

The murmurs of discontent—Capt. Gorbel, being a military man, thought of it as "disaffection"—among the crew of the R.S.S. *Indefeasible* had reached the point where they could no longer be ignored, well before the ship had come within fifty light years of its objective.

Sooner or later, Gorbel thought, sooner or later this idiotic seal-creature is going to notice them.

Capt. Gorbel wasn't sure whether he would be sorry or glad when the Adapted Man caught on. In a way, it would make things easier. But it would be an uncomfortable moment, not only for Hoqqueah and the rest of the pantrope team, but for Gorbel himself. Maybe it would be better to keep sitting on the safety valve until Hoqqueah and the other Altarians were put off on—what was its name again? Oh yes, Earth.

But the crew plainly wasn't going to let Gorbel put it off that long.

As for Hoqqueah, he didn't appear to have a noticing center anywhere in his brain. He was as little discommoded by the emotional undertow as he was by the thin and frigid air the Rigellian crew maintained inside the battlecraft. Secure in his coat of warm blubber, his eyes brown, liquid and merry, he sat in the forward greenhouse for most of each ship's day, watching the growth of the star Sol in the black skies ahead.

And he talked. Gods of all stars, how he talked! Capt. Gorbel already knew more about the ancient—the *very* ancient —history of the seeding program than he had had any desire to know, but there was still more coming. Nor was the seeding program Hoqqueah's sole subject. The Colonization Council delegate had had a vertical education, one which cut in a narrow shaft through many different fields of specialization— in contrast to Gorbel's own training, which had been spread horizontally over the whole subject of spaceflight without more than touching anything else.

Hoqqueah seemed to be making a project of enlarging the Captain's horizons, whether he wanted them enlarged or not.

"Take agriculture," he was saying at the moment. "This planet we're to seed provides an excellent argument for taking the long view of farm policy. There used to be jungles there; it was very fertile. But the people began their lives as farmers with the use of fire, and they killed themselves off in the same way."

"How?" Gorbel said automatically. Had he remained silent, Hoqqueah would have gone on anyhow; and it didn't pay to be impolite to the Colonization Council, even by proxy.

"In their own prehistory, fifteen thousand years before their official zero date, they cleared farmland by burning it off. Then they would plant a crop, harvest it, and let the jungle return. Then they burned the jungle off and went through the cycle again. At the beginning, they wiped out the greatest abundance of game animals Earth was ever to see, just by farming that way. Furthermore the method was totally destructive to the topsoil.

"But did they learn? No. Even after they achieved spaceflight, that method of farming was standard in most of the remaining jungle areas—even though the bare rock was showing through everywhere by that time."

Hoqqueah sighed. "Now, of course, there are no jungles. There are no seas, either. There's nothing but desert, naked rock, bitter cold, and thin, oxygen-poor air—or so the people would view it, if there were any of them left. *Tapa* farming wasn't solely responsible, but it helped."

Gorbel shot a quick glance at the hunched back of Lt. Averdor, his adjutant and navigator. Averdor had managed to avoid saying so much as one word to Hoqqueah or any of the other pantropists from the beginning of the trip. Of course he wasn't required to assume the diplomatic burdens involved—

150

those were Gorbel's crosses—but the strain of dodging even normal intercourse with the seal-men was beginning to tell on him.

Sooner or later, Averdor was going to explode. He would have nobody to blame for it but himself, but that wouldn't prevent everybody on board from suffering from it.

Including Gorbel, who would lose a first-class navigator and adjutant.

Yet it was certainly beyond Gorbel's authority to order Averdor to speak to an Adapted Man. He could only suggest that Averdor run through a few mechanical courtesies, for the good of the ship. The only response had been one of the stoniest stares Gorbel had ever seen, even from Averdor, with whom the Captain had been shipping for over thirty Galactic years.

And the worst of it was that Gorbel was, as a human being, wholly on Averdor's side.

"After a certain number of years, conditions change on *any* planet," Hoqqueah babbled solemnly, waving a flipper-like arm to include all the points of light outside the greenhouse. He was working back to his primary obsession: the seeding program. "It's only logical to insist that man be able to change with them—or, if he can't do that, he must establish himself somewhere else. Suppose he had colonized only the Earthlike planets? Not even those planets *remain* Earthlike forever, not in the biological sense."

"Why would we have limited ourselves to Earthlike planets in the first place?" Gorbel said. "Not that I know much about the place, but the specs don't make it sound like an optimum world."

"To be sure," Hoqqueah said, though as usual Gorbel didn't know which part of his own comment Hoqqueah was agreeing to. "There's no survival value in pinning one's race forever to one set of specs. It's only sensible to go on evolving with the universe, so as to stay independent of such things as the aging of worlds, or the explosions of their stars. And look at the results! Man exists now in so many forms that there's always a refuge *somewhere* for any threatened people. That's a great achievement—compared to it, what price the old arguments about sovereignty of form?"

"What, indeed?" Gorbel said, but inside his skull his other self was saying: Ah-ha, he smells the hostility after all. Once an Adapted Man, always an Adapted Man—and always fighting for equality with the basic human form. But it's no good, you seal-snouted bureaucrat. You can argue for the

151

rest of your life, but your whiskers will always wiggle when you talk.

And obviously you'll never stop talking.

"And as a military man yourself, you'd be the first to appreciate the military advantages, Captain," Hoqqueah added earnestly. "Using pantropy, man has seized thousands of worlds that would have been inacccessible to him otherwise. It's enormously increased our chances to become masters of the galaxy, to take most of it under occupation *without* stealing anyone else's planet in the process. An occupation without dispossession—let alone without bloodshed. Yet if some race other than man should develop imperial ambitions, and try to annex *our* planets, it will find itself enormously outnumbered."

"That's true," Capt. Gorbel said, interested in spite of himself. "It's probably just as well that we worked fast, way back there in the beginning. Before somebody else thought up the method, I mean. But, how come it *was* us? Seems to me that the first race to invent it should've been a race that already had it—if you follow me."

"Not quite, Captain. If you will give me an example—?"

"Well, we scouted a system once where there was a race that occupied two different planets, not both at the same time, but back and forth," Gorbel said. "They had a life-cycle that had three different forms. In the first form they'd winter over on the outermost of the two worlds. Then they'd change to another form that could cross space, mother-naked, without ships, and spend the rest of the year on the inner planet in the third form. Then they'd change back into the second form and cross back to the colder planet.

"It's a hard thing to describe. But the point is, this wasn't anything they'd worked out; it was natural to them. They'd evolved that way." He looked at Averdor again. "The navigation was tricky around there during the swarming season."

Avedor failed to rise to the bait.

"I see; the point is well taken," Hoqqueah said, nodding with grotesque thoughtfulness. "But let me point out to you, Captain, that being already able to do a thing doesn't aid you in thinking of it as something that needs to be perfected. Oh, I've seen races like the one you describe, too—races with polymorphism, sexual alteration of generation, metamorphosis of the insect life-history type, and so on. There's a planet named Lithia, about forty light years from here, where the dominant race undergoes complete evolutionary recapitulation *after* birth—not before it, as men do. But why should any of them think of form-changing as something extraordinary, and to be striven for? It's one of the commonplaces of their lives, after all."

A small bell chimed in the greenhouse. Hoqqueah got up at once, his movements precise and almost graceful despite his tubbiness. "Thus endeth the day," he said cheerfully. "Thank you for your courtesy, Captain."

He waddled out. He would, of course, be back tomorrow. And the day after that.

And the next day—unless the crewmen hadn't tarred and feathered the whole bunch by then.

If only, Gorbel thought distractedly, if only the damned Adapts weren't so quick to abuse their privileges! As a delegate of the Colonization Council, Hoqqueah was a person of some importance, and could not be barred from entering the greenhouse except in an emergency. But didn't the man know that he shouldn't use the privilege each and every day, on a ship manned by basic-form human beings most of whom could not enter the greenhouse at all without a direct order?

And the rest of the pantropists were just as bad. As passengers with the technical status of human beings, they could go almost anywhere in the ship that the crew could go—and they did, persistently and unapologetically, as though moving among equals. Legally, that was what they were—but didn't they know by this time that there was such a thing as prejudice? And that among common spacemen the prejudice against their kind—and against any Adapted Man—always hovered near the borderline of bigotry?

There was a slight hum as Averdor's power chair swung around to face the Captain. Like most Rigellian men, the lieutenant's face was lean and harsh, almost like that of an ancient religious fanatic, and the starlight in the greenhouse did nothing to soften it; but to Capt. Gorbel, to whom it was familiar down to its last line, it looked especially forbidding now.

"Well?" he said.

"I'd think you'd be fed to the teeth with that freak by this time," Averdor said without preamble. "Something's got to be done, Captain, before the crew gets so surly that we have to start handing out brig sentences."

"I don't like know-it-alls any better than you do," Gorbel said grimly. "Especially when they talk nonsense—and half of what this one says about space flight is nonsense, that much I'm sure of. But the man's a delegate of the Council. He's got a right to be up here if he wants to."

"You can bar anybody from the greenhouse in an emergency—even the ship's officers."

"I fail to see any emergency," Gorbel said stiffly.

"This is a hazardous part of the galazy—potentially, anyhow. It hasn't been visited for millennia. That star up ahead has nine planets besides the one we're supposed to land on, and I don't know how many satellites of planetary size. Suppose somebody on one of them lost his head and took a crack at us as we went by?"

Gorbel frowned. "That's reaching for trouble. Besides, the area's been surveyed recently at least once—otherwise we wouldn't be here."

"A sketch job. It's still sensible to take precautions. If there should be any trouble, there's many a Board of Review that would call it risky to have unreliable, second-class human types in the greenhouse when it breaks out."

"You're talking nonsense."

"Dammit, Captain, read between the lines a minute," Averdor said harshly. "I know as well as you do that there's going to be no trouble that we can't handle. And that no reviewing board would pull a complaint like that on *you* if there were. I'm just trying to give you an excuse to use on the seals."

"I'm listening."

"Good. The *Indefeasible* is the tightest ship in the Rigellian navy, her record's clean, and the crew's morale is almost a legend. We can't afford to start gigging the men for their personal prejudices—which is what it will amount to, if those seals drive them to breaking discipline. Besides, they've got a right to do their work without a lot of seal snouts poking continually over their shoulders."

"I can hear myself explaining that to Hoqqueah."

"You don't need to," Averdor said doggedly. "You can tell him, instead, that you're going to have to declare the ship on emergency status until we land. That means that the pantrope team, as passengers, will have to stick to their quarters. It's simple enough."

It was simple enough, all right. And decidedly tempting.

"I don't like it," Gorbel said. "Besides, Hoqqueah may be a know-it-all, but he's not entirely a fool. He'll see through it easily enough."

Averdor shrugged. "It's your command," he said. "But I don't see what he could do about it even if he did see through it. It'd be all on the log and according to regs. All he could report to the Council would be a suspicion—and they'd probably discount it. Everybody knows that these second-class types are quick to think they're being persecuted. It's my theory that that's why they *are* persecuted, a lot of the time at least."

"I don't follow you."

"The man I shipped under before I came on board the *Indefeasible*," Averdor said, "was one of those people who don't even trust themselves. They expect everybody they meet to slip a knife into them when their backs are turned. And there are always other people who make it almost a point of honor to knife a man like that, just because he seems to be asking for it. He didn't hold that command long."

"I see what you mean," Gorbel said. "Well, I'll think about it."

But by the next ship's day, when Hoqqueah returned to the greenhouse, Gorbel still had not made up his mind. The very fact that his own feelings were on the side of Averdor and the crew made him suspicious of Averdor's "easy" solution. The plan was tempting enough to blind a tempted man to flaws that might otherwise be obvious.

The Adapted Man settled himself comfortably and looked out through the transparent metal. "Ah," he said. "Our target is sensibly bigger now, eh, Captain? Think of it: in just a few days now, we will be—in the historical sense—home again."

And now it was riddles! "What do you mean?" Gorbel said.

"I'm sorry; I thought you knew. Earth is the home planet of the human race, Captain. There is where the basic form evolved."

Gorbel considered this unexpected bit of information cautiously. Even assuming that it was true—and it probably was, that would be the kind of thing Hoqqueah would know about a planet to which he was assigned—it didn't seem to make any special difference in the situation. But Hoqqueah had obviously brought it out for a reason. Well, he'd be trotting out the reason, too, soon enough; nobody would ever accuse the Altarian of being taciturn.

Nevertheless, he considered turning on the screen for a close look at the planet. Up to now he had felt not the slightest interest in it.

"Yes, there's where it all began," Hoqqueah said. "Of course at first it never occurred to those people that they might produce pre-adapted children. They went to all kinds of extremes to adapt their environment instead, or to carry it along with them. But they finally realized that with the planets, that

155

won't work. You can't spend your life in a spacesuit, or under a dome, either.

"Besides, they had had form trouble in their society from their earliest days. For centuries they were absurdly touchy over minute differences in coloring and shape, and even in thinking. They had regime after regime that tried to impose its own concept of the standard citizen on everybody, and enslaved those who didn't fit the specs."

Abruptly, Hoqqueah's chatter began to make Gorbel uncomfortable. It was becoming easier and easier to sympathize with Averdor's determination to ignore the Adapted Man's existence entirely.

"It was only after they'd painfully taught themselves that such differences really don't matter that they could go on to pantropy," Hoqqueah said. "It was the logical conclusion. Of course, a certain continuity of form had to be maintained, and has been maintained to this day. You cannot totally change the form without totally changing the thought processes. If you give a man the form of a cockroach, as one ancient writer foresaw, he will wind up thinking like a cockroach, not like a human being. We recognized that. On worlds where only extreme modifications of the human form would make it suitable—for instance, a planet of the gas giant type —no seeding is attempted. The Council maintains that such worlds are the potential property of other races than the human, races whose psychotypes would not have to undergo radical change in order to survive there."

Dimly, Capt. Gorbel saw where Hoqqueah was leading him, and he did not like what he saw. The seal-man, in his own maddeningly indirect way, was arguing his right to be considered an equal in fact as well as in law. He was arguing it, however, in a universe of discourse totally unfamiliar to Capt. Gorbel, with facts whose validity he alone knew and whose relevance he alone could judge. He was, in short, loading the dice, and the last residues of Gorbel's tolerance were evaporating rapidly.

"Of course there was resistance back there at the beginning," Hoqqueah said. "The kind of mind that had only recently been persuaded that colored men are human beings was quick to take the attitude that an Adapted Man—any Adapted Man—was the social inferior of the 'primary' or basic human type, the type that lived on Earth. But it was also a very old idea on the Earth that basic humanity inheres in the mind, not in the form.

"You see, Captain, all this might still have been prevented, had it been possible to maintain the attitude that changing

156

the form even in part makes a man less of a man than he was in the 'primary' state. But the day has come when that attitude is no longer tenable—a day that is the greatest of all moral watersheds for our race, the day that is to unite all our divergent currents of attitudes toward each other into one common reservoir of brotherhood and purpose. You and I are very fortunate to be on the scene to see it."

"Very interesting," Gorbel said coldly. "But all those things happened a long time ago, and we know very little about this part of the galaxy these days. Under the circumstances—which you'll find clearly written out in the log, together with the appropriate regulations—I'm forced to place the ship on emergency alert beginning tomorrow, and continuing until your team disembarks. I'm afraid that means that henceforth all passengers will be required to stay in quarters."

Hoqqueah turned and arose. His eyes were still warm and liquid, but there was no longer any trace of merriment in them.

"I know very well what it means," he said. "And to some extent I understand the need—though I had been hoping to see the planet of our birth first from space. But I don't think *you* quite understood *me*, Captain. The moral watershed of which I spoke is not in the past. It is now. It began the day that the Earth itself became no longer habitable for the so-called basic human type. The flowing of the streams toward the common reservoir will become bigger and bigger as word spreads through the galaxy that Earth itself has been seeded with Adapted Men. With that news will go a shock of recognition—the shock of realizing that the 'basic' types are now, and have been for a long time, a very small minority, despite their pretensions."

Was Hoqqueah being absurd enough to threaten—an unarmed, comical seal-man shaking a fist at the captain of the *Indefeasible*? Or—

"Before I go, let me ask you this one question, Captain. Down there is your home planet, and my team and I will be going out on its surface before long. Do you dare to follow us out of the ship?"

"And why should I?" Gorbel said.

"Why, to show the superiority of the basic type, Captain," Hoqqueah said softly. "Surely you cannot admit that a pack of seal-men are your betters, on your own ancestral ground!"

He bowed and went to the door. Just before he reached it, he turned and looked speculatively at Gorbel and at Lt.

157

Averdor, who was staring at him with an expression of rigid fury.

"Or can you?" he said. "It will be interesting to see how you manage to comport yourselves as a minority. I think you lack practice."

He went out. Both Gorbel and Averdor turned jerkily to the screen, and Gorbel turned it on. The image grew, steadied, settled down.

When the next trick came on duty, both men were still staring at the vast and tumbled desert of the Earth.

Galactic Cluster

Contents

TO KENNETH S. WHITE

Tomb Tapper

THE DISTANT glare of the atomic explosion had already faded
from the sky as McDonough's car whirred away from the
blacked-out town of Port Jervis and turned north. He was
making fifty m.p.h. on U.S. Route 209 using no lights but
his parkers, and if a deer should bolt across the road ahead
of him he would never see it until the impact. It was hard
enough to see the road.

But he was thinking, not for the first time, of the old joke
about the man who tapped train wheels.

He had been doing it, so the story ran, for thirty years. On
every working day he would go up and down both sides of
every locomotive that pulled into the yards and hit the
wheels with a hammer; first the drivers, then the trucks. Each
time, he would cock his head, as though listening for something in the sound. On the day of his retirement, he was
given a magnificent dinner, as befitted a man with long senior-
ity in the Brotherhood of Railway Trainmen—and somebody
stopped to ask him what he had been tapping for all those
years.

He had cocked his head as though listening for something,
but evidently nothing came. "I don't know," he said.

That's me, McDonough thought. I tap tombs, not trains.
But what am I listening for?

The speedometer said he was close to the turnoff for the
airport, and he pulled the dimmers on. There it was. There
was at first nothing to be seen, as the headlights swept along
the dirt road, but a wall of darkness deep as all night,
faintly edged at the east by the low domed hills of the
Neversink valley. Then another pair of lights snapped on
behind him, on the main highway, and came jolting after
McDonough's car, clear and sharp in the dust clouds he had
raised.

He swung the car to a stop beside the airport fence and
killed the lights; the other car followed. In the renewed blackness the faint traces of dawn on the hills were wiped out, as
though the whole universe had been set back an hour. Then
the yellow eye of a flashlight opened in the window of the
other car and stared into his face.

7

He opened the door. "Martinson?" he said tentatively.

"Right here," the adjutant's voice said. The flashlight's oval spoor swung to the ground. "Anybody else with you?"

"No. You?"

"No. Go ahead and get your equipment out. I'll open up the shack."

The oval spot of light bobbed across the parking area and came to uneasy rest on the combination padlock which held the door of the operations shack secure. McDonough flipped the dome light of his car on long enough to locate the canvas sling which held the components of his electro-encephalograph, and eased the sling out onto the sand.

He had just slammed the car door and taken up the burden when little chinks of light sprang into being in the blind windows of the shack. At the same time, cars came droning out onto the field from the opposite side, four of them, each with its wide-spaced unblinking slits of paired parking lights, and ranked themselves on either side of the landing strip. It would be dawn before long, but if the planes were ready to go before dawn, the cars could light the strip with their brights.

We're fast, McDonough thought, with brief pride. Even the Air Force thinks the Civil Air Patrol is just a bunch of amateurs, but we can put a mission in the air ahead of any other CAP squadron in this county. We can scramble.

He was getting his night vision back now, and a quick glance showed him that the windsock was flowing straight out above the black, silent hangar against the pearly false dawn. Aloft, the stars were paling without any cloud-dimming, or even much twinkling. The wind was steady north up the valley; ideal flying weather.

Small lumpy figures were running across the field from the parked cars toward the shack. The squadron was scrambling.

"Mac!" Martinson shouted from inside the shack. "Where are you? Get your junk in here and get started!"

McDonough slipped inside the door, and swung his EEG components onto the chart table. Light was pouring into the briefing room from the tiny office, dazzling after the long darkness. In the briefing room the radio blinked a tiny red eye, but the squadron's communications officer hadn't yet arrived to answer it. In the office, Martinson's voice rumbled softly, urgently, and the phone gave him back thin unintelligible noises, like an unteachable parakeet.

Then, suddenly, the adjutant appeared at the office door

and peered at McDonough. "What are you waiting for?" he said. "Get that mind reader of yours into the Cub on the double."

"What's wrong with the Aeronca? It's faster."

"Water in the gas; she ices up. We'll have to drain the tank. This is a hell of a time to argue." Martinson jerked open the squealing door which opened into the hangar, his hand groping for the light switch. McDonough followed him, supporting his sling with both hands, his elbows together. Nothing is quite so concentratedly heavy as an electronics chassis with a transformer mounted on it, and four of them make a back-wrenching load.

The adjutant was already hauling the servicing platform across the concrete floor to the cowling of the Piper Cub. "Get your stuff set," he said. "I'll fuel her up and check the oil."

"All right. Doesn't look like she needs much gas."

"Don't you ever stop talkin'? Let's move."

McDonough lowered his load to the cold floor beside the plane's cabin, feeling a brief flash of resentment. In daily life Martinson was a job printer who couldn't, and didn't, give orders to anybody, not even his wife. Well, those were usually the boys who let rank go to their heads, even in a volunteer outfit. He got to work.

Voices sounded from the shack, and then Andy Persons, the commanding officer, came bounding over the sill, followed by two sleepy-eyed cadets. "What's up?" he shouted. "That you, Martinson?"

"It's me. One of you cadets, pass me up that can. Andy, get the doors open, hey? There's a Russki bomber down north of us, somewhere near Howells. Part of a flight that was making a run on Schenectady."

"Did they get it?"

"No, they overshot, *way* over—took out Kingston instead. Stewart Field hit them just as they turned to regroup, and knocked this baby down on the first pass. We're supposed to——"

The rest of the adjutant's reply was lost in a growing, echoing roar, as though they were all standing underneath a vast trestle over which all the railroad trains in the world were crossing at once. The sixty-four-foot organ reeds of jets were being blown in the night zenith above the field—another hunting pack, come from Stewart Field to avenge the hydrogen agony that had been Kingston.

His head still inside the plane's greenhouse, McDonough

listened transfixed. Like most CAP officers, he was too old to be a jet pilot, his reflexes too slow, his eyesight too far over the line, his belly muscles too soft to take the five-gravity turns; but now and then he thought about what it might be like to ride one of those flying blowtorches, cruising at six hundred miles an hour before a thin black wake of kerosene fumes, or being followed along the ground at top speed by the double wave-front of the "supersonic bang." It was a noble notion, almost as fine as that of piloting the one-man Niagara of power that was a rocket fighter.

The noise grew until it seemed certain that the invisible jets were going to bullet directly through the hangar, and then dimmed gradually.

"The usual orders?" Persons shouted up from under the declining roar. "Find the plane, pump the live survivors, pick the corpses' brains? Who else is up?"

"Nobody," Martinson said, coming down from the ladder and hauling it clear of the plane. "Middletown squadron's deactivated; Montgomery hasn't got a plane; Newburgh hasn't got a field."

"Warwick has Group's L-16——"

"They snapped the undercarriage off it last week," Martinson said with gloomy satisfaction. "It's our baby, as usual. Mac, you got your ghoul-tools all set in there?"

"In a minute," McDonough said. He was already wearing the Walter goggles, pushed back up on his helmet, and the detector, amplifier, and power pack of the EEG were secure in their frames on the platform behind the Cub's rear seat. The "hair net"—the flexible network of electrodes which he would jam on the head of any dead man whose head had survived the bomber crash—was connected to them and hung in its clips under the seat, the leads strung to avoid fouling the plane's exposed control cables. Nothing remained to do now but to secure the frequency analyzer, which was the heaviest of the units and had to be bolted down just forward of the rear joystick so that its weight would not shift in flight. If the apparatus didn't have to be collimated after every flight, it could be left in the plane—but it did, and that was that.

"O.K.," he said, pulling his head out of the greenhouse. He was trembling slightly. These tomb-tapping expeditions were hard on the nerves. No matter how much training in the art of reading a dead mind you may have had, the actual experience is different, and cannot be duplicated from the long-stored corpses of the laboratory. The newly dead brain is an inferno, almost by definition.

"Good," Persons said. "Martinson, you'll pilot. Mac, keep on the air; we're going to refuel the Airoknocker and get it up by ten o'clock if we can. In any case we'll feed you any spottings we get from the Air Force as fast as they come in. Martinson, refuel at Montgomery if you have to; don't waste time coming back here. Got it?"

"Roger," Martinson said, scrambling into the front seat and buckling his safety belt. McDonough put his foot hastily into the stirrup and swung into the back seat.

"Cadets!" Persons said. "Pull chocks! Roll 'er!"

Characteristically, Persons himself did the heavy work of lifting and swinging the tail. The Cub bumped off the apron and out on the grass into the brightening morning.

"Switch off!" the cadet at the nose called. "Gas! Brakes!"

"Switch off, brakes," Martinson called back. "Mac, where to? Got any ideas?"

While McDonough thought about it, the cadet pulled the prop backwards through four turns. "Brakes! Contact!"

"Let's try up around the Otisville tunnel. If they were knocked down over Howells, they stood a good chance to wind up on the side of that mountain."

Martinson nodded and reached a gloved hand over his head. "Contact!" he shouted, and turned the switch. The cadet swung the prop, and the engine barked and roared; at McDonough's left, the duplicate throttle slid forward slightly as the pilot "caught" the engine. McDonough buttoned up the cabin, and then the plane began to roll toward the far, dim edge of the grassy field.

The sky got brighter. They were off again, to tap on another man's tomb, and ask of the dim voice inside it what memories it had left unspoken when it had died.

The Civil Air Patrol is, and has been since 1941, an auxiliary of the United States Air Force, active in coastal patrol and in air-sea rescue work. By 1954—when its ranks totaled more than eighty thousand men and women, about fifteen thousand of them licensed pilots—the Air Force had nerved itself up to designating CAP as its Air Intelligence arm, with the job of locating downed enemy planes and radioing back information of military importance.

Aerial search is primarily the task of planes which can fly low and slow. Air Intelligence requires speed, since the kind of tactical information an enemy wreck may offer can grow cold within a few hours. The CAP's planes, most of them single-engine, private-flying models, had already been proven ideal aerial search instruments; the CAP's radio net, with its more than seventy-five hundred fixed, mobile and airborne stations, was more than fast enough to get information to wherever it was needed while it was still hot.

But the expected enemy, after all, was Russia; and how many civilians, even those who know how to fly, navigate, or operate a radio transmitter, could ask anyone an intelligent question in Russian, let alone understand the answer?

It was the astonishingly rapid development of electrical methods for probing the brain which provided the answer— in particular the development, in the late fifties, of flicker-stimulus aimed at the visual memory. Abruptly, EEG technicians no longer needed to use language at all to probe the brain for visual images, and read them; they did not even need to know how their apparatus worked, let alone the brain. A few moments of flicker into the subject's eyes, on a frequency chosen from a table, and the images would come swarming into the operator's toposcope goggles—the frequency chosen without the slightest basic knowledge of electrophysiology, as a woman choosing an ingredient from a cookbook is ignorant of—and indifferent to—the chemistry involved in the choice.

It was that engineering discovery which put tomb-tappers into the back seats of the CAP's putt-putts when the war finally began—for the images in the toposcope goggles did not stop when the brain died.

The world at dawn, as McDonough saw it from three thousand feet, was a world of long sculptured shadows, almost as motionless and three-dimensional as a lunar landscape near the daylight terminator. The air was very quiet, and the Cub droned as gently through the blue haze as any bee, gaining altitude above the field in a series of wide climbing turns. At the last turn the plane wheeled south over a farm owned by someone Martinson knew, a man already turning his acres from the seat of his tractor, and Martinson waggled the plane's wings at him and got back a wave like the quivering of an insect's antenna. It was all deceptively normal.

Then the horizon dipped below the Cub's nose again and Martinson was climbing out of the valley. A lake passed below them, spotted with islands, and with the brown barracks of

Camp Cejwin, once a children's summer camp but now full of sleeping soldiers. Martinson continued south, skirting Port Jervis, until McDonough was able to pick up the main line of the Erie Railroad, going northeast toward Otisville and Howells. The mountain through which the Otisville tunnel ran was already visible as a smoky hulk to the far left of the dawn.

McDonough turned on the radio, which responded with a rhythmical sputtering; the Cub's engine was not adequately shielded. In the background, the C.O.'s voice was calling them: "Huguenot to L-4. Huguenot to L-4."

"L-4 here. We read you, Andy. We're heading toward Otisville. Smooth as glass up here. Nothing to report yet."

"We read you weak but clear. We're dumping the gas in the Airoknocker *crackle* ground. We'll follow as fast as possible. No new AF spottings yet. If *crackle*, call us right away. Over."

"L-4 to Huguenot. Lost the last sentence, Andy. Cylinder static. Lost the last sentence. Please read it back."

"All right, Mac. If you see the bomber, *crackle* right away. Got it? If you see *crackle*, call us right away. Got it? Over."

"Got it, Andy. L-4 to Huguenot, over and out."

"Over and out."

The railroad embankment below them went around a wide arc and separated deceptively into two. One of the lines had been pulled up years back, but the marks of the long-ago stacked and burned ties still striped the gravel bed, and it would have been impossible for a stranger to tell from the air whether or not there were any rails running over those marks; terrain from the air can be deceptive unless you know what it is supposed to look like, rather than what it does look like. Martinson, however, knew as well as McDonough which of the two rail spurs was the discontinued one, and banked the Cub in a gentle climbing turn toward the mountain.

The rectangular acres wheeled slowly and solemnly below them, brindled with tiny cows as motionless as toys. After a while the deceptive spur line turned sharply east into a woolly green woods and never came out again. The mountain got larger, the morning ground haze rising up its nearer side, as though the whole forest were smoldering sullenly there.

Martinson turned his head and leaned it back to look out of the corner of one eye at the back seat, but McDonough shook his head. There was no chance at all that the crashed bomber could be on this side of that heavy-shouldered mass of rock.

Martinson shrugged and eased the stick back. The plane bored up into the sky, past four thousand feet, past four thousand, five hundred. Lake Hawthorne passed under the Cub's fat little tires, an irregular sapphire set in the pommel of the mountain. The altimeter crept slowly past five thousand feet; Martinson was taking no chances on being caught in the downdraft on the other side of the hill. At six thousand, he edged the throttle back and leveled out, peering back through the plexiglas.

But there was no sign of any wreck on that side of the mountain, either.

Puzzled, McDonough forced up the top cabin flap on the right side, buttoned it into place against the buffeting slipstream, and thrust his head out into the tearing gale. There was nothing to see on the ground. Straight down, the knife-edge brow of the cliff from which the railroad tracks emerged again drifted slowly away from the Cub's tail; just an inch farther on was the matchbox which was the Otisville siding shack. A sort of shaking of pepper around the matchbox meant people, a small crowd of them—though there was no train due until the Erie's No. 6, which didn't stop at Otisville anyhow.

He thumped Martinson on the shoulder. The adjutant tilted his head back and shouted, "What?"

"Bank right. Something going on around the Otisville station. Go down a bit."

The adjutant jerked out the carburetor-heat toggle and pulled back the throttle. The plane, idling, went into a long, whistling glide along the railroad right of way.

"Can't go too low here," he said. "If we get caught in the downdraft, we'll get slammed right into the mountain."

"I know that. Go on about four miles and make an airline approach back. Then you can climb into the draft. I want to see what's going on down there."

Martinson shrugged and opened the throttle again. The Cub clawed for altitude, then made a half-turn over Howells for the bogus landing run.

The plane went into normal glide and McDonough craned his neck. In a few moments he was able to see what had happened down below. The mountain from this side was steep and sharp; a wounded bomber couldn't possibly have hoped to clear it. At night, on the other hand, the mouth of

the railroad tunnel was marked on all three sides, by the lights
of the station on the left, the neon sign of the tavern which
stood on the brow of the cliff in Otisville (POP. 3,000—HIGH
AND HEALTHY) and on the right by the Erie's own signal
standard. Radar would have shown the rest: the long regular
path of the embankment leading directly into that cul-de-sac
of lights, the beetling mass of contours which was the mountain. All these signs would mean "tunnel" in any language.

And the bomber pilot had taken the longest of all possible
chances: to come down gliding along the right of way, in the
hope of shooting his fuselage cleanly into that tunnel, leaving
behind his wings with their dangerous engines and fuel tanks.
It was absolutely insane, but that was what he had done.

And, miracle of miracles, he had made it. McDonough
could see the wings now, buttered into two-dimensional
profiles over the two pilasters of the tunnel. They had hit
with such force that the fuel in them must have been vaporized
instantly; at least, there was no sign of a fire. And no sign of
a fuselage, either.

The bomber's body was inside the mountain, probably halfway or more down the tunnel's one-mile length. It was in-
conceivable that there could be anything intelligible left of it;
but where one miracle has happened, two are possible.

No wonder the little Otisville station was peppered over
with the specks of wondering people.

"L-4 to Huguenot. L-4 to Huguenot. Andy, are you there?"

"We read you, Mac. Go ahead."

"We've found your bomber. It's in the Otisville tunnel.
Over."

"*Crackle* to L-4. You've lost your mind."

"That's where it is, all the same. We're going to try to
make a landing. Send us a team as soon as you can. Out."

"Huguenot to L-4. Don't be a *crackle* idiot, Mac, you
can't land there."

"Out," McDonough said. He pounded Martinson's shoulder
and gestured urgently downward.

"You want to land?" Martinson said. "Why didn't you say
so? We'll never get down on a shallow glide like this." He
cleared the engine with a brief burp on the throttle, pulled
the Cub up into a sharp stall, and slid off on one wing. The
whole world began to spin giddily.

Martinson was losing altitude. McDonough closed his eyes
and hung onto his back teeth.

Martinson's drastic piloting got them down to a rough landing, on the wheels, on the road leading to the Otisville station, slightly under a mile away from the mountain. They taxied the rest of the way. The crowd left the mouth of the tunnel to cluster around the airplane the moment it had come to a stop, but a few moments' questioning convinced Mc-Donough that the Otisvilleans knew very little. Some of them had heard "a turrible noise" in the early morning, and with the first light had discovered the bright metal coating the sides of the tunnel. No, there hadn't been any smoke. No, nobody heard any sounds in the tunnel. You couldn't see the other end of it, though; something was blocking it.

"The signal's red on this side," McDonough said thoughtfully while he helped the adjutant tie the plane down. "You used to run the PBX board for the Erie in Port, didn't you, Marty? If you were to phone the station master there, maybe we could get him to throw a block on the other end of the tunnel."

"If there's wreckage in there, the block will be on automatically."

"Sure. But we've got to go in there. I don't want the Number Six piling in after us."

Martinson nodded, and went inside the railroad station. McDonough looked around. There was, as usual, a motorized hand truck parked off the tracks on the other side of the embankment. Many willing hands helped him set it on the right of way, and several huskies got the one-lung engine started for him. Getting his own apparatus out of the plane and onto the truck, however, was a job for which he refused all aid. The stuff was just too delicate, for all its weight, to be allowed in the hands of laymen—and never mind that McDonough himself was almost as much of a layman in neurophysiology as they were; he at least knew the collimating tables and the cookbook.

"O.K.," Martinson said, rejoining them. "Tunnel's blocked at both ends. I talked to Ralph at the dispatcher's; he was steaming—says he's lost four trains already, and another due in from Buffalo in forty-four minutes. We cried a little about it. Do we go now?"

"Right now."

Martinson drew his automatic and squatted down on the front of the truck. The little car growled and crawled toward the tunnel. The spectators murmured and shook their heads knowingly.

Inside the tunnel it was as dark as always, and cold, with a damp chill which struck through McDonough's flight jacket and dungarees. The air was still, and in addition to its musty smell it had a peculiar metallic stench. Thus far, however, there was none of the smell of fuel or of combustion products which McDonough had expected. He found suddenly that he was trembling again, although he did not really believe that the EEG would be needed.

"Did you notice those wings?" Martinson said suddenly, just loud enough to be heard above the popping of the motor. The echoes distorted his voice almost beyond recognition.

"Notice them? What about them?"

"Too short to be bomber wings. Also, no engines."

McDonough swore silently. To have failed to notice a detail as gross as that was a sure sign that he was even more frightened than he had thought. "Anything else?"

"Well, I don't think they were aluminum; too tough. Titanium, maybe, or stainless steel. What have we got in here, anyhow? You *know* the Russkies couldn't get a fighter this far."

There was no arguing that. There was no answering the question, either—not yet.

McDonough unhooked the torch from his belt. Behind them, the white aperture of the tunnel's mouth looked no bigger than a nickel, and the twin bright lines of the rails looked forty miles long. Ahead, the flashlight revealed nothing but the slimy walls of the tunnel, coated with soot.

And then there was a fugitive bluish gleam. McDonough set the motor back down as far as it would go. The truck crawled painfully through the stifling blackness. The thudding of the engine was painful, as though his own heart were trying to move the heavy platform.

The gleam came closer. Nothing moved around it. It was metal, reflecting the light from his torch. Martinson lit his own and brought it into play.

The truck stopped, and there was absolute silence except for the ticking of water on the floor of the tunnel.

"It's a rocket," Martinson whispered. His torch roved over the ridiculously inadequate tail empennage facing them. It was badly crumpled. "In fair shape, considering. At the clip he was going, he must have slammed back and forth like an alarm clapper."

Cautiously they got off the truck and prowled around the gleaming, badly dented spindle. There were clean shears where the wings had been, but the stubs still remained, as though the metal itself had given to the impact before the joints could. That meant welded construction throughout, McDonough remembered vaguely. The vessel rested now roughly in the center of the tunnel, and the railroad tracks had spraddled under its weight. The fuselage bore no identifying marks, except for a red star at the nose; or rather, a red asterisk.

Martinson's torch lingered over the star for a moment, but the adjutant offered no comment. He went around the nose, McDonough trailing.

On the other side of the ship was the death wound; a small, ragged tear in the metal, not far forward of the tail. Some of the raw curls of metal were partially melted. Martinson touched one.

"Flak," he muttered. "Cut his fuel lines. Lucky he didn't blow up."

"How do we get in?" McDonough said nervously. "The cabin didn't even crack. And we can't crawl through that hole."

Martinson thought about it. Then he bent to the lesion in the ship's skin, took a deep breath, and bellowed at the top of his voice:

"*Hey* in there! Open up!"

It took a long time for the echoes to die away. McDonough was paralyzed with pure fright. Anyone of those distorted, ominous rebounding voices could have been an answer. Finally, however, the silence came back.

"So he's dead," Martinson said practically. "I'll bet even his footbones are broken, every one of 'em. Mac, stick your hair net in there and see if you can pick up anything."

"N-not a chance. I can't get anything unless the electrodes are actually t-touching the skull."

"Try it anyhow, and then we can get out of here and let the experts take over. I've about made up my mind it's a missile, anyhow. With this little damage, it could still go off."

McDonough had been repressing that notion since his first sight of the spindle. The attempt to save the fuselage intact, the piloting skill involved, and the obvious cabin windshield all argued against it; but even the bare possibility was somehow twice as terrifying, here under a mountain, as it would have been in the open. With so enormous a mass

of rock pressing down on him, and the ravening energies of
a sun perhaps waiting to break loose by his side——

No, no; it was a fighter, and the pilot might somehow still
be alive. He almost ran to get the electrode net off the truck.
He dangled it on its cable inside the flak tear, pulled the
goggles over his eyes, and flicked the switch with his thumb.

The Walter goggles made the world inside the tunnel no
darker than it actually was, but knowing that he would now
be unable to see any gleam of light in the tunnel, should one
appear from somewhere—say, in the ultimate glare of
hydrogen fusion—increased the pressure of blackness on his
brain. Back on the truck the frequency-analyzer began its
regular, meaningless peeping, scanning the possible cortical
output bands in order of likelihood: First the 0.5 to 3.5
cycles/second band, the delta wave, the last activity of the
brain detectable before death; then the four to seven c.p.s.
theta channel, the pleasure-scanning waves which went on
even during sleep; the alpha rhythm, the visual scanner, at
eight to thirteen c.p.s.; the beta rhythms at fourteen to thirty
c.p.s. which mirror the tensions of conscious computation,
not far below the level of real thought; the gamma band,
where——

The goggles lit.

. . . And still the dazzling sky-blue sheep are grazing in the
red field under the rainbow-billed and pea-green birds. . . .

McDonough snatched the goggles up with a gasp, and
stared frantically into the blackness, now swimming with residual images in contrasting colors, melting gradually as the
rods and cones in his retina gave up the energy they had absorbed from the scene in the goggles. Curiously, he knew at
once where the voice had come from: it had been his mother's reading to him, on Christmas Eve, a story called "A
Child's Christmas in Wales." He had not thought of it in well
over two decades, but the scene in the toposcope goggles had
called it forth irresistibly.

"What's the matter?" Martinson's voice said. "Get anything? Are you sick?"

"No," McDonough muttered. "Nothing."

"Then let's beat it. Do you make a noise like that over
nothing every day? My Uncle Crosby did, but then, he had
asthma."

Tentatively, McDonough lowered the goggles again. The
scene came back, still in the same impossible colors, and
almost completely without motion. Now that he was able

to look at it again, however, he saw that the blue animals were not sheep; they were too large, and they had faces rather like those of kittens. Nor were the enormously slow-moving birds actually birds at all, except that they did seem to be flying—in unlikely straight lines, with slow, mathematically even flappings of unwinglike wings; there was something vegetable about them. The red field was only a dazzling blur, hazing the feet of the blue animals with the huge, innocent kitten's faces. As for the sky, it hardly seemed to be there at all; it was as white as paper.

"Come on," Martinson muttered, his voice edged with irritation. "What's the sense of staying in this hole any more? You bucking for pneumonia?"

"There's . . . something alive in there."

"Not a chance," Martinson said. His voice was noticeably more ragged. "You're dreaming. You said yourself you couldn't pick up——"

"I know what I'm doing," McDonough insisted, watching the scene in the goggles. "There's a live brain in there. Something nobody's ever hit before. It's powerful—no mind in the books ever put out a broadcast like this. It isn't human."

"All the more reason to call in the AF and quit. We can't get in there anyhow. What do you mean, it isn't human? It's a Red, that's all."

"No, it isn't," McDonough said evenly. Now that he thought he knew what they had found, he had stopped trembling. He was still terrified, but it was a different kind of terror: the fright of a man who has at last gotten a clear idea of what it is he is up against. "Human beings just don't broadcast like this. Especially not when they're near dying. And they don't remember huge blue sheep with cat's heads on them, or red grass, or a white sky. Not even if they come from the USSR. Whoever it is in there comes from some place else."

"You read too much. What about the star on the nose?"

McDonough drew a deep breath. "What about it?" he said steadily. "It isn't the insignia of the Red Air Force. I saw that it stopped you, too. No air force I ever heard of flies a red asterisk. It isn't a *cocarde* at all. It's just what it is."

"An asterisk?" Martinson said angrily.

"No, Marty, I think it's a star. A symbol for a *real* star. The AF's gone and knocked us down a spaceship." He pushed the goggles up and carefully withdrew the electrode net from the hole in the battered fuselage.

"And," he said carefully, "the pilot, whatever he is, is still alive—and thinking about home, wherever *that* is."

Though the Air Force had been duly notified by the radio net of McDonough's preposterous discovery, it took its own time about getting a technical crew over to Otisville. It had to, regardless of how much stock it took in the theory. The nearest source of advanced Air Force EEG equipment was just outside Newburgh, at Stewart Field, and it would have to be driven to Otisville by truck; no AF plane slow enough to duplicate Martinson's landing on the road could have handled the necessary payload.

For several hours, therefore, McDonough could do pretty much as he liked with his prize. After only a little urging, Martinson got the Erie dispatcher to send an oxyacetylene torch to the Port Jervis side of the tunnel, on board a Diesel camelback. Persons, who had subsequently arrived in the Aeronca, was all for trying it immediately in the tunnel, but McDonough was restrained by some dim memory of high school experiments with magnesium, a metal which looked very much like this. He persuaded the C.O. to try the torch on the smeared wings first.

The wings didn't burn. They carried the torch into the tunnel, and Persons got to work with it, enlarging the flak hole.

"Is that what-is-it still alive?" Persons asked, cutting steadily.

"I think so," McDonough said, his eyes averted from the tiny sun of the torch. "I've been sticking the electrodes in there about once every five minutes. I get essentially the same picture. But it's getting steadily weaker."

"D'you think we'll reach it before it dies?"

"I don't know. I'm not even sure I want to."

Persons thought that over, lifting the torch from the metal. Then he said, "You've got something there. Maybe I better try that gadget and see what I think."

"No," McDonough said. "It isn't tuned to you."

"Orders, Mac. Let me give it a try. Hand it over."

"It isn't that, Andy. I wouldn't buck you, you know that; you made this squadron. But it's dangerous. Do you want to have an epileptic fit? The chances are nine to five that you would."

"Oh," Persons said. "All right. It's your show." He resumed cutting.

After a while McDonough said, in a remote, emotionless voice: "That's enough. I think I can get through there now, as soon as it cools."

"Suppose there's no passage between the tail and the nose?" Martinson said. "More likely there's a firewall, and we'd never be able to cut through that."

"Probably," McDonough agreed. "We couldn't run the torch near the fuel tanks, anyhow, that's for sure."

"Then what good——"

"If these people think anything like we do, there's bound to be some kind of escape mechanism—something that blows the pilot's capsule free of the ship. I ought to be able to reach it."

"And fire it in *here?*" Persons said. "You'll smash the cabin against the tunnel roof. That'll kill the pilot for sure."

"Not if I disarm it. If I can get the charge out of it, all firing it will do is open the locking devices; then we can take the windshield off and get in. I'll pass the charge out back to you; handle it gently. Let me have your flashlight, Marty, mine's almost dead."

Silently, Martinson handed him the light. He hesitated a moment, listening to the water dripping in the background. Then, with a deep breath, he said, "Well. Here goes nothin'."

He clambered into the narrow opening.

The jungle of pipes, wires and pumps before him was utterly unfamiliar in detail, but familiar in principle. Human beings, given the job of setting up a rocket motor, set it up in this general way. McDonough probed with the light beam, looking for a passage large enough for him to wiggle through.

There didn't seem to be any such passage, but he squirmed his way forward regardless, forcing himself into any opening that presented itself, no matter how small and contorted it seemed. The feeling of entrapment was terrible. If he were to wind up in a cul-de-sac, he would never be able to worm himself backwards out of this jungle of piping . . .

He hit his head a sharp crack on a metal roof, and the metal resounded hollowly. A tank of some kind, empty, or nearly empty. Oxygen? No, unless the stuff had evaporated long ago; the skin of the tank was no colder than any of the other surfaces he had encountered. Propellant, perhaps, or compressed nitrogen—something like that.

Between the tank and what he took to be the inside of the hull, there was a low freeway, just high enough for him to squeeze through if he turned his head sideways. There were occasional supports and ganglions of wiring to be writhed around, but the going was a little better than it had been, back in the engine compartment. Then his head lifted into a slightly larger space, made of walls that curved gently against each other: the front of the tank, he guessed, opposed to the floor of the pilot's capsule and the belly of the hull. Between the capsule and the hull, up rather high, was the outside curve of a tube, large in diameter but very short; it was encrusted with motors, small pumps, and wiring.

An air lock? It certainly looked like one. If so, the trick with the escape mechanism might not have to be worked at all—if indeed the escape device existed.

Finding that he could raise his shoulders enough to rest on his elbows, he studied the wiring. The thickest of the cables emerged from the pilot's capsule; that should be the power line, ready to activate the whole business when the pilot hit the switch. If so, it could be shorted out—provided that there was still any juice in the batteries.

He managed to get the big nippers free of his belt, and dragged forward into a position where he could use them, with considerable straining. He closed their needlelike teeth around the cable and squeezed with all his might. The jaws closed slowly, and the cusps bit in.

There was a deep, surging hum, and all the pumps and motors began to whirr and throb. From back the way he had come, he heard a very muffled distant shout of astonishment.

He hooked the nippers back into his belt and inched forward, raising his back until he was almost curled into a ball. By careful, small movements, as though he were being born, he managed to somersault painfully in the cramped, curved space, and get his head and shoulders back under the tank again, face up this time. He had to trail the flashlight, so that his progress backwards through the utter darkness was as blind as a mole's; but he made it, at long last.

The tunnel, once he had tumbled out into it again, seemed miraculously spacious—almost like flying.

"The damn door opened right up, all by itself," Martinson was chattering. "Scared me green. What'd you do—say 'Open sesame' or something?"

"Yeah," McDonough said. He rescued his electrode net from the hand truck and went forward to the gaping air lock. The door had blocked most of the rest of the tunnel, but it was open wide enough.

It wasn't much of an air lock. As he had seen from inside, it was too short to hold a man; probably it had only been intended to moderate the pressure drop between inside and outside, not prevent such a drop absolutely. Only the outer door had the proper bank-vault heaviness of a true air lock. The inner one, open, was now nothing but a narrow ring of serrated blades, machined to a Johannson-block finish so fine that they were airtight by virtue of molecular cohesion alone—a highly perfected iris diaphragm. McDonough wondered vaguely how the pinpoint hole in the center of the diaphragm was plugged when the iris was fully closed, but his layman's knowledge of engineering failed him entirely there; he could come up with nothing better than a vision of the pilot plugging that hole with a wad of well-chewed bubble gum.

He sniffed the damp, cold, still air. Nothing. If the pilot had breathed anything alien to Earth-normal air, it had already dissipated without trace in the organ pipe of the tunnel. He flashed his light inside the cabin.

The instruments were smashed beyond hope, except for a few at the sides of the capsule. The pilot had smashed them —or rather, his environment had.

Before him in the light of the torch was a heavy, transparent tank of iridescent greenish-brown fluid, with a small figure floating inside it. It had been the tank, which had broken free of its moorings, which had smashed up the rest of the compartment. The pilot was completely enclosed in what looked like an ordinary G-suit, inside the oil; flexible hoses connected to bottles on the ceiling fed him his atmosphere, whatever it was. The hoses hadn't broken, but something inside the G-suit had; a line of tiny bubbles was rising from somewhere near the pilot's neck.

He pressed the EEG electrode net against the tank and looked into the Walter goggles. The sheep with the kitten's faces were still there, somewhat changed in position; but almost all of the color had washed out of the scene. McDonough grunted involuntarily. There was now an atmosphere about the picture which hit him like a blow, a feeling of intense oppression, of intense distress . . .

"Marty," he said hoarsely. "Let's see if we can't cut into that tank from the bottom somehow." He backed down into the tunnel.

"Why? If he's got internal injuries——"

"The suit's been breached. It's filling with that oil from the bottom. If we don't drain the tank, he'll drown first."

"All right. Still think he's a man-from-Mars, Mac?"

"I don't know. It's too small to be a man, you can see that. And the memories aren't like human memories. That's all I know. Can we drill the tank some place?"

"Don't need to," Persons' echo-distorted voice said from inside the air lock. The reflections of his flashlight shifted in the opening like ghosts. "I just found a drain pet cock. Roll up your trouser cuffs, gents."

But the oil didn't drain out of the ship. Evidently it went into storage somewhere inside the hull, to be pumped back into the pilot's cocoon when it was needed again.

It took a long time. The silence came flooding back into the tunnel.

"That oil-suspension trick is neat," Martinson whispered edgily. "Cushions him like a fish. He's got inertia still, but no mass—like a man in free fall."

McDonough fidgeted, but said nothing. He was trying to imagine what the multicolored vision of the pilot could mean. Something about it was nagging at him. It was wrong. Why would a still-conscious and gravely injured pilot be solely preoccupied with remembering the fields of home? Why wasn't he trying to save himself instead—as ingeniously as he had tried to save the ship? He still had electrical power, and in that litter of smashed apparatus which he alone could recognize, there must surely be expedients which still awaited his trial. But he had already given up, though he knew he was dying.

Or did he? The emotional aura suggested a knowledge of things desperately wrong, yet there was no real desperation, no frenzy, hardly any fear—almost as though the pilot did not know what death was, or, knowing it, was confident that it could not happen to him. The immensely powerful, dying mind inside the G-suit seemed curiously uncaring and passive, as though it awaited rescue with supreme confidence —so supreme that it could afford to drift, in an oil-suspended floating dream of home, nostalgic and unhappy, but not really afraid.

And yet it was dying!

"Almost empty," Andy Persons' quiet, garbled voice said into the tunnel.

Clenching his teeth, McDonough hitched himself into the air lock again and tried to tap the fading thoughts on a higher frequency. But there was simply nothing to hear or see, though with a brain so strong, there should have been, at as short a range as this. And it was peculiar, too, that the visual dream never changed. The flow of thoughts in a powerful human mind is bewilderingly rapid; it takes weeks of analysis by specialists before its essential pattern emerges. This mind, on the other hand, had been holding tenaciously to this one thought—complicated though it was—for a minimum of two hours. A truly subidiot performance—being broadcast with all the drive of a super genius.

Nothing in the cookbook provided McDonough with any precedent for it.

The suited figure was now slumped against the side of the empty tank, and the shades inside the toposcope goggles suddenly began to be distorted with regular, wrenching blurs: pain waves. A test at the level of the theta waves confirmed it; the unknown brain was responding to the pain with terrible knots of rage, real blasts of it, so strong and uncontrolled that McDonough could not endure them for more than a second. His hand was shaking so hard that he could hardly tune back to the gamma level again.

"We should have left the oil there," he whispered. "We've moved him too much. The internal injuries are going to kill him in a few minutes."

"We couldn't let him drown, you said so yourself," Persons said practically. "Look, there's a seam on this tank that looks like a torsion seal. If we break it, it ought to open up like a tired clam. Then we can get him out of here."

As he spoke, the empty tank parted into two shell-like halves. The pilot lay slumped and twisted at the bottom, like a doll, his suit glistening in the light of the C.O.'s torch.

"Help me. By the shoulders, real easy. That's it; lift. Easy, now."

Numbly, McDonough helped. It was true that the oil would have drowned the fragile, pitiful figure, but this was no help, either. The thing came up out of the cabin like a marionette with all its strings cut. Martinson cut the last of them: the flexible tubes which kept it connected to the ship. The three of them put it down, sprawling bonelessly.

. . . AND STILL THE DAZZLING SKY-BLUE SHEEP ARE GRAZING IN THE RED FIELD . . .

Just like that, McDonough saw it.

A coloring book!

That was what the scene was. That was why the colors

were wrong, and the size referents. Of course the sheeplike animals did not look much like sheep, which the pilot could never have seen except in pictures. Of course the sheep's heads looked like the heads of kittens; everyone has seen kittens. Of course the brain was powerful out of all proportion to its survival drive and its knowledge of death; it was the brain of a genius, but a genius without experience. And of course, *this* way, the USSR could get a rocket fighter to the United States on a one-way trip.

The helmet fell off the body, and rolled off into the gutter which carried away the water condensing on the wall of the tunnel. Martinson gasped, and then began to swear in a low, grinding monotone. Andy Persons said nothing, but his light, as he played it on the pilot's head, shook with fury.

McDonough, his fantasy of space ships exploded, went back to the hand truck and kicked his tomb-tapping apparatus into small shards and bent pieces. His whole heart was a fuming caldron of pity and grief. He would never knock upon another tomb again.

The blond head on the floor of the tunnel, dreaming its waning dream of a colored paper field, was that of a little girl, barely eight years old.

King of the Hill

IT DID Col. Hal Gascoigne no good whatsoever to know that he was the only man aboard Satellite Vehicle 1. No good at all. He had stopped reminding himself of the fact some time back.

And now, as he sat sweating in the perfectly balanced air in front of the bombardier board, one of the men spoke to him again:

"Colonel, sir——"

Gascoigne swung around in the seat, and the sergeant—Gascoigne could almost remember the man's name—threw him a snappy Air Force salute.

"Well?"

"Bomb one is primed, sir. Your orders?"

"My orders?" Gascoigne said wonderingly. But the man was already gone. Gascoigne couldn't actually *see* the sergeant leave the control cabin, but he was no longer in it.

While he tried to remember, another voice rang in the

cabin, as flat and razzy as all voices sound on an intercom.

"Radar room. On target."

A regular, meaningless peeping. The timing circuit had cut in.

Or had it? There was nobody in the radar room. There was nobody in the bomb hold, either. There had never been anybody on board SV-1 but Gascoigne, not since he had relieved Grinnell—and Grinnell had flown the station up here in the first place.

Then who had that sergeant been? His name was . . . It was . . .

The hammering of the teletype blanked it out. The noise was as loud as a pom-pom in the echoing metal cave. He got up and coasted across the deck to the machine, gliding in the gravity-free cabin with the ease of a man to whom free fall is almost second nature.

The teletype was silent by the time he reached it, and at first the tape looked blank. He wiped the sweat out of his eyes. There was the message.

MNBVCXZ LKJ HGFDS PYTR AOIU EUIO QPALZM

He got out his copy of *The Well-Tempered Pogo* and checked the speeches of Grundoon the Beaver-Chile for the key letter-sequence on which the code was based. There weren't very many choices. He had the clear in ten minutes.

BOMB ONE WASHINGTON 1700 HRS TAMMANÁNY

There it was. That was what he had been priming the bomb for. But there should have been earlier orders, giving him the go-ahead to prime. He began to rewind the paper.

It was all blank.

And—*Washington?* Why would the Joint Chiefs of Staff order him——

"Colonel Gascoigne, sir."

Gascoigne jerked around and returned the salute. "What's your name?" he snapped.

"Sweeney, sir," the corporal said. Actually it didn't sound very much like Sweeney, or like anything else; it was just a noise. Yet the man's face looked familiar. "Ready with bomb two, sir."

The corporal saluted, turned, took two steps, and faded. He did not vanish, but he did not go out the door, either. He simply receded, became darker and harder to distinguish, and was no longer there. It was as though he and Gascoigne had disagreed about the effects of perspective in the glowing Earthlight, and Gascoigne had turned out to be wrong.

Numbly, he finished rewinding the paper. There was no doubt about it. There the order stood, black on yellow, as plain as plain. Bomb the capital of your own country at 1700 hours. Just incidentally, bomb your own home in the process, but don't give that a second thought. Be thorough, drop two bombs; don't worry about missing by a few seconds of arc and hitting Baltimore instead, or Silver Spring, or Milford, Del. CIG will give you the coordinates, but plaster the area anyhow. That's S.O.P.

With rubbery fingers, Gascoigne began to work the keys of the teletype. Sending on the frequency of Civilian Intelligence Group, he typed:

HELP SHOUT SERIOUS REPEAT SERIOUS PERSONNEL TROUBLE HERE STOP DON'T KNOW HOW LONG I CAN KEEP IT DOWN STOP URGENT GASCOIGNE SV ONE STOP

Behind him, the oscillator peeped rhythmically, timing the drive on the launching rack trunnion.

"Radar room. On target."

Gascoigne did not turn. He sat before the bombardier board and sweated in the perfectly balanced air. Inside his skull, his own voice was shouting:

STOP   STOP   STOP

That, as we reconstructed it afterwards, is how the SV-1 affair began. It was pure luck, I suppose, that Gascoigne sent his message direct to us. Civilian Intelligence Group is rarely called into an emergency when the emergency is just being born. Usually Washington tries to do the bailing job first. Then, when Washington discovers that the boat is still sinking, it passes the bailing can to us—usually with a demand that we transform it into a centrifugal pump, on the double.

We don't mind. Washington's failure to develop a government department similar in function to CIG is the reason why we're in business. The profits, of course, go to Affiliated Enterprises, Inc., the loose corporation of universities and industries which put up the money to build ULTIMAC— and ULTIMAC is, in turn, the reason why Washington comes running to CIG so often.

This time, however, it did not look like the big computer was going to be of much use to us. I said as much to Joan Hadamard, our social sciences division chief, when I handed her the message.

"Um," she said. "*Personnel* trouble? What does he mean? He hasn't got any personnel on that station."

This was no news to me. CIG provided the figures that got the SV-1 into its orbit in the first place, and it was on our advice that it carried only one man. The crew of a space vessel either has to be large or it has to be a lone man; there is no intermediate choice. And SV-1 wasn't big enough to carry a large crew—not to carry them and keep the men from flying at each other's throats sooner or later, that is.

"He means himself," I said. "That's why I don't think this is a job for the computer. It's going to have to be played person-to-person. It's my bet that the man's responsibility-happy; that danger was always implicit in the one-man recommendation."

"The only decent solution is a full complement," Joan agreed. "Once the Pentagon can get enough money from Congress to build a big station."

"What puzzles me is, why did he call us instead of his superiors?"

"That's easy. We process his figures. He trusts us. The Pentagon thinks we're infallible, and he's caught the disease from them."

"That's bad," I said.

"I've never denied it."

"No, what I mean is that it's bad that he called us instead of going through channels. It means that the emergency is at least as bad as he says it is."

I thought about it another precious moment longer while Joan did some quick dialing. As everybody on Earth—with the possible exception of a few Tibetans—already knew, the man who rode SV-1 rode with three hydrogen bombs immediately under his feet—bombs which he could drop with great precision on any spot on the Earth. Gascoigne was, in effect, the sum total of American foreign policy; he might as well have had "Spatial Supremacy" stamped on his forehead.

"What does the Air Force say?" I asked Joan as she hung up.

"They say they're a little worried about Gascoigne. He's a very stable man, but they had to let him run a month over his normal replacement time—why, they don't explain. He's been turning in badly garbled reports over the last week. They're thinking about giving him a dressing down."

"Thinking! They'd better be careful with that stuff, or

they'll hurt themselves. Joan, somebody's going to have to go up there. I'll arrange fast transportation, and tell Gascoigne that help is coming. Who should go?"

"I don't have a recommendation," Joan said. "Better ask the computer."

I did so—on the double.

ULTIMAC said: *Harris.*

"Good luck, Peter," Joan said calmly. Too calmly.

"Yeah," I said. "Or good night."

Exactly what I expected to happen as the ferry rocket approached SV-1, I don't now recall. I had decided that I couldn't carry a squad with me. If Gascoigne was really far gone, he wouldn't allow a group of men to disembark; one man, on the other hand, he might pass. But I suppose I did expect him to put up an argument first.

Nothing happened. He did not challenge the ferry, and he didn't answer hails. Contact with the station was made through the radar automatics, and I was put off on board as routinely as though I was being let into a movie—but a lot more rapidly.

The control room was dark and confusing, and at first I didn't see Gascoigne anywhere. The Earthlight coming through the observation port was brilliant, but beyond the edges of its path the darkness was almost absolute, broken only by the little stars of indicator lenses.

A faint snicking sound turned my eyes in the right direction. There was Gascoigne. He was hunched over the bombardier board, his back to me. In one hand he held a small tool resembling a ticket punch. Its jaws were nibbling steadily at a taut line of tape running between two spools; that had been the sound I'd heard. I recognized the device without any trouble; it was a programmer.

But why hadn't Gascoigne heard me come in? I hadn't tried to sneak up on him, there is no quiet way to come through an air lock anyway. But the punch went on snicking steadily.

"Colonel Gascoigne," I said. There was no answer. I took a step forward. "Colonel Gascoigne, I'm Harris of CIG. What are you doing?"

The additional step did the trick. "Stay away from me," Gascoigne growled, from somewhere way down in his chest. "I'm programming the bomb. Punching in the orders myself. Can't depend on my crew. Stay away."

"Give over for a minute. I want to talk to you."

"That's a new one," said Gascoigne, not moving. "Most of you guys were rushing to set up lauchings before you even reported to me. Who the hell are you, anyhow? There's nobody on board, I know *that* well enough."

"I'm Peter Harris," I said. "From CIG—you called us, remember? You asked us to send help."

"Doesn't prove a thing. Tell me something I *don't* know. Then maybe I'll believe you exist. Otherwise—beat it."

"Nothing doing. Put down that punch."

Gascoigne straightened slowly and turned to look at me. "Well, you don't vanish, I'll give you that," he said. "What did you say your name was?"

"Harris. Here's my ID card."

Gascoigne took the plastic-coated card tentatively, and then removed his glasses and polished them. The gesture itself was perfectly ordinary, and wouldn't have surprised me—except that Gascoigne was not wearing glasses.

"It's hard to see in here," he complained. "Everything gets so steamed up. Hm. All right, you're real. What do you want?"

His finger touched a journal. Silently, the tape began to roll from one spool to another.

"Gascoigne, stop that thing. If you drop any bombs there'll be hell to pay. It's tense enough down below as it is. And there's no reason to bomb anybody."

"Plenty of reason," Gascoigne muttered. He turned toward the teletype, exposing to me for the first time a hip holster cradling a large, black automatic. I didn't doubt that he could draw it with fabulous rapidity, and put the bullets just where he wanted them to go. "I've got orders. There they are. See for yourself."

Cautiously, I sidled over to the teletype and looked. Except for Gascoigne's own message to CIG, and one from Joan Hadamard announcing that I was on my way, the paper was totally blank. There had been no other messages that day unless Gascoigne had changed the roll, and there was no reason why he should have. Those rolls last close to forever.

"When did this order come in?"

"This morning some time. I don't know. Sweeney!" he bawled suddenly, so loud that the paper tore in my hands. "When did that drop order come through?"

Nobody answered. But Gascoigne said almost at once, "There, you heard him."

"I didn't hear anything but you," I said, "and I'm going to stop that tape. Stand aside."

"Not a chance, Mister," Gascoigne said grimly. "The tape rides."

"Who's getting hit?"

"Washington," Gascoigne said, and passed his hand over his face. He appeared to have forgotten the imaginary spectacles.

"That's where your home is, isn't it?"

"It sure is," Gascoigne said. "It sure as hell is, Mister. Cute, isn't it?"

It was cute, all right. The Air Force boys at the Pentagon were going to be given about ten milliseconds to be sorry they'd refused to send a replacement for Gascoigne along with me. *Replace him with who? We can't send his second alternate in anything short of a week. The man has to have retraining, and the first alternate's in the hospital with a ruptured spleen. Besides, Gascoigne's the best man for the job; he's got to be bailed out somehow.*

Sure. With a psychological centrifugal pump, no doubt. In the meantime the tape kept right on running.

"You might as well stop wiping your face, and turn down the humidity instead," I said. "You've already smudged your glasses again."

"Glasses?" Gascoigne muttered. He moved slowly across the cabin, sailing upright like a sea horse, to the blank glass of a closed port. I seriously doubted that he could see his reflection in it, but maybe he didn't really want to see it. "I messed them up, all right. Thanks." He went through the polishing routine again.

A man who thinks he is wearing glasses also thinks he can't see without them. I slid to the programmer and turned off the tape. I was between the spools and Gascoigne now —but I couldn't stay there forever.

"Let's talk a minute, Colonel," I said. "Surely it can't do any harm."

Gascoigne smiled, with a sort of childish craft. "I'll talk," he said. "Just as soon as you start that tape again. I was watching you in the mirror, *before* I took my glasses off."

The liar. I hadn't made a move while he'd been looking into that porthole. His poor pitiful weak old rheumy eyes had seen every move I made while he was polishing his "glasses." I shrugged and stepped away from the programmer.

"You start it," I said. "I won't take the responsibiltiy."

"It's orders," Gascoigne said woodenly. He started the tape running again. "It's their responsibility. What did you want to talk to me about, anyhow?"

"Colonel Gascoigne, have you ever killed anybody?"

He looked startled. "Yes, once I did," he said, almost eagerly. "I crashed a plane into a house. Killed the whole family. Walked away with nothing worse than a burned leg—good as new after a couple of muscle stabilizations. That's what made me shift from piloting to weapons; that leg's not quite good enough to fly with any more."

"Tough."

He snickered suddenly, explosively. "And now look at me," he said. "I'm going to kill my *own* family in a little while. And millions of other people. Maybe the whole world."

How long was "a little while"?

"What have you got against it?" I said.

"Against what—the world? Nothing. Not a damn thing. Look at me; I'm king of the hill up here. I can't complain."

He paused and licked his lips. "It was different when I was a kid," he said. "Not so dull, then. In those days you could get a real newspaper, that you could unfold for the first time yourself, and pick out what you wanted to read. Not like now, when the news comes to you predigested on a piece of paper out of your radio. That's what's the matter with it, if you ask me."

"What's the matter with what?"

"With the news—that's why it's always bad these days. Everything's had something done to it. The milk is homogenized, the bread is sliced, the cars steer themselves, the phonographs will produce sounds no musical instrument could make. Too much meddling, too many people who can't keep their hands off things. Ever fire a kiln?"

"Me?" I said, startled.

"No, I didn't think so. Nobody makes pottery these days. Not by hand. And if they did, who'd buy it? They don't want something that's been made. They want something that's been Done To."

The tape kept on traveling. Down below, there was a heavy rumble, difficult to identify specifically: something heavy being shifted on tracks, or maybe a freight lock opening.

"So now you're going to Do Something to the Earth," I said slowly.

"Not me. It's orders."

"Orders from inside, Colonel Gascoigne. There's nothing on the spools." What else could I do? I didn't have time to take him through two years of psychoanalysis and bring him to his own insight. Besides, I'm not licensed to practice medicine—not on Earth. "I didn't want to say so, but I have to now."

"Say what?" Gascoigne said suspiciously. "That I'm crazy or something?"

"No. I didn't say that. You did," I pointed out. "But I will tell you that that stuff about not liking the world these days is baloney. Or rationalization, if you want a nicer word. You're carrying a screaming load of guilt, Colonel, whether you're aware of it or not."

"I don't know what you're talking about. Why don't you just beat it?"

"No. And you know well enough. You fell all over yourself to tell me about the family you killed in your flying accident." I gave him ten seconds of silence, and then shot the question at him as hard as I could. "*What was their name?*"

"How do I know? Sweeney or something. Anything. I don't remember."

"Sure you do. Do you think that killing your own family is going to bring the Sweeneys back to life?"

Gascoigne's mouth twisted, but he seemed to be entirely unaware of the grimace. "That's all hogwash," he said. "I never did hold with that psychological claptrap. It's you that's handing out the baloney, not me."

"Then why are you being so vituperative about it? Hogwash, claptrap, baloney—you are working awfully hard to knock it down, for a man who doesn't believe in it."

"Go away," he said sullenly. "I've got my orders. I'm obeying them."

Stalemate. But there was no such thing as stalemate up here. Defeat was the word.

The tape traveled. I did not know what to do. The last bomb problem CIG had tackled had been one we had set up ourselves; we had arranged for a dud to be dropped in New York harbor, to test our own facilities for speed in determining the nature of the missile. The situation on board SV-1 was completely different——

Whoa. Was it? Maybe I'd hit something there.

"Colonel Gascoigne," I said slowly, "you might as well know now that it isn't going to work. Not even if you do get that bomb off."

"Yes, I can. What's to stop me?" He hooked one thumb in his belt, just above the holster, so that his fingers tips rested on the breech of the automatic.

"Your bombs. They aren't alive."

Gascoigne laughed harshly and waved at the controls. "Tell that to the counter in the bomb hold. Go ahead. There's a meter you can read, right there on the bombardier board."

"Sure," I said. "The bombs are radioactive, all right. Have you ever checked their half life?"

It was a long shot. Gascoigne was a weapons man; if it were possible to check half life on board the SV-1, he would have checked it. But I didn't think it was possible.

"What would I do that for?"

"You wouldn't, being a loyal airman. You believe what your superiors tell you. But I'm a civilian, Colonel. There's no element in those bombs that will either fuse or fission. The half life is too long for tritium or for lithium 6, and it's too short for uranium 235 or radio-thorium. The stuff is probably strontium 90—in short, nothing but a bluff."

"By the time I finished checking that," Gascoigne said, "the bomb would be launched anyhow. And you haven't checked it, either. Try another tack."

"I don't need to. You don't have to believe me. We'll just sit here and wait for the bomb drop, and then the point will prove itself. After that, of course, you'll be court-martialed for firing a wild shot without orders. But since you're prepared to wipe out your own family, you won't mind a little thing like twenty years in the guardhouse."

Gascoigne looked at the silently rolling tape. "Sure," he said, "I've got the orders, anyhow. The same thing would happen if I didn't obey them. If nobody gets hurt, so much the better."

A sudden spasm of emotion—I took it to be grief, but I could have been wrong—shook his whole frame for a moment. Again, he did not seem to notice it. I said:

"That's right. Not even your family. Of course the whole

world will know the station's a bluff, but if those are the orders——"

"I don't know," Gascoigne said harshly. "I don't know whether I even got any orders. I don't remember where I put them. Maybe they're not real." He looked at me confusedly, and his expression was frighteningly like that of a small boy making a confession.

"You know something?" he said. "I don't know what's real any more. I haven't been able to tell, ever since yesterday. I don't even know if you are real, or your ID card either. What do you think of that?"

"Nothing," I said.

"Nothing! Nothing! That's my trouble. Nothing! I can't tell what's nothing and what's something. You say the bombs are duds. All right. But what if *you're* the dud, and the bombs are real? Answer me that!"

His expression was almost triumphant now.

"The bombs are duds," I said. "And you've gone and steamed up your glasses again. Why don't you turn down the humidity, so you can see for three minutes hand running?"

Gascoigne leaned far forward, so far that he was perilously close to toppling, and peered directly into my face.

"Don't give me that," he said hoarsely. "Don't—give—me that—stuff."

I froze right where I was. Gascoigne watched my eyes for a while. Then, slowly, he put his hand on his forehead and began to wipe it downward. He smeared it over his face, in slow motion, all the way down to his chin.

Then he took the hand away and looked at it, as though it had just strangled him and he couldn't understand why. And finally he spoke.

"It—isn't true," he said dully. "I'm not wearing any glasses. Haven't worn glasses since I was ten. Not since I broke my last pair—playing King of the Hill."

He sat down before the bombardier board and put his head in his hands.

"You win," he said hoarsely. "I must be crazy as a loon. I don't know what I'm seeing and what I'm not. You better take this gun away. If I fired it I might even hit something."

"You're all right," I said. And I meant it; but I didn't waste any time all the same. The automatic first; then the tape. In that order, the sequence couldn't be reversed afterwards.

But the sound of the programmer's journal clicking to "Off" was as loud in that cabin as any gunshot.

"He'll be all right," I told Joan afterwards. "He pulled himself through. I wouldn't have dared to throw it at any other man that fast—but he's got guts."

"Just the same," Joan said, "they'd better start rotating the station captains faster. The next man may not be so tough—and what if *he's* a sleepwalker?"

I didn't say anything. I'd had my share of worries for that week.

"You did a whale of a job yourself, Peter," Joan said. "I just wish we could bank it in the machine. We might need the data later."

"Well, why can't we?"

"The Joint Chiefs of Staff say no. They don't say why. But they don't want any part of it recorded in ULTIMAC —or anywhere else."

I stared at her. At first it didn't seem to make sense. And then it did—and that was worse.

"Wait a minute," I said. "Joan—does that mean what I think it means? Is 'Spatial Supremacy' just as bankrupt as 'Massive Retaliation' was? Is it possible that the satellite— and the bombs . . . Is it possible that I was telling Gascoigne the truth about the bombs being duds?"

Joan shrugged.

"He that darkeneth counsel without wisdom," she said, "isn't earning his salary."

Common Time

". . . the days went slowly round and round, endless and uneventful as cycles in space. Time, and time-pieces! How many centuries did my hammock tell, as pendulum- like it swung to the ship's dull roll, and ticked the hours and ages."

—Herman Melville, in *Mardi*

Don't move.

It was the first thought that came into Garrard's mind when he awoke, and perhaps it saved his life. He lay where he was, strapped against the padding, listening to the round

hum of the engines. That in itself was wrong; he should be
unable to hear the overdrive at all.

He thought to himself: *Has it begun already?*

Otherwise everything seemed normal. The DFC-3 had
crossed over into interstellar velocity, and he was still alive,
and the ship was still functioning. The ship should at this
moment be traveling at 22.4 times the speed of light—a neat
4,157,000 miles per second.

Somehow Garrard did not doubt that it was. On both
previous tries, the ships had whiffed away toward Alpha Centauri at the proper moment when the overdrive should have
cut in; and the split second of residual image after they had
vanished, subjected to spectroscopy, showed a Doppler shift
which tallied with the acceleration predicted for that moment
by Haertel.

The trouble was not that Brown and Cellini hadn't gotten
away in good order. It was simply that neither of them had
ever been heard from again.

Very slowly, he opened his eyes. His eyelids felt terrifically
heavy. As far as he could judge from the pressure of the
couch against his skin, the gravity was normal; nevertheless,
moving his eyelids seemed almost an impossible job.

After long concentration, he got them fully open. The
instrument chassis was directly before him, extended over his
diaphragm on its elbow joint. Still without moving anything
but his eyes—and those only with the utmost patience—he
checked each of the meters. Velocity: 22.4 c. Operating temperature: normal. Ship temperature: 37° C. Air pressure:
778 mm. Fuel: No. 1 tank full, No. 2 tank full, No. 3 tank
full, No. 4 tank nine tenths full. Gravity: 1 g. Calendar:
stopped.

He looked at it closely, though his eyes seemed to focus
very slowly, too. It was, of course, something more than a
calendar—it was an all-purpose clock, designed to show him
the passage of seconds, as well as of the ten months his trip
was supposed to take to the double star. But there was no
doubt about it: the second hand was motionless.

That was the second abnormality. Garrard felt an impulse
to get up and see if he could start the clock again. Perhaps
the trouble had been temporary and safely in the past. Immediately there sounded in his head the injunction he had
drilled into himself for a full month before the trip had
begun—

Don't move!

Don't move until you know the situation as far as it can be known without moving. Whatever it was that had snatched Brown and Cellini irretrievably beyond human ken was potent, and totally beyond anticipation. They had both been excellent men, intelligent, resourceful, trained to the point of diminishing returns and not a micron beyond that point—the best men in the Project. Preparations for every knowable kind of trouble had been built into their ships, as they had been built into the DFC-3. Therefore, if there was something wrong nevertheless, it would be something that might strike from some commonplace quarter—and strike only once.

He listened to the humming. It was even and placid, and not very loud, but it disturbed him deeply. The overdrive was supposed to be inaudible, and the tapes from the first unmanned test vehicles had recorded no such hum. The noise did not appear to interfere with the overdrive's operation, or to indicate any failure in it. It was just an irrelevancy for which he could find no reason.

But the reason existed. Garrard did not intend to do so much as draw another breath until he found out what it was.

Incredibly, he realized for the first time that he had not in fact drawn one single breath since he had first come to. Though he felt not the slightest discomfort, the discovery called up so overwhelming a flash of panic that he very nearly sat bolt upright on the couch. Luckily—or so it seemed, after the panic had begun to ebb—the curious lethargy which had affected his eyelids appeared to involve his whole body, for the impulse was gone before he could summon the energy to answer it. And the panic, poignant though it had been for an instant, turned out to be wholly intellectual. In a moment, he was observing that his failure to breathe in no way discommoded him as far as he could tell —it was just there, waiting to be explained . . .

Or to kill him. But it hadn't, yet.

Engines humming; eyelids heavy; breathing absent; calendar stopped. The four facts added up to nothing. The temptation to move something—even if it were only a big toe—was strong, but Garrard fought it back. He had been awake only a short while—half an hour at most—and already had noticed four abnormalities. There were bound to be more, anomalies more subtle than these four; but available to close examination before he had to move. Nor was there anything in particular that he had to do, aside from caring for his own wants; the Project, on the chance that Brown's and Cellini's failure to return had resulted from some tampering with the overdrive, had made everything in the DFC-3 subject only to the computer. In a very real sense, Garrard was just along for the ride. Only when the overdrive was off could he adjust——

Pock.

It was a soft, low-pitched noise, rather like a cork coming out of a wine bottle. It seemed to have come just from the right of the control chassis. He halted a sudden jerk of his head on the cushions toward it with a flat fiat of will. Slowly, he moved his eyes in that direction.

He could see nothing that might have caused the sound. The ship's temperature dial showed no change, which ruled out a heat noise from differential contraction or expansion—the only possible explanation he could bring to mind.

He closed his eyes—a process which turned out to be just as difficult as opening them had been—and tried to visualize what the calendar had looked like when he had first come out of anesthesia. After he got a clear and—he was almost sure—accurate picture, Garrard opened his eyes again.

The sound had been the calendar, advancing one second. It was now motionless again, apparently stopped.

He did not know how long it took the second hand to make that jump, normally; the question had never come up. Certainly the jump, when it came at the end of each second, had been too fast for the eye to follow.

Belatedly, he realized what all this cogitation was costing him in terms of essential information. The calendar had moved. Above all and before anything else, he *must* know exactly how long it took it to move again . . .

He began to count, allowing an arbitrary five seconds lost. *One-and-a-six, one-and-a-seven, one-and-an-eight*——

Garrard had gotten only that far when he found himself plunged into hell.

First, and utterly without reason, a sickening fear flooded swiftly through his veins, becoming more and more intense. His bowels began to knot, with infinite slowness. His whole body became a field of small, slow pulses—not so much shaking him as putting his limbs into contrary joggling motions, and making his skin ripple gently under his clothing. Against the hum another sound became audible, a nearly subsonic thunder which seemed to be inside his head. Still the fear mounted, and with it came the pain, and the tenesmus—a boardlike stiffening of his muscles, particularly across his abdomen and his shoulders, but affecting his forearms almost as grievously. He felt himself beginning, very gradually, to double at the middle, a motion about which he could do precisely nothing—a terrifying kind of dynamic paralysis. . . .

It lasted for hours. At the height of it, Garrard's mind, even his very personality, was washed out utterly; he was only a vessel of horror. When some few trickles of reason began to return over that burning desert of reasonless emotion, he found that he was sitting up on the cushions, and that with one arm he had thrust the control chassis back on its elbow so that it no longer jutted over his body. His clothing was wet with perspiration, which stubbornly refused to evaporate or to cool him. And his lungs ached a little, although he could still detect no breathing.

What under God had happened? Was it this that had killed Brown and Cellini? For it would kill Garrard, too—of that he was sure, if it happened often. It would kill him even if it happened only twice more, if the next two such things followed the first one closely. At the very best it would make a slobbering idiot of him; and though the computer might bring Garrard and the ship back to Earth, it would not be able to tell the Project about this tornado of senseless fear.

The calendar said that the eternity in hell had taken three seconds. As he looked at it in academic indignation, it said *pock* and condescended to make the total seizure four seconds long. With grim determination, Garrard began to count again.

He took care to establish the counting as an absolutely even, automatic process which would not stop at the back of his mind no matter what other problem he tackled along with it, or what emotional typhoons should interrupt him. Really compulsive counting cannot be stopped by anything—not the transports of love nor the agonies of empires. Garrard knew the dangers in deliberately setting up such a mechanism in his mind, but he also knew how desperately he needed to time that clock tick. He was beginning to understand what had happened to him—but he needed exact measurement before he could put that understanding to use.

Of course there had been plenty of speculation on the possible effect of the overdrive on the subjective time of the pilot, but none of it had come to much. At any speed below the velocity of light, subjective and objective time were exactly the same as far as the pilot was concerned. For an observer on Earth, time aboard the ship would appear to be vastly slowed at near-light speeds; but for the pilot himself there would be no apparent change.

Since flight beyond the speed of light was impossible—although for slightly differing reasons—by both the current theories of relativity, neither theory had offered any clue as to what would happen on board a translight ship. They would not allow that any such ship could even exist. The Haertel transformation, on which, in effect, the DFC-3 flew, was nonrelativistic: it showed that the apparent elapsed time of a translight journey should be identical in ship-time, and in the time of observers at both ends of the trip.

But since ship and pilot were part of the same system, both covered by the same expression in Haertel's equation, it had never occurred to anyone that the pilot and the ship might keep different times. The notion was ridiculous.

One-and-a-sevenhundredone, one-and-a-sevenhundredtwo, one - and - a - sevenhundredthree, one - and - a - sevenhundred four . . .

The ship was keeping ship-time, which was identical with observer-time. It would arrive at the Alpha Centauri system in ten months. But the pilot was keeping Garrard-time, and it was beginning to look as though he wasn't going to arrive at all.

It was impossible, but there it was. Something—almost certainly an unsuspected physiological side effect of the overdrive field on human metabolism, an effect which naturally could not have been detected in the preliminary, robot-piloted tests of the overdrive—had speeded up Garrard's subjective apprehension of time, and had done a thorough job of it.

The second hand began a slow, preliminary quivering as the calendar's innards began to apply power to it. *Seventy-hundred-forty-one, seventy-hundred-forty-two, seventy-hundred-forty-three . . .*

At the count of 7,058 the second hand began the jump to the next graduation. It took it several apparent minutes to get across the tiny distance, and several more to come completely to rest. Later still, the sound came to him:

pock.

In a fever of thought, but without any real physical agitation, his mind began to manipulate the figures. Since it took him longer to count an individual number as the number became larger, the interval between the two calendar ticks probably was closer to 7,200 seconds than to 7,058. Figuring backward brought him quickly to the equivalence he wanted:

One second in ship-time was two hours in Garrard-time.

Had he really been counting for what was, for him, two whole hours? There seemed to be no doubt about it. It looked like a long trip ahead.

Just how long it was going to be struck him with stunning force. Time had been slowed for him by a factor of 7200. He would get to Alpha Centauri in just 72,000 months.

Which was—

Six thousand years!

2

Garrard sat motionless for a long time after that, the Nessus-shirt of warm sweat swathing him persistently, refusing even to cool. There was, after all, no hurry.

Six thousand years. There would be food and water and air for all that time, or for sixty or six hundred thousand years; the ship would synthesize his needs, as a matter of course, for as long as the fuel lasted, and the fuel bred itself. Even if Garrard ate a meal every three seconds of objective, or ship, time (which, he realized suddenly, he wouldn't be able to do, for it took the ship several seconds of objective time to prepare and serve up a meal once it was ordered; he'd be lucky if he ate once a day, Garrard-time), there would be no reason to fear any shortage of supplies. That had been one of the earliest of the possibilities for disaster that the Project engineers had ruled out in the design of the DFC-3.

But nobody had thought to provide a mechanism which would indefinitely refurbish Garrard. After six thousand years, there would be nothing left of him but a faint film of dust on the DFC-3's dully gleaming horizontal surfaces. His corpse might outlast him a while, since the ship itself was sterile—but eventually he would be consumed by the bacteria which he carried in his own digestive tract. He needed those bacteria to synthesize part of his B-vitamin needs while he lived, but they would consume him without compunction once he had ceased to be as complicated and delicately balanced a thing as a pilot—or as any other kind of life.

Garrard was, in short, to die before the DFC-3 had gotten fairly away from Sol; and when, after 12,000 apparent years, the DFC-3 returned to Earth, not even his mummy would be still aboard.

The chill that went through him at that seemed almost unrelated to the way he thought he felt about the discovery; it lasted an enormously long time, and insofar as he could characterize it at all, it seemed to be a chill of urgency and excitement—not at all the kind of chill he should be feeling at a virtual death sentence. Luckily it was not as intolerably violent as the last such emotional convulsion; and when it was over, two clock ticks later, it left behind a residuum of doubt.

Suppose that this effect of time-stretching was only mental? The rest of his bodily processes might still be keeping ship-time; Garrard had no immediate reason to believe otherwise. If so, he would be able to move about only on ship-time, too; it would take many apparent months to complete the simplest task.

But he would live, if that were the case. His mind would arrive at Alpha Centauri six thousand years older, and perhaps madder, than his body, but he would live.

If, on the other hand, his bodily movements were going to be as fast as his mental processes, he would have to be enormously careful. He would have to move slowly and exert as little force as possible. The normal human hand movement, in such a task as lifting a pencil, took the pencil from a state of rest to another state of rest by imparting to it an acceleration of about two feet per second per second—and, of course, decelerated it by the same amount. If Garrard were to attempt to impart to a two-pound weight, which was keeping ship-time, an acceleration of $14,440$ ft/sec^2 in his time, he'd have to exert a force of 900 pounds on it.

The point was not that it couldn't be done—but that it would take as much effort as pushing a stalled jeep. He'd never be able to lift that pencil with his forearm muscles alone; he'd have to put his back into the task.

And the human body wasn't engineered to maintain stresses of that magnitude indefinitely. Not even the most powerful professional weight-lifter is forced to show his prowess throughout every minute of every day.

Pock.

That was the calendar again; another second had gone by. Or another two hours. It had certainly seemed longer than a second, but less than two hours, too. Evidently subjective time was an intensively recomplicated measure. Even in this world of micro-time—in which Garrard's mind, at least, seemed to be operating—he could make the lapses between calendar ticks seem a little shorter by becoming actively interested in some problem or other. That would help, during the waking hours, but it would help only if the rest of his body were *not* keeping the same time as his mind. If it were not, then he would lead an incredibly active, but perhaps not intolerable, mental life during the many centuries of his awake-time, and would be mercifully asleep for nearly as long.

Both problems—that of how much force he could exert with his body, and how long he could hope to be asleep in his mind—emerged simultaneously into the forefront of his consciousness while he still sat inertly on the hammock, their terms still much muddled together. After the single tick of the calendar, the ship—or the part of it that Garrard could see from here—settled back into complete rigidity. The sound of the engines, too, did not seem to vary in frequency or amplitude, at least as far as his ears could tell. He was still not breathing. Nothing moved, nothing changed.

It was the fact that he could still detect no motion of his diaphragm or his rib cage that decided him at last. His body had to be keeping ship-time, otherwise he would have blacked out from oxygen starvation long before now. That assumption explained, too, those two incredibly prolonged, seemingly sourceless saturnalias of emotion through which he had suffered: they had been nothing more nor less than the response of his endocrine glands to the purely intellectual reactions he had experienced earlier. He had discovered that he was not breathing, had felt a flash of panic and had tried to sit up. Long after his mind had forgotten those two impulses, they had inched their way from his brain down his nerves to the glands and muscles involved, and actual, *physical* panic had supervened. When that was over, he actually *was* sitting up, though the flood of adrenalin had prevented his noticing the motion as he had made it. The later chill—less violent, and apparently associated with the discovery that he might die long before the trip was completed—actually had been his body's response to a much earlier mental command—the abstract fever of interest he had felt while computing the time differential had been responsible for it.

Obviously, he was going to have to be very careful with apparently cold and intellectual impulses of any kind—or he would pay for them later with a prolonged and agonizing glandular reaction. Nevertheless, the discovery gave him considerable satisfaction, and Garrard allowed it free play; it certainly could not hurt him to feel pleased for a few hours, and the glandular pleasure might even prove helpful if it caught him at a moment of mental depression. Six thousand years, after all, provided a considerable number of opportunities for feeling down in the mouth; so it would be best to encourage all pleasure moments, and let the after-reaction last as long as it might. It would be the instants of panic, of fear, of gloom, which he would have to regulate sternly the moment they came into his mind; it would be those which would otherwise plunge him into four, five, six, perhaps even ten, Garrard-hours of emotional inferno.

Pock.

There now, that was very good: there had been two Garrard-hours which he had passed with virtually no difficulty of any kind, and without being especially conscious of their passage. If he could really settle down and become used to this kind of scheduling, the trip might not be as bad as he had at first feared. Sleep would take immense bites out of it; and during the waking periods he could put in one hell of a lot of creative thinking. During a single day of ship time, Garrard could get in more thinking than any philosopher of Earth could have managed during an entire lifetime. Garrard could, if he disciplined himself sufficiently, devote his mind for a century to running down the consequences of a single thought, down to the last detail, and still have millennia left to go on to the next thought. What panoplies of pure reason could he not have assembled by the time 6,000 years had gone by? With sufficient concentration, he might come up with the solution to the Problem of Evil between breakfast and dinner of a single ship's day, and in a ship's month might put his finger on the First Cause!

Pock.

Not that Garrard was sanguine enough to expect that he would remain logical or even sane throughout the trip. The vista was still grim, in much of its detail. But the opportunities, too, were there. He felt a momentary regret that it hadn't been Haertel, rather than himself, who had been given such an opportunity—

Pock.

—for the old man could certainly have made better use of it than Garrard could. The situation demanded someone trained in the highest rigors of mathematics to be put to the best conceivable use. Still and all Garrard began to feel—

Pock.

—that he would give a good account of himself, and it tickled him to realize that (as long as he held onto his essential sanity) he would return—

Pock.

—to Earth after ten Earth months with knowledge centuries advanced beyond anything—

Pock.

—that Haertel knew, or that anyone could know—

Pock.

—who had to work within a normal lifetime. *Pck.* The whole prospect tickled him. *Pck.* Even the clock tick seemed more cheerful. *Pck.* He felt fairly safe now *Pck* in disregarding his drilled-in command *Pck* against moving *Pck*, since in any *Pck* event he *Pck* had already *Pck* moved *Pck* without *Pck* being *Pck* harmed *Pck* Pck Pck Pck Pck *pckpckpckpckpckpckpck.* . . .

He yawned, stretched, and got up. It wouldn't do to be too pleased, after all. There were certainly many problems that still needed coping with, such as how to keep the impulse toward getting a ship-time task performed going, while his higher centers were following the ramifications of some purely philosophical point. And besides . . .

And besides, he had just moved.

More than that; he had just performed a complicated maneuver with his body *in normal time!*

Before Garrard looked at the calendar itself, the message it had been ticking away at him had penetrated. While he had been enjoying the protracted, glandular backwash of his earlier feeling of satisfaction, he had failed to notice, at least consciously, that the calendar was accelerating.

Good-bye, vast ethical systems which would dwarf the Greeks. Good-bye, calculuses aeons advanced beyond the spinor calculus of Dirac. Good-bye, cosmologies by Garrard which would allot the Almighty a job as third-assistant-waterboy in an *n*-dimensional backfield.

Good-bye, also, to a project he had once tried to undertake in college—to describe and count the positions of love, of which, according to under-the-counter myth, there were supposed to be at least forty eight. Garrard had never been able to carry his tally beyond twenty, and he had just lost what was probably his last opportunity to try again.

The micro-time in which he had been living had worn off, only a few objective minutes after the ship had gone into overdrive and he had come out of the anesthetic. The long intellectual agony, with its glandular counterpoint, had come to nothing. Garrard was now keeping ship-time.

Garrard sat back down on the hammock, uncertain whether to be bitter or relieved. Neither emotion satisfied him in the end; he simply felt unsatisfied. Micro-time had been bad enough while it lasted; but now it was gone, and everything seemed normal. How could so transient a thing have killed Brown and Cellini? They were stable men, more stable, by his own private estimation, than Garrard himself. Yet he had come through it. Was there more to it than this?

And if there was—what, conceivably, could it be?

There was no answer. At his elbow, on the control chassis which he had thrust aside during that first moment of infinitely protracted panic, the calendar continued to tick. The engine noise was gone. His breath came and went in natural rhythm. He felt light and strong. The ship was quiet, calm, unchanging.

The calendar ticked, faster and faster. It reached and passed the first hour, ship-time, of flight in overdrive.

Pock.

Garrard looked up in surprise. The familiar noise, this time, had been the hour-hand jumping one unit. The minute-hand was already sweeping past the past half-hour. The second-hand was whirling like a propellor—and while he watched it, it speeded up to complete invisibility—

Pock.

Another hour. The half-hour already passed. *Pock.* Another hour. *Pock.* Another. *Pock. Pock. Pock, Pock, Pock, Pock, pck-pck-pck-pck-pckpckpckpck.* . . .

The hands of the calendar swirled toward invisibility as time ran away with Garrard. Yet the ship did not change. It stayed there, rigid, inviolate, invulnerable. When the date tumblers reached a speed at which Garrard could no longer read them, he discovered that once more he could not move —and that, although his whole body seemed to be aflutter like that of a hummingbird, nothing coherent was coming to him through his senses. The room was dimming, becoming redder; or no, it was . . .

But he never saw the end of the process, never was

allowed to look from the pinnacle of macro-time toward which the Haertel overdrive was taking him.

Pseudo-death took him first.

3

That Garrard did not die completely, and within a comparatively short time after the DFC-3 had gone into overdrive, was due to the purest of accidents; but Garrard did not know that. In fact, he knew nothing at all for an indefinite period, sitting rigid and staring, his metabolism slowed down to next to nothing, his mind almost utterly inactive. From time to time, a single wave of low-level metabolic activity passed through him—what an electrician might have termed a "maintenance turnover"—in response to the urgings of some occult survival urge; but these were of so basic a nature as to reach his consciousness not at all. This was the pseudo-death.

When the observer actually arrived, however, Garrard woke. He could make very little sense out of what he saw or felt even now; but one fact was clear: the overdrive was off—and with it the crazy alterations in time rates—and there was strong light coming through one of the ports. The first leg of the trip was over. It had been these two changes in his environment which had restored him to life.

The thing (or things) which had restored him to consciousness, however, was—it was what? It made no sense. It was a construction, a rather fragile one, which completely surrounded his hammock. No, it wasn't a construction, but evidently something alive—a living being, organized horizontally, that had arranged itself in a circle about him. No, it was a number of beings. Or a combination of all of these things.

How it had gotten into the ship was a mystery, but there it was. Or there they were.

"How do you hear?" the creature said abruptly. Its voice, or their voices, came at equal volume from every point in the circle, but not from any particular point in it. Garrard could think of no reason why that should be unusual.

"I—" he said. "Or we—we hear with our ears. Here."

His answer, with its unintentionally long chain of open vowel sounds, rang ridiculously. He wondered why he was speaking such an odd language.

"We-they wooed to pitch you-yours thiswise," the creature said. With a thump, a book from the DFC-3's ample library fell to the deck beside the hammock. "We wooed there and there and there for a many. You are the being-Garrard. We-they are the clinesterton beademung, with all of love."

"With all of love," Garrard echoed. The beademung's use of the language they both were speaking was odd; but again Garrard could find no logical reason why the beademung's usage should be considered wrong.

"Are—are you-they from Alpha Centauri?" he said hesitantly.

"Yes, we hear the twin radioceles, that show there beyond the gift-orifices. We-they pitched that the being-Garrard with most adoration these twins and had mind to them, soft and loud alike. How do you hear?"

This time the being-Garrard understood the question. "I hear Earth," he said. "But that is very soft, and does not show."

"Yes," said the beademung. "It is a harmony, not a first, as ours. The All-Devouring listens to lovers there, not on the radioceles. Let me-mine pitch you-yours so to have mind of the rodalent beademung and other brothers and lovers, along the channel which is fragrant to the being-Garrard."

Garrard found that he understood the speech without difficulty. The thought occurred to him that to understand a language on its own terms—without having to put it back into English in one's own mind—is an ability that is won only with difficulty and long practice. Yet, instantly his mind said, "But it *is* English," which of course it was. The offer the clinesterton beademung had just made was enormously hearted, and he in turn was much minded and of love, to his own delighting as well as to the beademungen; that almost went without saying.

There were many matings of ships after that, and the being-Garrard pitched the harmonies of the beademungen, leaving his ship with the many gift orifices in harmonic for the All-Devouring to love, while the beademungen made show of they-theirs.

He tried, also, to tell how he was out of love with the overdrive, which wooed only spaces and times, and made featurelings. The rodalent beademung wooed the overdrive, but it did not pitch he-them.

Then the being-Garrard knew that all the time was devoured, and he must hear Earth again.

"I pitch you-them to fullest love," he told the beade-

mungen, "I shall adore the radioceles of Alpha and Proxima
Centauri, 'on Earth as it is in Heaven.' Now the overdrive
my-other must woo and win me, and make me adore a
featureling much like silence."

"But you will be pitched again," the clinesterton beademung said. "After you have adored Earth. You are much
loved by Time, the All-Devouring. We-they shall wait for
this othering."

Privately Garrard did not faith as much, but he said,
"Yes, we-they will make a new wooing of the beademungen at some other radiant. With all of love."

On this the beademungen made and pitched adorations,
and in the midst the overdrive cut in. The ship with the
many gift orifices and the being-Garrard him-other saw the
twin radioceles sundered away.

Then, once more, came the pseudo-death.

4

When the small candle lit in the endless cavern of
Garrard's pseudo-dead mind, the DFC-3 was well inside
the orbit of Uranus. Since the sun was still very small and
distant, it made no spectacular display through the nearby
port, and nothing called him from the post-death sleep for
nearly two days.

The computers waited patiently for him. They were no
longer immune to his control; he could now tool the ship
back to Earth himself if he so desired. But the computers
were also designed to take into account the fact that he
might be truly dead by the time the DFC-3 got back. After
giving him a solid week, during which time he did nothing
but sleep, they took over again. Radio signals began to go
out, tuned to a special channel.

An hour later, a very weak signal came back. It was only
a directional signal, and it made no sound inside the DFC-3
—but it was sufficient to put the big ship in motion again.

It was that which woke Garrard. His conscious mind was
still glazed over with the icy spume of the pseudo-death;
and as far as he could see the interior of the cabin had not
changed one whit, except for the book on the deck—

The book. The clinesterton beademung had dropped it
there. But what under God was a clinesterton beademung?
And what was he, Garrard, crying about? It didn't make
sense. He remembered dimly some kind of experience out
there by the Centauri twins—

COMMON TIME 53

—the twin radioceles—

There was another one of those words. It seemed to have Greek roots, but he knew no Greek—and besides, why would Centaurians speak Greek?

He leaned forward and actuated the switch which would roll the shutter off the front port, actually a telescope with a translucent viewing screen. It showed a few stars, and a faint nimbus off on one edge which might be the Sun. At about one o'clock on the screen, was a planet about the size of a pea which had tiny projections, like teacup handles, on each side. The DFC-3 hadn't passed Saturn on its way out; at that time it had been on the other side of the Sun from the route the starship had had to follow. But the planet was certainly difficult to mistake.

Garrard was on his way home—and he was still alive and sane. Or was he still sane? These fantasies about Centaurians—which still seemed to have such a profound emotional effect upon him—did not argue very well for the stability of his mind.

But they were fading rapidly. When he discovered, clutching at the handiest fragments of the "memories," that the plural of *beademung* was *beademungen,* he stopped taking the problem seriously. Obviously a race of Centaurians who spoke Greek wouldn't also be forming weak German plurals. The whole business had obviously been thrown up by his unconscious.

But what *had* he found by the Centaurus stars?

There was no answer to that question but that incomprehensible garble about love, the All-Devouring, and beademungen. Possibly, he had never seen the Centaurus stars at all, but had been lying here, cold as a mackerel, for the entire twenty months.

Or had it been 12,000 years? After the tricks the overdrive had played with time, there was no way to tell what the objective date actually was. Frantically Garrard put the telescope into action. Where was the Earth? After 12,000 years—

The Earth was there. Which, he realized swiftly, proved nothing. The Earth had lasted for many millions of years; 12,000 years was nothing to a planet. The Moon was there, too; both were plainly visible, on the far side of the Sun— but not too far to pick them out clearly, with the telescope at highest power. Garrard could even see a clear sun-highlight on the Atlantic Ocean, not far east of Greenland; evidently the computers were bringing the DFC-3 in on the Earth from about 23° north of the plane of the ecliptic.

The Moon, too, had not changed. He could even see on its face the huge splash of white, mimicking the sun-high-light on Earth's ocean, which was the magnesium hydroxide landing beacon, which had been dusted over the Mare Vaporum in the earliest days of space flight, with a dark spot on its southern edge which could only be the crater Monilius.

But that again proved nothing. The Moon never changed. A film of dust laid down by modern man on its face would last for millennia—what, after all, existed on the Moon to blow it away? The Mare Vaporum beacon covered more than 4,000 square miles; age would not dim it, nor could man himself undo it—either accidentally, or on purpose—in anything under a century. When you dust an area that large on a world without atmosphere, it stays dusted.

He checked the stars against his charts. They hadn't moved; why should they have, in only 12,000 years? The pointer stars in the Dipper still pointed to Polaris. Draco, like a fantastic bit of tape, wound between the two Bears, and Cepheus and Cassiopeia, as it always had done. These constellations told him only that it was spring in the northern hemisphere of Earth.

But spring of what year?

Then, suddenly, it occurred to Garrard that he had a method of finding the answer. The Moon causes tides in the Earth, and action and reaction are always equal and opposite. The Moon cannot move things on Earth without itself being affected—and that effect shows up in the moon's angular momentum. The Moon's distance from the Earth increases steadily by 0.6 inches every year. At the end of 12,000 years, it should be 600 feet farther away from the Earth.

Was it possible to measure? Garrard doubted it, but he got out his ephemeris and his dividers anyhow, and took pictures. While he worked, the Earth grew nearer. By the time he had finished his first calculation—which was indecisive, because it allowed a margin for error greater than the distances he was trying to check—Earth and Moon were close enough in the telescope to permit much more accurate measurements.

Which were, he realized wryly, quite unnecessary. The computer had brought the DFC-3 back, not to an observed sun or planet, but simply to a calculated point. That Earth and Moon would not be near that point when the DFC-3 returned was not an assumption that the computer could make. That the Earth was visible from here was already good and sufficient proof that no more time had elapsed than had been calculated for from the beginning.

This was hardly new to Garrard; it had simply been retired to the back of his mind. Actually he had been doing all this figuring for one reason, and one reason only: because deep in his brain, set to work by himself, there was a mechanism that demanded counting. Long ago, while he was still trying to time the ship's calendar, he had initiated compulsive counting—and it appeared that he had been counting ever since. That had been one of the known dangers of deliberately starting such a mental mechanism; and now it was bearing fruit in these perfectly useless astronomical exercises.

The insight was healing. He finished the figures roughly, and that unheard moron deep inside his brain stopped counting at last. It had been pawing its abacus for twenty months now, and Garrard imagined that it was as glad to be retired as he was to feel it go.

His radio squawked, and said anxiously, "DFC-3, DFC-3. Garrard, do you hear me? Are you still alive? Everybody's going wild down here. Garrard, if you hear me, call us!"

It was Haertel's voice. Garrard closed the dividers so convulsively that one of the points nipped into the heel of his hand. "Haertel, I'm here. DFC-3 to the Project. This is Garrard." And then, without knowing quite why, he added: "With all of love."

Haertel, after all the hoopla was over, was more than interested in the time effects. "It certainly enlarges the manifold in which I was working," he said. "But I think we can account for it in the transformation. Perhaps even factor it out, which would eliminate it as far as the pilot is concerned. We'll see, anyhow."

Garrard swirled his highball reflectively. In Haertel's cramped old office, in the Project's administration shack, he felt both strange and as old, as compressed, constricted. He said, "I don't think I'd do that, Adolph. I think it saved my life."

"How?"

"I told you that I seemed to die after a while. Since I got

home, I've been reading; and I've discovered that the psychologists take far less stock in the individuality of the human psyche than you and I do. You and I are physical scientists, so we think about the world as being all outside our skins—something which is to be observed, but which doesn't alter the essential *I*. But evidently, that old solipsistic position isn't quite true. Our very personalities, really, depend in large part upon *all* the things in our environment, large and small, that exist outside our skins. If by some means you could cut a human being off from every sense impression that comes to him from outside, he would cease to exist as a personality within two or three minutes. Probably he would die."

"Unquote: Harry Stack Sullivan," Haertel said, dryly. "So?"

"So," Garrard said, "think of what a monotonous environment the inside of a spaceship is. It's perfectly rigid, still, unchanging, lifeless. In ordinary interplanetary flight, in such an environment, even the most hardened spaceman may go off his rocker now and then. You know the typical spaceman's psychosis as well as I do, I suppose. The man's personality goes rigid, just like his surroundings. Usually he recovers as soon as he makes port, and makes contact with a more-or-less normal world again.

"But in the DFC-3, I was cut off from the world around me much more severely. I couldn't look outside the ports— I was in overdrive, and there was nothing to see. I couldn't communicate with home, because I was going faster than light. And then I found I couldn't move either, for an enormous long while; and that even the instruments that are in constant change for the usual spaceman wouldn't be in motion for me. Even those were fixed.

"After the time rate began to pick up, I found myself in an even more impossible box. The instruments moved, all right, but then they moved *fast* for me to read them. The whole situation was now utterly rigid—and, in effect, I died. I froze as solid as the ship around me, and stayed that way as long as the overdrive was on."

"By that showing," Haertel said dryly, "the time effects were hardly your friends."

"But they were, Adolph. Look. Your engines act on subjective time; they keep it varying along continuous curves— from far-too-slow to far-too-fast—and, I suppose, back down again. Now, this is a *situation of continuous change*. It wasn't marked enough, in the long run, to keep me out of pseudo-death; but it was sufficient to protect me from being obliterated altogether, which I think is what happened to Brown and Cellini. Those men knew that they could shut down the overdrive if they could just get to it, and they killed themselves trying. But I knew that I just had to sit and take it— and, by my great good luck, your sine-curve time variation made it possible for me to survive."

"Ah, ah," Haertel said. "A point worth considering— though I doubt that it will make interstellar travel very popular!"

He dropped back into silence, his thin mouth pursed. Garrard took a grateful pull at his drink.

At last Haertel said: "Why are you in trouble over these Centaurians? It seems to me that you have done a good job. It was nothing that you were a hero—any fool can be brave—but I see also that you *thought*, where Brown and Cellini evidently only reacted. Is there some secret about what you found when you reached those two stars?"

Garrard said, "Yes, there is. But I've already told you what it is. When I came out of the pseudo-death, I was just a sort of plastic palimpsest upon which anybody could have made a mark. My own environment, my ordinary Earth environment, was a hell of a long way off. My present surroundings were nearly as rigid as they had ever been. When I met the Centaurians—if I did, and I'm not at all sure of that—*they* became the most important thing in my world, and my personality changed to accommodate and understand them. That was a change about which I couldn't do a thing.

"Possibly I did understand them. But the man who understood them wasn't the same man you're talking to now, Adolph. Now that I'm back on Earth, I don't understand that man. He even spoke English in a way that's gibberish to me. If I can't understand myself during that period—and I can't; I don't even believe that that man was the Garrard I know—what hope have I of telling you or the Project about the Centurians? They found me in a controlled environment, and they altered me by entering it. Now that they're gone, nothing comes through; I don't even understand why I think they spoke English!"

"Did they have a name for themselves?"

"Sure," Garrard said. "They were the beademungen."

"What did they look like?"

"I never saw them."

Haertel leaned forward. "Then . . ."

"I heard them. I think." Garrard shrugged, and tasted his Scotch again. He was home, and on the whole he was pleased.

But in his malleable mind he heard someone say, *On Earth, as it is in Heaven;* and then, in another voice, which might also have been his own (why had he thought "him-other"?), *It is later than you think.*

"Adolph," he said, "is this all there is to it? Or are we going to go on with it from here? How long will it take to make a better starship, a DFC-4?"

"Many years," Haertel said, smiling kindly. "Don't be anxious, Garrard. You've come back, which is more than the others managed to do, and nobody will ask you to go out again. I really think that it's hardly likely that we'll get another ship built during your lifetime; and even if we do, we'll be slow to launch it. We really have very little information about what kind of playground you found out there."

"I'll go," Garrard said. "I'm not afraid to go back—I'd like to go. Now that I know how the DFC-3 behaves, I could take it out again, bring you back proper maps, tapes, photos."

"Do you really think," Haertel said, his face suddenly serious, "that we could let the DFC-3 go out again? Garrard, we're going to take that ship apart practically molecule by molecule; that's preliminary to the building of any DFC-4. And no more can we let you go. I don't mean to be cruel, but has it occurred to you that this desire to go back may be the result of some kind of post-hypnotic suggestion? If so, the more badly you want to go back, the more dangerous to us all you may be. We are going to have to examine you just as thoroughly as we do the ship. If these beademungen wanted you to come back, they must have had a reason— and we have to know that reason."

Garrard nodded, but he knew that Haertel could see the slight movement of his eyebrows and the wrinkles forming in his forehead, the contractions of the small muscles which stop the flow of tears only to make grief patent on the rest of the face.

"In short," he said, *"don't move."*

Haertel looked politely puzzled. Garrard, however, could

say nothing more. He had returned to humanity's common time, and would never leave it again.

Not even, for all his dimly remembered promise, with all there was left in him of love.

A Work of Art

INSTANTLY, he remembered dying. He remembered it, however, as if at two removes—as though he were remembering a memory, rather than an actual event; as though he himself had not really been there when he died.

Yet the memory was all from his own point of view, not that of some detached and disembodied observer which might have been his soul. He had been most conscious of the rasping, unevenly drawn movements of the air in his chest. Blurring rapidly, the doctor's face had bent over him, loomed, come closer, and then had vanished as the doctor's head passed below his cone of vision, turned sideways to listen to his lungs.

It had become rapidly darker, and then, only then, had he realized that these were to be his last minutes. He had tried dutifully to say Pauline's name, but his memory contained no record of the sound—only of the rattling breath, and of the film of sootiness thickening in the air, blotting out everything for an instant.

Only an instant, and then the memory was over. The room was bright again, and the ceiling, he noticed with wonder, had turned a soft green. The doctor's head lifted again and looked down at him.

It was a different doctor. This one was a far younger man, with an ascetic face and gleaming, almost fey eyes. There was no doubt about it. One of the last conscious thoughts he had had was that of gratitude that the attending physician, there at the end, had not been the one who secretly hated him for his one-time associations with the Nazi hierarchy. The attending doctor, instead, had worn an expression amusingly proper for that of a Swiss expert called to the deathbed of an eminent man: a mixture of worry at the prospect of losing so eminent a patient, and complacency at the thought that, at the old man's age, nobody could blame this doctor if he died. At 85, pneumonia is a serious matter, with or without penicillin.

"You're all right now," the new doctor said, freeing his patient's head of a whole series of little silver rods which had been clinging to it by a sort of network cap. "Rest a minute and try to be calm. Do you know your name?"

He drew a cautious breath. There seemed to be nothing at all the matter with his lungs now; indeed, he felt positively healthy. "Certainly," he said, a little nettled. "Do you know yours?"

The doctor smiled crookedly. "You're in character, it appears," he said. "My name is Barkun Kris; I am a mind sculptor. Yours?"

"Richard Strauss."

"Very good," Dr. Kris said, and turned away. Strauss, however, had already been diverted by a new singularity. *Strauss* is a word as well as a name in German; it has many meanings—an ostrich, a bouquet; von Wolzogen had had a high old time working all the possible puns into the libretto of *Feuersnot*. And it happened to be the first German word to be spoken either by himself or by Dr. Kris since that twice-removed moment of death. The language was not French or Italian, either. It was most like English, but not the English Strauss knew; nevertheless, he was having no trouble speaking it and even thinking in it.

Well, he thought, *I'll be able to conduct* The Love of Danae *after all. It isn't every composer who can première his own opera posthumously.* Still, there was something queer about all this— the queerest part of all being that conviction, which would not go away, that he had actually been dead for just a short time. Of course medicine was making great strides, but . . .

"Explain all this," he said, lifting himself to one elbow. The bed was different, too, and not nearly as comfortable as the one in which he had died. As for the room, it looked more like a dynamo shed than a sickroom. Had modern medicine taken to reviving its corpses on the floor of the Siemanns-Schukert plant?

"In a moment," Dr. Kris said. He finished rolling some machine back into what Strauss impatiently supposed to be its place, and crossed to the pallet. "Now. There are many things you'll have to take for granted without attempting to understand them, Dr. Strauss. Not everything in the world today is explicable in terms of your assumptions. Please bear that in mind."

"Very well. Proceed."

"The date," Dr. Kris said, "is 2161 by your calendar— or, in other words, it is now two hundred and twelve years after your death. Naturally, you'll realize that by this time nothing remains of your body but the bones. The body you have now was volunteered for your use. Before you look into a mirror to see what it's like, remember that its physical difference from the one you were used to is all in your favor. It's in perfect health, not unpleasant for other people to look at, and its physiological age is about fifty."

A miracle? No, not in this new age, surely. It was simply a work of science. But what a science! This was Nietzsche's eternal recurrence and the immortality of the superman combined into one.

"And where is this?" the composer said.

"In Port York, part of the State of Manhattan, in the United States. You will find the country less changed in some respects than I imagine you anticipate. Other changes, of course, will seem radical to you; but it's hard for me to predict which ones will strike you that way. A certain resilience on your part will bear cultivating."

"I understand," Strauss said, sitting up. "One question, please; is it still possible for a composer to make a living in this century?"

"Indeed it is," Dr. Kris said, smiling. "As we expect you to do. It is one of the purposes for which we've—brought you back."

"I gather, then," Strauss said somewhat dryly, "that there is still a demand for my music. The critics in the old days——"

"That's not quite how it is," Dr. Kris said. "I understand some of your work is still played, but frankly I know very little about your current status. My interest is rather——"

A door opened somewhere, and another man came in. He was older and more ponderous than Kris and had a certain air of academicism; but he too was wearing the oddly tailored surgeon's gown, and looked upon Kris's patient with the glowing eyes of an artist.

"A success, Kris?" he said. "Congratulations."

"They're not in order yet," Dr. Kris said. "The final proof is what counts. Dr. Strauss, if you feel strong enough,

Dr. Seirds and I would like to ask you some questions. We'd like to make sure your memory is clear."

"Certainly. Go ahead."

"According to our records," Kris said, "you once knew a man whose initials were RKL; this was while you were conducting at the Vienna *Staatsoper.*" He made the double "a" at least twice too long, as though German were a dead language he was striving to pronounce in some "classical" accent. "What was his name, and who was he?"

"That would be Kurt List—his first name was Richard, but he didn't use it. He was assistant stage manager."

The two doctors looked at each other. "Why did you offer to write a new overture to *The Woman Without a Shadow,* and give the manuscript to the City of Vienna?"

"So I wouldn't have to pay the garbage removal tax on the Maria Theresa villa they had given me."

"In the back yard of your house at Garmisch-Partenkirchen there was a tombstone. What was written on it?"

Strauss frowned. That was a question he would be happy to be unable to answer. If one is to play childish jokes upon oneself, it's best not to carve them in stone, and put the carving where you can't help seeing it every time you go out to tinker with the Mercedes. "It says," he replied wearily, *"Sacred to the memory of Guntram, Minnesinger, slain in a horrible way by his father's own symphony orchestra."*

"When was *Guntram* premièred?"

"In—let me see—1894, I believe."

"Where?"

"In Weimar."

"Who was the leading lady?"

"Pauline de Ahna."

"What happened to her afterward?'"

"I married her. Is she . . ." Strauss began anxiously.

"No," Dr. Kris said. "I'm sorry, but we lack the data to reconstruct more or less ordinary people."

The composer sighed. He did not know whether to be worried or not. He had loved Pauline, to be sure; on the other hand, it would be pleasant to be able to live the new life without being forced to take off one's shoes every time one entered the house, so as not to scratch the polished hardwood floors. And also pleasant, perhaps, to have two o'clock in the afternoon come by without hearing Pauline's everlasting, *"Richard—jetzt komponiert!"*

"Next question," he said.

For reasons which Strauss did not understand, but was content to take for granted, he was separated from Drs. Kris and Seirds as soon as both were satisfied that the composer's memory was reliable and his health stable. His estate, he was given to understand, had long since been broken up—a sorry end for what had been one of the principal fortunes of Europe—but he was given sufficient money to set up lodgings and resume an active life. He was provided, too, with introductions which proved valuable.

It took longer than he had expected to adjust to the changes that had taken place in music alone. Music was, he quickly began to suspect, a dying art, which would soon have a status not much above that held by flower arranging back in what he thought of as his own century. Certainly it couldn't be denied that the trend toward fragmentation, already visible back in his own time, had proceeded almost to completion in 2161.

He paid no more attention to American popular tunes than he had bothered to pay in his previous life. Yet it was evident that their assembly-line production methods—all the ballad composers openly used a slide-rule-like device called a Hit Machine—now had their counterparts almost throughout serious music.

The conservatives these days, for instance, were the twelve-tone composers—always, in Strauss's opinions, a dryly mechanical lot, but never more so than now. Their gods—Berg, Schoenberg, von Webern were looked upon by the concert-going public as great masters, on the abstruse side perhaps, but as worthy of reverence as any of the Three B's.

There was one wing of the conservatives, however, which had gone the twelve-tone procedure one better. These men composed what was called "stochastic music," put together by choosing each individual note by consultation with tables of random numbers. Their bible, their basic text, was a volume called *Operational Aesthetics*, which in turn derived from a discipline called information theory; and not one word of it seemed to touch upon any of the techniques and customs of composition which Strauss knew. The ideal of this group was to produce music which would be "universal"—that is, wholly devoid of any trace of the composer's individuality, wholly a musical expression of the universal Laws of Chance. The Laws of Chance seemed to have a style of their own, all right; but to Strauss it seemed the style of an idiot child being taught to hammer a flat piano, to keep him from getting into trouble.

By far the largest body of work being produced, however, fell into a category misleadingly called "science-music." The term reflected nothing but the titles of the works, which dealt with space flight, time travel, and other subjects of a romantic or an unlikely nature. There was nothing in the least scientific about the music, which consisted of a mélange of clichés and imitations of natural sounds, in which Strauss was horrified to see his own time-distorted and diluted image.

The most popular form of science-music was a nine-minute composition called a concerto, though it bore no resemblance at all to the classical concerto form; it was instead a sort of free rhapsody after Rachmaninoff—long after. A typical one—"Song of Deep Space" it was called, by somebody named H. Valerion Krafft—began with a loud assault on the tam-tam, after which all the strings rushed up the scale in unison, followed at a respectful distance by the harp and one clarinet in parallel 6/4's. At the top of the scale cymbals were bashed together, *forte possibile*, and the whole orchestra launched itself into a major-minor, wailing sort of melody; the whole orchestra, that is, except for the French horns, which were plodding back down the scale again in what was evidently supposed to be a countermelody. The second phrase of the theme was picked up by a solo trumpet with a suggestion of tremolo; the orchestra died back to its roots to await the next cloudburst, and at this point—as any four-year-old could have predicted—the piano entered with the second theme.

Behind the orchestra stood a group of thirty women, ready to come in with a wordless chorus intended to suggest the eeriness of Deep Space—but at this point, too, Strauss had already learned to get up and leave. Atfer a few such experiences he could also count upon meeting in the lobby Sindi Noniss, the agent to whom Dr. Kris had introduced him, and who was handling the reborn composer's output—what there was of it thus far. Sindi had come to expect these walkouts on the part of his client, and patiently awaited them, standing beneath a bust of Gian Carlo Menotti; but he liked them less and less, and lately had been greeting them by turning alternately red and white like a toti-potent barber pole.

"You shouldn't have done it," he burst out after the Krafft incident. "You can't just walk out on a new Krafft composition. The man's the president of the Interplanetary Society for Contemporary Music. How am I ever going to persuade them that you're a contemporary if you keep snubbing them?"

"What does it matter?" Strauss said. "They don't know me by sight."

"You're wrong; they know you very well, and they're watching every move you make. You're the first major composer the mind sculptors ever tackled, and the ISCM would be glad to turn you back with a rejection slip."

"Why?"

"Oh," said Sindi, "there are lots of reasons. The sculptors are snobs; so are the ISCM boys. Each of them wants to prove to the other that their own art is the king of them all. And then there's the competition; it would be easier to flunk you than to let you into the market. I really think you'd better go back in. I could make up some excuse——"

"No," Strauss said shortly. "I have work to do."

"But that's just the point, Richard. How are we going to get an opera produced without the ISCM? It isn't as though you wrote theremin solos, or something that didn't cost so——"

"I have work to do," he said, and left.

And he did: work which absorbed him as had no other project during the last thirty years of his former life. He had scarcely touched pen to music paper—both had been astonishingly hard to find—when he realized that nothing in his long career had provided him with touchstones by which to judge what music he should write *now*.

The old tricks came swarming back by the thousands, to be sure: the sudden, unexpected key changes at the crest of a melody; the interval stretching; the piling of divided strings, playing in the high harmonics, upon the already tottering top of a climax; the scurry and bustle as phrases were passed like lightning from one choir of the orchestra to another; the flashing runs in the brass, the chuckling in the clarinets, the snarling mixtures of colors to emphasize dramatic tension— all of them.

But none of them satisfied him now. He had been content with them for most of a lifetime, and had made them do an astonishing amount of work. But now it was time to strike out afresh. Some of the tricks, indeed, actively repelled him: where had he gotten the notion, clung to for decades, that violins screaming out in unison somewhere in the stratosphere was a sound interesting enough to be worth repeating inside a single composition, let alone in all of them?

And nobody, he reflected contentedly, ever approached such a new beginning better equipped. In addition to the past lying available in his memory, he had always had a technical armamentarium second to none; even the hostile critics had granted him that. Now that he was, in a sense, composing his first opera—his first after fifteen of them!—he had every opportunity to make it a masterpiece.

And every such intention.

There were, of course, many minor distractions. One of them was that search for old-fashioned score paper, and a pen and ink with which to write on it. Very few of the modern composers, it developed, wrote their music at all. A large bloc of them used tape, patching together snippets of tone and sound snipped from other tapes, superimposing one tape on another, and varying the results by twirling an elaborate array of knobs this way or that. Almost all the composers of 3-V scores, on the other hand, wrote on the sound track itself, rapidly scribbling jagged wiggly lines which, when passed through a photocell-audio circuit, produced a noise reasonably like an orchestra playing music, overtones and all.

The last-ditch conservatives who still wrote notes on paper, did so with the aid of a musical typewriter. The device, Strauss had to admit, seemed perfected at last; it had manuals and stops like an organ, but it was not much more than twice as large as a standard letter-writing typewriter, and produced a neat page. But he was satisfied with his own spidery, highly-legible manuscript and refused to abandon it, badly though the one pen nib he had been able to buy coarsened it. It helped to tie him to his past.

Joining the ISCM had also caused him some bad moments, even after Sindi had worked him around the political road blocks. The Society man who examined his qualifications as a member had run through the questions with no more interest than might have been shown by a veterinarian examining his four thousandth sick calf.

"Had anything published?"

"Yes, nine tone poems, about three hundred songs, an——"

"Not when you were alive," the examiner said, somewhat disquietingly. "I mean since the sculptors turned you out again."

"Since the sculptors—ah, I understand. Yes, a string quartet, two song cycles, a——"

"Good. Alfie, write down 'songs.' Play an instrument?"

"Piano."

"Hm." The examiner studied his fingernails. "Oh, well. Do you read music? Or do you use a Scriber, or tape clips? Or a Machine?"

"I read."

"Here." The examiner sat Strauss down in front of a viewing lectern, over the lit surface of which an endless belt of translucent paper was traveling. On the paper was an immensely magnified sound track. "Whistle me the tune of that, and name the instruments it sounds like."

"I don't read that *Musiksticheln*," Strauss said frostily, "or write it, either. I use standard notation, on music paper."

"Alfie, write down 'Reads notes only.' " He laid a sheet of grayly printed music on the lectern above the ground glass. "Whistle me that."

"That" proved to be a popular tune called "Vangs, Snifters and Store-Credit Snooky" which had been written on a Hit Machine in 2159 by a guitar-faking politician who sang it at campaign rallies. (In some respects, Strauss reflected, the United States had indeed not changed very much.) It had become so popular that anybody could have whistled it from the title alone, whether he could read the music or not. Strauss whistled it, and to prove his bona fides added, "It's in the key of B flat."

The examiner went over to the green-painted upright piano and hit one greasy black key. The instrument was horribly out of tune—the note was much nearer to the standard 440/cps A than it was to B flat—but the examiner said, "So it is. Alfie, write down, 'Also read flats.' All right, son, you're a member. Nice to have you with us; not many people can read that old-style notation any more. A lot of them think they're too good for it."

"Thank you," Strauss said.

"My feeling is, if it was good enough for the old masters, it's good enough for us. We don't have people like them with us these days, it seems to me. Except for Dr. Krafft, of

course. They were *great* back in the old days—men like
Shilkrit, Steiner, Tiomkin, and Pearl . . . and Wilder and
Jannsen. Real goffin."

"Doch gewiss," Strauss said politely.

But the work went forward. He was making a little income
now, from small works. People seemed to feel a special
interest in a composer who had come out of the mind sculptors' laboratories; and in addition the material itself, Strauss
was quite certain, had merits of its own to help sell it.

It was the opera which counted, however. That grew and
grew under his pen, as fresh and new as his new life, as
founded in knowledge and ripeness as his long full memory.
Finding a libretto had been troublesome at first. While it
was possible that something existed that might have served
among the current scripts for 3-V—though he doubted it—
he found himself unable to tell the good from the bad
through the fog cast over both by incomprehensibly technical production directions. Eventually, and for only the
third time in his whole career, he had fallen back upon a
play written in a language other than his own, and—for
the first time—decided to set it in that language.

The play was Christopher Fry's *Venus Observed,* in all
ways a perfect Strauss opera libretto, as he came gradually to
realize. Though nominally a comedy, with a complex farcical
plot, it was a verse play with considerable depth to it, and a
number of characters who cried out to be brought by music
into three dimensions, plus a strong undercurrent of autum-
nal tragedy, of leaf-fall and apple-fall—precisely the kind of
contradictory dramatic mixture which von Hofmannsthal
had supplied him with in *The Knight of the Rose,* in *Ariadne
at Naxos,* and in *Arabella.*

Alas for von Hofmannsthal, but here was another long-
dead playwright who seemed nearly as gifted; and the musical opportunities were immense. There was, for instance, the
fire which ended act two; what a gift for a composer to whom
orchestration and counterpoint were as important as air and
water! Or take the moment where Perpetua shoots the apple
from the Duke's hand; in that one moment a single passing
reference could add Rossini's marmoreal *William Tell* to the
musical texture as nothing but an ironic footnote! And the
Duke's great curtain speech, beginning:

> Shall I be sorry for myself? In Mortality's name

I'll be sorry for myself. Branches and boughs.
Brown hills, the valleys faint with brume,
A burnish on the lake . . .

There was a speech for a great tragic comedian, in the
spirit of Falstaff; the final union of laughter and tears, punc-
tuated by the sleepy comments of Reedbeck, to whose son-
orous snore (trombones, no less than five of them, *con sor-
dini?*) the opera would gently end. . . .

What could be better? And yet he had come upon the play
only by the unlikeliest series of accidents. At first he had
planned to do a straight knockabout farce, in the idiom of
The Silent Woman, just to warm himself up. Remembering
that Zweig had adapted that libretto for him, in the old days,
from a play by Ben Jonson, Strauss had begun to search out
English plays of the period just after Jonson's, and had
promptly run aground on an awful specimen in heroic
couplets called *Venice Preserv'd,* by one Thomas Otway.
The Fry play had directly followed the Otway in the card
catalogue, and he had looked at it out of curiosity; why
should a Twentieth Century playwright be punning on a title
from the Eighteenth?

After two pages of the Fry play, the minor puzzle of the
pun disappeared entirely from his concern. His luck was
running again; he had an opera.

Sindi worked miracles in arranging for the performance.
The date of the première was set even before the score was
finished, reminding Strauss pleasantly of those heady days
when Fuerstner had been snatching the conclusion of *Elek-
tra* off his work table a page at a time, before the ink was
even dry, to rush it to the engraver before publication deadline. The situation now, however, was even more complicated,
for some of the score had to be scribed, some of it taped,
some of it engraved in the old way, to meet the new
techniques of performance; there were moments when Sindi
seemed to be turning quite gray.

But *Venus Observed* was, as usual, forthcoming complete
from Strauss's pen in plenty of time. Writing the music in
first draft had been hellishly hard work, much more like
being reborn than had been that confused awakening in
Barkun Kris's laboratory, with its overtones of being dead
instead; but Strauss found that he still retained all of his old

ability to score from the draft almost effortlessly, as undisturbed by Sindi's half-audible worrying in the room with him as he was by the terrifying supersonic bangs of the rockets that bulleted invisibly over the city.

When he was finished, he had two days still to spare before the beginning of rehearsals. With those, furthermore, he would have nothing to do. The techniques of performance in this age were so completely bound up with the electronic arts as to reduce his own experience—he, the master *Kapellmeister* of them all—to the hopelessly primitive.

He did not mind. The music, as written, would speak for itself. In the meantime he found it grateful to forget the months'-long preoccupation with the stage for a while. He went back to the library and browsed lazily through old poems, vaguely seeking texts for a song or two. He knew better than to bother with recent poets; they could not speak to him, and he knew it. The Americans of his own age, he thought, might give him a clue to understanding this America of 2161; and if some such poem gave birth to a song, so much the better.

The search was relaxing and he gave himself up to enjoying it. Finally he struck a tape that he liked: a tape read in a crackled old voice that twanged of Idaho as that voice had twanged in 1910, in Strauss's own ancient youth. The poet's name was Pound; he said, on the tape

> . . . *the souls of all men great*
> *At times pass through us,*
> *And we are melted into them, and are not*
> *Save reflexions of their souls.*
> *Thus I am Dante for a space and am*
> *One François Villon, ballard-lord and thief*
> *Or am such holy ones I may not write,*
> *Lest Blasphemy be writ against my name;*
> *This for an instant and the flame is gone.*
> *'Tis as in midmost us there glows a sphere*
> *Translucent, molten gold, that is the "I"*
> *And into this some form projects itself:*
> *Christus, or John, or eke the Florentine;*
> *And as the clear space is not if a form's*
> *Imposed thereon,*
> *So cease we from all being for the time,*
> *And these, the Masters of the Soul, live on.*

He smiled. That lesson had been written again and again,

from Plato onward. Yet the poem was a history of his own case, a sort of theory for the metempsychosis he had undergone, and in its formal way it was moving. It would be fitting to make a little hymn of it, in honor of his own rebirth, and of the poet's insight.

A series of solemn, breathless chords framed themselves in his inner ear, against which the words might be intoned in a high, gently bending hush at the beginning . . . and then a dramatic passage in which the great names of Dante and Villon would enter ringing like challenges to Time. . . . He wrote for a while in his notebook before he returned the spool to its shelf.

These, he thought, are good auspices.

And so the night of the première arrived, the audience pouring into the hall, the 3-V cameras riding on no visible supports through the air, and Sindi calculating his share of his client's earnings by a complicated game he played on his fingers, the basic law of which seemed to be that one plus one equals ten. The hall filled to the roof with people from every class, as though what was to come would be a circus rather than an opera.

There were, surprisingly, nearly fifty of the aloof and aristocratic mind sculptors, clad in formal clothes which were exaggerated black versions of their surgeon's gowns. They had bought a bloc of seats near the front of the auditorium, where the gigantic 3-V figures which would shortly fill the "stage" before them (the real singers would perform on a small stage in the basement) could not but seem monstrously out of proportion; but Strauss supposed that they had taken this into account and dismissed it.

There was a tide of whispering in the audience as the sculptors began to trickle in, and with it an undercurrent of excitement the meaning of which was unknown to Strauss. He did not attempt to fathom it, however; he was coping with his own mounting tide of opening-night tension, which, despite all the years, he had never quite been able to shake.

The sourceless, gentle light in the auditorium dimmed, and Strauss mounted the podium. There was a score before him, but he doubted that he would need it. Directly before him, poking up from among the musicians, were the inevitable 3-V snouts, waiting to carry his image to the singers in the basement.

The audience was quiet now. This was the moment. His

baton swept up and then decisively down, and the prelude
came surging up out of the pit.

For a little while he was deeply immersed in the always
tricky business of keeping the enormous orchestra together
and sensitive to the flexing of the musical web beneath his
hand. As his control firmed and became secure, however,
the task became slightly less demanding, and he was able
to pay more attention to what the whole sounded like.

There was something decidedly wrong with it. Of course
there were the occasional surprises as some bit of orchestral
color emerged with a different *Klang* than he had expected;
that happened to every composer, even after a lifetime of
experience. And there were moments when the singers, entering upon a phrase more difficult to handle than he had
calculated, sounded like someone about to fall off a tightrope
(although none of them actually fluffed once; they were as
fine a troupe of voices as he had ever had to work with).

But these were details. It was the over-all impression that
was wrong. He was losing not only the excitement of the
première—after all, that couldn't last at the same pitch all
evening—but also his very interest in what was coming from
the stage and the pit. He was gradually tiring; his baton arm
becoming heavier; as the second act mounted to what should
have been an impassioned outpouring of shining tone, he was
so bored as to wish he could go back to his desk to work
on that song.

Then the act was over; only one more to go. He scarcely
heard the applause. The twenty minutes' rest in his dressing
room was just barely enough to give him the necessary
strength.

And suddenly, in the middle of the last act, he understood.
There was nothing new about the music. It was the old
Strauss all over again—but weaker, more dilute than ever.
Compared with the output of composers like Krafft, it doubt-
less sounded like a masterpiece to this audience. But he knew.

The resolutions, the determination to abandon the old
clichés and mannerisms, the decision to say something new—
they had all come to nothing against the force of habit. Being
brought to life again meant bringing to life as well all those
deeply graven reflexes of his style. He had only to pick up
his pen and they overpowered him with easy automatism, no

more under his control than the jerk of a finger away from a flame.

His eyes filled; his body was young, but he was an old man, an old man. Another thirty-five years of this? Never. He had said all this before, centuries before. Nearly a half century condemned to saying it all over again, in a weaker and still weaker voice, aware that even this debased century would come to recognize in him only the burnt husk of greatness?—no; never, never.

He was aware, dully, that the opera was over. The audience was screaming its joy. He knew the sound. They had screamed that way when *Day of Peace* had been premièred, but they had been cheering the man he had been, not the man that *Day of Peace* showed with cruel clarity he had become. Here the sound was even more meaningless: cheers of ignorance, and that was all.

He turned slowly. With surprise, and with a surprising sense of relief, he saw that the cheers were not, after all, for him.

They were for Dr. Barkun Kris.

Kris was standing in the middle of the bloc of mind sculptors, bowing to the audience. The sculptors nearest him were shaking his hand one after the other. More grasped at it as he made his way to the aisle, and walked forward to the podium. When he mounted the rostrum and took the composer's limp hand, the cheering became delirious.

Kris lifted his arm. The cheering died instantly to an intent hush.

"Thank you," he said clearly. "Ladies and gentlemen, before we take leave of Dr. Strauss, let us again tell him what a privilege it has been for us to hear this fresh example of his mastery. I am sure no farewell could be more fitting."

The ovation lasted five minutes, and would have gone another five if Kris had not cut it off.

"Dr. Strauss," he said, "in a moment, when I speak a certain formulation to you, you will realize that your name is Jerom Bosch, born in our century and with a life in it all your own. The superimposed memories which have made you assume the mask, the *persona,* of a great composer will be gone. I tell you this so that you may understand why these people here share your applause with me."

A wave of assenting sound.

"The art of mind sculpture—the creation of artificial personalities for aesthetic enjoyment—may never reach such a pinnacle again. For you should understand that as Jerom Bosch you had no talent for music at all; indeed, we searched a long time to find a man who was utterly unable to carry even the simplest tune. Yet we were able to impose upon such unpromising material not only the personality, but the genius, of a great composer. That genius belongs entirely to you—to the *persona* that thinks of itself as Richard Strauss. None of the credit goes to the man who volunteered for the sculpture. That is your triumph, and we salute you for it."

Now the ovation could no longer be contained. Strauss, with a crooked smile, watched Dr. Kris bow. This mind sculpturing was a suitably sophisticated kind of cruelty for this age; but the impulse, of course, had always existed. It was the same impulse that had made Rembrandt and Leonardo turn cadavers into art works.

It deserved a suitably sophisticated payment under the *lex talionis:* an eye for an eye, a tooth for a tooth—and a failure for a failure.

No, he need not tell Dr. Kris that the "Strauss" he had created was as empty of genius as a hollow gourd. The joke would always be on the sculptor, who was incapable of hearing the hollowness of the music now preserved on the 3-V tapes.

But for an instant a surge of revolt poured through his blood stream. *I am I,* he thought. *I am Richard Strauss until I die, and will never be Jerom Bosch, who was utterly unable to carry even the simplest tune.* His hand, still holding the baton, came sharply up, though whether to deliver or to ward off a blow he could not tell.

He let it fall again, and instead, at last, bowed—not to the audience, but to Dr. Kris. He was sorry for nothing, as Kris turned to him to say the word that would plunge him back into oblivion, except that he would now have no chance to set that poem to music.

To Pay the Piper

THE MAN in the white jacket stopped at the door marked *Re-Education Project—Col. H. H. Mudgett, Commanding Officer* and waited while the scanner looked him over. He had been through that door a thousand times, but the scanner

made as elaborate a job of it as if it had never seen him
before.

It always did, for there was always in fact a chance that it
had never seen him before, whatever the fallible human beings
to whom it reported might think. It went over him from gray,
crew-cut poll to reagent-proof shoes, checking his small wiry
body and lean profile against its stored silhouettes, tasting and
smelling him as dubiously as if he were an orange held in
storage two days too long.

"Name?" it said at last.

"Carson, Samuel, 32-454-0698."

"Business?"

"Medical director, Re-Ed One."

While Carson waited, a distant, heavy concussion came
rolling down upon him through the mile of solid granite above
his head. At the same moment, the letters on the door—and
everything else inside his cone of vision—blurred distressingly,
and a stab of pure pain went lancing through his head. It was
the supersonic component of the explosion, and it was harmless—except that it always both hurt and scared him.

The light on the door-scanner, which had been glowing
yellow up to now, flicked back to red again and the machine
began the whole routine all over; the sound bomb had reset it.
Carson patiently endured its inspection, gave his name, serial
number, and mission once more, and this time got the green.
He went in, unfolding as he walked the flimsy square of cheap
paper he had been carrying all along.

Mudgett looked up from his desk and said at once: "What
now?"

The physician tossed the square of paper down under
Mudgett's eyes. "Summary of the press reaction to Hamelin's
speech last night," he said. "The total effect is going against
us, Colonel. Unless we can change Hamelin's mind, this outcry
to re-educate civilians ahead of soldiers is going to lose the
war for us. The urge to live on the surface again has been
mounting for ten years; now it's got a target to focus on.
Us."

Mudgett chewed on a pencil while he read the summary;
a blocky, bulky man, as short as Carson and with hair as
gray and close-cropped. A year ago, Carson would have told
him that nobody in Re-Ed could afford to put stray objects
in his mouth even once, let alone as a habit; now Carson just
waited. There wasn't a man—or a woman or a child—of
America's surviving thirty-five million "sane" people who

didn't have some such tic. Not now, not after twenty-five years of underground life.

"He knows it's impossible, doesn't he?" Mudgett demanded abruptly.

"Of course he doesn't," Carson said impatiently. "He doesnt know any more about the real nature of the project than the people do. He thinks the 'educating' we do is in some sort of survival technique. . . . That's what the papers think, too, as you can plainly see by the way they loaded that editorial."

"Um. If we'd taken direct control of the papers in the first place . . ."

Carson said nothing. Military control of every facet of civilian life was a fact, and Mudgett knew it. He also knew that an appearance of freedom to think is a necessity for the human mind—and that the appearance could not be maintained without a few shreds of the actuality.

"Suppose we do this," Mudgett said at last. "Hamelin's position in the State Department makes it impossible for us to muzzle him. But it ought to be possible to explain to him that no unprotected human being can live on the surface, no matter how many Merit Badges he had for woodcraft and first aid. Maybe we could even take him on a little trip topside; I'll wager he's never seen it."

"And what if he dies up there?" Carson said stonily. "We lose three-fifths of every topside party as it is—and Hamelin's an inexperienced——"

"Might be the best thing, mightn't it?"

"*No*," Carson said. "It would look like we'd planned it that way. The papers would have the populace boiling by the next morning."

Mudgett groaned and nibbled another double row of indentations around the barrel of the pencil. "There must be something," he said.

"There is."

"Well?"

"Bring the man here and show him just what we *are* doing. Re-educate *him*, if necessary. Once we told the newspapers that he'd taken the course . . . well, who knows, they just might resent it. Abusing his clearance privileges and so on."

"We'd be violating our basic policy," Mudgett said slowly. " 'Give the Earth back to the men who fight for it.' Still, the idea has some merits. . . ."

"Hamelin is out in the antechamber right now," Carson said. "Shall I bring him in?"

The radioactivity never did rise much beyond a mildly hazardous level, and that was only transient, during the second week of the war—the week called the Death of Cities. The small shards of sanity retained by the high commands on both sides dictated avoiding weapons with a built-in backfire; no cobalt bombs were dropped, no territories permanently poisoned. Generals still remembered that unoccupied territory, no matter how devastated, is still unconquered territory.

But no such considerations stood in the way of biological warfare. It was controllable: you never released against the enemy any disease you didn't yourself know how to control. There would be some slips, of course, but the margin for error . . .

There were some slips. But for the most part, biological warfare worked fine. The great fevers washed like tides around and around the globe, one after another. In such cities as had escaped the bombings, the rumble of truck convoys carrying the puffed heaped corpses to the mass graves became the only sound except for sporadic small-arms fire; and then that too ceased, and the trucks stood rusting in rows.

Nor were human beings the sole victims. Cattle fevers were sent out. Wheat rusts, rice molds, corn blights, hog choleras, poultry enteritises, fountained into the indifferent air from the hidden laboratories, or were loosed far aloft, in the jet-stream, by rocketing fleets. Gelatin capsules pullulating with gill-rots fell like hail into the great fishing grounds of Newfoundland, Oregon, Japan, Sweden, Portugal. Hundreds of species of animals were drafted as secondary hosts for human diseases, were injected and released to carry the blessings of the laboratories to their mates and litters. It was discovered that minute amounts of the tetracycline series of antibiotics, which had long been used as feed supplements to bring farm animals to full market weight early, could also be used to raise the most whopping Anopheles and Aëdes mosquitoes anybody ever saw, capable of flying long distances against the wind and of carrying a peculiarly interesting new strain of the malarial parasite and the yellow fever virus. . . .

By the time it had ended, everyone who remained alive was a mile under ground.

For good.

"I still fail to understand why," Hamelin said, "if, as you claim, you have methods of re-educating soldiers for surface life, you can't do so for civilians as well. Or instead."

The Under Secretary, a tall, spare man, bald on top, and with a heavily creased forehead, spoke with the odd neutral accent—untinged by regionalism—of the trained diplomat, despite the fact that there had been no such thing as a foreign service for nearly half a century.

"We're going to try to explain that to you," Carson said. "But we thought that, first of all, we'd try to explain once more why we think it would be bad policy—as well as physically out of the question.

"Sure, everybody wants to go topside as soon as it's possible. Even people who are reconciled to these endless caverns and corridors hope for something better for their children—a glimpse of sunlight, a little rain, the fall of a leaf. That's more important now to all of us than the war, which we don't believe in any longer. That doesn't even make any military sense, since we haven't the numerical strength to occupy the enemy's territory any more, and they haven't the strength to occupy ours. We understand all that. But we also know that the enemy is intent on prosecuting the war to the end. Extermination is what they say they want, on their propaganda broadcasts, and your own Department reports that they seem to mean what they say. So we can't give up fighting them; that would be simple suicide. Are you still with me?"

"Yes, but I don't see——"

"Give me a moment more. If we have to continue to fight, we know this much: that the first of the two sides to get men on the surface again—so as to be able to *attack* important targets, not just keep them isolated in seas of plagues—will be the side that will bring this war to an end. They know that, too. We have good reason to believe that they have a re-education project, and that it's about as far advanced as ours is."

"Look at it this way," Colonel Mudgett burst in unexpectedly. "What we have now is a stalemate. A saboteur occasionally locates one of the underground cities and lets the pestilences into it. Sometimes on our side, sometimes on theirs. But that only happens sporadically, and it's just more of this mutual extermination business—to which we're committed, willy-nilly, for as long as they are. If we can get troops onto the surface first, we'll be able to scout out their important installations in short order, and issue them a surrender ultimatum with teeth in it. They'll take it. The only other course is the sort of slow, mutual suicide we've got now."

Hamelin put the tips of his fingers together. "You gentlemen lecture me about policy as if I had never heard the word before. I'm familiar with your arguments for sending soldiers first. You assume that you're familiar with all of mine for starting with civilians, but you're wrong, because some of them haven't been brought up at all outside the Department. I'm going to tell you some of them, and I think they'll merit your close attention."

Carson shrugged. "I'd like nothing better than to be convinced, Mr. Secretary. Go ahead."

"You of all people should know, Dr. Carson, how close our underground society is to a psychotic break. To take a single instance, the number of juvenile gangs roaming these corridors of ours has increased 400 per cent since the rumors about the Re-Education Project began to spread. Or another: the number of individual crimes without motive—crimes committed just to distract the committer from the grinding monotony of the life we all lead—has now passed the total of all other crimes put together.

"And as for actual insanity—of our thirty-five million people still unhospitalized, there are four million cases *of which we know*, each one of which should be committed right now for early paranoid schizophrenia—except that were we to commit them, our essential industries would suffer a manpower loss more devastating than anything the enemy has inflicted upon us. Every one of those four million persons is a major hazard to his neighbors and to his job, but how can we do without them? And what can we do about the unrecognized, subclinical cases, which probably total twice as many? How long can we continue operating without a collapse under such conditions?"

Carson mopped his brow. "I didn't suspect that it had gone that far."

"It has gone that far," Hamelin said icily, "and it is accelerating. Your own project has helped to accelerate it. Colonel Mudgett here mentioned the opening of isolated cities to the pestilences. Shall I tell you how Louisville fell?"

"A spy again, I suppose," Mudgett said.

"No, Colonel. Not a spy. A band of—of vigilantes, of mutineers. I'm familiar with your slogan, 'The Earth to those who fight for it.' Do you know the counterslogan that's circulating among the people?"

They waited. Hamelin smiled and said: " 'Let's die on the surface.' "

"They overwhelmed the military detachment there, put the city administration to death, and blew open the shaft to the surface. About a thousand people actually made it to the top. Within twenty-four hours the city was dead—as the ring-leaders had been warned would be the outcome. The warning didn't deter them. Nor did it protect the prudent citizens who had no part in the affair."

Hamelin leaned forward suddenly. "People won't wait to be told when it's their turn to be re-educated. They'll be tired of waiting, tired to the point of insanity of living at the bottom of a hole. They'll just go.

"And that, gentlemen, will leave the world to the enemy . . . or, more likely, the rats. They alone are immune to every-thing by now."

There was a long silence. At last Carson said mildly: "Why aren't we immune to everything by now?"

"Eh? Why—the new generations. They've never been exposed."

"We still have a reservoir of older people who lived through the war: people who had one or several of the new diseases that swept the world, some as many as five, and yet recovered. They still have their immunities. We know; we've tested them. We know from sampling that no new disease has been introduced by either side in over ten years now. Against all the known ones, we have immunization techniques, anti-sera, antibiotics, and so on. I suppose you get your shots every six months like all the rest of us; we should all be very hard to infect now, and such infections as do take should run mild courses." Carson held the Under Secretary's eyes grimly. "Now, answer me this question: why is it that, despite all these protections, every single person in an opened city dies?"

"I don't know," Hamelin said, staring at each of them in turn. "By your showing some of them should recover."

"They should," Carson said. "But nobody does. Why? Because the very nature of disease has changed since we all went underground. There are now abroad in the world a number of mutated bacterial strains which can by-pass the immunity mechanisms of the human body altogether. What this means in simple terms is that, should such a germ get into

your body, your body wouldn't recognize it as an invader. It
would manufacture no antibodies against the germ. Consequently, the germ could multiply without any check, and—you
would die. So would we all."

"I see," Hamelin said. He seemed to have recovered his
composure extraordinarily rapidly. "I am no scientist, gentlemen, but what you tell me makes our position sound perfectly
hopeless. Yet obviously you have some answer."

Carson nodded. "We do. But it's important for you to
understand the situation, otherwise the answer will mean
nothing to you. So: is it perfectly clear to you now, from what
we've said so far, that no amount of re-educating a man's
brain, be he soldier or civilian, will allow him to survive on
the surface?"

"Quite clear," Hamelin said, apparently ungrudgingly.
Carson's hopes rose by a fraction of a millimeter. "But if you
don't re-educate his brain, what can you re-educate? His
reflexes, perhaps?"

"No," Carson said. "His lymph nodes, and his spleen."

A scornful grin began to appear on Hamelin's thin lips.
"You need better public relations counsel than you've been
getting," he said. "If what you say is true—as of course I
assume it is—then the term 're-educate' is not only inappropriate, it's downright misleading. If you had chosen a less
suggestive and more accurate label in the beginning, I wouldn't
have been able to cause you half the trouble I have."

"I agree that we were badly advised there," Carson said.
"But not entirely for those reasons. Of course the name is
misleading; that's both a characteristic and a function of the
names of top secret projects. But in this instance the name
'Re-Education,' bad as it now appears, subjected the men
who chose it to a fatal temptation. You see, though it is
misleading, it is also entirely accurate."

"Word games," Hamelin said.

"Not at all," Mudgett interposed. "We were going to spare
you the theoretical reasoning behind our project, Mr. Secretary, but now you'll just have to sit still for it. The fact is
that the body's ability to distinguish between its own cells and
those of some foreign tissue—a skin graft, say, or a bacterial
invasion of the blood—isn't an inherited ability. It's a learned
reaction. Furthermore, if you'll think about it a moment,
you'll see that it has to be. Body cells die, too, and have to be
disposed of; what would happen if removing those dead cells
provoked an antibody reaction, as the destruction of foreign

cells does? We'd die of anaphylactic shock while we were still infants.

"For that reason, the body has to learn how to scavenge selectively. In human beings, that lesson isn't learned completely until about a month after birth. During the intervening time, the newborn infant is protected by antibodies that it gets from the colestrum, the 'first milk' it gets from the breast during the three or four days immediately after birth. It can't generate its own; it isn't allowed to, so to speak, until it's learned the trick of cleaning up body residues *without* triggering the antibody mechanisms. Any dead cells marked 'personal' have to be dealt with some other way."

"That seems clear enough," Hamelin said. "But I don't see its relevance."

"Well, we're in a position now where that differentiation between the self and everything outside the body doesn't do us any good any more. These mutated bacteria have been 'selfed' by the mutation. In other words, some of their protein molecules, probably desoxyribonucleic acid molecules, carry configurations or 'recognition units' identical with those of our body cells, so that the body can't tell one from another."

"But what has all this to do with re-education?"

"Just this," Carson said. "What we do here is to impose upon the cells of the body—all of them—a new set of recognition units for the guidance of the lymph nodes and the spleen, which are the organs that produce antibodies. The new units are highly complex, and the chances of their being duplicated by bacterial evolution, even under forced draft, are too small to worry about. That's what Re-Education is. In a few moments, if you like, we'll show you just how it's done."

Hamelin ground out his fifth cigarette in Mudgett's ash tray and placed the tips of his fingers together thoughtfully. Carson wondered just how much of the concept of recognition-marking the Under Secretary had absorbed. It had to be admitted that he was astonishingly quick to take hold of abstract ideas, but the self-marker theory of immunity was—like everything else in immunology—almost impossible to explain to laymen, no matter how intelligent.

"This process," Hamelin said hesitantly, "it takes a long time?"

"About six hours per subject, and we can handle only one man at a time. That means that we can count on putting no more than seven thousand troops into the field by the turn

of the century. Every one will have to be a highly trained
specialist, if we're to bring the war to a quick conclusion."

"Which means no civilians," Hamelin said. "I see. I'm
not entirely convinced, but—by all means let's see how it's
done."

Once inside, the Under Secretary tried his best to look
everywhere at once. The room cut into the rock was roughly
two hundred feet high. Most of it was occupied by the bulk
of the Re-Education Monitor, a mechanism as tall as a fifteen-
story building, and about a city block square. Guards watched
it on all sides, and the face of the machine swarmed with
technicians.

"Incredible," Hamelin murmured. "That enormous object
can process only one man at a time?"

"That's right," Mudgett said. "Luckily it doesn't have to
treat all the body cells directly. It works through the blood,
re-selfing the cells by means of small changes in the serum
chemistry."

"What kind of changes?"

"Well," Carson said, choosing each word carefully, "that's
more or less a graveyard secret, Mr. Secretary. We can tell
you this much: the machine uses a vast array of crystalline,
complex sugars which *behave* rather like the blood-group-
and-type proteins. They're fed into the serum in minute
amounts, under feedback control of second-by-second analysis
of the blood. The computations involved in deciding upon
the amount and the precise nature of each introduced chemical
are highly complex. Hence the size of the machine. It is,
in its major effect, an artificial kidney."

"I've seen artificial kidneys in the hospitals," Hamelin said,
frowning. "They're rather compact affairs."

"Because all they do is remove waste products from the
patient's blood, and restore the fluid and electrolyte balance.
Those are very minor renal functions in the higher mammals.
The organ's main duty is chemical control of immunity. If
Burnet and Fenner had known that back in 1949, when the
selfing theory was being formulated, we'd have had Re-
Education long before now."

"Most of the machine's size is due to the computation section," Mudgett emphasized. "In the body, the brain stem
does those computations, as part of maintaining homeostasis.
But we can't reach the brain stem from outside; it's not under
conscious control. Once the body is re-selfed, it will retrain

the thalamus where we can't." Suddenly, two swinging doors
at the base of the machine were pushed apart and a mobile
operating table came through, guided by two attendants. There
was a form on it, covered to the chin with a sheet. The face
above this sheet was immobile and almost as white.

Hamelin watched the table go out of the huge cavern with
visibly mixed emotions. He said: "This process—it's painful?"

"No, not exactly," Carson said. The motive behind the
question interested him hugely, but he didn't dare show it.
"But any fooling around with the immunity mechanisms can
give rise to symptoms—fever, general malaise, and so on.
We try to protect our subjects by giving them a light shock
anesthesia first."

"Shock?" Hamelin repeated. "You mean electroshock? I
don't see how——"

"Call it stress anesthesia instead. We give the man a
steroid drug that counterfeits the anesthesia the body itself
produces in moments of great stress—on the battlefield, say,
or just after a serious injury. It's fast, and free of aftereffects.
There's no secret about that, by the way; the drug involved is
21-hydroxypregnane-3,20-dione sodium succinate, and it dates
all the way back to 1955."

"Oh," the Under Secretary said. The ringing sound of the
chemical name had had, as Carson had hoped, a ritually
soothing effect.

"Gentlemen," Hamelin said hesitantly. "Gentlemen, I have
a—a rather unusual request. And, I am afraid, a rather selfish one." A brief, nervous laugh. "Selfish in both senses, if
you will pardon me the pun. You need feel no hesitation in
refusing me, but——"

Abruptly he appeared to find it impossible to go on. Carson
mentally crossed his fingers and plunged in.

"You would like to undergo the process yourself?" he said.

"Well, yes. Yes, that's exactly it. Does that seem in-
consistent? I should know, should I not, what it is that I'm
advocating for my following? Know it intimately, from
personal experience, not just theory? Of course I realize that
it would conflict with your policy, but I assure you I wouldn't
turn it to any political advantage—none whatsoever. And
perhaps it wouldn't be too great a lapse of policy to process
just one civilian among your seven thousand soldiers."

Subverted, by God! Carson looked at Mudgett with a
firmly straight face. It wouldn't do accept too quickly.

But Hamelin was rushing on, almost chattering now. "I

can understand your hesitation. You must feel that I'm trying
to gain some advantage, or even to get to the surface ahead
of my fellow men. If it will set your minds at rest, I would
be glad to enlist in your advance army. Before five years are
up, I could surely learn some technical skill which would
make me useful to the expedition. If you would prepare
papers to that effect, I'd be happy to sign them."

"That's hardly necessary," Mudgett said. "After you're Re-
Educated, we can simply announce the fact, and say that
you've agreed to join the advance party when the time comes."

"Ah," Hamelin said. "I see the difficulty. No, that would
make my position quite impossible. If there is no other
way . . ."

"Excuse us a moment," Carson said. Hamelin bowed, and
the doctor pulled Mudgett off out of earshot.

"Don't overplay it," he murmured. "You're tipping our
hand with that talk about a press release, Colonel. He's offering
us a bribe—but he's plenty smart enough to see that the price
you're suggesting is that of his whole political career; he
won't pay that much."

"What then?" Mudgett whispered hoarsely.

"Get somebody to prepare the kind of informal contract
he suggested. Offer to put it under security seal so we won't
be able to show it to the press at all. He'll know well enough
that such a seal can be broken if our policy ever comes before
a presidential review—and that will restrain him from forcing
such a review. Let's not demand too much. Once he's been
Re-Educated, he'll have to live the rest of the five years with
the knowledge that he *can* live topside any time he wants to
try it—and he hasn't had the discipline our men have had.
It's my bet that he'll goof off before the five years are up—and
good riddance."

They went back to Hamelin, who was watching the machine
and humming in a painfully abstracted manner.

"I've convinced the Colonel," Carson said, "that your services in the army might well be very valuable when the time
comes, Mr. Secretary. If you'll sign up, we'll put the papers
under security seal for your own protection, and then I think
we can fit you into our treatment program today."

"I'm grateful to you, Dr. Carson," Hamelin said. "Very
grateful indeed."

Five minutes after his injection, Hamelin was as peaceful
as a flounder and was rolled through the swinging doors. An

hour's discussion of the probable outcome, carried on in the privacy of Mudgett's office, bore very little additional fruit, however.

"It's our only course," Carson said. "It's what we hoped to gain from his visit, duly modified by circumstances. It all comes down to this: Hamelin's compromised himself, and he knows it."

"But," Mudgett said, "suppose he was right? What about all that talk of his about mass insanity?"

"I'm sure it's true," Carson said, his voice trembling slightly despite his best efforts at control. "It's going to be rougher than ever down here for the next five years, Colonel. Our only consolation is that the enemy must have exactly the same problem; and if we can beat them to the surface——"

"*Hsst!*" Mudgett said. Carson had already broken off his sentence. He wondered why the scanner gave a man such a hard time outside that door, and then admitted him without any warning to the people on the other side. Couldn't the damned thing be trained to knock?

The newcomer was a page from the haemotology section. "Here's the preliminary rundown on your 'student X,' Dr. Carson," he said.

The page saluted Mudgett and went out. Carson began to read. After a moment, he also began to sweat.

"Colonel, look at this. I was wrong after all. Disastrously wrong. I haven't seen a blood-type distribution pattern like Hamelin's since I was a medical student, and even back then it was only a demonstration, not a real live patient. Look at it from the genetic point of view—the migration factors."

He passed the protocol across the desk. Mudgett was not by background a scientist, but he was an enormously able administrator, of the breed that makes it its business to know the technicalities on which any project ultimately rests. He was not much more than halfway through the tally before his eyebrows were gaining altitude like shock waves.

"Carson, we can't let that man into the machine! He's——"

"He's already in it, Colonel, you know that. And if we interrupt the process before it runs to term, we'll kill him."

"Let's kill him, then," Mudgett said harshly. "Say he died while being processed. Do the country a favor."

"That would produce a hell of a stink. Besides, we have no proof."

Mudgett flourished the protocol excitedly.

"That's not proof to anyone but a haemotologist."

"But Carson, the man's a saboteur!" Mudgett shouted. "Nobody but an Asiatic could have a typing pattern like this! And he's no melting-pot product, either—he's a classical mixture, very probably a Georgian. And every move he's made since we first heard of him has been aimed directly at us—aimed directly at tricking us into getting him into the machine!"

"I think so too," Carson said grimly. "I just hope the enemy hasn't many more agents as brilliant."

"One's enough," Mudgett said. "He's sure to be loaded to the last cc of his blood with catalyst poisons. Once the machine starts processing his serum, we're done for—it'll take us years to reprogram the computer, if it can be done at all. It's *got* to be stopped!"

"Stopped?" Carson said, astonished. "But it's already stopped. That's not what worries me. The machine stopped it fifty minutes ago."

"It can't have! How could it? It has no relevant data!"

"Sure it has." Carson leaned forward, took the cruelly chewed pencil away from Mudgett, and made a neat check beside one of the entries on the protocol. Mudgett stared at the checked item.

"Platelets Rh VI?" he mumbled. "But what's that got to do with . . . Oh. Oh, I see. That platelet type doesn't exist at all in our population now, does it? Never seen it before myself, at least."

"No," Carson said, grinning wolfishly. "It never was common in the West, and the pogrom of 1981 wiped it out. That's something the enemy couldn't know. But the machine knows it. As soon as it gives him the standard anti-IV desensitization shot, his platelets will begin to dissolve—and he'll be rejected for incipient thrombocytopenia." He laughed. "For his own protection! But——"

"But he's getting nitrous oxide in the machine, and he'll be held six hours under anesthesia anyhow—also for his own protection," Mudgett broke in. He was grinning back at Carson like an idiot. "When he comes out from under, he'll assume that he's been re-educated, and he'll beat it back to the enemy to report that he's poisoned our machine, so that they can be sure they'll beat us to the surface. And he'll go the fastest way: *overland*."

"He will," Carson agreed. "Of course he'll go overland, and of course he'll die. But where does that leave us? We won't be able to conceal that he was treated here, if there's any sort of inquiry at all. And his death will make everything we do here look like a fraud. Instead of paying our Pied Piper—and great jumping Jehoshaphat, look at his name! They were rubbing our noses in it all the time! Nevertheless, we didn't pay the piper; we killed him. And 'platelets Rh VI' won't be an adequate excuse for the press, or for Hamelin's following."

"It doesn't worry me," Mudgett rumbled. "Who'll know? He won't die in our labs. He'll leave here hale and hearty. He won't die until he makes a break for the surface. After that we can compose a fine obituary for the press. Heroic government official, on the highest policy level—couldn't wait to lead his followers to the surface—died of being too much in a hurry—Re-Ed Project sorrowfully reminds everyone that no technique is foolproof . . ."

Mudgett paused long enough to light a cigarette, which was a most singular action for a man who never smoked. "As a matter of fact, Carson," he said, "it's a natural."

Carson considered it. It seemed to hold up. And "Hamelin" would have a death certificate as complex as he deserved— not officially, of course, but in the minds of everyone who knew the facts. His death, when it came, would be due directly to the thrombocytopenia which had caused the Re-Ed machine to reject him—and thrombocytopenia is a disease of infants. *Unless ye become as little children . . .*

That was a fitting reason for rejection from the new kingdom of Earth: anemia of the newborn.

His pent breath went out of him in a long sigh. He hadn't been aware that he'd been holding it. "It's true," he said softly. "That's the time to pay the piper."

"When?" Mudget said.

"When?" Carson said, surprised. "Why, *before* he takes the children away."

Nor Iron Bars

THE *Flyaway II*, which was large enough to carry a hundred passengers, seemed twice as large to Gordon Arpe with only the crew on board—large and silent, with the silence of its orbit a thousand miles above the Earth.

"When are they due?" Dr. (now Captain) Arpe said, for at least the fourth time. His second officer, Friedrich Oestreicher, looked at the chronometer and away again with boredom.

"The first batch will be on board in five minutes," he said harshly. "Presumably they've all reached SV-One by now. It only remains to ferry them over."

Arpe nibbled at a fingernail. Although he had always been the tall, thin, and jumpy type, nail-biting was a new vice to him.

"I still think it's insane to be carrying passengers on a flight like this," he said.

Oestreicher said nothing. Carrying passengers was no novelty to him. He had been captain of a passenger vessel on the Mars run for ten years, and looked it: a stocky hard-muscled youngster of thirty, whose crew cut was going gray despite the fact that he was five years younger than Arpe. He was second in command of the *Flyaway II* only because he had no knowledge of the new drive. Or, to put it another way, Arpe was captain only because he was the only man who did understand it, having invented it. Either way you put it didn't sweeten it for Oestreicher, that much was evident.

Well, the first officer would be the acting captain most of the time, anyhow. Arpe admitted that he himself had no knowledge of how to run a space ship. The thought of passengers, furthermore, came close to terrifying him. He hoped to have as little contact with them as possible.

But dammitall, it *was* crazy to be carrying a hundred laymen—half of them women and children, furthermore—on the maiden flight of an untried interstellar drive, solely on the belief of one Dr. Gordon Arpe that his brain child would work. Well, that wasn't the sole reason, of course. The whole Flyaway project, of which Arpe had been head, believed it would work, and so did the government.

And then there was the First Expedition to Centaurus, presumably still in flight after twelve years; they had elected to do it the hard way, on ion drive, despite Garrard's spectacular solo round trip, the Haertel overdrive which had made that possible being adjudged likely to be damaging to the sanity of a large crew. Arpe's discovery had been a totally unexpected breakthrough, offering the opportunity to rush a new batch of trained specialists to help the First Expedition colonize, arriving only a month or so after the First had landed. And if you are sending help, why not send families, too—the families the First Expedition had left behind?

Which also explained the two crews. One of them consisted of men from the Flyaway project, men who had built various parts of the drive, or designed them, or otherwise knew them intimately. The other was made up of men who had served some time—in some cases, as long as two full hitches—in the Space Service under Oestreicher. There was some overlapping, of course. The energy that powered the drive field came from a Nernst-effect generator: a compact ball of fusing hydrogen, held together in mid-combustion chamber by a hard magnetic field, which transformed the heat into electricity to be bled off perpendicular to the magnetic lines of force. The same generator powered the ion rockets of ordinary interplanetary flight, and so could be serviced by ordinary crews. On the other hand, Arpe's new attempt to beat the Lorenz-Fitzgerald equation involved giving the whole ship negative mass, a concept utterly foreign to even the most experienced spaceman. Only a physicist who knew Dirac holes well enough to call them "Pam" would have thought of the notion at all.

But it would work. Arpe was sure of that. A body with negative mass could come very close to the speed of light before the Fitzgerald contraction caught up with it, and without the wild sine-curve variation in subjective time which the non-Fitzgeraldian Haertel overdrive enforced on the passenger. If the field could be maintained successfully in spite of the contraction, there was no good reason why the velocity of light could not be passed; under such conditions, the ship would not be a material object at all.

And polarity in mass does not behave like polarity in electromagnetic fields. As gravity shows, where mass is concerned like attracts like, and unlikes repel. The very charging of the field should fling the charged object away from the Earth at a considerable speed.

The unmanned models had not been disappointing. They had vanished instantly, with a noise like a thunderclap. And since every atom in the ship was affected evenly, there ought to be no sensible acceleration, either—which is a primary requirement for an ideal drive. It looked good . . .

But not for a first test with a hundred passengers!

"Here they come," said Harold Stauffer, the second officer. Sandy-haired and wiry, he was even younger than Oestreicher, and had the small chin combined with handsome features which is usually called "a weak face." He was, Arpe already knew, about as weak as a Diesel locomotive; so much for physiognomy. He was pointing out the viewplate.

Arpe started and followed the pointing finger. At first he saw nothing but the doughnut with the peg in the middle which was Satellite Vehicle 1, as small as a fifty-cent piece at this distance. Then a tiny sliver of flame near it disclosed the first of the ferries, coming toward them.

"We had better get down to the air lock," Oestreicher said.

"All right," Arpe responded abstractedly. "Go ahead. I still have some checking to do."

"Better delegate it," Oestreicher said. "It's traditional for the captain to meet passengers coming on board. They expect it. And this batch is probably pretty scared, considering what they've undertaken. I wouldn't depart from routine with them if I were you, sir."

"I can run the check," Stauffer said helpfully. "If I get into any trouble on the drive, sir, I can always call your gang chief. He can be the judge of whether or not to call you."

Outgeneraled, Arpe followed Oestreicher down to the air lock.

The first ferry stuck its snub nose into the receiving area; the nose promptly unscrewed and tipped upward. The first passenger out was a staggering two-year-old, as bundled up as though it had been dressed for "the cold of space," so that nobody could have told whether it was a boy or a girl. It fell down promptly, got up again without noticing, and went charging straight ahead, shouting "Bye-bye-see-you, bye-bye-see-you, bye-bye——" Then it stopped, transfixed, looking about the huge metal cave with round eyes.

"Judy?" a voice cried from inside the ferry. "Judy! Judy, wait for Mommy!"

After a moment, the voice's owner emerged: a short, fair girl, perhaps eighteen. The baby by this time had spotted the crew member who had the broadest grin, and charged him shouting "Daddy Daddy Daddy Daddy Daddy Daddy" like a machine gun. The woman followed, blushing.

The crewman was not embarrassed. It was obvious that he had been called Daddy before by infants on three planets and five satellites, with what accuracy he might not have been able to guarantee. He picked up the little girl and poked her gently.

"Hi-hi, Judy," he said. "I see you. Where's Judy? *I* see her."

Judy crowed and covered her face with her hands; but she was peeking.

"Something's wrong here," Arpe murmured to Oestreicher. "How can a man who's been traveling toward Centaurus for twelve years have a two-year-old daughter?"

"Wouldn't raise the question if I were you, sir," Oestreicher said through motionless lips. "Passengers are never a uniform lot. Best to get used to it."

The aphorism was being amply illustrated. Next to leave the ferry was an old woman who might possibly have been the mother of one of the crewmen of the First Centaurus expedition; by ordinary standards she was in no shape to stand a trip through space, and surely she would be no help to anybody when she arrived. She was followed by a striking brunette girl in close-fitting, close-cut leotards, with a figure like a dancer. She might have been anywhere between 21 and 41 years old; she wore no ring, and the hard set of her otherwise lovely face did not suggest that she was anybody's wife. Oddly, she also looked familiar. Arpe nudged Oestreicher and nodded toward her.

"Celia Gospardi," Oestreicher said out of the corner of his mouth. "Three-V comedienne. You've seen her, sir, I'm sure."

And so he had; but he would never have recognized her, for she was not smiling. Her presence here defied any explanation he could imagine.

"Screened or not, there's something irregular about this," Arpe said in a low voice. "Obviously there's been a slip in the interviewing. Maybe we can turn some of this lot back."

Oestreicher shrugged. "It's your ship, sir," he said. "I advise against it, however."

Arpe scarcely heard him. If some of these passengers were really as unqualified as they looked . . . and there would be no time to send up replacements . . . At random, he started with the little girl's mother.

"Excuse me, ma'am . . ."

The girl turned with surprise, and then with pleasure. "Yes, Captain!"

"Uh, it occurs to me that there may have been, uh, an error. The *Flyaway II's* passengers are strictly restricted to technical colonists and to, uh, legal relatives of the First Centaurus Expedition. Since your Judy looks to be no more than two, and since it's been twelve years since . . ."

The girl's eyes had already turned ice-blue; she rescued him, after a fashion, from a speech he had suddenly realized he could never have finished. "Judy," she said levelly, "is the granddaughter of Captain Willoughby of the First Expedition. I am his daughter. I am sorry my husband isn't alive to pin your ears back, Captain. Any further questions?"

Arpe left the field without stopping to collect his wounded. He was stopped in mid-retreat by a thirteen-year-old boy wearing astonishingly thick glasses and a thatch of hair that went in all directions in dirty blond cirri.

"Sir," the boy said, "I understood that this was to be a new kind of ship. It looks like an SC-Forty-seven freighter to me. Isn't it?"

"Yes," Arpe said. "Yes, that's what it is. That is, it's the same hull. I mean, the engines and fittings are new."

"*Uh*-huh," the boy said. He turned his back and resumed prowling.

The noise was growing louder as the reception area filled. Arpe was uncomfortably aware that Oestreicher was watching him with something virtually indistinguishable from contempt, but still he could not get away; a small, compact man in a gray suit had hold of his elbow.

"Captain Arpe, I'm Forrest of the President's Commission, to disembark before departure," he said in a low murmur, so rapidly that one syllable could hardly be told from another. "We've checked you out and you seem to be in good shape. Just want to remind you that your drive is more important than anything else on board. Get the passengers where they want to go by all means if it's feasible, but if it isn't, *the government wants that drive back*. That means jettisoning the passengers without compunction if necessary. Dig?"

"All right." That had been pounded into him almost from the beginning of his commission, but suddenly it didn't seem to be as clear-cut a proposition, not now, not after the passengers were actually arriving in the flesh. Filled with a sudden, unticketable emotion, almost like horror, Arpe shook the government man off. Bidding tradition be damned, he got back to the bridge as fast as he could go, leaving Oestreicher to cope with the remaining newcomers. After all, Oestreicher was supposed to know how.

But the rest of the ordeal still loomed ahead of him. The ship could not actually take off until "tomorrow," after a twelve-hour period during which the passengers would get used to their quarters, and got enough questions answered to prevent their wandering into restricted areas of the ship.

And there was still the traditional Captain's Dinner to be
faced up to: a necessary ceremony during which the passengers got used to eating in free fall, got rid of their first
awkwardness with the tools of space, and got to know each
other, with the officers to help them. It was an initial step
rather than a final one, as was the Captain's Dinner on the
seas.

"Stauffer, how did the check-out go?"

"Mr. Stauffer, please, sir," the second officer said politely.
"All tight, sir. I asked your gang chief to sign the log with
me, which he did."

"Very good. Thank you—uh, Mr. Stauffer. Carry on."

"Yes, sir."

It looked like a long evening. Maybe Oestreicher would
be willing to forgo the Captain's Dinner. Somehow, Arpe
doubted that he would.

He wasn't willing, of course. He had already arranged for
it long ago. Since there was no salon on the converted
freighter, the dinner was held in one of the smaller holds,
whose cargo had been strapped temporarily in the corridors.
The whole inner surface of the hold was taken up by the
saddle-shaped tables, to which the guests hitched themselves
by belt hooks; service arrived from way up in the middle
of the air.

Arpe's table was populated by the thirteen-year-old boy he
had met earlier, a ship's nurse, two technicians from the
specialists among the colonist-passengers, a Nernst-generator
officer, and Celia Gospardi, who sat next to him. Since she
had no children of her own with her, she had not been placed
at one of the tables allocated to children and parents; besides,
she was a celebrity.

Arpe was appalled to discover that she was not the only
celebrity on board. At the very next table down was Daryon
Hammersmith, the man the newscasts called "The Conqueror
of Titan." There was no mistaking the huge-shouldered,
flamboyant explorer and his heavy voice; he was a natural
center of attention, especially among the women. He was
bald, but this simply made him look even more like a
Prussian officer of the old school, and as overpoweringly,
cruelly masculine as a hunting panther.

For several courses Arpe could think of nothing at all
to say. He rather hoped that this blankness of mind would
last; maybe the passengers would gather that he was aloof by

nature, and . . . But the silence at the captain's table was becoming noticeable, especially against the noise the children were making elsewhere. Next door, Hammersmith appeared to be telling stories.

And what stories! Arpe knew very little about the satellites, but he was somehow quite sure that there were no snow tigers on Titan who gnawed away the foundations of buildings, nor any three-eyed natives who relished frozen man-meat warmed just until its fluids changed from Ice IV to Ice III. If there were, it was odd that Hammersmith's own book about the Titan expedition had mentioned neither. But the explorer was making Arpe's silence even more conspicuous; he *had* to say something.

"Miss Gospardi—we're honored to have you with us. You have a husband among the First Expedition, I suppose?"

"Yes, worse luck," she said, gnawing with even white teeth at a drumstick. "My fifth."

"Oh. Well, if at first you don't succeed—isn't that how it goes? You're undertaking quite a journey to be with him again. I'm glad you feel so certain now."

"I'm certain," she said calmly. "It's a long trip, all right. But he made a big mistake when he thought it'd be too long for *me*."

The thirteen-year-old was watching her like an owl. It looked like a humid night for him.

"Of course, Titan's been tamed down considerably since my time," Hammersmith was booming jovially. "I'm told the new dome there is almost cozy, except for the wind. That wind—I still dream about it now and then."

"I admire your courage," Arpe said to the 3-V star, beginning to feel faintly courtly. Maybe he had talents he had neglected; he seemed to be doing rather well so far.

"It isn't courage," the woman said, freeing a piece of bread from the clutches of the Lazy Spider. "It's desperation. I hate space flight. I should know, I've had to make that Moon circuit for show dates often enough. But I'm going to get that lousy coward back if it's the last thing I do."

She took a full third out of the bread slice in one precise, gargantuan nibble.

"I wouldn't have thought of it if I hadn't lost my sixth husband to Peggy Walton. That skirt-chaser; I must have been out of my mind. But Johnny didn't bother to divorce me before he ran off on this Centaurus safari. That was a mistake. I'm going to haul *him* back by his *scruff*."

She folded the rest of the bread and snapped it delicately in two. The thirteen-year-old winced and looked away.

"No, I can't say that I miss Titan much," Hammersmith said, in a meditative tone which nevertheless carried the entire length of the hold. "I like planets where the sky is clear most of the time. My hobby is microastronomy—as a matter of fact I have some small reputation in the field, strictly as an amateur. I understand the stars should be unusually clear and brilliant in the Centaurus area, but of course there's nothing like open space for really serious work."

"To tell the truth," Celia went on, although for Arpe's money she had told more than enough truth already, "I'm scared to death of this bloated coffin of yours. But what the hell, I'm dead anyhow. On Earth, everybody knows I can't stay married two years, no matter how many fan letters I get. Or how many proposals, honorable or natural. It's no good to me any more that three million men say they love me. I know what they mean. Every time I take one of them up on it, he vanishes."

The folded snippet of bread vanished without a sound.

"Are you really going to be a colonist?" someone asked Hammersmith.

"Not for a while, anyhow," the explorer said. "I'm taking my fiancée there—" at least two score feminine faces fell with an almost audible thud—"to establish our home, but I hope I'll be pushing on ahead with a calibration cruiser. I have a theory that our Captain's drive may involve some navigational difficulties. And I'll be riding my hobby the while; the arrangement suits me nicely."

Arpe was sure his ears could be seen to be flapping. He was virtually certain that there was no such discipline as microastronomy, and he was perfectly certain that any collimation-cruising (Hammersmith even had the wrong word) the Arpe drive required was going to be done by one Gordon Arpe, except over his dead body.

"*This* man," Celia Gospardi went on implacably, "I'm going to hold, if I have to chase him all over the galaxy. I'll teach him to run away from *me* without making it legal first."

Her fork stabbed a heart of lettuce out of the Lazy Spider and turned it in the gout of Russian dressing the Spider had shot into the air after it. "What does he think he got himself into, anyhow—the Foreign Legion?" she asked nobody in particular. *"Him?* He couldn't find his way out of a super market without a map."

Arpe was gasping like a fish. The girl was smiling warmly at him, from the midst of a cloud of musky perfume against which the ship's ventilators labored in vain. He had never felt less like the captain of a great ship. In another second he would be squirming. He was already blushing.

"Sir . . ."

It was Oestreicher, bending at his ear. Arpe almost broke his tether with gratitude. "Yes, Mr. Oestreicher?"

"We're ready to start dogging down; SV-One has asked us to clear the area a little early, in view of the heavy traffic involved. If you could excuse yourself, we're needed on the bridge."

"Very good. Ladies and gentlemen, please excuse me; I have duties. I hope you'll see the dinner through, and have a good time."

"Is something wrong?" Celia Gospardi said, looking directly into his eyes. His heart went *boomp!* like a form-stamper.

"Nothing wrong," Oestreicher said smoothly from behind him. "There's always work to do in officer's country. Ready, Captain?"

Arpe kicked himself away from the table into the air, avoiding a floating steward only by a few inches. Oestreicher caught up with him in time to prevent his running head-on into the side of a bulkhead.

"We've allowed two hours for the passengers to finish eating and bed down," Oestreicher reported in the control room. "Then we'll start building the field. You're sure we don't need any preparations against acceleration?"

Arpe was recovering; now that the questions were technical, he knew where he was. "No, none at all. The field doesn't mean a thing while it's building. It has to reach a threshold before it takes effect. Once it crosses that point on the curve, it takes effect totally, all at once. Nobody should feel a thing."

"Good. Then we can hit the hammocks for a few hours. I suggest, sir, that Mr. Stauffer take the first watch; I'll take the second; that will leave you on deck when the drive actually fires, if it can be delayed that long. I already have us on a slight retrocurve from SV-One."

"It can be delayed as long as we like. It won't cross the threshold till we close that key."

"That was my understanding," Oestreicher said. "Very

good, sir. Then let's stand the usual watches and get under
way at the fixed time. By then we'll be at apogee so far as
the satellite station is concerned. It would be best to observe
normal routine, right up to the moment when the voyage
itself becomes unavoidably abnormal."

This was wisdom, of course. Arpe could do nothing but
nod, though he doubted very much that he would manage to
get to sleep before his trick came up. The bridge emptied,
except for Stauffer and a j.g. from the Nernst gang, and the
ship quieted.

In the morning, while the passengers were still asleep, Arpe
closed the key.

The *Flyaway II* vanished without a sound.

2

Mommy   Mommy   Mommy   Mommy   Mommy
Mommy

I dream I see him Johnny I love you he's going down
the ladder into the pit and I can't follow and he's gone already and it's time for the next act

Spaceship I'm flying it and Bobby can see me and all the
people

Some kind of emergency but then why not the alarms
Got to ring Stauffer

Daddy? Daddy? Bye-bye-see you? Daddy

Where's the bottle I knew I shouldn't of gotten sucked
into that game

The wind   always the wind

Falling falling why can't I stop falling will I die if I
stop

Two point eight three four Two point eight three four I
keep thinking two point eight three four that's what the
meter says two point eight three four

Somebody stop that wind I tell you it talks I tell you I
hear it words in the wind

Johnny don't go. I'm riding an elephant and he's trying
to go down the ladder after you and it's going to break

No alarms. All well. But can't think. Can't Mommy ladder
spaceship think for bye-bye-see-you two windy Daddy bottle
seconds straight. What's the bottle trouble game matter anyhow? Where's that two point eight three four physicist, what's-
his-bye-bye-name, Daddy, Johnny, Arpe!

will I die if I stop

I love you

the wind
two point
Mommy
STOP.
STOP. STOP. Arpe. Arpe. Where are you? Everyone else,
stop thinking. STOP. We're reading one another's minds.
Everyone try to stop before we go nuts. Captain Arpe, do
you hear me? Come to the bridge. Arpe, do you hear me?
I hear you. I'm on my way. My God.
You there at the field tension meter
two point eight three four
Yes, you. Concentrate, try not to pay attention to anything
else.
Yes, sir. 2.834. 2.834. 2.834.
You people with children, try to soothe them, bed them
down again. Mr. Hammersmith!
The wind . . . Yes?
Wake up. We need your help. Oestreicher here. Star deck
on the double please. A hey-rube.
But . . . Right, Mr. Oestreicher. On the way.

As the first officer's powerful personality took hold, the
raging storm of emotion and dream subsided gradually to a
sort of sullen background sea of fear, marked with fleeting
whitecaps of hysteria, and Arpe found himself able to think
his own thoughts again. There was no doubt about it: everyone on board the *Flyaway II* had become suddenly and
totally telepathic.

But what could be the cause? It couldn't be the field. Not
only was there nothing in the theory to account for it, but the
field had already been effective for nearly an hour, at this
same intensity, without producing any such pandemonium.

"My conclusion also," Oestreicher said as Arpe came onto
the bridge. "Also you'll notice that we can now see out of the
ship, and that the outside sensing instruments are registering
again. Neither of those things was true up to a few minutes
ago; we went blind as soon as the threshold was crossed."

"Then what's the alternative?" Arpe said. He found that it
helped to speak aloud; it diverted him from the undercurrent
of the intimate thoughts of everyone else. "It must be
characteristic of the space we're in, then, wherever that is.
Any clues?"

"There's a sun outside," Stauffer said, "and it has planets.

I'll have the figures for you in a minute. This I can say right away, though: It isn't Alpha Centauri. Too dim."

Somehow, Arpe hadn't expected it to be. Alpha Centauri was in normal space, and this was obviously anything but normal. He caught the figures as they surfaced in Stauffer's mind: Diameter of primary—about a thousand miles (could that possibly be right? Yes, it was correct. But incredible). Number of planets—six. Diameter of outermost planet—about a thousand miles; distance from primary—about 50 million miles.

"What kind of a screwy system is this?" Stauffer protested. "Six planets inside six astronomical units, and the outermost one as big as its sun? It's dynamically impossible."

It certainly was, and yet it was naggingly familiar. Gradually the truth began to dawn on him; there was only one kind of system in which both primary and planet were consistently 1/50,000 of the distance of the outermost orbit. He suppressed it temporarily, partly to see whether or not it was possible to conceal a thought from the others under these circumstances.

"Check the orbital distances, Mr. Stauffer. There should be only two figures involved."

"Two, sir? For six planets?"

"Yes. You'll find two of the bodies occupying the same distance, and the other four at the fifty-million-mile distance."

"Great Scott," Oestreicher said. "Don't tell me we've gotten ourselves inside an atom, sir!"

"Looks like it. Tell me, Mr. Oestreicher, did you get that from my mind, or derive it from what I said?"

"I doped it out," Oestreicher said, puzzled.

"Good; now we know something else: It *is* possible to suppress a thought in this medium. I've been holding the thought 'carbon atom' just below the level of my active consciousness for several minutes."

Oestreicher frowned, and thought: *That's good to know, it increases the possibility of controlling panic and . . .* Slowly, like a sinking ship, the rest of the thought went under. The first officer was practicing.

"You're right about the planets, sir," Stauffer reported. "I suppose this means that they'll all turn out to be the same size, and that there'll be no ecliptic, either."

"Necessarily. They're electrons. That 'sun' is the nucleus."

"But how did it happen?" Oestreicher demanded.

"I can only guess. The field gives us negative mass. We've

never encountered negative mass in nature anywhere but in the microcosm. Evidently that's the only realm where it *can* exist—ergo, as soon as we attained negative mass, we were collapsed into the microcosm."

"Great," Oestreicher grunted. "Can we get out, sir?"

"I don't know. Positive mass is allowable in the microcosm, so if we turned off the field, we might just keep right on staying here. We'll have to study it out. What interests me more right now is this telepathy; there must be some rationale for it."

He thought about it. Until now, he had never believed in telepathy at all; its reported behavior in the macrocosm had been so contrary to all known physical laws that it had been easier to assume that it didn't exist. But the laws of the macrocosm didn't apply down here; this was the domain of quantum mechanics—though telepathy didn't obey that scholium either. Was it possible that the "parapsychological" fields were a part of the fine structure of this universe, as the electromagnetic fields of this universe itself were the fine structure of the macrocosm? If so, any telepathic effects that turned up in the macrocosm would be traces only, a leakage or residuum, fleeting and wayward, beyond all hope of control. . . .

Oestreicher, he noticed, was following his reasoning with considerable interest. "I'm not used to thinking of electrons as having any fine structure," he said.

"Well, all the atomic particles have spin, and to measure that, you have to have some kind of point *on* the particle being translated from one position in space to another—at least by analogy. I would say that the analogy's established now; all we have to do is look out the port."

"You mean we might land on one of those things, sir?" Stauffer asked.

"I should think so," Arpe said, "if we think there's something to be gained by it. I'll leave that up to Mr. Oestreicher."

"Why not?" Oestreicher said, adding, to Arpe's surprise, "The research chance alone oughtn't to be passed up."

Suddenly, the background of fear, which Arpe had more and more become able to ignore, began to swell ominously; huge combers of pure panic were beginning to race over it.

"Oof," Oestreicher said. "We weren't covering enough—we forgot that they could pick up every unguarded word we said. And they don't like the idea."

They didn't. Individual thoughts were hard to catch, but

the main tenor was plain. These people had signed up to go
to Centaurus, and that was where they wanted to go. The
good possibility that they were trapped on the atomic-
size level was terrifying enough, but taking the further risk
of landing on an electron . . .

Abruptly Arpe felt, almost without any words to go with
it, the raw strength of Hammersmith throwing itself Canute-
like against the tide. The explorer's mind had not been in
evidence at all since the first shock; evidently he had quickly
discovered for himself the trick of masking. For a moment
the sheer militancy of Hammersmith's counterstroke seemed
to have a calming effect. . . .

One thread of pure terror lifted above the mass. It was
Celia Gospardi; she had just awakened, and her shell of
bravado had been stripped completely. Following that soundless scream, the combers of panic became higher, more
rapid. . . .

"We'll have to do something about that woman," Oestreicher said tensely. Arpe noted with interest that he was
masking the thought he was speaking, quite a difficult technical trick; he tried to mask it also in the reception. "She's
going to throw the whole ship into an uproar. You were
talking to her at some length last night, sir; maybe you'd
better try."

"All right," Arpe said reluctantly, taking a step toward
the door. "I gather she's still in her——"

Flup!

Celia Gospardi *was* in her stateroom.

So was Captain Arpe.

She stifled a small vocal scream as she recognized him.
"Don't be alarmed," he said quickly, though he was almost
as alarmed as she was. "Listen, Mr. Oestreicher and everybody else: be careful about making any sudden movements
with some definite destination in mind. You're likely to arrive
there without having crossed the intervening distance. It's a
characteristic of the space we're in."

*I read you, sir. So teleportation is an energy-level jump?
That could be nasty, all right.*

"It's—nice of you—to try to—quiet me," the girl said
timidly. Arpe noticed covertly that she could not mask worth
a damn. He would have to be careful in what he said, for
she would effectively make every word known throughout the
ship. It was too bad, in a way. Attractive as she was in her
public role, she was downright beautiful when frightened.

"Please do try to keep a hold on yourself, Miss Gospardi," he said. "There really doesn't seem to be any immediate danger. The ship is sound and her mechanisms are all operating as they should. We have supplies for a full year, and unlimited power; we ought to be able to get away. There's nothing to be frightened about."

"I can't help it," she said desperately. "I can't even think straight. My thoughts keep getting all mixed up with everybody else's."

"We're all having that trouble to some extent," Arpe said. "If you concentrate, you'll find that you can filter the other thoughts out about ninety per cent. And you'll have to try, because if you remain frightened you'll panic other people—especially the children. They're defenseless against adult emotions even *without* telepathy."

"I—I'll try."

"Good for you." With a slight smile, he added, "After all, if you think as little of your fifth husband as you say, you should welcome a little delay en route."

It was entirely the wrong thing to say. At once, way down at the bottom of her mind, a voice cried out in soundless anguish: *But I love him!*

Tears were running down her cheeks. Helplessly, Arpe left.

He walked carefully, in no hurry to repeat the unnerving teleportation jump. In the main companionway he was waylaid by a junior officer almost at once.

"Excuse me, sir. I have a report here from the ship's surgeon. Dr. Hoyle said it might be urgent and that I'd better bring it to you personally."

"Oh. All right, what is it?"

"Dr. Hoyle's compliments, sir, and he suggests that oxygen tension be checked. He has an acute surgical emergency—a passenger—which suggests that we may be running close to nine thousand."

Arpe tried to think about this, but it did not convey very much to him, and what it did convey was confusing. He knew that space ships, following a tradition laid down long ago in atmospheric flight, customarily expressed oxygen tension in terms of feet of altitude on Earth; but 9000 feet—though it would doubtless cause some discomfort—did not seem to represent a dangerously low concentration. And he could see no connection at all between a slightly depleted oxygen level and an acute surgical emergency. Besides, he was too flustered over Celia Gospardi.

The interview had not ended at all the way he had hoped.
But perhaps it was better to have left her grief-stricken than
panic-stricken. Of course, if she broadcast her grief all over
the ship, there were plenty of other people to receive it,
people who had causes for grief as real as hers.

"Grief inactivates," Oestreicher said as Arpe re-entered the
bridge. "Even at its worst, it doesn't create riots. Cheer up,
sir. I couldn't have done any better, I'm sure of that."

"Thank you, Mr. Oestreicher," Arpe said, flushing. Evidently he had forgotten to mask; "thinking out loud" was
more than a cliché down here. To cover, he proffered Hoyle's
confusing message.

"Oh?" Oestreicher strode to the mixing board and scanned
the big Bourdon gages with a single sweeping glance. "He's
right. We're pushing eight-seven hundred right now. Once we
cross ten thousand we'll have to order everybody into masks.
I *thought* I was feeling a little light-headed. Mr. Stauffer,
order an increase in pressure, and get the bubble crew going,
on double."

"Right." Stauffer shot out.

"Mr. Oestreicher, what's this all about?"

"We've sprung a major leak, sir—or, more likely, quite a
few major leaks. We've got to find out where all this air is
going. We may have killed Hoyle's patient already."

Arpe groaned. Surprisingly, Oestreicher grinned.

"Everything leaks," he said in a conversational tone. "That's
the first law of space. On the Mars run, when we disliked a
captain, we used to wish him an interesting trip. This one is
interesting."

"You're a psychologist, Mr. Oestreicher," Arpe said, but
he managed to grin back. "Very well; what's the program
now? I feel some weight."

"We were making a rocket approach to the nearest electron, sir, and we seem to be moving. I see no reason why we
should suspend that. Evidently the Third Law of Motion isn't
invalid down here."

"Which is a break," Stauffer said gloomily from the door.
"I've got the bubble crew moving, Mr. Oestreicher, but it'll
take a while. Captain, what are we seeing by? Gamma waves?
Space itself doesn't seem to be dark here."

"Gamma waves are too long," Arpe said. "Probably de
Broglie waves. The illuminated sky is probably a demonstration of Obler's Paradox: it's how *our* space would look if the
stars were evenly scattered throughout. That makes me think

we must be inside a fairly large body of matter. And the nearest one was SV-One."

"Oh-ho," Stauffer said. "And what happens to us when a cosmic ray primary comes charging through here and disrupts our atom?"

Arpe smiled. "You've got the answer to that already. Have you detected any motion in this electron we're approaching?"

"Not much—just normal planetary motion. About fourteen miles a second—expectable for the orbit."

"Which wouldn't be expectable at all unless we were living on an enormously accelerated time scale. By our home time scale we haven't been here a billionth of a second yet. We could spend the rest of our lives here without seeing a free neutron or a cosmic primary."

"That's a relief," Stauffer said; but he sounded a little dubious.

They fell silent as the little world grew gradually in the ports. There was no visible surface detail on it, and the albedo was high. As they came closer, the reasons for both effects became evident, for with each passing moment the outlines of the body grew fuzzier. It seemed to be imbedded in a sort of thick haze.

"Close enough," Oestreicher ruled. "We can't land the *Flyaway* anyhow; we'll have to put a couple of people off in a tender. Any suggestions, sir?"

"I'm going," Arpe said immediately. "I wouldn't miss an opportunity like this for anything."

"Can't blame you, sir," Oestreicher said. "But that body doesn't look like it has any solid core. What if you just sank right through to the center?"

"That's not likely," Arpe said. "I've got a small increment of negative mass, and I'll retain it by picking up the ship's field with an antenna. The electron's light, but what mass it has is positive; in other words, it will repel me slightly. I won't sink far."

"Well then, who's to go with you?" Oestreicher said, masking every word with great care. "One trained observer should be enough, but you'll need an anchor man. I'm astonished that we haven't heard from Hammersmith already—have you noticed how tightly he shut down as soon as this subject came up?"

"So he did," Arpe said, baffled. "I haven't heard a peep out of him for the last hour. Well, that's his problem; maybe he had enough after Titan."

"How about Miss Gospardi?" Stauffer suggested. "It seems to reassure her to be with you, Captain, and it'll give her something new to think about. And it'll take an incipient panic center out of the ship long enough to let the other people calm down."

"Good enough," Arpe said. "Mr. Stauffer, order the gig broken out."

3

The little world had a solid surface, after all, though it blended so gradually into the glittering haze of its atmosphere that it was very hard to see. Arpe and the girl seemed to be walking waist-deep in some swirling, opalescent substance that was bearing a colloidal metallic dust, like minute sequins. The faint repulsions against their space suits could not be felt as such; it seemed instead that they were walking in a gravitational field about a tenth that of the Earth.

"It's terribly quiet," Celia said.

The suit radios, Arpe noted, were not working. Luckily, the thought-carrying properties of the medium around them were unchanged.

"I'm not at all sure that this stuff would carry sound," he answered. "It isn't a gas as we know it, anyhow. It's simply a manifestation of indefiniteness. The electron never knows exactly where it is; it just trails off at its boundaries into not being anywhere in particular."

"Well, it's eerie. How long do we have to stay here?"

"Not long. I just want to get some idea of what it's like."

He bent over. The surface, he saw, was covered with fine detail, though again he was unable to make much sense of it. Here and there he saw tiny, crooked rills of some brilliantly shiny substance, rather like mercury, and—yes, there was an irregular puddle of it, and it showed a definite meniscus. When he pushed his finger into it, the puddle dented deeply, but it did not break and wet his glove. Its surface tension must be enormous; he wondered if it were made entirely of identical subfundamental particles. The whole globe seemed to be covered by a network of these shiny threads.

Now that his eyes were becoming acclimated, he saw that the "air," too, was full of these shining veins, making it look distinctly marbled. The veins offered no impediment to their walking; somehow, there never seemed to be any in their immediate vicinity, though there were always many of them just ahead. As the two moved, their progress seemed to be accompanied by vagrant, small emotional currents, without visible cause or source, too fugitive to identify.

"What is that silvery stuff?" Celia demanded fearfully.

"Celia, I haven't the faintest idea. What kind of particle could possibly be submicroscopic to an electron? It'd take a century of research right here on the spot to work up even an educated guess. This is all strange and new, utterly outside any experience man has ever had. I doubt that any words exist to describe it accurately."

The ground, too, seemed to vary in color. In the weak light it was hard to tell what the colors were. The variations appeared as shades of gray, with a bluish or greenish tinge here and there.

The emotional waves became a little stronger, and suddenly Arpe recognized the dominant one.

It was pain.

On a hunch, he turned suddenly and looked behind him. A twin set of broad black bootprints, as solid and sharply defined as if they had been painted, were marked out on the colored patches.

"I don't like the look of that," he said. "Our ship itself is almost of planetary mass in this system, and we're far too big for this planet. How do we know what all this fine detail means? But we're destroying it wherever we step, all the same. Forests, cities, the cells of some organism, something unguessable—we've got to go back right now."

"Believe me, I'm willing," the girl said.

The oldest footprints, those that they had made getting out of the tender, were beginning to grow silvery at the edges, as though with hoarfrost, or with whatever fungus might attack a shadow. Or was it seepage of the same substance that made up the rills? Conjecture multiplied endlessly without answer here. Arpe hated to think of the long oval blot the tender itself would leave behind on the landscape. He could only hope that the damage would be self-repairing; there was something about this place that was peculiarly . . . organic.

He lifted the tender quickly and took it out of the opalescent atmosphere with a minimum of ceremony, casting ahead for guidance to pick up the multifarious murmur of the minds on board the *Flyaway II*.

Only when he noticed that he was searching the sky visually

for the ship did he realize that he was not getting anything.

"Celia? You can hear me all right telepathically, can't you?"

"Clear as a bell. It makes me feel much better, Captain."

"Then what's wrong with the ship? I don't pick up a soul."

She frowned. "Why, neither do I. Where . . ."

Arpe pointed ahead. "There she is, right where we left her. We could hear them all well enough at this distance when we were on the way down. Why can't we now?"

He gunned the tender, all caution forgotten. His arrival in the *Flyaway II*'s air lock was noisy, and he lost several minutes jockeying the little boat into proper seal. They both fell out of it in an inelegant scramble.

There was nobody on board the *Flyaway II*. Nobody but themselves.

The telepathic silence left no doubt in Arpe's or Celia's mind, but they searched the huge vessel thoroughly to make sure. It was deserted.

"Captain!" Celia cried. Her panic was coming back full force. "What happened? Where could they have gone? There isn't any place——"

"I know there isn't. I don't know. Calm down a minute, Celia, and let me think." He sat down on a stanchion and stared blindly at the hull for a moment. Breathing the thinning air was a labor in itself; he found himself wishing they had not shucked their suits. Finally he got up and went back to the bridge, with the girl clinging desperately to his elbow.

Everything was in order. It was as if the whole ship had been deserted simultaneously in an instant. Oestreicher's pipe sat snugly in its clip by the chart board; though it was empty of any trace of the self-oxygenating mixture Oestreicher's juniors had dubbed "Old Gunpowder," the bowl was still hot.

"It can't have happened more than half an hour ago," he whispered. "As if they all did a jump at once—like the one that put me into your stateroom. But where to?"

Suddenly it dawned on him. There was only one answer. Of course they had gone nowhere.

"What is it?" Celia cried. "I can see what you're thinking, but it doesn't make sense!"

"It makes perfect sense—in *this* universe," he said grimly. "Celia, we're going to have to work fast, before Oestreicher makes some stab in the dark that might be irrevocable.

Luckily everything's running as though the crew were still here to tend it—which in fact happens to be true—so maybe two of us will be enough to do what we have to do. But you're going to have to follow instructions fast, accurately, and without stopping for an instant to ask questions."

"What are you going to do?"

"Shut down the field. No, don't protest, you haven't the faintest idea what that means, so you've no grounds for protest. Sit down at that board over there and watch my mind every instant. The moment I think of what you're to do next, do it. Understand?"

"No, but——"

"You understand well enough. All right, let's go."

Rapidly he began to step down the Nernst current going into the field generators, mentally directing Celia in the delicate job of holding the fusion sphere steady against the diminished drain. Within a minute he had the field down to just above the threshold level; the servos functioned without a hitch, and so, not very much to his surprise, did those aspects of the task which were supposed to be manned at all times.

"All right, now I'm going to cut it entirely. There'll be a big backlash on your board. See that master meter right in front of you at the head of the board? The black knob marked 'Back EMF' is cued to it. When I pull this switch, the meter will kick over to some reading above the red line. At the same instant, you roll the knob down to *exactly* the same calibration. If you back it down too far, the Nernst will die and we'll have no power at all. If you don't go down far enough, the Nernst will detonate. You've got to catch it on the nose. Understand?"

"I—think so."

"Good," he said. He hoped it would be good. Normally the rolloff was handled wholly automatically, but by expending the energy evenly into the dying field; they did not dare to chance that here. He could only pray that Celia's first try would be fast. "Here we go. Five seconds, four, three, two, one, *cut*."

Celia twisted the dial.

For an instant, nothing happened. Then——

Pandemonium.

"Nernst crew chief, report! What are you doing? No orders were——"

"Captain! Miss Gospardi! Where did you spring from?"

This was Oestreicher. He was standing right at Arpe's elbow.

"Stars! Stars!" Stauffer was shouting simultaneously. "Hey, look! Stars! We're *back!*"

There was a confused noise of many people shouting in the belly of the *Flyaway II*. But in Arpe's brain there was blessed silence; the red foaming of raw thoughts by the hundreds was no more. His mind was his own again.

"Good for you, Celia," he said. It was a sort of prayer. "We were in time."

"How did you do it, sir?" Oestreicher was saying. "We couldn't figure it out. We were following your exploration of the electron from here, and suddenly the whole planet just vanished. So did the whole system. We were floating in another atom entirely. We thought we'd lost you for good."

Arpe grinned weakly. "Did you know that you'd left the ship behind when you jumped?"

"But—impossible, sir. It was right here all the time."

"Yes, that too. It was exercising its privilege to be in two places at the same time. As a body with negative mass, it had some of the properties of a Dirac hole; as such, it had to be echoed somewhere else in the universe by an electron, like a sink and a source in calculus. Did you wind up in one of the shells of the second atom?"

"We did," Stauffer said. "We couldn't move out of it, either."

"That's why I killed the field," Arpe explained. "I couldn't know what you would do under the circumstances, but I *was* pretty sure that the ship would resume its normal mass when the field went down. A mass that size, of course, can't exist in the microcosm, so the ship had to snap back. And in the macrocosm it isn't possible for a body to be in two places at the same time. So here we are, gentlemen—reunited."

"Very good, sir," Stauffer said; but the second officer's voice seemed to be a little deficient in hero worship. "But where is here?"

"Eh? Excuse me, Mr. Stauffer, but don't you know?"

"No, sir," Stauffer said. "All I can tell you is that we're nowhere near home, and nowhere near the Centauri stars, either. We appear to be lost, sir."

His glance flicked over to the Bourdon gages.

"Also," he added quietly, "we're still losing air."

The general alarm had alarmed nobody but the crew, who alone knew how rarely it was sounded. As for the bubble gang, the passengers who knew what that meant mercifully kept their mouths shut—perhaps Hammersmith had blustered them into silence—and the rest, reassured at seeing the stars again, were only amused to watch full-grown, grim-looking men stalking the corridors blowing soap bubbles into the air. After a while, the bubble gang vanished; they were working between the hulls.

Arpe was baffled and restive. "Look here," he said suddenly. "This surgical emergency of Hoyle's—I'd forgotten about it, but it seems to have some bearing on this air situation. Let's——"

"He's on his way, sir," Oestreicher said. "I put a call on the bells for him as soon as—ah, here he is now."

Hoyle was a plump, smooth-faced man with a pursed mouth and an expression of perpetual reproof. He looked absurd in his naval whites. He was also four times a Haber medal winner for advances in space medicine.

"It was a ruptured spleen," he said primly. "A dead giveaway that we were losing oxygen. I was operating when I had the captain called, or I'd have been more explicit."

"Aha," Oestreicher said. "Your patient's a Negro, then."

"A female Negro—an eighteen-year-old girl, and incidentally one of the most beautiful women I've seen in many, many years."

"What has her color got to do with it?" Arpe demanded, feeling somewhat petulant at Oestreicher's obvious instant comprehension of the situation.

"Everything," Hoyle said. "Like many people of African extraction, she has sicklemia—a hereditary condition in which some of the red blood cells take on a characteristic sicklelike shape. In Africa it was pro-survival, because sicklemic people are not so susceptible to malaria as are people with normal erythrocytes. But it makes them less able to take air that's poor in oxygen—that was discovered back in the 1940s, during the era of unpressurized high altitude airplane flight. It's nothing that can't be dealt with by keeping sufficient oxygen in the ambient air, but . . ."

"How is she?" Arpe said.

"Dying," Hoyle said bluntly. "What else? I've got her in a tent but we can't keep that up forever. I need normal

pressure in my recovery room—or if we can't do that, get
her back to Earth *fast*."

He saluted sloppily and left. Arpe looked helplessly at
Stauffer, who was taking spectra as fast as he could get them
onto film, which was far from fast enough for Arpe, let
alone the computer. The first attempt at orientation—Schmidt
spherical films of the apparent sky, in the hope of identifying
at least one constellation, however distorted—had come to
nothing. Neither the computer nor any of the officers had
been able to find a single meaningful relationship.

"Is it going to do us any good if we do find the Sun?"
Oestreicher said. "If we make another jump, aren't we going
to face the same situation?"

"Here's S Doradus," Stauffer announced. "That's a beginning, anyhow. But it sure as hell isn't in any position I can
recognize."

"We're hoping to find the source of the leak," Arpe reminded the first officer. "But if we don't, I think I can calculate a fast jump—in-again-out-again. I hope we won't have to
do it, though. It would involve shooting for a very heavy
atom—heavy enough to be unstable——"

"Looking for the Sun?" a booming, unpleasantly familiar
voice broke in from the bulkhead. It was Hammersmith, of
course. Dogging his footsteps was Dr. Hoyle, looking even
more disapproving than ever.

"See here, Mr. Hammersmith," Arpe said. "This is an
emergency. You've got no business being on the bridge at all."

"You don't seem to be getting very far with the job,"
Hammersmith observed, with a disparaging glance at Stauffer.
"And it's my life as much as it's anybody else's. It's high
time I gave you a hand."

"We'll get along," Oestreicher said, his face red. "Your
stake in the matter is no greater than any other passenger's——"

"Ah, that's not quite true," Dr. Hoyle said, almost regretfully. "The emergency is medically about half Mr. Hammersmith's."

"Nonsense," Arpe said sharply. "If there's any urgency
beyond what affects us all, it affects your patient primarily."

"Yes, quite so," Dr. Hoyle said, spreading his hands. "She
is Mr. Hammersmith's fiancée."

After a moment, Arpe discovered that he was angry—not
with Hammersmith, but with himself, for being stunned by
the announcement. There was nothing in the least unlikely

about such an engagement, and yet it had never entered his head even as a possibility. Evidently his unconscious still had prejudices he had extirpated from his conscious mind thirty-five years ago.

"Why have you been keeping it a secret?" he asked slowly.

"For Helen's protection," Hammersmith said, with considerable bitterness. "On Centaurus we may get a chance at a reasonable degree of privacy and acceptance. But if I'd kept her with me on the ship, she'd have been stared at and whispered over for the entire trip. She preferred to stay below."

An ensign came in, wearing a space suit minus the helmet, and saluted clumsily. After he got the space suit arm up, he just left it there, resting his arm inside it. He looked like a small doll some child had managed to stuff inside a larger one.

"Bubble team reporting, sir," he said. "We were unable to find any leaks, sir."

"You're out of your mind," Oestreicher said sharply. "The pressure is still dropping. There's a hole somewhere you could put your head through."

"No, sir," the ensign said wearily. "There are no such holes. The entire ship is leaking. The air is going right out through the metal. The rate of loss is perfectly even, no matter where you test it."

"Osmosis!" Arpe exclaimed.

"What do you mean, sir?" Oestreicher said.

"I'm not sure, Mr. Oestreicher. But I've been wondering all along—I guess we all have—just how this whole business would affect the ship structurally. Evidently it weakened the molecular bonds of everything on board—and now we have good structural titanium behaving like a semipermeable membrane! I'll bet it's specific for oxygen, furthermore; a 20 per cent drop in pressure is just about what we're getting here."

"What about the effect on people?" Oestreicher said.

"That's Dr. Hoyle's department," Arpe said. "But I rather doubt that it affects living matter. That's in an opposite state of entropy. But when we get back, I want to have the ship measured. I'll bet it's several meters bigger in both length and girth than it was when it was built."

"*If* we get back," Oestreicher said, his brow dark.

"Is this going to put the kibosh on your drive?" Stauffer asked gloomily.

"It's going to make interstellar flight pretty expensive,"

Arpe admitted. "It looks like we'll have to junk a ship after one round trip."

"Well, we effectively junked the *Flyaway I* after one *one-way* trip," Oestreicher said reflectively. "That's progress, of a sort."

"Look here, all this jabber isn't getting us anywhere," Hammersmith said. "Do you want me to bail you out, or not? If not, I'd rather be with Helen than standing around listening to you."

"What do you propose to do," Arpe said, finding it impossible not to be frosty, "that we aren't doing already?"

"Teach you your business," Hammersmith said. "I presume you've established our distance from S Doradus for a starter. Once I have that, I can use the star as a beacon, to collimate my next measurements. Then I want the use of an image amplifier, with a direct-reading microvoltmeter tied into the circuit; you ought to have such a thing, as a routine instrument."

Stauffer pointed it out silently.

"Good." Hammersmith sat down and began to scan the stars with the amplifier. The meter silently reported the light output of each, as minute pulses of electricity. Hammersmith watched it with a furious intensity. At last he took off his wrist chronometer and begun to time the movements of the needle with the stop watch.

"Bull's-eye," he said suddenly.

"The Sun?" Arpe asked, unable to keep his tone from dripping with disbelief.

"No. That one is DQ Herculis—an old nova. It's a micro-variable. It varies by four hundredths of a magnitude every sixty-four seconds. Now we have two stars to fill our para-meters; maybe the computer could give us the Sun from those? Let's try it, anyhow."

Stauffer tried it. The computer had decided to be obtuse today. It did, however, narrow the region of search to a small sector of sky, containing approximately sixty stars.

"Does the Sun do something like that?" Oestreicher said. "I knew it was a variable star in the radio frequencies, but what about visible light?"

"If we could mount an RF antenna big enough, we'd have the Sun in a moment," Hammersmith said in a preoccupied voice. "But with light it's more complicated. . . . Um. If *that's* the Sun, we must be even farther away from it than I thought.

Dr. Hoyle, will you take my watch, please, and take my pulse?"

"Your pulse?" Hoyle said, startled. "Are you feeling ill? The air is——"

"I feel fine, I've breathed thinner air than this and lived," Hammersmith said irritably. "Just take my pulse for a starter, then take everyone else's here and give me the average. I'd use the whole shipload if I had the time, but I don't. If none of you experts knows what I'm doing I'm not going to waste what time I've got explaining it to you now. Goddam it, there are lives involved, remember?"

His lips thinned, Arpe nodded silently to Hoyle; he did not trust himself to speak. The physician shrugged his shoulders and began collecting pulse rates, starting with the big explorer. After a while he had an average and passed it to Hammersmith on a slip of paper torn from his report book.

"Good," Hammersmith said. "Mr. Stauffer, please feed this into Bessie there. Allow for a permitted range of variation of two per cent, and bleed the figure out into a hundred and six increments and decrements each; then tell me what the percentage is now. Can do?"

"Simple enough." Stauffer programmed the tape. The computer jammered out the answer almost before the second officer had stopped typing; Stauffer handed the strip of paper over to Hammersmith.

Arpe watched with reluctant fascination. He had no idea what Hammersmith was doing, but he was beginning to believe that there was such a science as microastronomy after all.

Thereafter, there was a long silence while Hammersmith scanned one star after another. At last he sighed and said:

"There you are. This ninth magnitude job I'm lined up on now. That's the Sun. Incidentally we are a little closer to Alpha Centauri than we are from home—though God knows we're a long way from either."

"How can you be sure?" Arpe said.

"I'm not sure. But I'm as sure as I can be at this distance. Pick the one you want to go to, make the jump, and I'll explain afterwards. We can't afford to kill any more time with lectures."

"No," Arpe said. "I will do no such thing. I'm not going to throw away what will probably be our only chance—the ship isn't likely to stand more than one more jump—on a calculation that I don't even know the rationale of."

"And what's the alternative?" Hammersmith demanded, sneering slightly. "Sit here and die of anoxia—and just sheer damn stubbornness?"

"I am the captain of this vessel," Arpe said, flushing. "We do not move until I get a satisfactory explanation of your pretensions. Do you understand me? That's my order; it's final."

For a few moments the two men glared at each other, stiff-necked as idols, each the god of his own pillbox-universe.

Hammersmith's eyelids drooped. All at once, he seemed too tired to care.

"You're wasting time," he said. "Surely it would be faster to check the spectrum."

"Excuse me, Captain," Stauffer said excitedly. "I just did that. And I think that star *is* the Sun. It's about eight hundred light-years away——"

"Eight hundred light-years!"

"Yes, sir, at least that. The spectral lines are about half missing, but all the ones that are definite enough to measure match nicely with the Sun's. I'm not so sure about the star Mr. Hammersmith identifies as A Centaurus, but at the very least it's a spectroscopic double, and it *is* about fifty light-years closer."

"My God," Arpe muttered. "Eight hundred."

Hammersmith looked up again, his expression curiously like that of a St. Bernard whose cask of brandy has been spurned. "Isn't that sufficient?" he said hoarsely. "In God's name, let's get going. She's dying while we stand around here nit-picking!"

"No rationale, no jump," Arpe said stonily. Oestreicher shot him a peculiar glance out of the corners of his eyes. In that moment, Arpe felt his painfully accumulated status with the first officer shatter like a Prince Rupert's drop; but he would not yield.

"Very well," Hammersmith said gently. "It goes like this. The Sun is a variable star. With a few exceptions, the pulses don't exceed the total average emission—the solar constant—by more than two per cent. The over-all period is 273 months. Inside that, there are at least sixty-three subordinate cycles. There's one of 212 days. Another one lasts only a fraction over six and a half days—I forget the exact period, but it's 1/1250 of the main cycle, if you want to work it out on Bessie there."

"I guessed something like that," Arpe said. "But what good does it do us? We have no tables for it——"

"These cycles have effects," Hammersmith said. "The six-and-a-half-day cycle strongly influences the weather on Earth, for instance. And the 212-day cycle is reflected one-for-one *in the human pulse rate.*"

"Oho," Oestreicher said. "Now I see. It's—Captain, this means that we can *never* be lost! Not so long as the Sun is detectable at all, whether we can identify it or not! We're carrying the only beacon we need right in our blood!"

"Yes," Hammersmith said. "That's how it goes. It's better to take an average of all the pulses available, since one man might be too excited to give you an accurate figure. I'm that overwrought myself. I wonder if it's patentable? No, a law of nature, I suppose; besides, too easily infringed, almost like a patent on shaving. . . . But it's true, Mr. Oestreicher. You may go as far afield as you please, but your Sun stays in your blood. You never really leave home."

He lifted his head and looked at Arpe with hooded, bloodshot eyes.

"Now can we go, please?" he said, almost in a whisper. "And, Captain—if this delay has killed Helen, you will answer to me for it, if I have to chase you to the smallest, most remote star that God ever made."

Arpe swallowed. "Mr. Stauffer," he said, "prepare for jump."

"Where to, sir?" the second officer said. "Back home—or to destination?"

And there was the crux. After the next jump the *Flyaway II* would not be spaceworthy any more. If they used it up making Centaurus, they would be marooned; they would have made their one round trip one-way. Besides . . . *your drive is more important than anything else on board. Get the passengers where they want to go by all means if it's feasible, but if it isn't, the government wants that drive back. . . . Understand?*

"We contracted with the passengers to go to Centaurus," Arpe said, sitting down before the computer. "That's where we'll go."

"Very good, sir," Oestreicher said. They were the finest three words Arpe had ever heard in his life.

The Negro girl, exquisite even in her still and terrible coma, was first off the ship into the big ship-to-shore ferry.

Hammersmith went with her, his big face contorted with anguish.

Then the massive job of evacuating everybody else began. Everyone—passengers and ship's complement alike—was wearing a mask now. After the jump through the heavy cosmic-ray primary that Arpe had picked, a stripped nucleus which happened to be going toward Centaurus anyhow, the *Flyaway II* was leaking air as though she were made of something not much better than surgical gauze. She was through.

Oestreicher turned to Arpe and held out his hand. "A great achievement, sir," the first officer said. "It'll be cut and dried into a routine after it's collimated—but they won't even know that back home until the radio word comes through, better than four years from now. I'm glad I was along while it was still new."

"Thank you, Mr. Oestreicher. You won't miss the Mars run?"

"They'll need interplanetary captains here too, sir." He paused. "I'd better go help Mr. Stauffer with the exodus."

"Right. Thank you, Mr. Oestreicher."

Then he was alone. He meant to be last off the ship; after living with Oestreicher and his staff for so long, he had come to see that traditions do not grow from nothing. After a while, however, the bulkhead-lock swung heavily open, and Dr. Hoyle came in.

"Skipper, you're bushed. Better knock it off."

"No," Arpe said in a husky voice, not turning away from watching through the viewplate the flaming departure of the ferry for the green and brown planet, so wholly Earthlike except for the strange shapes of its continents, a thousand miles below. "Hoyle, what do you think? Has she still got a chance?"

"I don't know. It will be nip and tuck. Maybe. Wilson—he was ship's surgeon on the *Flyaway I*—will pick her up as she lands. He's not young any more, but he was as good as they came; and with a surgeon it isn't age that matters, it's how frequently you operate. But . . . she was on the way out for a long time. She may be a little . . ."

He stopped.

"Go on," Arpe said. "Give it to me straight. I know I was wrong."

"She was low on oxygen for a long time," Hoyle said, without looking at Arpe. "It may be that she'll be a little simple-minded when she recovers. Or it may not; there's no predicting these things. But one thing's for sure; she'll never dare go into space again. Not even back to Earth. The next slight drop in oxygen tension will kill her. I even advised against airplanes for her, and Wilson concurs."

Arpe swallowed. "Does Hammersmith know that?"

"Yes," Hoyle said, "he knows it. But he'll stick with her. He loves her."

The ferry carrying the explorer and his fiancée, and Captain Willoughby's daughter and her Judy, and many others, was no longer visible. Sick at heart, Arpe watched Centaurus III turn below him.

That planet was the gateway to the stars—for everyone on it but Daryon and Helen Hammersmith. The door that had closed behind them when they had boarded the ferry was for them no gateway to any place. It was only the door to a prison.

But it was also, Arpe realized suddenly, a prison which would hold a great teacher—not of the humanities, but of Humanity. Arpe, not so imprisoned, had no such thing to teach.

It was true that he knew how to do a great thing—how to travel to the stars. It was true that he had taken Celia Gospardi and the others where they had wanted to go. It was true that he was now a small sort of hero to his crew; and it was true that he—Dr. Gordon Arpe, sometime laboratory recluse, sometime *ersatz* space-ship captain, sometime petty hero, had been kissed good-bye by a 3-V star.

But it was also over. From now on he could do no more than sit back and watch others refine the Arpe drive; the four-year communication gap between Centaurus and home would shut him out of those experiments as though he were a Cro-Magnon Man—or Daryon Hammersmith. When next Arpe saw an Earth physicist, he wouldn't have the smallest chance of understanding a word the man said.

That was a prison, too; a prison Capt. Gordon Arpe had fashioned himself, and then had thrown away the key.

"Beg pardon, Captain?"

"Oh. Sorry, Dr. Hoyle. Didn't realize you were still here." Arpe looked down for the last time on the green-and-brown planet, and drew a long breath. "I said, 'So be it.' "

Beep

JOSEF FABER lowered his newspaper slightly. Finding the girl on the park bench looking his way, he smiled the agonizingly embarrassed smile of the thoroughly married nobody caught bird-watching, and ducked back into the paper again.

He was reasonably certain that he looked the part of a middle-aged, steadily employed, harmless citizen enjoying a Sunday break in the bookkeeping and family routines. He was also quite certain, despite his official instructions, that it wouldn't make the slightest bit of difference if he didn't. These boy-meets-girl assignments always came off. Jo had never tackled a single one that had required him.

As a matter of fact, the newspaper, which he was supposed to be using only as a blind, interested him a good deal more than his job did. He had only barely begun to suspect the obvious ten years ago when the Service had snapped him up; now, after a decade as an agent, he was still fascinated to see how smoothly the really important situations came off. The *dangerous* situations—not boy-meets-girl.

This affair of the Black Horse Nebula, for instance. Some days ago the papers and the commentators had begun to mention reports of disturbances in that area, and Jo's practiced eye had picked up the mention. Something big was cooking.

Today it had boiled over—the Black Horse Nebula had suddenly spewed ships by the hundreds, a massed armada that must have taken more than a century of effort on the part of a whole star cluster, a production drive conducted in the strictest and most fanatical kind of secrecy. . . .

And, of course, the Service had been on the spot in plenty of time. With three times as many ships, disposed with mathematical precision so as to enfilade the entire armada the moment it broke from the nebula. The battle had been a massacre, the attack smashed before the average citizen could even begin to figure out what it had been aimed at—and good had triumphed over evil once more.

Of course.

Furtive scuffings on the gravel drew his attention briefly. He looked at his watch, which said 14:58:03. That was the time, according to his instructions, when boy had to meet girl.

He had been given the strictest kind of orders to let nothing interfere with this meeting—the orders always issued on boy-meets-girl assignments. But, as usual, he had nothing to do but observe. The meeting was coming off on the dot, without any prodding from Jo. They always did.

Of course.

With a sigh, he folded his newspaper, smiling again at the couple—yes, it was the right man, too—and moved away, as if reluctantly. He wondered what would happen were he to pull away the false mustache, pitch the newspaper on the grass, and bound away with a joyous whoop. He suspected that the course of history would not be deflected by even a second of arc, but he was not minded to try the experiment.

The park was pleasant. The twin suns warmed the path and the greenery without any of the blasting heat which they would bring to bear later in the summer. Randolph was altogether the most comfortable planet he had visited in years. A little backward, perhaps, but restful, too.

It was also slightly over a hundred light-years away from Earth. It would be interesting to know how Service head-quarters on Earth could have known in advance that boy would meet girl at a certain spot on Randolph, precisely at 14:58:03.

Or how Service headquarters could have ambushed with micrometric precision a major interstellar fleet, with no more preparation than a few days' buildup in the newspapers and video could evidence.

The press was free, on Randolph as everywhere. It reported the news it got. Any emergency concentration of Service ships in the Black Horse area, or anywhere else, would have been noticed and reported on. The Service did not forbid such reports for "security" reasons or for any other reasons. Yet there had been nothing to report but that (a) an armada of staggering size had erupted with no real warning from the Black Horse Nebula, and that (b) the Service had been ready.

By now, it was a commonplace that the Service was always ready. It had not had a defect or a failure in well over two centuries. It had not even had a fiasco, the alarming-sounding technical word by which it referred to the possibility that a boy-meets-girl assignment might not come off.

Jo hailed a hopper. Once inside he stripped himself of the

mustache, the bald spot, the forehead creases—all the make-up which had given him his mask of friendly innocuousness.

The hoppy watched the whole process in the rear-view mirror. Jo glanced up and met his eyes.

"Pardon me, mister, but I figured you didn't care if I saw you. You must be a Service man."

"That's right. Take me to Service HQ, will you?"

"Sure enough." The hoppy gunned his machine. It rose smoothly to the express level. "First time I ever got close to a Service man. Didn't hardly believe it at first when I saw you taking your face off. You sure looked different."

"Have to, sometimes," Jo said, preoccupied.

"I'll bet. No wonder you know all about everything before it breaks. You must have a thousand faces each, your own mother wouldn't know you, eh? Don't you care if I know about your snooping around in disguise?"

Jo grinned. The grin created a tiny pulling sensation across one curve of his cheek, just next to his nose. He stripped away the overlooked bit of tissue and examined it critically.

"Of course not. Disguise is an elementary part of Service work. Anyone could guess that. We don't use it often, as a matter of fact—only on very simple assignments."

"Oh." The hoppy sounded slightly disappointed, as melo-drama faded. He drove silently for about a minute. Then, speculatively: "Sometimes I think the Service must have time-travel, the things they pull. . . . Well, here you are. Good luck, mister."

"Thanks."

Jo went directly to Krasna's office. Krasna was a Randolpher. Earth-trained, and answerable to the Earth office, but otherwise pretty much on his own. His heavy, muscular face wore the same expression of serene confidence that was characteristic of Service officials everywhere—even some that, technically speaking, had no faces to wear it.

"Boy meets girl," Jo said briefly. "On the nose and on the spot."

"Good work, Jo. Cigarette?" Krasna pushed the box across his desk.

"Nope, not now. Like to talk to you, if you've got time."

Krasna pushed a button, and a toadstoollike chair rose out of the floor behind Jo. "What's on your mind?"

"Well," Jo said carefully. "I'm wondering why you patted me on the back just now for not doing a job."

"You did a job."

"I did not," Jo said flatly. "Boy would have met girl, whether I'd been here on Randolph or back on Earth. The course of true love always runs smooth. It has in all my boy-meets-girl cases, and it has in the boy-meets-girl cases of every other agent with whom I've compared notes."

"Well, good," Krasna said, smiling. "That's the way we like to have it run. And that's the way we expect it to run. But, Jo, we like to have somebody on the spot, somebody with a reputation for resourcefulness, just in case there's a snag. There almost never is, as you've observed. But—if there were?"

Jo snorted. "If what you're trying to do is to establish preconditions for the future, any interference by a Service agent would throw the eventual result farther *off* the track. I know that much about probability."

"And what makes you think that we're trying to set up the future?"

"It's obvious even to the hoppies on your own planet; the one that brought me here told me he thought the Service had time-travel. It's especially obvious to all the individuals and governments and entire populations that the Service has bailed out of serious messes for centuries, with never a single failure." Jo shrugged. "A man can be asked to safeguard only a small number of boy-meets-girl cases before he realizes, as an agent, that what the Service is safeguarding is the future children of those meetings. Ergo—the Service *knows* what those children are to be like, and has reason to want their future existence guaranteed. What other conclusion is possible?"

Krasna took out a cigarette and lit it deliberately; it was obvious that he was using the maneuver to cloak his response.

"None," he admitted at last. "We have some foreknowledge, of course. We couldn't have made our reputation with espionage alone. But we have obvious other advantages: genetics, for instance, and operations research, the theory of games, the Dirac transmitter—it's quite an arsenal, and of course there's a good deal of prediction involved in all those things."

"I see that," Jo said. He shifted in his chair, formulating all he wanted to say. He changed his mind about the cigarette and helped himself to one. "But these things don't add up to infallibility—and that's a qualitative difference, Kras. Take this affair of the Black Horse armada. The moment the armada appeared, we'll assume, Earth heard about it by Dirac, and started to assemble a counterarmada. But it takes *finite time* to bring together a concentration of ships and men, even if your message system is instantaneous.

"The Service's counterarmada was *already on hand*. It had been building there for so long and with so little fuss that nobody even noticed it concentrating until a day or so before the battle. Then planets in the area began to sit up and take notice, and be uneasy about what was going to break. But not very uneasy; the Service always wins—that's been a statistical fact for centuries. *Centuries*, Kras. Good Lord, it takes almost as long as that, in straight preparation, to pull some of the tricks we've pulled! The Dirac gives us an advantage of ten to twenty-five years in really extreme cases out on the rim of the Galaxy, but no more than that."

He realized that he had been fuming away on the cigarette until the roof of his mouth was scorched, and snubbed it out angrily. "That's a very different thing," he said, "than knowing in a general way how an enemy is likely to behave, or what kind of children the Mendelian laws say a given couple should have. It means that we've some way of reading the future in minute detail. That's in flat contradiction to everything I've been taught about probability, but I have to believe what I see."

Krasna laughed. "That's a very able presentation," he said. He seemed genuinely pleased. "I think you'll remember that you were first impressed into the Service when you began to wonder why the news was always good. Fewer and fewer people wonder about that nowadays; it's become a part of their expected environment." He stood up and ran a hand through his hair. "Now you've carried yourself through the next stage. Congratulations, Jo. You've just been promoted!"

"I have?" Jo said incredulously. "I came in here with the notion that I might get myself fired."

"No. Come around to this side of the desk, Jo, and I'll play you a little history." Krasna unfolded the desktop to expose a small visor screen. Obediently Jo rose and went around the desk to where he could see the blank surface. "I had a standard indoctrination tape sent up to me a week ago, in the expectation that you'd be ready to see it. Watch."

Krasna touched the board. A small dot of light appeared in the center of the screen and went out again. At the same time, there was a small *beep* of sound. Then the tape began to unroll and a picture clarified on the screen.

"As you suspected," Krasna said conversationally, "the Service is infallible. How it got that way is a story that started several centuries back.

2

Dana Lje—her father had been a Hollander, her mother born in the Celebes—sat down in the chair which Captain Robin Weinbaum had indicated, crossed her legs, and waited, her blue-black hair shining under the lights.

Weinbaum eyed her quizzically. The conqueror Resident who had given the girl her entirely European name had been paid in kind, for his daughter's beauty had nothing fair and Dutch about it. To the eye of the beholder, Dana Lje seemed a particularly delicate virgin of Bali, despite her Western name, clothing and assurance. The combination had already proven piquant for the millions who watched her television column, and Weinbaum found it no less charming at first hand.

"As one of your most recent victims," he said, "I'm not sure that I'm honored, Miss Lje. A few of my wounds are still bleeding. But I am a good deal puzzled as to why you're visiting me now. Aren't you afraid that I'll bite back?"

"I had no intention of attacking you personally, and I don't think I did," the video columnist said seriously. "It was just pretty plain that our intelligence had slipped badly in the Erskine affair. It was my job to say so. Obviously you were going to get hurt, since you're head of the bureau —but there was no malice in it."

"Cold comfort," Weinbaum said dryly. "But thank you, nevertheless."

The Eurasian girl shrugged. "That isn't what I came here about, anyway. Tell me, Captain Weinbaum—have you ever heard of an outfit calling itself Interstellar Information?"

Weinbaum shook his head. "Sounds like a skip-tracing firm. Not an easy business, these days."

"That's just what I thought when I first saw their letter-head," Dana said. "But the letter under it wasn't one that a private-eye outfit would write. Let me read part of it to you."

Her slim fingers burrowed in her inside jacket pocket and emerged again with a single sheet of paper. It was plain typewriter bond, Weinbaum noted automatically: she had brought only a copy with her, and had left the original of the letter at home. The copy, then, would be incomplete—probably seriously.

"It goes like this: 'Dear Miss Lje: As a syndicated video commentator with a wide audience and heavy responsibilities, you need the best sources of information available. We would like you to test our service, free of charge, in the hope of proving to you that it is superior to any other source of news on Earth. Therefore, we offer below several predictions concerning events to come in the Hercules and the so-called "Three Ghosts" areas. If these predictions are fulfilled 100 per cent—no less—we ask that you take us on as your correspondents for those areas, at rates to be agreed upon later. If the predictions are wrong in *any* respect, you need not consider us further.' "

"H'm," Weinbaum said slowly. "They're confident cusses —and that's an odd juxtaposition. The Three Ghosts make up only a little solar system, while the Hercules area could include the entire star cluster—or maybe even the whole constellation, which is a hell of a lot of sky. This outfit seems to be trying to tell you that it has thousands of field correspondents of its own, maybe as many as the government itself. If so, I'll guarantee that they're bragging."

"That may well be so. But before you make up your mind, let me read you one of the two predictions." The letter rustled in Dana Lje's hand. " 'At 03:16:10, on Year Day, 2090, the Hess-type interstellar liner *Brindisi* will be attacked in the neighborhood of the Three Ghosts system by four——' "

Weinbaum sat bolt upright in his swivel chair. "Let me see that letter!" he said, his voice harsh with repressed alarm.

"In a moment," the girl said, adjusting her skirt composedly. "Evidently I was right in riding my hunch. Let me go on reading: '—by four heavily armed vessels flying the lights of the navy of Hammersmith II. The position of the liner at that time will be at coded co-ordinates 88-A-theta-88-aleph-D and-per-se-and. It will——' "

"Miss Lje," Weinbaum said. "I'm sorry to interrupt you again, but what you've said already would justify me in jailing you at once, no matter how loudly your sponsors might scream. I don't know about this Interstellar Information outfit, or whether or not you did receive any such letter as the one you pretend to be quoting. But I can tell you that you've shown yourself to be in possession of information that only yours truly and four other men are supposed to know. It's already too late to tell you that everything you say may be held against you; all I can say now is, it's high time you clammed up!"

"I thought so," she said, apparently not disturbed in the least. "Then that liner *is* scheduled to hit those co-ordinates, and the coded time co-ordinate corresponds with the predicted Universal Time. Is it also true that the *Brindisi* will be carrying a top-secret communication device?"

"Are you deliberately trying to make me imprison you?" Weinbaum said, gritting his teeth. "Or is this just a stunt, designed to show me that my own bureau is full of leaks?"

"It could turn into that," Dana admitted. "But it hasn't, yet. Robin, I've been as honest with you as I'm able to be. You've had nothing but square deals from me up to now. I wouldn't yellow-screen you, and you know it. If this unknown outfit has this information, it might easily have gotten it from where it hints that it got it: from the field."

"Impossible."

"Why?"

"Because the information in question hasn't even reached my *own* agents in the field yet—it couldn't possibly have leaked as far as Hammersmith II or anywhere else, let alone to the Three Ghosts system! Letters have to be carried on ships, you know that. If I were to send orders by ultrawave to my Three Ghosts agent, he'd have to wait three hundred and twenty-four years to get them. By ship, he can get them in a little over two months. These particular orders have only been under way to him five days. Even if somebody has read them on board the ship that's carrying them, they couldn't possibly be sent on to the Three Ghosts any faster than they're traveling now."

Dana nodded her dark head. "All right. Then what are we left with but a leak in your headquarters here?"

"What, indeed," Weinbaum said grimly. "You'd better tell me who signed this letter of yours."

"The signature is J. Shelby Stevens."

Weinbaum switched on the intercom. "Margaret, look in the business register for an outfit called Interstellar Information and find out who owns it."

Dana Lje said, "Aren't you interested in the rest of the prediction?"

"You bet I am. Does it tell you the name of this communications device?"

"Yes," Dana said.

"What is it?"

"The Dirac communicator."

Weinbaum groaned and turned on the intercom again. "Margaret, send in Dr. Wald. Tell him to drop everything and gallop. Any luck with the other thing?"

"Yes, sir," the intercom said. "It's a one-man outfit, wholly owned by a J. Shelby Stevens, in Rico City. It was first registered this year."

"Arrest him, on suspicion of espionage."

The door swung open and Dr. Wald came in, all six and a half feet of him. He was extremely blond, and looked awkward, gentle, and not very intelligent.

"Thor, this young lady is our press nemesis, Dana Lje. Dana, Dr. Wald is the inventor of the Dirac communicator, about which you have so damnably much information."

"It's out *already?*" Dr. Wald said, scanning the girl with grave deliberation.

"It is, and lots more—*lots* more. Dana, you're a good girl at heart, and for some reason I trust you, stupid though it is to trust anybody in this job. I should detain you until Year Day, videocasts or no videocasts. Instead, I'm just going to ask you to sit on what you've got, and I'm going to explain why."

"Shoot."

"I've already mentioned how slow communication is between star and star. We have to carry all our letters on ships, just as we did locally before the invention of the telegraph. The overdrive lets us beat the speed of light, but not by much of a margin over really long distances. Do you understand that?"

"Certainly," Dana said. She appeared a bit nettled, and Weinbaum decided to give her the full dose at a more rapid pace. After all, she could be assumed to be better informed than the average layman.

"What we've needed for a long time, then," he said, "is some virtually instantaneous method of getting a message from somewhere to anywhere. Any time lag, no matter how small it seems at first, has a way of becoming major as longer and longer distances are involved. Sooner or later we must have this instantaneous method, or we won't be able to get messages from one system to another fast enough to hold our jurisdiction over outlying regions of space."

"Wait a minute," Dana said. "I'd always understood that ultrawave is faster than light."

"Effectively it is; physically it isn't. You don't understand that?"

She shook her dark head.

"In a nutshell," Weinbaum said, "ultrawave is radiation, and all radiation in free space is limited to the speed of light. The way we hype up ultrawave is to use an old application of wave-guide theory, whereby the real transmission of energy is at light speed, but an imaginary thing called "phase velocity" is going faster. But the gain in speed of transmission isn't large—by ultrawave, for instance, we get a message to Alpha Centauri in one year instead of nearly four. Over long distances, that's not nearly enough extra speed."

"Can't it be speeded further?" she said, frowning.

"No. Think of the ultrawave beam between here and Centaurus III as a caterpillar. The caterpillar himself is moving quite slowly, just at the speed of light. But the pulses which pass along his body are going forward faster than he is—and if you've ever watched a caterpillar, you'll know that that's true. But there's a physical limit to the number of pulses you can travel along that caterpillar, and we've already reached that limit. We've taken phase velocity as far as it will go.

"That's why we need something faster. For a long time our relativity theories discouraged hope of anything faster—even the high-phase velocity of a guided wave didn't contradict those theories; it just found a limited, mathematically imaginary loophole in them. But when Thor here began looking into the question of the velocity of propagation of a Dirac pulse, he found the answer. The communicator he developed does seem to act over long distances, *any* distance, instantaneously—and it may wind up knocking relativity into a cocked hat."

The girl's face was a study in stunned realization. "I'm not sure I've taken in all the technical angles," she said. "But if I'd had any notion of the political dynamite in this thing——"

"—you'd have kept out of my office," Weinbaum said grimly. "A good thing you didn't. The *Brindisi* is carrying a model of the Dirac communicator out to the periphery for a final test; the ship is supposed to get in touch with me from out there at a given Earth time, which we've calculated very elaborately to account for the residual Lorentz and Milne transformations involved in overdrive flight, and for a lot of other time phenomena that wouldn't mean anything at all to you.

"If that signal arrives here at the given Earth time, then —aside from the havoc it will create among the theoretical physicists whom we decide to let in on it—we will really have our instant communicator, and can include all of occupied space in the same time zone. And we'll have a terrific advantage over any lawbreaker who has to resort to ultra-wave locally and to letters carried by ships over the long haul."

"Not," Dr. Wald said sourly, "if it's already leaked out."

"It remains to be seen how much of it has leaked," Weinbaum said. "The principle is rather esoteric, Thor, and the name of the thing alone wouldn't mean much even to a trained scientist. I gather that Dana's mysterious informant didn't go into technical details . . . or did he?"

"No," Dana said.

"Tell the truth, Dana. I know that you're suppressing some of that letter."

The girl started slightly. "All right—yes, I am. But nothing technical. There's another part of the prediction that lists the number and class of ships you will send to protect the *Brindisi*—the prediction says they'll be sufficient, by the way —and I'm keeping that to myself, to see whether or not it comes true along with the rest. If it does, I think I've hired myself a correspondent."

"If it does," Weinbaum said, "you've hired yourself a jailbird. Let's see how much mind reading J. Whatsit Stevens can do from the subcellar of Fort Yaphank."

3

Weinbaum let himself into Stevens's cell, locking the door behind him and passing the keys out to the guard. He sat down heavily on the nearest stool.

Stevens smiled the weak benevolent smile of the very old, and laid his book aside on the bunk. The book, Weinbaum knew—since his office had cleared it—was only a volume of pleasant, harmless lyrics by a New Dynasty poet named Nims.

"Were our predictions correct, Captain?" Stevens said. His voice was high and musical, rather like that of a boy soprano.

Weinbaum nodded. "You still won't tell us how you did it?"

"But I already have," Stevens protested. "Our intelligence

network is the best in the Universe, Captain. It is superior even to your own excellent organization, as events have shown."

"Its results are superior, that I'll grant," Weinbaum said glumly. "If Dana Lje had thrown your letter down her disposal chute, we would have lost the *Brindisi* and our Dirac transmitter both. Incidentally, did your original letter predict accurately the number of ships we would send?"

Stevens nodded pleasantly, his neatly trimmed white beard thrusting forward slightly as he smiled.

"I was afraid so," Weinbaum leaned forward. "Do you have the Dirac transmitter, Stevens?"

"Of course, Captain. How else could my correspondents report to me with the efficiency you have observed?"

"Then why don't our receivers pick up the broadcasts of your agents? Dr. Wald says it's inherent in the principle that Dirac 'casts are picked up by *all* instruments tuned to receive them, bar none. And at this stage of the game there are so few such broadcasts being made that we'd be almost certain to detect any that weren't coming from our own operatives."

"I decline to answer that question, if you'll excuse the impoliteness," Stevens said, his voice quavering slightly. "I am an old man, Captain, and this intelligence agency is my sole source of income. If I told you how we operated, we would no longer have any advantage over your own service, except for the limited freedom from secrecy which we have. I have been assured by competent lawyers that I have every right to operate a private investigation bureau, properly licensed, upon any scale that I may choose; and that I have the right to keep my methods secret, as the so-called 'intellectual assets' of my firm. If you wish to use our services, well and good. We will provide them, with absolute guarantees on all information we furnish you, for an appropriate fee. But our methods are our own property."

Robin Weinbaum smiled twistedly. "I'm not a naïve man, Mr. Stevens," he said. "My service is hard on naïveté. You know as well as I do that the government can't allow you to operate on a free-lance basis, supplying top-secret information to anyone who can pay the price, or even free of charge to video columnists on a 'test' basis, even though you arrive at every jot of that information independently of espionage—which I still haven't entirely ruled out, by the way. If you can duplicate this *Brindisi* performance at will, we will have to have your services exclusively. In short, you become a hired civilian arm of my own bureau."

"Quite," Stevens said, returning the smile in a fatherly way. "We anticipated that, of course. However, we have contracts with other governments to consider; Erskine, in particular. If we are to work exclusively for Earth, necessarily our price will include compensation for renouncing our other accounts."

"Why should it? Patriotic public servants work for their government at a loss, if they can't work for it any other way."

"I am quite aware of that. I am quite prepared to renounce my other interests. But I do require to be paid."

"How much?" Weinbaum said, suddenly aware that his fists were clenched so tightly that they hurt.

Stevens appeared to consider, nodding his flowery white poll in senile deliberation. "My associates would have to be consulted. Tentatively, however, a sum equal to the present appropriation of your bureau would do, pending further negotiations."

Weinbaum shot to his feet, eyes wide. "You old buccaneer! You know damned well that I can't spend my entire appropriation on a single civilian service! Did it ever occur to you that most of the civilian outfits working for us are on cost-plus contracts, and that our civilian executives are being paid just a credit a year, by their own choice? You're demanding nearly two thousand credits an hour from your own government, and claiming the legal protection that the government affords you at the same time, in order to let those fanatics on Erskine run up a higher bid!"

"The price is not unreasonable," Stevens said. "The service is worth the price."

"That's where you're wrong! We have the discoverer of the machine working for us. For less than half the sum you're asking, we can find the application of the device that you're trading on—of that you can be damned sure."

"A dangerous gamble, Captain."

"Perhaps. We'll soon see!" Weinbaum glared at the placid face. "I'm forced to tell you that you're a free man, Mr. Stevens. We've been unable to show that you came by your information by any illegal method. You had classified facts in your possession, but no classified documents, and it's your privilege as a citizen to make guesses, no matter how educated.

"But we'll catch up with you sooner or later. Had you

been reasonable, you might have found yourself in a very good position with us, your income as assured as any political income can be, and your person respected to the hilt. Now, however, you're subject to censorship—you have no idea how humiliating that can be, but I'm going to see to it that you find out. There'll be no more newsbeats for Dana Lje, or for anyone else. I want to see every word of copy that you file with any client outside the bureau. Every word that is of use to me will be used, and you'll be paid the statutory one cent a word for it—the same rate that the FBI pays for anonymous gossip. Everything I don't find useful will be killed without clearance. Eventually we'll have the modification of the Dirac that you're using, and when that happens, you'll be so flat broke that a pancake with a harelip could spit right over you."

Weinbaum paused for a moment, astonished at his own fury.

Stevens's clarinetlike voice began to sound in the window-less cavity. "Captain, I have no doubt that you can do this to me, at least incompletely. But it will prove fruitless. I will give you a prediction, at no charge. It is guaranteed, as are all our predictions. It is this: *You will never find that modification.* Eventually, I will give it to you, on my own terms, but you will never find it for yourself, nor will you force it out of me. In the meantime, not a word of copy will be filed with you; for, despite the fact that you are an arm of the government, I can well afford to wait you out."

"Bluster," Weinbaum said.

"Fact. Yours is the bluster—loud talk based on nothing more than a hope. I, however, *know* whereof I speak. . . . But let us conclude this discussion. It serves no purpose; you will need to see my points made the hard way. Thank you for giving me my freedom. We will talk again under different circumstances on—let me see; ah, yes, on June 9 of the year 2091. That year is, I believe, almost upon us."

Stevens picked up his book again, nodding at Weinbaum, his expression harmless and kindly, his hands showing the marked tremor of *paralysis agitans*. Weinbaum moved help-lessly to the door and flagged the turnkey. As the bars closed behind him, Stevens's voice called out: "Oh, yes; and a Happy New Year, Captain."

Weinbaum blasted his way back into his own office, at least twice as mad as the proverbial nest of hornets, and at the same time rather dismally aware of his own probable future. If Stevens's second prediction turned out to be as phenomenally accurate as his first had been, Capt. Robin Weinbaum would soon be peddling a natty set of second-hand uniforms.

He glared down at Margaret Soames, his receptionist. She glared right back; she had known him too long to be intimidated.

"Anything?" he said.

"Dr. Wald's waiting for you in your office. There are some field reports, and a couple of Diracs on your private tape. Any luck with the old codger?"

"That," he said crushingly, "is Top Secret."

"Poof. That means that nobody still knows the answer but J. Shelby Stevens."

He collapsed suddenly. "You're so right. That's just what it does mean. But we'll bust him wide open sooner or later. We've *got* to."

"You'll do it," Margaret said. "Anything else for me?"

"No. Tip off the clerical staff that there's a half holiday today, then go take in a stereo or a steak or something yourself. Dr. Wald and I have a few private wires to pull . . . and unless I'm sadly mistaken, a private bottle of aquavit to empty."

"Right," the receptionist said. "Tie one on for me, Chief. I understand that beer is the best chaser for aquavit—I'll have some sent up."

"If you should return after I am suitably squiffed," Weinbaum said, feeling a little better already, "I will kiss you for your thoughtfulness. *That* should keep you at your stereo at least twice through the third feature."

As he went on through the door of his own office, she said demurely behind him, "It certainly should."

As soon as the door closed, however, his mood became abruptly almost as black as before. Despite his comparative youth—he was now only fifty-five—he had been in the service a long time, and he needed no one to tell him the possible consequences which might flow from possession by a private citizen of the Dirac communicator. If there was ever to be a Federation of Man in the Galaxy, it was within the power of J. Shelby Stevens to ruin it before it had fairly gotten started. And there seemed to be nothing at all that could be done about it.

"Hello, Thor," he said glumly. "Pass the bottle."

"Hello, Robin. I gather things went badly. Tell me about it."

Briefly, Weinbaum told him. "And the worst of it," he finished, "is that Stevens himself predicts that we won't find the application of the Dirac that he's using, and that eventually we'll have to buy it at his price. Somehow I believe him—but I can't see how it's possible. If I were to tell Congress that I was going to spend my entire appropriation for a single civilian service, I'd be out on my ear within the next three sessions."

"Perhaps that isn't his real price," the scientist suggested. "If he wants to barter, he'd naturally begin with a demand miles above what he actually wants."

"Sure, sure . . . but frankly, Thor, I'd hate to give the old reprobate even a single credit if I could get out of it." Weinbaum sighed. "Well, let's see what's come in from the field."

Thor Wald moved silently away from Weinbaum's desk while the officer unfolded it and set up the Dirac screen. Stacked neatly next to the ultraphone—a device Weinbaum had been thinking of, only a few days ago, as permanently outmoded—were the tapes Margaret had mentioned. He fed the first one into the Dirac and turned the main toggle to the position labeled START.

Immediately the whole screen went pure white and the audio speakers emitted an almost instantly end-stopped blare of sound—a *beep* which, as Weinbaum already knew, made up a continuous spectrum from about 30 cycles per second to well above 18,000 cps. Then both the light and the noise were gone as if they had never been, and were replaced by the familiar face and voice of Weinbaum's local ops chief in Rico City.

"There's nothing unusual in the way of transmitters in Stevens's offices here," the operative said without preamble. "And there isn't any local Interstellar Information staff, except for one stenographer, and she's as dumb as they come. About all we could get from her is that Stevens is 'such a sweet old man.' No possibility that she's faking it; she's genuinely stupid, the kind that thinks Betelgeuse is something Indians use to darken their skins. We looked for some sort of list or code table that would give us a line on Stevens's field staff, but that was another dead end. Now we're maintaining a twenty-four-hour Dinwiddie watch on the place from a joint across the street. Orders?"

Weinbaum dictated to the blank stretch of tape which followed: "Margaret, next time you send any Dirac tapes in here, cut that damnable *beep* off them first. Tell the boys in Rico City that Stevens has been released, and that I'm proceeding for an Order In Security to tap his ultraphone and his local lines—this is one case where I'm sure we can persuade the court that tapping's necessary. Also—and be damned sure you code this—tell them to proceed with the tap immediately and to maintain it regardless of whether or not the court O.K.s it. I'll thumbprint a Full Responsibility Confession for them. We can't afford to play pat-a-cake with Stevens—the potential is just too damned big. And oh, yes, Margaret, send the message by carrier, and send out general orders to everybody concerned not to use the Dirac again except when distance and time rule every other medium out. Stevens has already admitted that he can receive Dirac 'casts."

He put down the mike and stared morosely for a moment at the beautiful Eridanean scrollwood of his desktop. Wald coughed inquiringly and retrieved the aquavit.

"Excuse me, Robin," he said, "but I should think that would work both ways."

"So should I. And yet the fact is that we've never picked up so much as a whisper from either Stevens or his agents. I can't think of any way that could be pulled, but evidently it can."

"Well, let's rethink the problem, and see what we get," Wald said. "I didn't want to say so in front of the young lady, for obvious reasons—I mean Miss Lje, of course, not Margaret—but the truth is that the Dirac is essentially a simple mechanism in principle. I seriously doubt that there's any way to transmit a message from it which can't be detected—and an examination of the theory with that proviso in mind might give us something new."

"What proviso?" Weinbaum said. Thor Wald left him behind rather often these days.

"Why, that a Dirac transmission doesn't *necessarily* go to all communicators capable of receiving it. If that's true, then the reasons why it is true should emerge from the theory."

"I see. O.K., proceed on that line. I've been looking at Stevens's dossier while you were talking, and it's an absolute desert. Prior to the opening of the office in Rico City, there's no dope whatever on J. Shelby Stevens. The man as good as rubbed my nose in the fact that he's using a pseud when I first talked to him. I asked him what the 'J' in his name stood for, and he said, 'Oh, let's make it Jerome.' But who the man behind the pseud *is* . . ."

"Is it possible that he's using his own initials?"

"No," Weinbaum said. "Only the dumbest ever do that, or transpose syllables, or retain any connection at all with their real names. Those are the people who are in serious emotional trouble, people who drive themselves into anonymity, but leave clues strewn all around the landscape— those clues are really a cry for help, for discovery. Of course we're working on that angle—we can't neglect anything— but J. Shelby Stevens isn't that kind of case, I'm sure." Weinbaum stood up abruptly. "O.K., Thor—what's first on your technical program?"

"Well . . . I suppose we'll have to start with checking the frequencies we use. We're going on Dirac's assumption— and it works very well, and always has—that a positron in motion through a crystal lattice is accompanied by de Broglie waves which are transforms of the waves of an electron in motion somewhere else in the Universe. Thus if we control the frequency and path of the positron, we control the placement of the electron—we cause it to appear, so to speak, in the circuits of a communicator somewhere else. After that, reception is just a matter of amplifying the bursts and reading the signal."

Wald scowled and shook his blond head. "If Stevens is getting out messages which we don't pick up, my first assumption would be that he's worked out a fine-tuning circuit that's more delicate than ours, and is more or less sneaking his messages under ours. The only way that could be done, as far as I can see at the moment, is by something really fantastic in the way of exact frequency control of his positron gun. If so, the logical step for us is to go back to the beginning of our tests and rerun our diffractions to see if we can refine our measurements of positron frequencies."

The scientist looked so inexpressibly gloomy as he offered this conclusion that a pall of hopelessness settled over Weinbaum in sheer sympathy. "You don't look as if you expected that to uncover anything new."

"I don't. You see, Robin, things are different in physics now than they used to be in the twentieth century. In those days, it was always presupposed that physics was limitless —the classic statement was made by Weyl, who said that

'It is the nature of a real thing to be inexhaustible in content.' We know now that that's not so, except in a remote, associational sort of way. Nowadays, physics is a defined and self-limited science; its scope is still prodigious, but we can no longer think of it as endless.

"This is better established in particle physics than in any other branch of the science. Half of the trouble physicists of the last century had with Euclidean geometry—and hence the reason why they evolved so many recomplicated theories of relativity—is that it's a geometry of lines, and thus can be subdivided infinitely. When Cantor proved that there really is an infinity, at least mathematically speaking, that seemed to clinch the case for the possibility of a really infinite physical universe, too."

Wald's eyes grew vague, and he paused to gulp down a slug of the licorice-flavored aquavit which would have made Weinbaum's every hair stand on end.

"I remember," Wald said, "the man who taught me theory of sets at Princeton, many years ago. He used to say: 'Cantor teaches us that there are many kinds of infinities. *There* was a crazy old man!' "

Weinbaum rescued the bottle hastily. "So go on, Thor."

"Oh." Wald blinked. "Yes. Well, what we know now is that the geometry which applies to ultimate particles, like the positron, isn't Euclidean at all. It's Pythagorean—a geometry of points, not lines. Once you've measured one of those points, and it doesn't matter what kind of quantity you're measuring, you're down as far as you can go. At that point, the Universe becomes discontinuous, and no further refinement is possible.

"And I'd say that our positron-frequency measurements have already gotten that far down. There isn't another element in the Universe denser than plutonium, yet we get the same frequency values by diffraction through plutonium crystals that we get through osmium crystals—there's not the slightest difference. If J. Shelby Stevens is operating in terms of fractions of those values, then he's doing what an organist would call 'playing in the cracks'—which is certainly something you can *think* about doing, but something that's in actuality impossible to do. *Hoop.*"

"Hoop?" Weinbaum said.

"Sorry. A hiccup only."

"Oh. Well, maybe Stevens has rebuilt the organ?"

"If he has rebuilt the metrical frame of the Universe to

accommodate a private skip-tracing firm," Wald said firmly, "I for one see no reason why we can't countercheck him —hoop—by declaring the whole cosmos null and void."

"All right, all right," Weinbaum said, grinning. "I didn't mean to push your analogy right over the edge—I was just asking. But let's get to work on it anyhow. We can't just sit here and let Stevens get away with it. If this frequency angle turns out to be as hopeless as it seems, we'll try something else."

Wald eyed the aquavit bottle owlishly. "It's a very pretty problem," he said. "Have I ever sung you the song we have in Sweden called 'Nat-og-Dag?' "

"*Hoop*," Weinbaum said, to his own surprise, in a high falsetto. "Excuse me. No. Let's hear it."

The computer occupied an entire floor of the Security building, its seemingly identical banks laid out side by side on the floor along an advanced pathological state of Peano's "space-filling curve." At the current business end of the line was a master control board with a large television screen at its center, at which Dr. Wald was stationed, with Weinbaum looking, silently but anxiously, over his shoulder.

The screen itself showed a pattern which, except that it was drawn in green light against a dark gray background, strongly resembled the grain in a piece of highly polished mahogany. Photographs of similar patterns were stacked on a small table to Dr. Wald's right; several had spilled over onto the floor.

"Well, there it is," Wald sighed at length. "And I won't struggle to keep myself from saying 'I told you so.' What you've had me do here, Robin, is to reconfirm about half the basic postulates of particle physics—which is why it took so long, even though it was the first project we started." He snapped off the screen. "There are no cracks for J. Shelby to play in. That's definite."

"If you'd said 'That's flat,' you would have made a joke," Weinbaum said sourly. "Look . . . isn't there still a chance of error? If not on your part, Thor, then in the computer? After all, it's set up to work only with the unit charges of modern physics; mightn't we have to disconnect the banks that contain that bias before the machine will follow the fractional-charge instructions we give it?"

" 'Disconnect,' he says," Wald groaned, mopping his brow reflectively. "The bias exists everywhere in the machine, my friend, because it functions everywhere on those same unit charges. It wasn't a matter of subtracting banks; we had to add one with a bias all its own, to countercorrect the corrections the computer would otherwise apply to the instructions. The technicians thought I was crazy. Now, five months later, I've proved it."

Weinbaum grinned in spite of himself. "What about the other projects?"

"All done—some time back, as a matter of fact. The staff and I checked every single Dirac tape we've received since you released J. Shelby from Yaphank, for any sign of intermodulation, marginal signals, or anything else of the kind. There's nothing, Robin, absolutely nothing. That's our net result, all around."

"Which leaves us just where we started," Weinbaum said. "All the monitoring projects came to the same dead end; I strongly suspect that Stevens hasn't risked any further calls from his home office to his field staff, even though he seemed confident that we'd never intercept such calls—as we haven't. Even our local wire tapping hasn't turned up anything but calls by Stevens's secretary, making appointments for him with various clients, actual and potential. Any information he's selling these days he's passing on in person—and not in his office, either, because we've got bugs planted all over that and haven't heard a thing."

"That must limit his range of operation enormously," Wald objected.

Weinbaum nodded. "Without a doubt—but he shows no signs of being bothered by it. He can't have sent any tips to Erskine recently, for instance, because our last tangle with that crew came out very well for us, even though we had to use the Dirac to send the orders to our squadron out there. If he overheard us, he didn't even try to pass the word. Just as he said, he's sweating us out—" Weinbaum paused. "Wait a minute, here comes Margaret. And by the length of her stride, I'd say she's got something particularly nasty on her mind."

"You bet I do," Margaret Soames said vindictively. "And it'll blow plenty of lids around here, or I miss my guess. The I. D. squad has finally pinned down J. Shelby Stevens. They did it with the voice-comparator alone."

"How does that work?" Wald said interestedly.

"Blink microphone," Weinbaum said impatiently. "Isolates inflections on single, normally stressed syllables and matches them. Standard I. D. searching technique, on a case of this kind, but it takes so long that we usually get the quarry by other means before it pays off. Well, don't stand there like a dummy, Margaret. Who is he?

" 'He,' " Margaret said, "is your sweetheart of the video waves, Miss Dana Lje."

"They're crazy!" Wald said, staring at her.

Weinbaum came slowly out of his first shock of stunned disbelief. "No, Thor," he said finally. "No, it figures. If a woman is going to go in for disguises, there are always two she can assume outside her own sex: a young boy, and a very old man. And Dana's an actress; that's no news to us."

"But—but why did she do it, Robin?"

"That's what we're going to find out right now. So we wouldn't get the Dirac modification by ourselves, eh! Well, there are other ways of getting answers besides particle physics. Margaret, do you have a pick-up order out for that girl?"

"No," the receptionist said. "This is one chestnut I wanted to see you pull out for yourself. You give me the authority, and I send the order—not before."

"Spiteful child. Send it, then, and glory in my gritted teeth. Come on, Thor—let's put the nutcracker on this chestnut."

As they were leaving the computer floor, Weinbaum stopped suddenly in his tracks and began to mutter in an almost inaudible voice.

Wald said, "What's the matter, Robin?"

"Nothing. I keep being brought up short by those predictions. What's the date?"

"M'm . . . June 9. Why?"

"It's the exact date that 'Stevens' predicted we'd meet again, damn it! Something tells me that this isn't going to be as simple as it looks."

If Dana Lje had any idea of what she was in for—and considering the fact that she was 'J. Shelby Stevens' it had to be assumed that she did—the knowledge seemed not to make her at all fearful. She sat as composedly as ever before Weinbaum's desk, smoking her eternal cigarette, and waited, one dimpled knee pointed directly at the bridge of the officer's nose.

"Dana," Weinbaum said, "this time we're going to get all the answers, and we're not going to be gentle about it. Just

in case you're not aware of the fact, there are certain laws
relating to giving false information to a security officer, under
which we could heave you in prison for a minimum of fifteen
years. By application of the statutes on using communications
to defraud, plus various local laws against transvestism,
pseudonymity and so on, we could probably pile up enough
additional short sentences to keep you in Yaphank until you
really *do* grow a beard. So I'd advise you to open up."

"I have every intention of opening up," Dana said. "I
know, practically word for word, how this interview is going
to proceed, what information I'm going to give you, just
when I'm going to give it to you—and what you're going to
pay me for it. I knew all that many months ago. So there
would be no point in my holding out on you."

"What you're saying, Miss Lje," Thor Wald said in a resigned voice, "is that the future is fixed, and that you can
read it, in every essential detail."

"Quite right, Dr. Wald. Both those things are true."

There was a brief silence.

"All right," Weinbaum said grimly. "Talk."

"All right, Captain Weinbaum, pay me," Dana said calmly.

Weinbaum snorted.

"But I'm quite serious," she said. "You still don't know
what I know about the Dirac communicator. I won't be
forced to tell it, by threat of prison or by any other threat.
You see, I know for a fact that you aren't going to send me
to prison, or give me drugs, or do anything else of that kind.
I know for a fact, instead, that you are going to pay me—so
I'd be very foolish to say a word until you do. After all, it's
quite a secret you're buying. Once I tell you what it is, you
and the entire service will be able to read the future as I do,
and then the information will be valueless to me."

Weinbaum was completely speechless for a moment.
Finally he said, "Dana, you have a heart of purest brass, as
well as a knee with an invisible gunsight on it. I say that
I'm *not* going to give you my appropriation, regardless of
what the future may or may not say about it. I'm not going
to give it to you because the way my government—and yours
—runs things makes such a price impossible. Or is that really
your price?"

"It's my real price . . . but it's also an alternative. Call
it my second choice. My first choice, which means the price
I'd settle for, comes in two parts: (a) to be taken into your
service as a responsible officer; and, (b) to be married to
Captain Robin Weinbaum."

Weinbaum sailed up out of his chair. He felt as though copper-colored flames a foot long were shooting out of each of his ears.

"Of all the——" he began. There his voice failed completely.

From behind him, where Wald was standing, came something like a large, Scandinavian-model guffaw being choked into insensibility.

Dana herself seemed to be smiling a little.

"You see," she said, "I don't point my best and most accurate knee at every man I meet."

Weinbaum sat down again, slowly and carefully. "Walk, do not run, to nearest exit," he said. "Women and childlike security officers first. Miss Lje, are you trying to sell me the notion that you went through this elaborate hanky-panky—beard and all—out of a burning passion for my dumpy and underpaid person?"

"Not entirely," Dana Lje said. "I want to be in the bureau, too, as I said. Let me confront you, though, Captain, with a fact of life that doesn't seem to have occurred to you at all. Do you accept as a fact that I can read the future in detail, and that that, to be possible at all, means that the future is fixed?"

"Since Thor seems able to accept it, I suppose I can too—provisionally."

"There's nothing provisional about it," Dana said firmly. "Now, when I first came upon this—uh, this gimmick—quite a while back, one of the first things that I found out was that I was going to go through the 'J. Shelby Stevens' masquerade, force myself onto the staff of the bureau, and marry you, Robin. At the time, I was both astonished and completely rebellious. I didn't want to be on the bureau staff; I liked my free-lance life as a video commentator. I didn't want to marry you, though I wouldn't have been averse to living with you for a while—say a month or so. And above all, the masquerade struck me as ridiculous.

"But the facts kept staring me in the face. I *was* going to do all those things. There were no alternatives, no fanciful 'branches of time,' no decision-points that might be altered to make the future change. My future, like yours, Dr. Wald's, and everyone else's, was fixed. It didn't matter a snap whether or not I had a decent motive for what I was going to do; I was going to do it anyhow. Cause and effect, as I could see for myself, just don't exist. One event follows another because events are just as indestructible in space-time as matter and energy are.

"It was the bitterest of all pills. It will take me many years to swallow it completely, and you too. Dr. Wald will come around a little sooner, I think. At any rate, once I was intellectually convinced that all this was so, I had to protect my own sanity. I knew that I couldn't alter what I was going to do, but the least I could do to protect myself was to supply myself with motives. Or, in other words, just plain rationalizations. That much, it seems, we're free to do; the consciousness of the observer is just along for the ride through time, and can't alter events—but it can comment, explain, invent. That's fortunate, for none of us could stand going through motions which were truly free of what we think of as personal significances.

"So I supplied myself with the obvious motives. Since I was going to be married to you and couldn't get out of it, I set out to convince myself that I loved you. Now I do. Since I was going to join the bureau staff, I thought over all the advantages that it might have over video commentating, and found that they made a respectable list. Those are my motives.

"But I had no such motives at the beginning. Actually, there are never motives behind actions. All actions are fixed. What we called motives evidently are rationalizations by the helpless observing consciousness, which is intelligent enough to smell an event coming—and, since it cannot avert the event, instead cooks up reasons for wanting it to happen."

"Wow," Dr. Wald said, inelegantly but with considerable force.

"Either 'wow' or 'balderdash' seems to be called for—I can't quite decide which," Weinbaum agreed. "We know that Dana is an actress, Thor, so let's not fall off the apple tree quite yet. Dana, I've been saving the *really* hard question for the last. That question is: *How?* How did you arrive at this modification of the Dirac transmitter? Remember, we know your background, where we didn't know that of 'J. Shelby Stevens.' You're not a scientist. There were some fairly high-powered intellects among your distant relatives, but that's as close as you come."

"I'm going to give you several answers to that question," Dana Lje said. "Pick the one you like best. They're all true, but they tend to contradict each other here and there.

"To begin with, you're right about my relatives, of course.

If you'll check your dossier again, though, you'll discover that those so-called 'distant' relatives were the last surviving members of my family besides myself. When they died, second and fourth and ninth cousins though they were, their estates reverted to me, and among their effects I found a sketch of a possible instantaneous communicator based on de Broglie-wave inversion. The material was in very rough form, and mostly beyond my comprehension, because I am, as you say, no scientist myself. But I was interested; I could see, dimly, what such a thing might be worth—and not only in money.

"My interest was fanned by two coincidences—the kind of coincidences that cause-and-effect just can't allow, but which seem to happen all the same in the world of unchangeable events. For most of my adult life, I've been in communications industries of one kind or another, mostly branches of video. I had communications equipment around me constantly, and I had coffee and doughnuts with communications engineers every day. First I picked up the jargon; then, some of the procedures; and eventually a little real knowledge. Some of the things I learned can't be gotten any other way. Some other things are ordinarily available only to highly educated people like Dr. Wald here, and came to me by accident, in horseplay, between kisses, and a hundred other ways—all natural to the environment of a video network."

Weinbaum found, to his own astonishment, that the "between kisses" clause did not sit very well in his chest. He said, with unintentional brusqueness: "What's the other coincidence?"

"A leak in your own staff."

"Dana, you ought to have that set to music."

"Suit yourself."

"I can't suit myself," Weinbaum said petulantly. "I work for the government. Was this leak direct to you?"

"Not at first. That was why I kept insisting to you in person that there might be such a leak, and why I finally began to hint about it in public, on my program. I was hoping that you'd be able to seal it up inside the bureau before my first rather tenuous contact with it got lost. When I didn't succeed in provoking you into protecting yourself, I took the risk of making direct contact with the leak myself—and the first piece of secret information that came to me through it was the final point I needed to put my Dirac communicator together. When it was all assembled, it did more than just communicate. It predicted. And I can tell you why."

Weinbaum said thoughtfully, "I don't find this very hard to accept, so far. Pruned of the philosophy, it even makes some sense of the 'J. Shelby Stevens' affair. I assume that by letting the old gentleman become known as somebody who knew more about the Dirac transmitter than I did, and who wasn't averse to negotiating with anybody who had money, you kept the leak working through you—rather than transmitting data directly to unfriendly governments."

"It did work out that way," Dana said. "But that wasn't the genesis or the purpose of the Stevens masquerade. I've already given you the whole explanation of how that came about."

"Well, you'd better name me that leak, before the man gets away."

"When the price is paid, not before. It's too late to prevent a getaway, anyhow. In the meantime, Robin, I want to go on and tell you the other answer to your question about how I was able to find this particular Dirac secret, and you didn't. What answers I've given you up to now have been cause-and-effect answers, with which we're all more comfortable. But I want to impress on you that all apparent cause-and-effect relationships are accidents. There is no such thing as a cause, and no such thing as an effect. I found the secret because I found it; that event was fixed; that certain circumstances seem to explain why I found it, in the old cause-and-effect terms, is irrelevant. Similarly, with all your superior equipment and brains, you didn't find it for one reason, and one reason alone: because you didn't find it. The history of the future says you didn't."

"I pays my money and I takes no choice, eh?" Weinbaum said ruefully.

"I'm afraid so—and I don't like it any better than you do."

"Thor, what's your opinion of all this?"

"It's just faintly flabbergasting," Wald said soberly. "However, it hangs together. The deterministic universe which Miss Lje paints was a common feature of the old relativity theories, and as sheer speculation has an even longer history. I would say that, in the long run, how much credence we place in the story as a whole will rest upon her method of, as she calls it, reading the future. If it is demonstrable beyond any doubt, then the rest becomes perfectly credible—philosophy and all. If it doesn't, then what remains is an admirable job of acting, plus some metaphysics which, while self-consistent, is not original with Miss Lje."

"That sums up the case as well as if I'd coached you, Dr. Wald," Dana said. "I'd like to point out one more thing. If I can read the future, then 'J. Shelby Stevens' never had any need for a staff of field operatives, and he never needed to send a single Dirac message which you might intercept. All he needed to do was to make predictions from his readings, which he knew to be infallible; no private espionage network had to be involved."

"I see that," Weinbaum said dryly. "All right, Dana, let's put the proposition this way: *I do not believe you.* Much of what you say is probably true, but in totality I believe it to be false. On the other hand, if you're telling the whole truth, you certainly deserve a place on the bureau staff—it would be dangerous as hell *not* to have you with us—and the marriage is a more or less minor matter, except to you and me. You can have that with no strings attached; I don't want to be bought, any more than you would.

"So: if you will tell me where the leak is, we will consider that part of the question closed. I make that condition not as a price, but because I don't want to get myself engaged to somebody who might be shot as a spy within a month."

"Fair enough," Dana said. "Robin, your leak is Margaret Soames. She is an Erskine operative, and nobody's bubble-brain. She's a highly trained technician."

"Well, I'll be damned," Weinbaum said in astonishment. "Then she's already flown the coop—she was the one who first told me we'd identified you. She must have taken on that job in order to hold up delivery long enough to stage an exit."

"That's right. But you'll catch her, day after tomorrow. And you are now a hooked fish, Robin."

There was another suppressed burble from Thor Wald.

"I accept the fate happily," Weinbaum said, eying the gunsight knee. "Now, if you will tell me how you work your swami trick, and if it backs up everything you've said to the letter, as you claim, I'll see to it that you're also taken into the bureau and that all charges against you are quashed. Otherwise, I'll probably have to kiss the bride between the bars of a cell."

Dana smiled. "The secret is very simple. It's in the beep."

Weinbaum's jaw dropped. "The beep? The Dirac noise?"

"That's right. You didn't find it out because you considered the beep to be just a nuisance, and ordered Miss Soames to

cut it off all tapes before sending them in to you. Miss
Soames, who had some inkling of what the beep meant, was
more than happy to do so, leaving the reading of the beep
exclusively to 'J. Shelby Stevens'—who she thought was going
to take on Erskine as a client."

"Explain," Thor Wald said, looking intense.

"Just as you assumed, every Dirac message that is sent is
picked up by every receiver that is capable of detecting it.
Every receiver—including the first one ever built, which is
yours, Dr. Wald, through the hundreds of thousands of them
which will exist throughout the Galaxy in the twenty-fourth
century, to the untold millions which will exist in the thirtieth
century, and so on. The Dirac beep is the simultaneous reception of *every one of the Dirac messages which have ever
been sent, or ever will be sent*. Incidentally, the cardinal
number of the total of those messages is a relatively small
and of course finite number; it's far below really large finite
numbers such as the number of electrons in the universe,
even when you break each and every message down into
individual 'bits' and count those."

"Of course," Dr. Wald said softly. "Of course! But, Miss
Lje . . . how do you tune for an individual message? We
tried fractional positron frequencies, and got nowhere."

"I didn't even know fractional positron frequencies existed,"
Dana confessed. "No, it's simple—so simple that a lucky
layman like me could arrive at it. You tune individual
messages out of the beep by time lag, nothing more. All the
messages arrive at the same instant, in the smallest fraction
of time that exists, something called a 'chronon.' "

"Yes," Wald said. "The time it takes one electron to move
from one quantum-level to another. That's the Pythagorean
point of time measurement."

"Thank you. Obviously no gross physical receiver can respond to a message that brief, or at least that's what I
thought at first. But because there are relay and switching
delays, various forms of feedback and so on, in the apparatus
itself, the beep arrives at the output end as a complex pulse
which has been 'splattered' along the time axis for a full
second or more. That's an effect which you can exaggerate
by recording the 'splattered' beep on a high-speed tape, the
same way you would record any event that you wanted to
study in slow motion. Then you tune up the various failure-
points in your receiver, to exaggerate one failure, minimize

all the others, and use noise-suppressing techniques to cut out the background."

Thor Wald frowned. "You'd still have a considerable garble when you were through. You'd have to sample the messages——"

"Which is just what I did; Robin's little lecture to me about the ultrawave gave me that hint. I set myself to find out how the ultrawave channel carries so many messages at once, and I discovered that you people sample the incoming pulses every thousandth of a second and pass on one pip only when the wave deviates in a certain way from the mean. I didn't really believe it would work on the Dirac beep, but it turned out just as well: 90 percent as intelligible as the original transmission after it came through the smearing device. I'd already got enough from the beep to put my plan in motion, of course—but now every voice message in it was available, and crystal-clear: If you select three pips every thousandth of second, you can even pick up an intelligible transmission of music—a little razzy, but good enough to identify the instruments that are playing—and that's a very close test of any communications device."

"There's a question of detail here that doesn't quite follow," said Weinbaum, for whom the technical talk was becoming a little too thick to fight through. "Dana, you say that you knew the course this conversation was going to take—yet it isn't being Dirac-recorded, nor can I see any reason why any summary of it would be sent out on the Dirac afterwards."

"That's true, Robin. However, when I leave here, I will make such a transcast myself, on my own Dirac. Obviously I will—because I've *already* picked it up, from the beep."

"In other words, you're going to call yourself up—months ago."

"That's it," Dana said. "It's not as useful a technique as you might think at first, because it's dangerous to make such broadcasts while a situation is still developing. You can safely 'phone back' details only after the given situation has gone to completion, as a chemist might put it. Once you know, however, that when you use the Dirac you're dealing with time, you can coax some very strange things out of the instrument."

She paused and smiled. "I have heard," she said conversationally, "the voice of the President of our Galaxy, in 3480, announcing the federation of the Milky Way and the

Magellanic Clouds. I've heard the commander of a world-line cruiser, traveling from 8873 to 8704 along the world line of the planet Hathshepa, which circles a star on the rim of NGC 4725, calling for help across eleven million light-years—but what kind of help he was calling for, or will be calling for, is beyond my comprehension. And many other things. When you check on me, you'll hear these things too—and you'll wonder what many of them mean.

"And you'll listen to them even more closely than I did, in the hope of finding out whether or not anyone was able to understand in time to help."

Weinbaum and Wald looked dazed.

Her voice became a little more somber. "Most of the voices in the Dirac beep are like that—they're cries for help, which you can overhear decades or centuries before the senders get into trouble. You'll feel obligated to answer every one, to try to supply the held that's needed. And you'll listen to the succeeding messages and say: 'Did we—will we get there in time? Did we understand in time?'

"And in most cases you won't be sure. You'll know the future, but not what most of it means. The farther into the future you travel with the machine, the more incomprehensible the messages become, and so you're reduced to telling yourself that time will, after all, have to pass by at its own pace, before enough of the surrounding events can emerge to make those remote messages clear.

"The long-run effect, as far as I can think it through, is not going to be that of omniscience—of our consciousness being extracted entirely from the time stream and allowed to view its whole sweep from one side. Instead, the Dirac in effect simply slides the bead of consciousness forward from the present a certain distance. Whether it's five hundred or five thousand years still remains to be seen. At that point the law of diminishing returns sets in—or the noise factor begins to overbalance the information, take your choice—and the observer is reduced to traveling in time at the same old speed. He's just a bit ahead of himself."

"You've thought a great deal about this," Wald said slowly. "I dislike to think of what might have happened had some less conscientious person stumbled on the beep."

"That wasn't in the cards," Dana said.

In the ensuing quiet, Weinbaum felt a faint, irrational sense of let-down, of something which had promised more than had been delivered—rather like the taste of fresh bread as compared to its smell, or the discovery that Thor Wald's Swedish "folk song" *Nat-og-Dag* was only Cole Porter's *Night and Day* in another language. He recognized the feeling: it was the usual emotion of the hunter when the hunt is over, the born detective's professional version of the *post coitum tristre*. After looking at the smiling, supple Dana Lje a moment more, however, he was almost content.

"There's one more thing," he said. "I don't want to be insufferably skeptical about this—but I want to see it work. Thor, can we set up a sampling and smearing device such as Dana describes and run a test?"

"In fifteen minutes," Dr. Wald said. "We have most of the unit in already assembled form on our big ultrawave receiver, and it shouldn't take any effort to add a high-speed tape unit to it. I'll do it right now."

He went out. Weinbaum and Dana looked at each other for a moment, rather like strange cats. Then the security officer got up, with what he knew to be an air of somewhat grim determination, and seized his fiancée's hands, anticipating a struggle.

That first kiss was, by intention at least, mostly *pro forma*. But by the time Wald padded back into the office, the letter had been pretty thoroughly superseded by the spirit. The scientist harrumphed and set his burden on the desk. "This is all there is to it," he said, "but I had to hunt all through the library to find a Dirac record with a beep still on it. Just a moment more while I make connections. . . ."

Weinbaum used the time to bring his mind back to the matter at hand, although not quite completely. Then two tape spindles began to whir like so many bees, and the end-stopped sound of the Dirac beep filled the room. Wald stopped the apparatus, reset it, and started the smearing tape very slowly in the opposite direction.

A distant babble of voices came from the speaker. As Weinbaum leaned forward tensely, one voice said clearly and loudly above the rest:

"Hello, Earth bureau. Lt. T. L. Matthews at Hercules Station NGC 6341, transmission date 13-22-2091. We have the last point on the orbit curve of your dope-runners plotted, and the curve itself points to a small system about twenty-five light-years from the base here; the place hasn't even got a name on our charts. Scouts show the home planet at least twice as heavily fortified as we anticipated, so we'll need another cruiser. We have a 'can-do' from you in the beep for us, but we're waiting as ordered to get it in the present. NGC 6341 Matthews out."

After the first instant of stunned amazement—for no amount of intellectual willingness to accept could have prepared him for the overwhelming fact itself—Weinbaum had grabbed a pencil and begun to write at top speed. As the voice signed out he threw the pencil down and looked excitedly at Dr. Wald.

"Seven months ahead," he said, aware that he was grinning like an idiot. "Thor, you know the trouble we've had with that needle in the Hercules haystack! This orbit-curve trick must be something Matthews has yet to dream up—at least he hasn't come to me with it yet, and there's nothing in the situation as it stands now that would indicate a closing time of six months for the case. The computers said it would take three more years."

"It's new data," Dr. Wald agreed solemnly.

"Well, don't stop there, in God's name! Let's hear some more!"

Dr. Wald went through the ritual, much faster this time. The speaker said:

"Nausentampen. Eddettompic. Berobsilom. Aimkaksetchoc. Sanbetogmow. Datdectamset. Domatrosmin. Out."

"My word," Wald said. "What's all that?"

"That's what I was talking about," Dana Lje said. "At least half of what you get from the beep is just as incomprehensible. I suppose it's whatever has happened to the English language, thousands of years from now."

"No, it isn't," Weinbaum said. He had resumed writing, and was still at it, despite the comparative briefness of the transmission. "Not this sample, anyhow. That, ladies and gentlemen, is code—no language consists exclusively of four-syllable words, of that you can be sure. What's more, it's a version of our code. I can't break it down very far—it takes a full-time expert to read this stuff—but I get the date and some of the sense. It's March 12, 3022, and there's some kind of a mass evacuation taking place. The message seems to be a routing order."

"But why will we be using code?" Dr. Wald wanted to know. "It implies that we think somebody might overhear us—somebody else with a Dirac. That could be very messy."

"It could indeed," Weinbaum said. "But we'll find out, I imagine. Give her another spin, Thor."

"Shall I try for a picture this time?"

Weinbaum nodded. A moment later, he was looking squarely into the green-skinned face of something that looked like an animated traffic signal with a helmet on it. Though the creature had no mouth, the Dirac speaker was saying quite clearly, "Hello, Chief. This is Thammos NGC 2287, transmission date Gor 60, 302 by my calendar, July 2, 2973 by yours. This is a lousy little planet. Everything stinks of oxygen, just like Earth. But the natives accept us and that's the important thing. We've got your genius safely born. Detailed report coming later by paw. NGC 2287 Thammos out."

"I wish I knew my New General Catalogue better," Weinbaum said. "Isn't that M 41 in Canis Major, the one with the red star in the middle? And we'll be using non-humanoids there! What *was* that creature, anyhow? Never mind, spin her again."

Dr. Wald spun her again. Weinbaum, already feeling a little dizzy, had given up taking notes. That could come later, all that could come later. Now he wanted only scenes and voices, more and more scenes and voices from the future. They were better than aquavit, even with a beer chaser.

4

THE INDOCTRINATION tape ended, and Krasna touched a button. The Dirac screen darkened, and folded silently back into the desk.

"They didn't see their way through to us, not by a long shot," he said. "They didn't see, for instance, that when one section of the government becomes nearly all-knowing—no matter how small it was to begin with—it necessarily becomes all of the government that there is. Thus the bureau turned into the Service and pushed everyone else out.

"On the other hand, those people did come to be afraid that a government with an all-knowing arm might become a rigid dictatorship. That couldn't happen and didn't happen, because the more you know, the wider your field of possible operation becomes and the more fluid and dynamic a society you need. How could a rigid society expand to other star systems, let alone other galaxies? It couldn't be done."

"I should think it could," Jo said slowly. "After all, if you know in advance what everybody is going to do . . ."

"But we don't, Jo. That's just a popular fiction—or, if

you like, a red herring. Not all of the business of the cosmos is carried on over the Dirac, after all. The only events we can ever overhear are those which are transmitted as a message. Do you order your lunch over the Dirac? Of course you don't. Up to now, you've never said a word over the Dirac in your life.

"And there's much more to it than that. All dictatorships are based on the proposition that government can somehow control a man's thoughts. We know now that the consciousness of the observer is the only free thing in the Universe. Wouldn't we look foolish trying to control that, when our entire physics shows that it's impossible to do so? That's why the Service is in no sense a thought police. We're interested only in acts. We're an Event Police."

"But why?" Jo said. "If all history is fixed, why do we bother with these boy-meets-girl assignments, for instance? The meetings will happen anyhow."

"Of course they will," Krasna agreed immediately. "But look, Jo. Our interests as a government depend upon the future. We operate *as if* the future is as real as the past, and so far we haven't been disappointed: the Service is 100 per cent successful. But that very success isn't without its warnings. What would happen if we *stopped* supervising events? We don't know, and we don't dare take the chance. Despite the evidence that the future is fixed, we have to take on the role of the caretaker of inevitability. We believe that nothing can possibly go wrong . . . but we have to act on the philosophy that history helps only those who help themselves.

"That's why we safeguard huge numbers of courtships right through to contract, and even beyond it. We have to see to it that *every single person who is mentioned in any Dirac 'cast gets born*. Our obligation as Event Police is to make the events of the future possible, because those events are crucial to our society—even the smallest of them. It's an enormous task, believe me, and it gets bigger and bigger every day. Apparently it always will."

"Always?" Jo said. "What about the public? Isn't it going to smell this out sooner or later? The evidence is piling up at a terrific rate."

"Yes and no," Krasna said. "Lots of people are smelling it out right now, just as you did. But the number of new people we need in the Service grows faster—it's always ahead of the number of laymen who follow the clues to the truth."

Jo took a deep breath. "You take all this as if it were as commonplace as boiling an egg, Kras," he said. "Don't you ever wonder about some of the things you get from the beep? That 'cast Dana Lje picked up from Canes Venatici, for instance, the one from the ship that was traveling backward in time? How is that possible? What could be the purpose? Is it——"

"*Pace, pace,*" Krasna said. "I don't know and I don't care. Neither should you. That event is too far in the future for us to worry about. We can't possibly know its context yet, so there's no sense in trying to understand it. If an Englishman of around 1600 had found out about the American Revolution, he would have thought it a tragedy; an Englishman of 1950 would have a very different view of it. We're in the same spot. The messages we get from the really far future have no contexts as yet."

"I think I see," Jo said. "I'll get used to it in time, I suppose, after I use the Dirac for a while. Or does my new rank authorize me to do that?"

"Yes, it does. But, Jo, first I want to pass on to you a rule of Service etiquette that must never be broken. You won't be allowed anywhere near a Dirac mike until you have it burned into your memory beyond any forgetfulness."

"I'm listening, Kras, believe me."

"Good. This is the rule: *The date of a Serviceman's death must never be mentioned in a Dirac 'cast.*"

Jo blinked, feeling a little chilly. The reason behind the rule was decidedly tough-minded, but its ultimate kindness was plain. He said, "I won't forget that. I'll want that protection myself. Many thanks, Kras. What's my new assignment?"

"To begin with," Krasna said, grinning, "as simple a job as I've ever given you, right here on Randolph. Skin out of here and find me that cab driver—the one who mentioned time-travel to you. He's uncomfortably close to the truth; closer than you were in one category.

"Find him, and bring him to me. The Service is about to take in a new raw recruit!"

This Earth of Hours

THE ADVANCE squadron was coming into line as Master Sergeant Oberholzer came onto the bridge of the *Novoe Washingtongrad*, saluted, and stood stiffly to the left of Lieutenant Campion, the exec, to wait for orders. The bridge was crowded and crackling with tension, but after twenty years in the Marines it was all old stuff to Oberholzer. The *Hobo* (as most of the enlisted men called her, out of earshot of the brass) was at the point of the formation, as befitted a virtually indestructible battleship already surfeited with these petty conquests. The rest of the cone was sweeping on ahead, in the swift enveloping maneuver which had reduced so many previous planets before they had been able to understand what was happening to them.

This time, the planet at the focus of all those shifting conic sections of raw naval power was a place called Callë. It was showing now on a screen that Oberholzer could see, turning as placidly as any planet turned when you were too far away from it to see what guns it might be pointing at you. Lieutenant Campion was watching it too, though he had to look out of the very corners of his eyes to see it at all.

If the exec were caught watching the screen instead of the meter board assigned to him, Captain Hammer would probably reduce him to an ensign. Nevertheless, Campion never took his eyes off the image of Callë. This one was going to be rough.

Captain Hammer was watching, too. After a moment he said, "Sound!" in a voice like sandpaper.

"By the pulse six, sir," Lieutenant Spring's voice murmured from the direction of the 'scope. His junior, a very raw youngster named Rover, passed him a chit from the plotting table. "For that read: By the briefs five eight nine, sir," the invisible navigator corrected.

Oberholzer listened without moving while Captain Hammer muttered under his breath to Flo-Mar 12-Upjohn, the only civilian allowed on the bridge—and small wonder, since he was the Consort of State of the Matriarchy itself. Hammer had long ago become accustomed enough to his own bridge to be able to control who overheard him, but

156

12-Upjohn's answering whisper must have been audible to every man there.

"The briefing said nothing about a second inhabited planet," the Consort said, a little peevishly. "But then there's very little we *do* know about this system—that's part of our trouble. What makes you think it's a colony?"

"A colony from Callë, not one of ours," Hammer said, in more or less normal tones; evidently he had decided against trying to keep only half of the discussion private. "The electromagnetic 'noise' from both planets has the same spectrum—the energy level, the output, is higher on Callë, that's all. That means similar machines being used in similar ways. And let me point out, Your Excellency, that the outer planet is in opposition to Callë now, which will put it precisely in our rear if we complete this maneuver."

"*When* we complete this maneuver," 12-Upjohn said firmly. "Is there any evidence of communication between the two planets?"

Hammer frowned. "No," he admitted.

"Then we'll regard the colonization hypothesis as unproved —and stand ready to strike back hard if events prove us wrong. I think we have a sufficient force here to reduce *three* planets like Callë if we're driven to that pitch."

Hammer grunted and resigned the argument. Of course it was quite possible that 12-Upjohn was right; he did not lack for experience—in fact, he wore the Silver Earring, as the most-traveled Consort of State ever to ride the Standing Wave. Nevertheless Oberholzer repressed a sniff with difficulty. Like all the military, he was a colonial; he had never seen the Earth, and never expected to; and, both as a colonial and as a Marine who had been fighting the Matriarchy's battles all his adult life, he was more than a little contemptuous of Earthmen, with their tandem names and all that they implied. Of course it was not the Consort of State's fault that he had been born on Earth, and so had been named only Marvin 12 out of the misfortune of being a male; nor that he had married into Florence Upjohn's cabinet, that being the only way one could become a cabinet member, and Marvin 12 having been taught from birth to believe such a post the highest honor a man might covet. All the same, neither 12-Upjohn nor his entourage of drones filled Oberholzer with confidence.

Nobody, however, had asked M. Sgt. Richard Oberholzer what he thought, and nobody was likely to. As the chief of all the non-Navy enlisted personnel on board the *Hobo*, he was expected to be on the bridge when matters were ripening toward criticality; but his duty there was to listen, not to proffer advice. He could not in fact remember any occasion when an officer had asked his opinion, though he had received—and executed—his fair share of near-suicidal orders from bridges long demolished.

"By the pulse five point five," Lieutenant Spring's voice sang.

"Sergeant Oberholzer," Hammer said.

"Aye, sir."

"We are proceeding as per orders. You may now brief your men and put them into full battle gear."

Oberholzer saluted and went below. There was little enough he could tell the squad—as 12-Upjohn had said, Callë's system was nearly unknown—but even that little would improve the total ignorance in which they had been kept till now. Luckily, they were not much given to asking questions of a strategic sort; like impressed spacehands everywhere, the huge mass of the Matriarchy's interstellar holdings meant nothing to them but endlessly riding the Standing Wave, with battle and death lurking at the end of every jump. Luckily also, they were inclined to trust Oberholzer, if only for the low cunning he had shown in keeping most of them alive, especially in the face of unusually Crimean orders from the bridge.

This time Oberholzer would need every ounce of trust and erg of obedience they would give him. Though he never expected anything but the worst, he had a queer cold feeling that this time he was going to get it. There were hardly any data to go on yet, but there had been something about Callë that looked persuasively like the end of the line.

Very few of the forty men in the wardroom even looked up as Oberholzer entered. They were checking their gear in the dismal light of the fluorescents, with the single-mindedness of men to whom a properly wound gun-tube coil, a properly set face-shield gasket, a properly fueled and focused vaulting jet, have come to mean more than parents, children, retirement pensions, the rule of law, or the logic of empire. The only man to show any flicker of interest was Sergeant Cassirir—as was normal, since he was Oberholzer's understudy—and he did no more than look up from over the straps of his antigas suit and say, "Well?"

"Well," Oberholzer said, "now hear this."

There was a sort of composite jingle and clank as the men lowered their gear to the deck or put it aside on their bunks.

"We're investing a planet called Callë in the Canes Venatici cluster," Oberholzer said, sitting down on an olive-drab canvas pack stuffed with lysurgic acid grenades. "A cruiser called the *Assam Dragon*—you were with her on her shakedown, weren't you, Himber?—touched down here ten years ago with a flock of tenders and got swallowed up. They got two or three quick yells for help out and that was that—nothing anybody could make much sense of, no weapons named or description of the enemy. So here we are, loaded for the kill."

"Wasn't any Calley in command of the *Assam Dragon* when I was aboard," Himber said doubtfully.

"Nah. Place was named for the astronomer who spotted her, from the rim of the cluster, a hundred years ago," Oberholzer said. "Nobody names planets for ship captains. Anybody got any sensible questions?"

"Just what kind of trouble are we looking for?" Cassirir said.

"That's just it —we don't know. This is closer to the center of the Galaxy than we've ever gotten before. It may be a population center too; could be that Callë is just one piece of a federation, at least inside its own cluster. That's why we've got the boys from Momma on board; this one could be damn important."

Somebody sniffed. "If this cluster is full of people, how come we never picked up signals from it?"

"How do you know we never did?" Oberholzer retorted. "For all I know, maybe that's why the *Assam Dragon* came here in the first place. Anyhow that's not our problem. All we're——"

The lights went out. Simultaneously, the whole mass of the *Novoe Washingtongrad* shuddered savagely, as though a boulder almost as big as she was had been dropped on her.

Seconds later, the gravity went out too.

2

Flo-Mar 12-Upjohn knew no more of the real nature of the disaster than did the wardroom squad, nor did anybody on the bridge, for that matter. The blow had been inde-tectable until it struck, and then most of the fleet was simply annihilated; only the *Hobo* was big enough to survive the blow, and she survived only partially—in fact, in five pieces. Nor did the Consort of State ever know by what miracle the section he was in hit Callé still partially under power; he was not privy to the self-salvaging engineering principles of battleships. All he knew—once he struggled back to consciousness—was that he was still alive, and that there was a broad shaft of sunlight coming through a top-to-bottom split in one wall of what had been his office aboard ship.

He held his ringing head for a while, then got up in search of water. Nothing came out of the dispenser, so he unstrapped his dispatch case from the underside of his desk and produced a pint palladium flask of vodka. He had screwed up his face to sample this—at the moment he would have preferred water—when a groan reminded him that there might be more than one room in his suddenly shrunken universe, as well as other survivors.

He was right on both counts. Though the ship section he was in consisted mostly of engines of whose function he had no notion, there were also three other staterooms. Two of these were deserted, but the third turned out to contain a battered member of his own staff, by name Robin One.

The young man was not yet conscious and 12-Upjohn regarded him with a faint touch of despair. Robin One was perhaps the last man in space that the Consort of State would have chosen to be shipwrecked with.

That he was utterly expendable almost went without saying; he was, after all, a drone. When the perfection of sperm electrophoresis had enabled parents for the first time to predetermine the sex of their children, the predictable result had been an enormous glut of males—which was directly accountable for the present regime on Earth. By the time the people and the lawmakers, thoroughly frightened by the crazy years of fashion upheavals, "beefcake," polyandry, male prostitution, and all the rest, had come to their senses, the Matriarchy was in to stay; a weak electric current had overturned civilized society as drastically as the steel knife had demoralized the Eskimos.

Though the tide of excess males had since receded somewhat, it had left behind a wrack, of which Robin One was a bubble. He was a drone, and hence superfluous by definition—fit only to be sent colonizing, on diplomatic missions or otherwise thrown away.

Superfluity alone, of course, could hardly account for his

presence on 12-Upjohn's staff. Officially, Robin One was an interpreter; actually—since nobody could know the language the Consort of State might be called upon to understand on this mission—he was a poet, a class of unattached males with special privileges in the Matriarchy, particularly if what they wrote was of the middling-difficult or Hillyer Society sort. Robin One was an eminently typical member of this class, distractible, sulky, jealous, easily wounded, homosexual, lazy except when writing, and probably (to give him the benefit of the doubt, for 12-Upjohn had no ear whatever for poetry) the second-worst poet of his generation.

It had to be admitted that assigning 12-Upjohn a poet as an interpreter on this mission had not been a wholly bad idea, and that if Hildegard Muller of the Interstellar Understanding Commission had not thought of it, no mere male would have been likely to—least of all Bar-Rob 4-Agberg, Director of Assimilation. The nightmare of finding the whole of the center of the Galaxy organized into one vast federation, much older than Earth's, had been troubling the State Department for a long time, at first from purely theoretical considerations—all those heart-stars were much older than those in the spiral arms, and besides, where star density in space is so much higher, interstellar travel does not look like quite so insuperable an obstacle as it long had to Earthmen —and later from certain practical signs, of which the obliteration of the *Assam Dragon* and her tenders had been only the most provocative. Getting along with these people on the first contact would be vital, and yet the language barrier might well provoke a tragedy wanted by neither side, as the obliteration of Nagasaki in World War II had been provoked by the mistranslation of a single word. Under such circumstances, a man with a feeling for strange words in odd relationships might well prove to be useful, or even vital.

Nevertheless, it was with a certain grim enjoyment that 12-Upjohn poured into Robin One a good two-ounce jolt of vodka. Robin coughed convulsively and sat up, blinking.

"Your Excellency—how—what's happened? I thought we were dead. But we've got lights again, and gravity."

He was observant, that had to be granted. "The lights are ours but the gravity is Callë's," 12-Upjohn explained tersely. "We're in a part of the ship that cracked up."

"Well, it's good that we've got power."

"We can't afford to be philosophical about it. Whatever

shape it's in, this derelict is a thoroughly conspicuous object and we'd better get out of it in a hurry."

"Why?" Robin said. "We were supposed to make contact with these people. Why not just sit here until they notice and come to see us?"

"Suppose they just blast us to smaller bits instead? They didn't stop to parley with the fleet, you'll notice."

"This is a different situation," Robin said stubbornly. "I wouldn't have stopped to parley with that fleet myself, if I'd had the means of knocking it out first. It didn't look a bit like a diplomatic mission. But why should they be afraid of a piece of a wreck?"

The Consort of State stroked the back of his neck reflectively. The boy had a point. It was risky; on the other hand, how long would they survive foraging in completely unknown territory? And yet obviously they couldn't stay cooped up in here forever—especially if it was true that there was already no water.

He was spared having to make up his mind by a halloo from the direction of the office. After a startled stare at each other, the two hit the deck running.

Sergeant Oberholzer's face was peering grimly through the split in the bulkhead.

"Oho," he said. "So you *did* make it." He said something unintelligible to some invisible person outside, and then squirmed through the breach into the room, with considerable difficulty, since he was in full battle gear. "None of the officers did, so I guess that puts you in command."

"In command of what?" 12-Upjohn said dryly.

"Not very much," the Marine admitted. "I've got five men surviving, one of them with a broken hip, and a section of the ship with two drive units in it. It would lift, more or less, if we could jury-rig some controls, but I don't know where we'd go in it without supplies or a navigator—or an overdrive, for that matter." He looked about speculatively. "There was a Standing Wave transceiver in this section, I think, but it'd be a miracle if it still functioned."

"Would you know how to test it?" Robin asked.

"No. Anyhow we've got more immediate business than that. We've picked up a native. What's more, he speaks English—must have picked it up from the *Assam Dragon*. We started to ask him questions, but it turns out he's some sort of top official, so we brought him over here on the off chance that one of you was alive."

"What a break!" Robin One said explosively.

"A whole series of them," 12-Upjohn agreed, none too happily. He had long ago learned to be at his most suspicious when the breaks seemed to be coming his way. "Well, better bring him in."

"Can't," Oberholzer said. "Apologies, Your Excellency, but he wouldn't fit. You'll have to come to him."

3

It was impossible to imagine what sort of stock the Callëan had evolved from. He seemed to be a thoroughgoing mixture of several different phyla. Most of him was a brown, segmented tube about the diameter of a barrel and perhaps twenty-five feet long, rather like a cross between a python and a worm. The front segments were carried upright, raising the head a good ten feet off the ground.

Properly speaking, 12-Upjohn thought, the Callëan really had no head, but only a front end, marked by two enormous faceted eyes and three upsetting simple eyes which were usually closed. Beneath these there was a collar of six short, squidlike tentacles, carried wrapped around the creature in a ropy ring. He was as impossible-looking as he was fearsome, and 12-Upjohn felt at a multiple disadvantage from the beginning.

"How did you learn our language?" he said, purely as a starter.

"I learned it from you," the Callëan said promptly. The voice was unexpectedly high, a quality which was accentuated by the creature's singsong intonation; 12-Upjohn could not see where it was coming from. "From your ship which I took apart, the dragon-of-war."

"Why did you do that?"

"It was evident that you meant me ill," the Callëan sang. "At that time I did not know that you were sick, but that became evident at the dissections."

"Dissections! You dissected the crew of the *Dragon?*"

"All but one."

There was a growl from Oberholzer. The Consort of State shot him a warning glance.

"You may have made a mistake," 12-Upjohn said. "A natural mistake, perhaps. But it was our purpose to offer you trade and peaceful relationships. Our weapons were only precautionary."

"I do not think so," the Callëan said, "and I never make

mistakes. That you make mistakes is natural, but it is not
natural to me."

12-Upjohn felt his jaw dropping. That the creature meant
what he said could not be doubted; his command of the
language was too complete to permit any more sensible
interpretation. 12-Upjohn found himself at a loss; not only
was the statement the most staggering he had ever heard
from any sentient being, but while it was being made he had
discovered how the Callëan spoke: the sounds issued at low
volume from a multitude of spiracles or breath-holes all
along the body, each hole producing only one pure tone,
the words and intonations being formed in mid-air by intermodulation—a miracle of co-ordination among a multitude
of organs obviously unsuitable for sound-forming at all. This
thing was formidable—that would have been evident even
without the lesson of the chunk of the *Novoe Washingtongrad* canted crazily in the sands behind them.

Sands? He looked about with a start. Until that moment
the Callëan had so hypnotized his attention that he had forgotten to look at the landscape, but his unconscious had
registered it. Sand, and nothing but sand. If there were
better parts of Callë than this desert, they were not visible
from here, all the way to the horizon.

"What do you propose to do with us?" he said at last.
There was really nothing else to say; cut off in every possible
sense from his home world, he no longer had any base from
which to negotiate.

"Nothing," the Callëan said. "You are free to come and
go as you please."

"You're no longer afraid of us?"

"No. When you came to kill me I prevented you, but you
can no longer do that."

"There you've made a mistake, all right," Oberholzer said,
lifting his rifle toward the multicolored, glittering jewels of
the Callëan's eyes. "You know what this is—they must have
had them on the *Dragon*."

"Don't be an idiot, Sergeant," 12-Upjohn said sharply.
"We're in no position to make any threats." Nor, he added
silently, should the Marine have called attention to his gun
before the Callëan had taken any overt notice of it.

"I know what it is," the creature said. "You cannot kill
me with that. You tried it often before and found you could
not. You would remember this if you were not sick."

"I never saw anything that I couldn't kill with a Sussmann

flamer," Oberholzer said between his teeth. "Let me try it on the bastard, Your Excellency."

"Wait a minute," Robin One said, to 12-Upjohn's astonishment. "I want to ask some questions—if you don't mind, Your Excellency?"

"I don't mind," 12-Upjohn said after an instant. Anything to get the Marine's crazy impulse toward slaughter sidetracked. "Go ahead."

"Did you dissect the crew of the *Assam Dragon* personally?" Robin asked the Callëan.

"Of course."

"Are you the ruler of this planet?"

"Yes."

"Are you the only person in this system?"

"No."

Robin paused and frowned. Then he said: "Are you the only person of your species in your system?"

"No. There is another on Xixobrax—the fourth planet."

Robin paused once more, but not, it seemed to 12-Upjohn, as though he were in any doubt; it was only as though he were gathering his courage for the key question of all. 12-Upjohn tried to imagine what it might be, and failed.

"How many of you are there?" Robin One said.

"I cannot answer that. As of the instant you asked me that question, there were eighty-three hundred thousand billion, one hundred and eighty nine million, four hundred and sixty five thousand, one hundred and eighty; but now the number has changed, and it goes on changing."

"Impossible," 12-Upjohn said, stunned. "Not even two planets could support such a number—and you'd never allow a desert like this to go on existing if you had even a fraction of that population to support. I begin to think, sir, that you are a type normal to my business: the ordinary, unimaginative liar."

"He's not lying," Robin said, his voice quivering. "It all fits together. Just let me finish, sir, please. I'll explain, but I've got to go through to the end first."

"Well," 12-Upjohn said, helplessly, "all right, go ahead." But he was instantly sorry, for what Robin One said was:

"Thank you. I have no more questions."

The Callëan turned in a great liquid wheel and poured away across the sand dunes at an incredible speed. 12-Upjohn shouted after him, without any clear idea of what it was that he was shouting—but no matter, for the Callëan took no notice. Within seconds, it seemed, he was only a thread-worm in the middle distance, and then he was gone. They were all alone in the chill desert air.

Oberholzer lowered his rifle bewilderedly. "He's fast," he said to nobody in particular. "Cripes, but he's fast. I couldn't even keep him in the sights."

"That proves it," Robin said tightly. He was trembling, but whether with fright or elation, 12-Upjohn could not tell; possibly both.

"It had better prove something," the Consort of State said, trying hard not to sound portentous. There was something about this bright remote desert that made empty any possible pretense to dignity. "As far as I can see, you've just lost us what may have been our only chance to treat with these creatures . . . just as surely as the sergeant would have done it with his gun. Explain, please."

"I didn't really catch on until I realized that he was using the second person singular when he spoke to us," Robin said. If he had heard any threat implied in 12-Upjohn's charge, it was not visible; he seemed totally preoccupied. "There's no way to tell them apart in modern English. We thought he was referring to us as 'you' plural, but he wasn't, any more than his 'I' was a plural. He thinks we're all a part of the same personality—including the men from the *Dragon*, too—*just as he is himself*. That's why he left when I said I had no more questions. He can't comprehend that each of us has an independent ego. For him such a thing doesn't exist."

"Like ants?" 12-Upjohn said slowly. "I don't see how an advanced technology . . . but no, I do see. And if it's so, it means that any Callëan we run across could be their chief of state, but that no one of them actually is. The only other real individual is next door, on the fourth planet—another hive ego."

"Maybe not," Robin said. "Don't forget that he thinks we're part of one, too."

12-Upjohn dismissed that possibility at once. "He's sure to know his own system, after all. . . . What alarms me is the population figure he cited. It's got to be at least clusterwide— and from the exactness with which he was willing to cite it, for a given instant, he had to have immediate access to it. An instant, effortless census."

"Yes," Robin said. "Meaning mind-to-mind contact, from

one to all, throughout the whole complex. That's what started me thinking about the funny way he used pronouns."

"If that's the case, Robin, we are *spurlos versenkt*. And my pronoun includes the Earth."

"They may have some limitations," Robin said, but it was clear that he was only whistling in the dark. "But at least it explains why they butchered the *Dragon's* crew so readily —and why they're willing to let us wander around their planet as if we didn't even exist. We don't, for them. They can't have any respect for a single life. No wonder they didn't give a damn for the sergeant's gun!"

His initial flush had given way to a marble paleness; there were beads of sweat on his brow in the dry hot air, and he was trembling harder than ever. He looked as though he might faint in the next instant, though only the slightest of stutters disturbed his rush of words. But for once the Consort of State could not accuse him of agitation over trifles.

Oberholzer looked from one to the other, his expression betraying perhaps only disgust, or perhaps blank incomprehension—it was impossible to tell. Then, with a sudden sharp *snick* which made them both start, he shot closed the safety catch on the Sussmann.

"Well," he said in a smooth cold empty voice, "now we know what we'll eat."

4

Their basic and dangerous division of plans and purposes began with that.

Sergeant Oberholzer was not a fool, as the hash marks on his sleeve and the battle stars on his ribbons attested plainly; he understood the implications of what the Callëan had said—at least after the Momma's boy had interpreted them; and he was shrewd enough not to undervalue the contribution the poor terrified fairy had made to their possible survival on this world. For the moment, however, it suited the Marine to play the role of the dumb sergeant to the hilt. If a full understanding of what the Callëans were like might reduce him to a like state of trembling impotence, he could do without it.

Not that he really believed that any such thing could happen to him; but it was not hard to see that Momma's boys were halfway there already—and if the party as a whole

hoped to get anything done, they had to be jolted out of it
as fast as possible.

At first he thought he had made it. "Certainly not!" the
Consort of State said indignantly. "You're a man, sergeant,
not a Callëan. Nothing the Callëans do is any excuse for
your behaving otherwise than as a man."

"I'd rather eat an enemy than a friend," Oberholzer said
cryptically. "Have you got any supplies inside there?"

"I—I don't know. But that has nothing to do with it."

"Depends on what you mean by 'it.' But maybe we can
argue about that later. What are your orders, Your
Excellency?"

"I haven't an order in my head," 12-Upjohn said with
sudden, disarming frankness. "We'd better try to make some
sensible plans first, and stop bickering. Robin, stop snuffling,
too. The question is, what can we do besides trying to survive,
and cherishing an idiot hope for a rescue mission?"

"For one thing, we can try to spring the man from the
Dragon's crew that these worms have still got alive," Oberholzer said. "If that's what he meant when he said they
dissected all but one."

"That doesn't seem very feasible to me," 12-Upjohn said.
"We have no idea where they're holding him——"

"Ask them. This one answered every question you asked
him."

"—and even supposing that he's near by, we couldn't
free him from a horde of Callëans, no matter how many
dead bodies they let you pile up. At best, sooner or later
you'd run out of ammunition."

"It's worth trying," Oberholzer said. "We could use the
manpower."

"What for?" Robin One demanded. "He'd be just one more
mouth to feed. At the moment, at least, they're feeding him."

"For raising ship," Oberholzer retorted. "*If* there's any
damn chance of welding our two heaps of junk together and
getting off this mudball. We ought to look into it, anyhow."

Robin One was looking more alarmed by the minute. If
the prospect of getting into a fight with the Callëans had
scared him, Oberholzer thought, the notion of hard physical
labor evidently was producing something close to panic.

"Where could we go?" he said. "Supposing that we could
fly such a shambles at all?"

"I don't know," Oberholzer said. "We don't know what's
possible yet. But anything's better than sitting around here

and starving. First off, I want that man from the *Dragon*."

"I'm opposed to it," 12-Upjohn said firmly. "The Calléans are leaving us to our own devices now. If we cause any real trouble they may well decide that we'd be safer locked up, or dead. I don't mind planning to lift ship if we can—but no military expeditions."

"Sir," Oberholzer said, "military action on this planet is what I was sent here for. I reserve the right to use my own judgment. You can complain, if we ever get back—but I'm not going to let a man rot in a worm-burrow while I've got a gun on my back. You can come along or not, but we're going."

He signaled to Cassirir, who seemed to be grinning slightly. 12-Upjohn stared at him for a moment, and then shook his head.

"We'll stay," he said. "Since we have no water, Sergeant, I hope you'll do us the kindness of telling us where your part of the ship lies."

"That way, about two kilometers," Oberholzer said. "Help yourself. If you want to settle in there, you'll save us the trouble of toting Private Hannes with us on a stretcher."

"Of course," the Consort of State said. "We'll take care of him. But, Sergeant . . ."

"Yes, Your Excellency?"

"If this stunt of yours still leaves us all alive afterwards, and we do get back to any base of ours, I will *certainly* see to it that a complaint is lodged. I'm not disowning you now because it's obvious that we'll all have to work together to survive, and a certain amount of amity will be essential. But don't be deceived by that."

"I understand, sir," Oberholzer said levelly. "Cassirir, let's go. We'll backtrack to where we nabbed the worm, and then follow his trail to wherever he came from. Fall in."

The men shouldered their Sussmanns. 12-Upjohn and Robin One watched them go. At the last dune before the two would go out of sight altogether, Oberholzer turned and waved, but neither waved back. Shrugging, Oberholzer resumed plodding.

"Sarge?"

"Yeah?"

"How *do* you figure to spring this joker with only four guns?"

"Five guns if we spring him—I've got a side arm," Oberholzer reminded him. "We'll play it by ear, that's all. I want to see just how serious these worms are about leaving us alone, and letting us shoot them if we feel like it. I've got a hunch that they aren't very bright, one at a time, and don't react fast to strictly local situations. If this whole planet is like one huge body, and the worms are its brain cells, then we're germs—and maybe it'd take more than four germs to make the body do anything against us that counted, at least fast enough to do any good."

Cassirir was frowning absurdly; he did not seem to be taking the theory in without pain. Well, Cassirir had never been much of a man for tactics.

"Here's where we found the guy," one of the men said, pointing at the sand.

"That's not much of a trail," Cassirir said. "If there's any wind it'll be wiped out like a shot."

"Take a sight on it, that's all we need. You saw him run off—straight as a ruled line, no twists or turns around the dunes or anything. Like an army ant. If the trail sands over, we'll follow the sight. It's a cinch it leads someplace."

"All right," Cassirir said, getting out his compass. After a while the four of them resumed trudging.

There were only a few drops of hot, flat-tasting water left in the canteens, and their eyes were gritty and red from dryness and sand, when they topped the ridge that overlooked the nest. The word sprang instantly into Oberholzer's mind, though perhaps he had been expecting some such thing ever since Robin One had compared the Calléans to ants.

It was a collection of rough white spires, each perhaps fifty feet high, rising from a common doughlike mass which almost filled a small valley. There was no greenery around it and no visible source of water, but there were three roads, two of them leading into oval black entrances which Oberholzer could see from here. Occasionally—not often—a Callëan would scuttle out and vanish, or come speeding over the horizon and dart into the darkness. Some of the spires bore masts carrying what seemed to be antennae or more recondite electronic devices, but there were no windows to be seen; and the only sound in the valley, except for the dry dusty wind, was a subdued composite hum.

"Man!" Cassirir said, whispering without being aware of it. "It must be as black as the ace of spades in there. Anybody got a torch?"

Nobody had. "We won't need one anyhow," Oberholzer

said confidently. "They've got eyes, and they can see in desert sunlight. That means they can't move around in total darkness. Let's go—I'm thirsty."

They stumbled down into the valley and approached the nearest black hole cautiously. Sure enough, it was not as black as it had appeared from the hill; there was a glow inside, which had been hidden from them against the contrast of the glaringly lit sands. Nevertheless, Oberholzer found himself hanging back.

While he hesitated, a Callëan came rocketing out of the entrance and pulled to a smooth, sudden stop.

"You are not to get in the way," he said, in exactly the same piping singsong voice the other had used.

"Tell me where to go and I'll stay out of your way," Oberholzer said. "Where is the man from the warship that you didn't dissect?"

"In Gnitonis, halfway around the world from here."

Oberholzer felt his shoulders sag, but the Callëan was not through. "You should have told me that you wanted him," he said. "I will have him brought to you. Is there else that you need?"

"Water," Oberholzer said hopefully.

"That will be brought. There is no water you can use here. Stay out of the cities; you will be in the way."

"How else can we eat?"

"Food will be brought. You should make your needs known; you are of low intelligence and helpless. I forbid nothing, I know you are harmless, and your life is short in any case; but I do not want you to get in the way."

The repetition was beginning to tell on Oberholzer, and the frustration created by his having tried to use a battering ram against a freely swinging door was compounded by his mental picture of what the two Momma's boys would say when the squad got back.

"Thank you," he said, and bringing the Sussmann into line, he trained it on the Callëan's squidlike head and squeezed the trigger.

It was at once established that the Callëans were as mortal to Sussmann flamers as is all other flesh and blood; this one made a very satisfactory corpse. Unsatisfied, the flamer bolt went on to burn a long slash in the wall of the nest, not far above the entrance. Oberholzer grounded the rifle and waited to see what would happen next; his men hefted their weapons tensely.

For a few minutes there was no motion but the random twitching of the headless Calléan's legs. Evidently he was still not entirely dead, though he was a good four feet shorter than he had been before, and plainly was feeling the lack. Then, there was a stir inside the dark entrance.

A ten-legged animal about the size of a large rabbit emerged tentatively into the sunlight, followed by two more, and then by a whole series of them, perhaps as many as twenty. Though Oberholzer had been unabashed by the Calléans themselves, there was something about these things that made him feel sick. They were coal black and shiny, and they did not seem to have any eyes; their heavily armored heads bore nothing but a set of rudimentary palps and a pair of enormous pincers, like those of a June beetle.

Sightless or no, they were excellent surgeons. They cut the remains of the Calléan swiftly into sections, precisely one metamere to a section, and bore the carrion back inside the nest. Filled with loathing, Oberholzer stepped quickly forward and kicked one of the last in the procession. It toppled over like an unstable kitchen stool, but regained its footing as though nothing had happened. The kick had not hurt it visibly, though Oberholzer's toes felt as though he had kicked a Victorian iron dog. The creature, still holding its steak delicately in its living tongs, mushed implacably after the others back into the dubiety of the nest. Then all that was left in the broiling sunlight was a few pools of blackening blood seeping swiftly into the sand.

"Let's get out of here," Cassirir said raggedly.

"Stand fast," Oberholzer growled. "If they're mad at us, I want to know about it right now."

But the next Calléan to pass them, some twenty eternal minutes later, hardly even slowed down. "Keep out of the way," he said, and streaked away over the dunes. Snarling, Oberholzer caromed a bolt after him, but missed him clean.

"All right," he said. "Let's go back. No hitting the canteens till we're five kilometers past the mid-point cairn. March!"

The men were all on the verge of prostration by the time that point was passed, but Oberholzer never once had to enforce the order. Nobody, it appeared, was eager to come to an end on Callé as a series of butcher's cuts in the tongs of a squad of huge black beetles.

5

"I know what they think," the man from the *Assam Dragon* said. "I've heard them say it often enough."

He was a personable youngster, perhaps thirty, with blond wavy hair which had been turned almost white by the strong Callëan sunlight: his captors had walked him for three hours every day on the desert. He had once been the *Assam Dragon's* radioman, a post which in interstellar flight is a branch of astronomy, not of communications; nevertheless, Oberholzer and the marines called him Sparks, in deference to a tradition which, 12-Upjohn suspected, the marines did not even know existed.

"Then why wouldn't there be a chance of our establishing better relations with the 'person' on the fourth planet?" 12-Upjohn said. "After all, there's never been an Earth landing there."

"Because the 'person' on Xixobrax is a colony of Callë, and knows everything that goes on here. It took the two planets in co-operation to destroy the fleet. There's almost full telepathic communion between the two—in fact, all through the Central Empire. The only rapport that seems to weaken over short distances—interplanetary distances—is the sense of identity. That's why each planet has an 'I' of its own, its own ego. But it's not the kind of ego we know anything about. Xixobrax wouldn't give us any better deal than Callë has, any more than I'd give Callë a better deal than you would, Your Excellency. They have common purposes and allegiances. All the Central Empire seems to be like that."

12-Upjohn thought about it; but he did not like what he thought. It was a knotty problem, even in theory.

Telepathy among men had never amounted to anything. After the pioneer exploration of the microcosm with the Arpe Effect—the second of two unsuccessful attempts at an interstellar drive, long before the discovery of the Standing Wave—it had become easy to see why this would be so. Psi forces in general were characteristic only of the subspace in which the primary particles of the atom had their being; their occasional manifestations in the macrocosm were statistical accidents, as weak and indirigible as spontaneous radioactive decay.

Up to now this had suited 12-Upjohn. It had always seemed to him that the whole notion of telepathy was a

dodge—an attempt to by-pass the plain duty of each man
to learn to know his brother, and, if possible, to learn to
love him; the telepathy fanatics were out to short-circuit the
task, to make easy the most difficult assignment a human
being might undertake. He was well aware, too, of the bias
against telepathy which was inherent in his profession of
diplomat; yet he had always been certain of his case, hazy
though it was around the edges. One of his proofs was that
telepathy's main defenders invariably were incorrigibly lazy
writers, from Upton Sinclair and Theodore Dreiser all the
way down to . . .

All the same, it seemed inarguable that the whole center
of the Galaxy, an enormously diverse collection of peoples
and cultures, was being held together in a common and
strife-free union by telepathy alone, or perhaps by telepathy
and its even more dubious adjuncts: a whole galaxy held
together by a force so unreliable that two human beings
sitting across from each other at a card table had never
been able to put it to an even vaguely practicable use.

Somewhere, there was a huge hole in the argument.

While he had sat helplessly thinking in these circles, even
Robin One was busy, toting power packs to the welding crew
which was working outside to braze together on the desert the
implausible, misshapen lump of metal which the Marine
sergeant was fanatically determined would become a ship
again. Now the job was done, though no shipwright would
admire it, and the question of where to go with it was being
debated in full council. Sparks, for his part, was prepared
to bet that the Calleans would not hinder their departure.

"Why would they have given us all this oxygen and stuff
if they were going to prevent us from using it?" he said
reasonably. "They know what it's for—even if they have
no brains, collectively they're plenty smart enough."

"*No* brains?" 12-Upjohn said. "Or are you just exag-
gerating?"

"No brains," the man from the *Assam Dragon* insisted.
"Just lots of ganglia. I gather that's the way all of the races
of the Central Empire are organized, regardless of other
physical differences. That's what they mean when they say
we're all sick—hadn't you realized that?"

"No," 12-Upjohn said in slowly dawning horror. "You
had better spell it out."

"Why, they say that's why we get cancer. They say that

the brain is the ultimate source of all tumors, and is itself a tumor. They call it 'hostile symbiosis.' "

"Malignant?"

"In the long run. Races that develop them kill themselves off. Something to do with solar radiation; animals on planets of Population II stars develop them, Population I planets don't."

Robin One hummed an archaic twelve-tone series under his breath. There were no words to go with it, but the Consort of State recognized it; it was part of a chorale from a twentieth-century American opera, and the words went: *Weep, weep beyond time for this Earth of hours.*

"If fits," he said heavily. "So to receive and use a weak field like telepathy, you need a weak brain. Human beings will never make it."

"Earthworms of the galaxy, unite," Robin One said.

"They already have," Sergeant Oberholzer pointed out. "So where does all this leave us?"

"It means," 12-Upjohn said slowly, "that this Central Empire, where the stars are almost all Population I, is spreading out toward the spiral arms where the Earth lies. Any cluster civilizations they meet are natural allies—clusters are purely Population I—and probably have already been mentally assimilated. Any possible natural allies *we* meet, going around Population II stars, we may well pick a fight with instead."

"That's not what I meant," Sergeant Oberholzer said.

"I know what you meant; but this changes things. As I understand it, we have a chance of making a straight hop to the nearest Earth base, if we go on starvation rations——"

"—and if I don't make more than a point zero five per cent error in plotting the course," Sparks put in.

"Yes. On the other hand, we can make *sure* of getting there by going in short leaps via planets known to be inhabited, but never colonized and possibly hostile. The only other possibility is Xixobrax, which I think we've ruled out. Correct?"

"Right as rain," Sergeant Oberholzer said. "Now I see what you're driving at, Your Excellency. The only thing is— you didn't mention that the stepping stone method will take us the rest of our lives."

"So I didn't," 12-Upjohn said bleakly. "But I hadn't forgotten it. The other side of *that* coin is that it will be even longer than that before the Matriarchy and the Central Empire collide."

"After which," Sergeant Oberholzer said with a certain relish, "I doubt that it'll be a Matriarchy, whichever wins. Are you calling for a vote, sir?"

"Well—yes, I seem to be."

"Then let's grasshopper," Sergeant Oberholzer said unhesitatingly. "The boys and I can't fight a point zero five per cent error in navigation—but for hostile planets, we've got the flamers."

Robin One shuddered. "I don't mind the fighting part," he said unexpectedly. "But I *do* simply loathe the thought of being an old, old man when I get home. All the same, we do have to get the word back."

"You're agreeing with the sergeant?"

"Yes, that's what I said."

"I agree," Sparks said. "Either way we may not make it, but the odds are in favor of doing it the hard way."

"Very good," 12-Upjohn said. He was uncertain of his exact emotion at this moment; perhaps gloomy satisfaction was as close a description as any. "I make it unanimous. Let's get ready."

The sergeant saluted and prepared to leave the cabin; but suddenly he turned back.

"I didn't think very much of either of you, a while back," he said brutally. "But I'll tell you this: there must be something about brains that involves guts, too. I'll back 'em any time against any critter that lets itself be shot like a fish in a barrel—whatever the odds."

The Consort of State was still mulling that speech over as the madman's caricature of an interstellar ship groaned and lifted its lumps and angles from Callë. Who knows, he kept telling himself, who knows, it might even be true.

But he noticed that Robin One was still humming the chorale from *Psyche and Eros*; and ahead the galactic night was as black as death.

The End

Science Fiction from SIGNET

SIGNET Science Fiction You'll Enjoy

Buy them at your local

bookstore or use coupon

on next page for ordering.

Ø

Exciting Fiction from SIGNET